A Kiss—and They Were Destiny's Slaves

Nothing woke her, nothing she could remember. But suddenly her heart was pounding fiercely and her eyes shot open.

Standing over her, in the shadows, was a man. The moon fell across them. Victoria found herself staring into the Duke's eyes.

His eyes still upon hers, he reached for her, and when his lips touched hers she panicked, pushing against him, struggling to break free.

His lips were insistent, forcing hers apart, his tongue touching hers, something within her bursting, fire coursing through her veins . . .

He pulled her down to the floor, hungrily searching her lips, both of them gasping when he finally lifted his head.

"Tell me to stop," he whispered at her harshly. "For God's sake, tell me to stop . . ."

Books by Sheila O'Hallion

Fire and Innocence
Masquerade of Hearts

Published by POCKET BOOKS

Masquerade of Hearts

Sheila O'Hallion

POCKET BOOKS, a Simon & Schuster division of
Gulf & Western Corporation, New York, N.Y. 10020

This novel is a work of historical fiction. Names, characters, places and incidents relating to non-historical figures are either the product of the author's imagination or are used fictitiously. Any resemblance of such non-historical incidents, places or figures to actual events or locales or persons, living or dead, is entirely coincidental.

Another *Original* publication of POCKET BOOKS

 POCKET BOOKS, a division of Simon & Schuster, Inc.
1230 Avenue of the Americas, New York, N.Y. 10020

ISBN: 0-671-54423-3

First Pocket Books printing March 1987

10 9 8 7 6 5 4 3 2 1

POCKET and colophon are registered trademarks of Simon & Schuster, Inc.

Printed in the U.S.A.

Masquerade of Hearts

Chapter 1

BLUSTERY MARCH WINDS WHIPPED through the streets of London, pie men and street sellers holding on to their hats as they shouted out their wares. It was 1880, the forty-third year of Queen Victoria's reign, and the new century was still twenty years distant. But the cacophony of progress was all around: people, horses, and machinery filling the streets and assaulting the senses with noise, fumes, and smoke.

Pulling out around a slow-moving coach, a hired hansom cab careened through traffic, speeding past victorias and landaus as it hurtled westward. Inside the hansom a young woman clung desperately to the bench as the driver sent them racing around a corner, nearly colliding with a group of rowdy young gentlemen. A pie flew by the cab. Victoria Leggett turned back in her seat to see the well-dressed young men, still in the street, still buying pies and throwing them at each other amid raucous laughter. The sounds of their hilarity were punctuated by the metal shop signs all around banging up against the storefronts in the wind.

Victoria's feet were wedged atop her scuffed portmanteau, the entire world rushing haphazardly forward, breaking her young heart in two. Resolutely she forced back the tears that were ready to spill, smoothing the worn fabric of her second-best gown's brown skirt, telling herself she was being foolish. Hearts don't break in two, she told herself,

1

pulling her cape closer about her against London's cold, soot-laden air.

It had to be faced. All of it. Every single last miserable bit of it.

She was an orphan and now she had lost the only home she had ever known and the position that had ensured her way in the world. She was entirely alone. And she was riding miles and miles from London to the estate of a peer of the realm whom she did not know, who was not expecting her, and upon whom her entire future depended.

And there was no money for a return fare home. Home, she told herself ruefully, if such you could call this noisy, noisome city whose cruelty had closed down Mercy House. Had forced her to embark upon this perilous journey with nothing to aid her but her own determination not to end up in London's home for the poor.

She dozed after a bit. The steady rush of the carriage, the sudden gusts of wind, the sounds of the horse and carriage as it traversed the much-traveled roads, lulled Victoria into the rest she had not found in the night just past. Her tired head drooped forward, a tumble of russet-colored curls falling toward closed celadon eyes that dreamed uneasy dreams behind their gray-green irises.

The sounds out beyond the covered carriage were slowly fading away as they left the city. The Thames road followed the river as it wound westward, early spring greenery replacing the close-packed buildings and the noise of the city.

Something of the changed sounds and smells penetrated Victoria's dreams, awakening her. She no longer heard the harsh street sellers' cries, the smells of soot and people were gone too, replaced by the sweet scents of fresh grasses and country-clean air and the distant lowing of cattle.

She opened her eyes to see a stout gray church tower rising in the distance ahead of the cab. Below the church a tiny village of plaster-faced, half-timbered houses sat in the soft spring sunlight. Victoria stared at the red and brown tiled roofs and the great expanse of sloping meadow that stretched out all around the little village. Pale yellow buttercups blanketed the meadow, tall green beechwoods rising beyond it. Dark green fir trees and yews edged away toward a narrow track that turned riverward. When the hansom cab reached the track it turned onto it, the driver humming to himself as his horse dutifully headed over a hump in the narrow lane, a mansion now visible beside the river.

The great mansion had long ago been named for the willow trees that drooped delicately downward toward the Thames water in the distance. A long driveway wound up across gently rising ground toward the huge gray-stone house itself, an avenue of lime trees shading the freshly raked gravel.

Victoria stared at the house, which loomed larger and larger, her frightened eyes widening as its vastness bore in upon her. It was bigger than the whole of Mercy House itself, as large as a palace. The cab followed the drive, circling away from the river. Victoria glanced back toward its blue-green surfaces sparkling in the soft sunshine. Then she turned to face the huge house, swallowing hard.

Ivy trails softened its hard square lines, rosebushes crowding up close to one long side of the mansion, shades of rose-madder, claret, crimson, and ruby mixing with vermilions, pinks, and old gold.

They passed under a wrought-iron gate and soon came to a halt, the driver pulling on the reins, stopping next to stone steps. Twenty feet wide, each a few shallow inches high, they rose one above the next toward a large oak door. Banded in iron, it stood forbiddingly closed, the shadow of the house looming across the horse and carriage.

The driver wrapped the reins loosely around the brake, climbing down and reaching to help the young woman inside his cab. She took the hand that reached in toward her, allowing its grasp to steady her descent, her feet upon the gravel before she realized she was irretrievably set upon a course that led to the challenge of that closed doorway.

She tried to smile, the grizzled old man staring at her oddly. "You sure you be all right, miss?" he asked, peering at her with rheumy eyes that had seen most of what this modern world had to offer, for good and for bad. "This be the place?" His doubts came through, his eyes sparing her the embarrassment of studying her shabby attire. "I can pull round back." He offered. She shook her head, the auburn curls peeping out around the tiny feathered hat she wore, a gift from the matron before Mercy House closed its doors forever.

"This will be fine," Victoria told the man. "Please see to my bag."

And still he hesitated. "Shouldn't you be seeing to—that is, in case there's been a mix-up—"

Her heart-shaped chin set resolutely, she met the man's eye. "There is no mistake. And no going back," she added ambiguously, earning a sideways glance as he bent to his task.

Victoria Leggett turned toward the doorway a few shallow steps above the broad porch, hearing the driver huffing and puffing with the weight of her ungainly battered case. Even the portmanteau was a castoff, acquired from one of the most fortunate of Mercy House's inhabitants. The lucky young girl had come to Mercy House when she was but eight, this very portmanteau filled with clothes and toys, the woman who brought her crying copiously and vowing that matters should be made right. And right they were made, not two years later, when a great gray-bearded giant of a man had come to claim the child, staring down with moist eyes and calling her granddaughter. Hugging her close while hundreds of pairs of envious eyes found windows and doors and chinks in the wall to peer through. She was carried off, the lucky one, in a coach and four. The gray-bearded man was the girl's grandfather, Victoria had been told, that man having just learned the story of the terrible fate that had led his grandchild to Mercy House two long years before.

The sound of the portmanteau, left behind and given to Victoria, brought her thoughts unwillingly back to the task at hand. She reached into her almost empty purse, dispensing the few bob she had left into the driver's hand.

He looked down at it doubtfully, then at the girl before him, her slim young figure pulled up straight, her expression resolute. He tipped his cap, climbing up onto his perch and unhooking the reins before he looked back at Victoria. "It might be best as how I should wait," he said.

Victoria shook her head. She smiled, though he never knew how false a smile it was she gave him. "That will be fine. Thank you."

She swallowed, her heart beating as if the wings of a huge bird had been trapped within her breast, and watched the carriage turn about, listening to the horses' hooves as they beat their way back down the narrow drive. It was not until the hansom cab disappeared beyond the lacy lines of the wrought-iron gate that she turned around to face the forbidding door.

She walked up toward it with a resolute step, raising her small hand and making a fist around the bell pull that hung alongside the door.

At the sound of the pealing bells within, her strength of purpose deserted her. Her eyes closed against the enormity of the task before her, squeezing tight as if she might open them to find all this a dream.

And so Michael Dennis Flaherty's first glimpse of the girl who was to change his master's life showed a chit of a girl in mouse-brown clothes, her red curls tumbling about a tattered hat, her eyes squeezed closed, and her hands clasped tightly together.

"Yes?" He used his most dismissive tone, learned from the English staff who suffered his existence with the least good grace they could manage.

Gray-green eyes flew open to stare up at the swarthy, husky hulk before her. Michael Flaherty had reached his fifties with his bulging muscles intact, a few wrinkles curling about his open Irish face, and a laughter in his eyes that all the English had not been able to discipline. But at this moment he looked like the most prepossessing of retainers to the young girl who stared up at him.

"I'm to see the Duke of Bereshaven." She spoke in a clear, true voice, the quaver beneath her words barely discernible.

"Oh you are, are you? And who told you to come here, then?"

The fear that invaded her huge eyes would have melted a stone. "Is this not The Willows? Is he not here?" Thoughts of the wasted fare, the distance from London and civilization, the emptiness of her purse, all brought forth a desperation that was evident in her voice.

5

"The Willows it is. And who's this to be asking if he's here?"

"I am Victoria Leggett." She spoke with more assurance than she felt, determined to brazen it out. "I am the duke's new amanuensis."

"His what!" The burly man stared down at her from beneath bushy black eyebrows.

She raised her chin. "Sir Thomas Poysner sent me."

This stopped the big man. He stared at her for a long moment. "He did, did he?"

"Yes." Definite, combative, the word stood alone, not followed by others.

Mike Flaherty hesitated and then stepped back, letting her walk inside. "Then I'd best let him know you're here."

"Thank you." The hint of condescension in her tone pleased her. Victoria stepped forward, becoming more secure with each step she took.

The man motioned her toward a paneled oak bench along the far wall of the wide central hall. He waited until she sat down upon it, smoothing her skirts as he walked past her toward a far door on the other side of the hall.

Victoria was left alone, staring down at the polished marble floor with its mottled black and white markings. Beyond her rows of solid oak doors were spaced along either side of a hallway that stretched back within the house.

A chandelier, huge and elaborate, hung suspended from the high ceiling, its tiny crystal prisms tinkling gently in the breeze that carried down the hall from some hidden door, drawing her gaze upward as if in prayer.

A maid, dressed all in black except for her small white cap, came out of a doorway nearby. She stared at Victoria, then quickly bent her head, scurrying past, disappearing behind a green baize door to one side of the oak bench.

And still Victoria sat. The silence began to dissolve into small household sounds as her ears became accustomed to the house.

Beyond the green baize door, down the servants' hall, which led to a kitchen and butler's pantry and all the rooms of service that kept the great house operating smoothly, small sounds of movement could be heard. The murmur of voices came near and then drifted farther away. Someone shut a cupboard door with a loud and definite push.

The hall itself was silent, Victoria's own breathing loud in the quiet until a tall grandfather's clock began to chime. When it finished sounding the quarter hour, its steady deep-cadenced tick ... tock filled Victoria's ears, the clock's pendulum in concert with her own heart, each tick beating with her heart, each tock reverberating through her body.

"What the bloody hell do you mean, bags!" A man's voice, deep, powerful, and at the moment loud with irritation carried down the hall toward Victoria, bringing her to stiff attention in her seat. She clasped her hands together, praying silently for strength.

The sound of the voice was accompanied by the slamming of doors, the sound of booted feet slapping against marble, and soon Victoria found herself staring at the tallest man she had ever seen.

"Well!?"

The giant barked at her, the Irishman who had let her in coming up behind him. Victoria quickly stood up, curtsying as she replied: "Good morning, your grace."

There was a moment's hesitation as he stared down at the red-haired wench who slowly righted herself, standing a full foot shorter than himself when she straightened up. About five-foot-three, with the skin foreigners call English rose, she was breathtaking. Even in her shabby dun-colored clothes she possessed a regal stance, a presence that belied her humble possessions.

He knew nothing of the wild beating of her heart as he stared down at her. "What is the meaning of this?" He asked, glowering, his brown eyes black in the shadowy light, his glossy brown-black hair disheveled. He looked as if he had recently come in from the winds that blew out beyond the castlelike stillness of this huge hall. Or as if he was in the habit of running his hand through his hair, disarranging it into a tumble of thick dark curls.

"Well!?" He barked again when she did not immediately reply.

"Sir! Your grace," she amended, her eyes lowering again,

7

"You have advertised for the position of amanuensis. I am here in reply."

"Advertised!" He stared at her as if she were demented.

"You are in need of secretarial help. An amanuensis," Victoria added quickly. "You have let this be known."

"Yes! But I have not advertised!" His scandalized tone spoke volumes.

"Sir Thomas Poysner told me of the position."

There was a sudden stillness. When she found her courage, she braved staring up at him, seeing his unreadable expression gazing back at her. He looked to be in his thirties or so. And he was used to authority, that was apparent from his un-self-conscious management of himself and his household. From the servant who had answered her ring. But then of course, as cousin to the Queen, he would be used to having his own way.

"Sir Thomas recommends you?" the Duke of Bereshaven was asking.

She stared at him. "You are the duke, are you not?"

"Why do you ask?" He looked nonplussed, as if no one had ever had the temerity to ask such a question of him.

"Well?" she demanded.

"I am." He made the briefest bow imaginable. "As of these months, at any rate." He watched her more carefully. "Why the question?"

She took her courage in her hands. "I was told the Duke of Bereshaven was in need of an experienced amanuensis with strong secretarial skills. I am surprised that Sir Thomas has not apprised you of my coming. I should have thought he would have done so, since he is the one who told me of your need and is said to be a close associate of Your Grace's."

He stared at her. "Yes. You would suppose so, wouldn't you?"

"As I said," she replied calmly.

"I would too," he agreed. "Let's ask him, shall we?"

"What?" Her assurance faltered, her eyes widening.

"I think we both should confront him, what do you say?"

"I—" She swallowed. "It is a long ride from London."

"As you must well know, having just made it." He

watched her. "I understand from my man that you have trunks waiting upon the steps."

"One, sir. I mean your grace. Only one."

"Then Sir Thomas assured you that the position would be yours."

She hesitated. "One hardly would come all this way otherwise. Would one?" she asked the man who stared down at her with eyes that held strange lights now. He almost looked amused.

"One would not think so." he replied. "But then one seldom knows what another would do. Does one?"

Not knowing what to reply, she remained silent. He was studying her. "I am sure you are as curious as I am why Sir Thomas did not prepare anyone for your arrival."

"Perhaps," she began, "perhaps—after all, he is so busy and with so much on his mind . . ."

"Perhaps it has merely slipped his mind that he promised you employment on my staff?" the Duke supplied helpfully.

"Yes. Exactly!" She smiled up at him.

He nodded slowly. "Perhaps," he agreed. "Shall we ask him?" He repeated his earlier words.

Her eyes were wide, their gray-green depths reflecting a mixture of emotions. "I assure you I am fully qualified—"

"Sir Thomas would hardly recommend less, would he?" the duke said mildly.

"If you would care to put my abilities to the test before you send for him—I mean, he is a very busy man and one would hate to bother him unneedfully . . ."

"Of course." The duke stepped back, motioning her toward where he stood. "If you will follow me . . ."

For one brief moment she panicked. Glancing back toward the closed front door, she imagined herself fleeing out it, racing down the slopes of the buttercup-carpeted meadow, leaving this dark-eyed man and his insolent expression behind as she fled toward security. But security was gone. Mercy House was gone. Closed. And the only hope lay in brazening this moment out. She stood up, following the duke down the wide hall toward a closed door.

Telling herself she was fully capable of all the duties an amanuensis must carry out, she walked through the doorway and stopped in her tracks.

Before her was Sir Thomas Poysner. He was just turning away from the fireplace, still warming his hands behind him as the logs sparked up the chimney. His long legs spread wide apart on the Turkey carpet, he stared at her, his expression one of total disbelief.

"Victoria!" His surprise was apparent to all ears.

Her cheeks burned. Her heart pounded. Her knees buckled, the curtsy she gave involuntary. She sank almost to the floor before Mike Flaherty reached to help her.

"My lord . . ." she was saying as Mike lifted her up, his strong arm the only support she had.

Poysner was looking toward the duke, who shrugged. Still Sir Thomas stared. "Edward, what is the meaning of this?"

Edward Albert, ninth Duke of Bereshaven, shrugged. "The wench said you sent her."

"I did not!" Victoria found her voice and flared out, only to stop immediately upon seeing the men's eyes turn toward her. "I—I mean," she continued, "that I did not precisely say . . . that is, what I meant to say was that you felt I would be worthy of the position. Of amanuensis," she clarified, watching Sir Thomas.

Sir Thomas could feel her desperation and glanced at the duke. "Edward, we should talk."

"We should. Yes," the duke agreed. "Here. And now," he added, waiting for the solicitor to continue.

"I did tell the girl about the position," Sir Thomas said, seeing the duke's expression change.

The duke straightened up, glancing at the chit of a girl and walking toward the fireplace, his voice brusque when at last he spoke. "So you told her. And what else did you tell her? Promise her?" Edward's voice became colder.

"I promised nothing, obviously. There was nothing I could promise. When I found you were no longer maintaining your London residence but instead had removed to The Willows, I told her it would be impractical to apply."

"And yet here she is." Edward spoke as if Victoria were no longer in the room.

"My lords, may I remind you that I *am* here?" Both men turned to face her, Edward glancing at Mike, who grinned broadly behind the girl.

10

Seeing the duke's eyes upon him, Mike spoke freely. "She's got spirit."

"And I will do anything necessary to procure this position," Victoria put in quickly, seeing her chance.

Dead silence met her words. "I beg your pardon?" the duke said finally in a frigid tone.

"And well you should. Your grace," she added after a moment. "You've not even asked about my skills. You dismissed me out of hand."

"Yes." He drew himself even straighter, his backbone stiff. "Miss Whatever-your-name-is, I am perfectly aware of the overriding fact of your unsuitability as to—as to *gender*. That in itself is sufficient reason to give pause."

"Oh bosh!" She saw his shock. Even Sir Thomas looked startled. "I'm bloody good at what I do and yet every position I interview for, they tell me they only hire men! Then why pay lip service to jobs for women? Well? I was trained in all the secretarial skills. I have taught them as well. There is none you can hire who could serve you better."

"Really!" Edward Albert replied, scandalized. He turned toward Sir Thomas. "I have never seen such a lack of breeding . . . such a—" The duke turned back to glance toward Victoria. "Such lack of sensibility."

Mike grinned. "She reminds me of an Irish lass. Proud and full of vinegar." He spoke as did no servant, an easy familiarity to his conversation when he addressed the duke. "You aren't, are you lass? Irish, that is?"

She shook her head. "I don't know. I was left as a child at Mercy House." Her head came up then, to challenge the complacent man who stood across the room, looking down his aristocratic nose at her. "Mercy House is an orphanage for homeless girls. Or it was until the funds ran out and it had to close. There's not a lot of call for your kind of 'sensibility' when you don't know where your food is coming from."

"It's true," Sir Thomas said. "That is, about the home closing down," he added quickly, seeing Edward's expression. "The girl had nowhere to turn. She probably spent her last farthing getting here."

"I did," Victoria told them both, her little chin up now, pride keeping her voice from quavering.

"And had nowhere to leave her belongings, I suppose." The duke's tone was caustic, his expression disbelieving.

"I suppose I could have left them behind," she told him, meeting his eye. "But I could not have gone back to get them, so what was the point? I have no money, no home, and no relatives. If you do not take me in, I do not know what shall become of me."

"Why you bold little—" Edward cut the words off before he went further. "No one has ever forced me into any decision, let alone a chit such as you!"

"After all, Edward—" Sir Thomas began, only to be stopped by the Duke's upraised hand.

"Don't tell me, Thomas, I shall not listen. You have created this situation and you shall have your hands full remedying it. What you do with her once you return her to the city is your concern, not mine." He turned away. "There is work to be continued in the study. I shall await you there."

Mike Flaherty started after the duke, stopping one brief moment to grin down at the girl. "Don't worry, he's not so bad once you get to know him."

"I fear I shall not be here long enough to find that out," she told him.

"Now, don't you go worrying so." Mike grinned and then left.

Sir Thomas tried to smile. "At least you seem to have won his servant over."

"Is he truly? A servant I mean? He speaks in such a familiar way toward the duke."

Sir Thomas smiled faintly. "Not any more than you yourself."

"That's different." She searched for the ways in which it was different but found she could not explain what she meant.

He saw that she was trembling. "Victoria, have you eaten today?"

"I did not have time," she lied.

"I thought as much." He walked to a cord by the fireplace.

"It's all right!" she said quickly. "I do not want any favors from him!"

"My dear girl, you've asked for a much bigger favor than a bite to eat, you know."

"I have not! I work hard and earn each penny I make."

"I'm sorry, I did not mean that. I meant—well, the way you appeared on the doorstep. After all, you could hardly think he would simply take you in."

Tears came then, unbidden. Unable to keep them back any longer, tired and afraid and bewildered, she ducked her head, dabbing at them with a tiny square of darned lace. "I thought he would at least interview me," she said through soft sobs.

"Oh, my dear girl, please—" Sir Thomas looked pained, unsure what to do with a crying female. He pulled on his own large linen handkerchief, bringing it to her and handing it over. "It's not as bad as all that."

"Yes. It is," she told him, sniffling. "How can you say it's not?"

"What I mean is, that is I meant to say, that, after all . . . I mean . . ." He trailed off, his pale blue eyes worried as he searched her woebegone face. "Oh dash it all, let me talk to him!"

"It won't help," Victoria said through her tears as Sir Thomas started toward the door. "He won't care." Tear-filled green eyes looked beseechingly into his own, an unspoken plea in them.

"We'll just see about that," Sir Thomas said as he left.

Victoria sank to the soft cushions of a heavily upholstered blue velvet sofa, her frail shoulders bent forward, her head down. A soft cough made her look up to see a young maid standing in the doorway. "You rang, miss?" the girl asked, curiosity in her eyes as she stared at the handkerchief and the red-rimmed eyes of the young woman seated across the room.

"Oh . . . Sir Thomas wished some . . . tea . . . and scones if you have them."

The girl's expression did not change. "We have them, miss. Would you like them in here, then?"

"Yes. I mean, I think he would. Thank you."

"You're welcome, miss." The girl left, Victoria listening to her walk across the marble-floored hall outside. She listened for Sir Thomas's return, holding her breath and praying silently, taking a deep breath to calm herself when she heard footsteps again approaching the open door.

After a moment the tall, dark-eyed duke appeared. He stopped in the doorway, framed by it as he stared at her, his expression unreadable. "Sir Thomas feels that since you are here, you can be useful. He is dictating correspondence concerning certain estate matters."

She stood up quickly, before he could change his mind. "Oh yes, your grace. I should be most happy to do what I can." She started toward him, missing her step a little as she hurried forward. She almost tripped, and the duke stepped forward to help her. His hand grabbed her elbow, keeping her upright. "Are you all right?" he asked.

"Fine. Thank you." She stared up at those eyes that had looked at her so coldly before. Concern showed in them now, a gentleness in his voice as he felt her trembling beneath his touch.

"You are sure you're quite well?"

She tried to smile, tried to look away when he began to search her face, when he stared at the red rims of her eyes. "Yes, thank you."

She walked on past him, out into the hall, waiting then for him to show her the way. When he came out and started toward the back of the house, the young maid appeared, a tray in hand. She stopped when she saw the duke leading Victoria away.

The duke glanced at the tray. "What's that?"

"Tea and biscuits for the"—the girl saw Victoria shake her head quickly—"for Sir Thomas, your grace," the girl finished, seeing Victoria's grateful smile.

"He needs nothing, we just had our meal." Victoria followed the duke toward a far door, the maid watching them go in before turning back toward the kitchen.

The door the duke led Victoria to opened onto a smallish room filled with books, memorabilia, and heavy dark furniture from some long-ago age. The walls were papered with a dark print of exotic birds, their plumage darkened with age, blending now into the dark green background of palm fronds and forest vistas.

Sir Thomas smiled encouragingly at Victoria as she stood in the doorway, the Duke of Bereshaven walking past her, on across the room.

"Really, Thomas, you must do something about that great appetite of yours," the duke was saying.

Sir Thomas glanced from the duke to Victoria as Edward continued, "I sent the girl away; you hardly need a tray when we just finished the midday meal."

"I—that is to say—perhaps Miss Leggett would like some refreshment . . ."

The duke looked toward the girl. "Come in then, come along. If you're to be any use, you can't stand in the doorway forever." He watched her move forward. "Do you wish to aid and abet this glutton's appetite?"

"No." She spoke softly, swallowing hard against the hunger pang that grabbed at her stomach.

Sir Thomas looked worried. "I say, don't browbeat the girl. You are hungry, are you not, child? Speak. It's all right."

"It's perfectly all right," the duke added, leaning back in his chair and banging his fists down onto the wide mahogany desk before him. "If we are to waste the afternoon discussing such nonsense and then watching this chit eat scones, we shall never finish!"

"I'm not hungry," Victoria said very loudly. Gaining control of her voice, she spoke again. "I am here to assist you in your work."

"Are you sure . . ." Sir Thomas began.

"Capital!" the duke interjected. "Then, shall we *begin!*" He badgered his solicitor until Sir Thomas finally returned to the task at hand.

"We were discussing the disposition of your Irish holdings," the lawyer said.

The duke's eyes hooded over. "My father sold them off."

"That was his intention. However, his death prevented the finalization of the contracts."

The duke stood up, his eyes searching the middle distance

15

as if answers lay there. When he spoke, his tone was mild. "It then becomes my decision."

When he said no more, Sir Thomas replied, "Yes, of course."

The duke walked to the tall windows that looked out toward the rosebushes. Staring past the budding blossoms, he spoke again, his voice as far away as his eyes. "I was born there. In Ireland."

"Yes," Sir Thomas said when the duke did not continue. "As to the disposition of the lands . . ."

The duke did not reply immediately. "I was seven when my father brought us here . . . twenty-eight years ago . . . the Famine." He spoke as if the others were not in the room. But when he turned back to face Victoria and his solicitor, his eyes hardened. "I shall not quite yet sell off the Irish estates, Thomas. That shall wait until I've thought it over."

"But your father had agreed—"

The Duke smiled, but there was no humor in his eyes. "My father, the late duke, had no love for Ireland, or things Irish. Including his late wife and his sons. Suffice it to say that he died prematurely, for the purposes of those who wished to buy our lands. I have been duke only a scant two months but I *am* duke. They shall have to abide by my decision."

When he finished speaking, he looked toward Victoria. "Had you not best sit? If you are to construct these letters I fail to see how it can be done standing up."

Conscious of his eyes upon her, she walked slowly toward Sir Thomas and sat on the chair he held out for her. She reached for the pen and inkwell, pulling a piece of parchment from the pile to one side of the desk. Holding it firmly, smoothing it out, she dipped the pen into the ink and then looked up, waiting for them to dictate their thoughts.

Sir Thomas began to speak, phrasing his letter in lawyers' jargon, speaking faster as he went on. Edward watched the girl's small white hand fly quickly across the page, carving ink figures into the parchment as fast as Sir Thomas spoke. The beginning of a grudging admiration made him turn away, his hands clasped behind his back, his gaze on the grounds outside again as he turned back toward the windows. The even cadences of his solicitor's words, the light scratching of the pen's nib across the parchment, were the only sounds to be heard in the room behind him. Outside the gardeners were pruning bushes, swapping lazy jokes as birds called to each other overhead, the day lengthening, the grounds of The Willows vibrant with life.

Chapter 2

THE SUN HAD CLIMBED much higher, the wind still whip-ping great white clouds across the pale blue afternoon sky outside the study where Victoria still worked.

The duke was reading a long legal document as Sir Thomas ended another missive. "Please see that the required information reaches his grace at the earliest opportunity as new papers must be drawn up once the above terms are agreed to." Sir Thomas leafed through the last of the letters he held, looking over at Edward, who glanced up when he spoke. "Do you wish some reply sent to Butts?"

"I shall attend to that later," the duke answered.

"I must repeat my earlier advice. To involve yourself, in any way, with the Irish party will surely lead to problems."

Victoria heard their words through a numbness that was beginning to encroach upon her thoughts. She struggled against it, biting her lower lip hard as she bent to copy the letters dictated, telling herself that her employment de-pended upon her completion of this task.

There was nowhere else to go, no one else to turn to; only her secretarial skills and her determination could save her from the poor house or worse.

"Edward, you are to meet with the Queen this very week. What could you say to her if you embarked on any such association! A member of her own family, a peer of the realm, and in league with her greatest enemies!"

"Enough!" the duke's voice barked out, straightening

18

Victoria's spine, turning her to look toward the two men who stood before each other. "I shall do what I feel must be done and my decisions will not be based upon the Queen's wishes or any others but my own."

"You worry me," Sir Thomas said, staring into eyes that gave no hint of the man's inner thoughts. "You are so new to the responsibility, the position. To antagonize the Crown at such a moment in your career could lead to ruin."

"You assume that I intend to align myself with the Irish cause."

Thomas Poysner watched the man who was but five years younger than himself. Hoping the duke meant what he seemed to be saying, the solicitor hesitated before replying. "If I misread your intentions, I apologize."

"Fine. Let's end this discussion."

Sir Thomas stiffened. "If you wish to dismiss my opinions, I assure you I am ready to leave."

The duke waved the man's words away, turning toward the girl who sat wide-eyed across the room. "Thomas, don't go all pomp and circumstance on me. You have made your views abundantly clear. Why continue to yammer on about them?"

The duke spoke with wry good humor but Sir Thomas was not to be placated by easy words and casual good humor. "I am not aware that I have ever been guilty of 'yammering' on about anything."

"Good Lord." The duke still looked toward Victoria. "Can you tell this champion of yours that there is no cause for pettishness. I may not say things with the best of court manners but surely he's used to that by now."

Victoria stood up, feeling her head reel as she did so, the movement bringing a dizzy spin to the chambers. "Sir Thomas is the kindest of men and the most loyal of friends. Anyone who cannot treat him with courtesy is—is—" Victoria found herself at a loss for words, the room still spinning slowly about her. She reached for the support of the smooth dark-wood desk as she moved around it to face the duke.

"Is?" The duke stared down at her, curious.

She tried to glare at him but her eyes were no longer focusing. A small part of her brain was telling her to hush up, to say nothing that would endanger her position here, but the rest of her brain was shouting loud and clear that she *had* no position here. That this duke would as soon turn her out as look at her. The thought itself angered her; all the worry of these last weeks, all the fear that had kept her awake the long night before, all the hopes she had nursed, the dreams she had spun—all were coming tumbling down upon her as she looked up at this man who held her future in his hands. "You are ungrateful, arrogant, and cruel!" she told him, amazed at herself. She felt her knees buckling even as she wondered to herself if she could actually have voiced the words she heard in her mind.

The last thing she saw was the look of surprise and concern in the Duke of Bereshaven's eyes.

Edward saw the young girl staring up at him, saw her swaying toward him, and instinctively reached out to prevent her fall. Sir Thomas moved quickly to help, a strangled oath escaping his lips. "Now look what you've done!"

Edward had his arms full of Victoria, reaching to cushion her fall, her head slumped against his shoulder, her body limp in his arms. "I!" The duke sounded insulted. "*I* have done nothing! You are the one who sent her on this fool's errand. You should have known I would never hire a woman!"

"Yes! I should have realized you were as pigheaded as your father! Meanwhile, the girl's starving to death and fainting dead away!"

"Starving—"

"Why the bloody hell do you think I ordered food!"

"Well, why didn't you say so? She herself said she wanted none!"

"She wants the job, you bloody imbecile—she was afraid of you!" Sir Thomas heard his own words, his high-pitched angry voice, and subsided, staring down at the girl. "I'll take her," he said then.

"You'll do nothing of the sort." Edward reached beneath her, lifting her up into his arms. "Open the door. We must get her to a bed." He started across the room, Sir Thomas moving quickly to open the door before Edward reached it.

Passing his solicitor, the duke almost smiled. "I must say you show none of the diplomatic skills you are so anxious I should learn."

Sir Thomas expostulated mildly as Edward walked into the marble-floored hall. "Make yourself useful," Edward told him. "Ring for Michael and tell him to send for the doctor." Edward had started up the grand staircase, Victoria enfolded in his arms. "And hurry before we have the wench die on our hands." Under his breath, as he trudged up the stairs, he spoke again, looking down at the top of her head, auburn curls tumbling in disarray, her hat pushed to one side. "I think you've probably planned just such an occurrence, haven't you, if only to disrupt my day. You wish my household to be like every penny dreadful, filled with tales of the murder of poor working girls at the hands of the aristocracy."

Victoria heard his voice but could not place it. The sound came from a long way away, the words a jumble in the soft floating place where she heard them. She felt as if she were being carried down long corridors of shadows, carried onward by strong arms, shielded from harm. She could feel the warmth, the strength, that surrounded her but was unable to name it, having never felt it before.

And so she floated up, content to bask in the warmth she felt, reason as far away as reality. Slowly, slowly, she came awake, feeling the soft yellow silk of the duke's waistcoat against her cheek, feeling the strength of his arms as he carried her down a long corridor of closed doors.

A woman appeared, uniformed and capped, her face swimming before the gray-green eyes that opened and closed again. Victoria heard a door open and then felt herself lifted away from his body, his arms placing her down onto the cool white sheets of a tall, narrow bed.

Her eyes opened, staring up into his.

He was bent over her, his arms still around her, laying her back on the white cotton bedding. Behind them Sir Thomas and the housekeeper came into the room; Mike was talking to someone in the hall.

Edward stared down at Victoria's eyes, his lips hovering

scant inches from the full soft curves of her mouth. His hands were full of her, the soft scent of lilacs filling his nostrils.

She felt the strength of his arms, the gentleness of his hands, her eyes full of wonder. She had never felt a man's hands in all the long years she could remember. No men worked at Mercy House, save the elderly doctor whom she had never had to endure, the tales of his lechery rampant among the young charges who should have been shielded from such stories. Their words had been just that to Victoria, mere words, unlinked to reality, to the drab days that followed one after another down through the years of her youth.

But now she felt something she could not name. A quick surge of sweetly bitter feeling that she did not want to end. His eyes seemed filled with worlds she could merely glimpse, worlds she wanted to explore. She could feel him pulling away, his arms withdrawing from around her as he laid her back upon the bed, leaving her bereft. Her small hand reached to touch his arm, the shock of feeling that coursed through her transmitted to him, making him hesitate.

Her eyes looked up into his, her hand lying atop his sleeve. As he moved, her hand moved, slowly, down his sleeve until she touched his bare wrist. She felt a tremor pulsing through him and it made her tremble too, her eyes liquid and yielding as she stared up at him.

He reached to cover her hand with his, the warmth of her touch quickening his pulse.

"Is she all right?" Sir Thomas asked from nearby.

"What?" Edward spoke, his control over his voice unsure. "Yes." He began to straighten up again, her hand still in his, his eyes unable to tear themselves away from hers. "She's coming awake."

He could feel the slight pressure of her hand as it tried to keep him near, and then let go, letting him pull away to stand straight at the side of the bed.

"Victoria?" Sir Thomas leaned over the bed. "Can you hear me?"

She swallowed, nodding, her hand now flat against the sheets. She could still feel the warmth of his touch. "Yes, I can hear you," she told Sir Thomas, her eyes searching for Edward as he stepped farther back. "Yes." Her voice was very soft, very weak. "Thank you. I'm so sorry."

"Sorry? Don't be silly! Edward, come tell this girl she's nothing to feel sorry for!"

Edward's face swam into view beside Sir Thomas's. "He's right, you know. Except that you should have had the sense to say you were hungry."

"Yes . . ." She smiled tentatively up at the man whose arms had enfolded her, had carried her here. "Thank you . . ."

He shook his head. "Nothing of the kind."

"Dr. Fry." Michael's voice came from the doorway, a tiny little man coming in beside him, putting down his bag to peer closely at the patient on the narrow bed.

He reached to pull her eyelids up and down before clucking to himself, reaching back toward his bag to rummage within it.

"She needs food." A woman's voice spoke from the opposite side of the bed. Victoria's eyes turned toward the plumpish woman who stood there, arms akimbo, glaring at the doctor. "A bit of soup and tea and all will be well."

"We shall see," the doctor said in his most enigmatic fashion. "There may be more complicated matters here than one would think."

The housekeeper stood her ground, staring directly at the duke. "Well, your grace, do I see to some food for this poor girl or do we wait for some mumbo-jumbo from his highness the doctor here?"

"I beg your pardon!" The doctor drew himself up to his full height, trying unsuccessfully to stare the woman down.

"I've had enough truck with doctors to tell you what I think of them if you've not got delicate ears," she told the men stoutly.

"Fix the soup, Bess," the duke said quietly. "It can't hurt," he said when the doctor glared at him. "And it just might help."

"Aye, and a bit of whiskey will bring her round straightaway," Mike was saying.

"We have to be careful," Sir Thomas added.

"Yes. Thanks to you," the duke told him.

"Me!"

"You sent her here, did you not?"

Victoria heard them arguing as from a vast distance. She felt the doctor poking about at her, clucking to himself. But she left them all to their bickering, floating back toward the strong arms that had held her close, savoring the sweet security she had felt when his strength had enfolded her.

"Edward . . ." A woman came into the room. "What's happened here?" Her voice was harsh, authoritarian.

The Duke's reply came slowly. "Aunt Judith, please leave us. This is no concern of yours."

"No concern! Who is this girl and why is she here? I have a right to ask. I will not permit decadent practices in my household."

Edward grew visibly colder. "May I remind you," he said quietly, "that this is my household?"

She stiffened, looking from him to Sir Thomas as if to enlist aid. When she found none forthcoming, she left without a word.

After the door closed Sir Thomas cleared his throat. "Edward, after all, you know she did not mean what she said to be taken in that light."

"How do you know?" Edward asked him, staring him down. "How precisely do you think she meant it? How many shades of meaning are there to the word *decadent?* Well? And as to 'my' household—does that also lend itself to interpretation?"

"She is your father's sister."

"Of that I am well aware. And of her opinion of me I am also well aware." Edward looked toward the bed. "Doctor, what is your verdict?"

"The girl needs rest."

"Yes," Edward said dryly. "I could have told you that and spared you coming all this way."

"I beg your pardon?" The doctor stood up, putting his tools away within his bag, looking up when the housekeeper reappeared with a tray of tea and bread and butter. "Good. Please see that she eats," he told the woman, earning a murderous look before he turned, smiling, toward the duke. "As you suggested, your grace, the girl has been deprived.

24

The good Lord alone knows for how long. She needs rest and bland food for the moment. Soon she will be as good as new."

"Soon?" The duke scowled.

"Doctor," Sir Thomas interjected, pulling him aside, "what the duke means is for how long must the poor girl be bedridden?"

The doctor shrugged. "It's hard to tell. She is young, she should regain her strength quickly. But for the time being it is not advisable for her to do much. She should be kept as still as possible."

The duke walked closer to the bed, staring down at the girl who was slowly drinking from a tiny porcelain cup the housekeeper held to her lips. "Do you hear him?" the duke asked Victoria.

Victoria's eyes followed the sound of his voice, looking up at him as the woman she did not know put the tea to her lips. She swallowed a little, then turned her lips away, still watching the dark-haired, dark-eyed man. "Yes," she said softly. "But I am fine, I assure you."

"And he assures me that you must be kept low for the time being."

"No. Please . . ." She tried to sit up, the housekeeper forcing her back to the pillows. "I'm all right," Victoria insisted, her weak voice belying her words.

"Stay still." His voice stopped her agitation. She stared up at him, losing herself in the depths of his dark eyes. "I shall tell you when you may get up," he continued, watching her sink back against the pillows as if exhausted with the effort of trying to leave them. "Do you hear me?"

She nodded, her eyes filling with tears. "Thank you," she said, tears choking her words, turning away from him so he would not see her undone.

The duke looked awkwardly away and then nodded curtly toward the doctor. Striding past Sir Thomas, he spoke as he left the room. "See to her comfort. I shall want to discuss matters with you before you go, Thomas. I shall be below."

He was gone; Victoria stared toward the doorway and then saw Sir Thomas watching her, his expression puzzled, vague feelings of unease pricking at him. She accepted the spoonful of soup the housekeeper brought to her lips, her eyes following Sir Thomas now as he paced the room end to end, back and forth, over and over.

"Please—" she told him when he had traversed it several times over, "Please, do not worry . . . I am well taken care of. I am fine."

The housekeeper looked up at the lawyer. "If you're worried about the girl, don't be, . . . she's in good hands and she'll be going nowhere for the time being."

Sir Thomas stared at the housekeeper, then his eyes traveled to meet Victoria's. "Aye. That's what I'm afraid of."

He said no more before he left them to each other, the doctor walking out with him, regaling him with medical facts as they walked away down the hall.

The sounds of their voices fell back toward Victoria and the housekeeper, who smiled at her young charge. "I don't know what you're about, young lady, or how you've managed it, but I think you're here to stay for a while."

Victoria smiled at the woman, her eyes closing with the effort. "Oh, I hope so," she said. "I hope so . . ."

She drifted off to sleep, the plain, plump woman watching the young girl for a long moment before gathering up the tray and starting out toward the kitchens below.

The room lay in silence then, only Victoria's steady breathing breaking the stillness, the hours of the day creeping slowly by.

Evening crept up upon Victoria with the same steadiness. One moment she was closing her eyes against the late-slanting rays of the afternoon sun and the next she found herself opening her eyes to blink at the brightness of the fire in the grate, the room beyond the arc of brightness shrouded in dark shadows, blackness filling the view beyond the window.

The sound of someone whispering came toward her as she lay upon the bed. "He can't come here, Edward. You must not let him." The woman's voice was low; she pleaded her case softly. "It will be the end of everything if he does."

"Don't you think I want to stop him? There's no way I can." Bitterness colored the duke's reply. "Don't you know if there were any way at all, I'd use it?" The words were wrenched out of him, the force of the feeling behind them turning him away from her, the shadows resolving themselves into two figures near the closed door to the hall.

He came forward, stopping in front of the grate. Resting his hands on the narrow mantel, he stared down at the flames. His face and figure were still in shadows, sudden bursts of reddish light from the leaping fire flaring out to highlight his anguished face and the white silk of his waistcoat beneath the black evening clothes that blended into the shadows around him.

The woman stepped closer, staring down into the fire, her blond hair the only clear feature to be made out as she stood beside him. "What's to become of us?" she asked softly, expecting no reply.

After a space of silent moments she turned and saw Victoria's open eyes. "Good evening," the woman said, startling the duke, who straightened up, looking toward the bed.

"Is she awake?" he asked.

"Yes." The blond woman came nearer the bed, smiling down at Victoria.

The duke hesitated by the fireplace. "I shall be in my study," he said as he left.

The woman stopped beside Victoria, straightening the coverlet a little, sitting down after a moment on the narrow wood chair the housekeeper had brought near earlier. "Are you feeling better?" she asked, gentle concern in her eyes.

Victoria nodded, moving against the soft goose down of the pillows propped under her head. "Thank you, yes. I'm sorry to be such a bother—"

"Don't be silly, we're just glad you're better."

Victoria stared at the woman. She was all soft roundnesses. In her thirties perhaps, with creamy skin and large blue eyes that watched Victoria carefully at the moment.

"I understand you are very good at your work," the blond woman said, a small smile hovering about her mouth. "Even, it seems, when you are ready to faint dead away."

"Your grace, I assure you, I am normally the healthiest of people—" Victoria began earnestly.

"I'm no one's 'grace,' Miss Leggett. Or may I call you Victoria? I am Sylvia, the duke's sister-in-law."

"Oh." Victoria stared at the vision before her, the woman's face fading in and out of view as she found her eyes closing of their own accord. She struggled to keep them open.

"Don't fight the doctor's medicine, Victoria. It's meant to help you rest. And when you wake, we shall get you fattened up so that you can proceed to find a proper position. Shhh . . . there's nothing to fret about. I shall sit by you until you sleep."

Sylvia's voice was soothing, memories of a kind helper years ago at Mercy House conjured up with her words . . . I shall sit by you until you sleep, child . . . no more tears for your lost folks, there's no reason to fear . . . sleep now. . . . The words came echoing back from childhood, the lonely child once more hugging her bedclothes close, afraid of the dark. Of the future. Of the loneliness that ached within her heart.

Her last thought was of the duke's arms, strong around her, the comfort of them coming back to smooth her brow as she drifted off to sleep.

Chapter 3

MORNING BROUGHT THE TALL grim-faced woman the duke had called Aunt Judith. She stood in the doorway, staring in toward the awakening Victoria.

When she saw Victoria's eyes open, she spoke. "I have no idea what you think you are about. This is a decent house and I shall see to it that it stays so."

"Please—" Victoria cleared her throat, trying to sit up.

"Don't try your pleases on me, miss." The woman turned away, shutting the door behind her.

Fear welled up again, filling Victoria with dread. She could hardly stay in a household that wanted no part of her. She threw off the covers and stood, only to sit quickly down, her head spinning at the sudden movement. If only she had planned more carefully, if only she had eaten something before coming—but if she had, she told herself ruefully, she would not have had enough money left to make the journey. She had chosen a slim chance over none.

Her shoulders drooped as she thought of the endless interviews she had trudged to over the last months. Through winter's sleet and snow, through wind and bitter cold, to offices where every pair of eyes were averted from her, the men within them treating her as a leper. One even upbraiding her for trying to take the bread out of some poor man's mouth, of taking the bread from his children's mouths as well. She had come close to telling the sour-breathed gentleman in the green eyeshade that whether he thought so or not, she had to have bread too, for she had found no way to live on air alone. But she had said none of it. She had sat with her hands folded in her lap, had suffered the polite refusals, the impolite refusals, and even the knowing eyes, the smiling invitation to discuss her situation over a glass of sherry later that night. In her rooms, if she preferred, in order to be discreet. After all, there were ways and ways for a nice-looking young woman to earn her keep in the world. Some gentlemen were more than kind.

She had found a blank stare helpful. And bland questions about the meaning of the words until at last they would think her dull-witted and not worth the effort.

She shivered, the fire in the grate banked down and almost out. March winds blew hard out beyond the stone walls of the house, the entire world presenting a grim and forbidding picture to Victoria's worried eyes this early spring morning. The room was cold, chilling her further as she stood up, moving slowly so as not to make her head begin to spin again.

She reached for her petticoat, unhooking the night robe someone had unpacked from her bag. Her brown traveling dress had been hung in the wardrobe. And her gray, her best black, her old blue gown. She stared at her things laid out and hung up, neatly put away. Her heart leaped to her throat, a tiny ray of hope forming within the dark cloud of her worry. They would not have unpacked her things if she were to be thrust out today. There might be hope of a second chance. After all, she was here, and he did need an amanuensis. It might be possible, she kept telling herself as she dressed, even if the grim-faced Aunt Judith did not approve.

Downstairs the young maid was carrying a tray toward the stairwell. "Oh! I was to bring this to you, miss."

"I thought I'd best be up," Victoria told her shyly.

The girl smiled. "Me mum always says you lose your strength laying about. 'Course how she'd know when she's never had a day off in her life is beyond me." The girl hesitated, her voice lowering when she continued. "Mr. Flaherty says you're to stay."

Sudden hope shone in Victoria's face, her words eager. "Who said I should stay?"

"Mr. Flaherty, the duke's man. You met him yesterday. The Irish gentleman."

"The duke's man?" Victoria repeated, wondering if his words meant the duke had said so himself.

"Oh yes, he came back from Ireland with them all those years ago. Inseparable they are, Mr. Flaherty being more like a father than the duke's own was, they say." The young maid stopped, wondering if she'd said too much.

"What's your name?" Victoria asked her.

"I'm Nancy, miss." She bobbed a little curtsy, still holding the tray of tea and toast.

"I'm Victoria, Nancy. There's no need to call me miss."

"Oh yes, miss!" Nancy replied earnestly. "Mr. Dodd, he that was secretary to the old duke, he was always to be called Mr. Dodd. And you are to be Miss Leggett. Mr. Flaherty told us."

"Did Mr. Dodd retire?" Victoria asked the girl.

"Not exactly," Nancy replied. She looked hesitant to say more. "If you like, I can show you to the dining room and Lady Sylvia."

"Is Lady Judith there?" Victoria's expression made Nancy smile.

"She's up and out early, Lady Judith is. You'll not be bothered by her this morning."

"Good," Victoria said faintly, realizing afterward she had said it out loud. "I mean, thank you. If you would show me the way—"

"It's just along here, then." Nancy led the way down the long main hall that ran the length of the house, stopping briefly by closed double doors. "This is the formal dining room, but breakfast is served in the morning room," she said as she moved on, Victoria coming slowly behind, her stomach fluttering with unease as well as hunger, the huge strange house closed away within itself.

Nancy led Victoria to a narrow door at the end of the hall. Just beyond it, French doors opened up onto a stone terrace, the Thames visible far away across the lawns. Weeping willows drooped elegantly toward the riverbank in the distance.

The maid waited for Victoria to open the door. Then she walked back toward the green baize door, reaching for a piece of cold toast from the tray she still held.

The morning room was bright and cheerful, a fire roaring away in a narrow Dutch tile–covered fireplace. Two-inch-wide stripes of lemon yellow and cream repeated over and over again in the wallpaper that reached from midway up the wall to just below the ceiling. Above and below the wallpaper dark oak paneling lent a dignified air to the little room.

Across the table, looking up to smile at Victoria, Sylvia sat before a plate of kippers and toast. Her creamy blond beauty fit the room, her welcoming motion carrying Victoria forward. "Good for you, to be up and about so soon. How was your night? Were you comfortable?"

"Yes, but I must apologize for making such a spectacle of myself. I didn't mean to be thrust upon your household so awkwardly."

"Nonsense. Come eat. We don't want you fainting away again, do we? The dishes are all along the sideboard there. We serve ourselves breakfast, as much as we like, so you must eat for both yesterday and today too."

Victoria walked to the long bow-legged sideboard, reaching for a plate and looking toward the covered serving dishes.

"Don't be shy."

"It's not that. This is almost like at the home," Victoria said, reaching for a cover, revealing poached eggs. She reached for a spoon. "Except of course our dishes were not so pretty, nor were they matched. But we always helped ourselves along a line and then sat to table where we chose."

"Edward said you came from a home for girls."

"Yes. Mercy House. There were seventeen girls. Children I mean. And four of us working there, not including Matron. Until Lady Ashbrook passed away and the city closed it down."

"What will become of the children now?"

Victoria took a sausage from another plate and a slice of toasted bread as she replied, trying to keep her voice steady. "I'm not sure. We were told they were being transferred to good homes, but I fear they have wound up in London Orphanage. One ran away, I know; she was fourteen and said she could make her own way. I fear what will become of her."

"How beastly. And there was no warning?"

"None whatsoever." Victoria brought her plate to the table, hesitating and then sitting down opposite Lady Sylvia. "Lady Ashbrook had seemed in the best of health. Her heart gave out suddenly and then it was found that she had not made a proper will—she of course had not planned upon becoming ill—then solicitors said she was too ill to make one, for her mind was wandering. Or so said her relatives. She had cousins in Warwickshire, it turned out. She'd never been close to them but they had barristers who petitioned the court to allow them control of her estate. They were quite unpleasant about the school. And so it closed."

"You poor child. And you've never known another home?"

Victoria shook her head. "No."

"Sir Thomas said as much. Well, you shall now. At least until we can get you on your feet and situated."

"I *am* on my feet," Victoria pointed out. "And I am a very well trained secretary. If the duke will only give me a chance to prove my worth, I am sure I can satisfy him."

"Yes. Well . . . " Sylvia smiled sadly at the young girl. "We shall see."

"It is not unheard of for women to do such work. Truly, there are many gentlemen, peers, who have used female amanuenses to great advantage. And there is a book, Sir Thomas told me, a book the duke wished to complete."

"A book? Oh, you mean his father's history. Yes, I suppose he is planning on going forward with it. But you see—" Sylvia searched for words that would not offend. "Those of whom you speak, and I myself know of a gentleman of our acquaintance whose amanuensis is indeed a lady . . . " Sylvia saw Victoria's hopeful look. "This lady is, well, just that you see. A lady. And his relative at that, a cousin of some sort or another. So the situation is quite different."

"A lady," Victoria repeated slowly, her cheeks burning.

33

"And a relative," Sylvia added quickly. "More tea?"

"No. Thank you." Victoria looked down at her plate. Then back up to meet the other woman's kind blue eyes. Sylvia looked pained to have had to bring up such a delicate subject.

"I cannot tell you that I am a lady. Or baseborn. Or any other fact, since I know no facts of my origins. But I assure you I have been taught in a most careful manner."

"Yes, of course you have," Sylvia said gently. "Unfortunately, Lady Ashbrook had an—unfortunate—reputation within court circles."

"She was unblemished!" Victoria interjected quickly, her voice rising in defense of the woman who had given her the only home she had ever known.

"Of course, please—I understand." Sylvia spoke quickly too, smiling, trying to calm the girl. "I only meant that her association with those who have been most adamantly vocal in their support of women's freedoms had cast a pall over her. And her—associates."

"You do not believe women should be free?" Victoria asked, astonished.

"But we *are* free," Sylvia replied. "In every important way. And, as the Queen herself says, women are the lesser vessel after all. We are not meant to have our heads in books."

"Why ever not?"

"It addles the brain."

Victoria stared at the woman across from her. A kind woman. Gentle and beautiful and kind. "Do you really think that?"

"The Queen herself has said so. We are not meant for riotous freedoms; we would not know what to do with them. We would abuse the privileges granted us in the end. Then where would we be? Unsure of ourselves, unprotected by gentlemen, all alone in the world—"

Victoria swallowed. "Perhaps because I have always been alone in the world, unaided by father or brother or gentleman, I do not feel that it is so impossible to function alone."

"But my dear, even now, it is a man whose largess you must depend upon for work."

"Not largess, surely! I would not expect to be kept on for

34

any reason other than that I did my work well and gave value for my salary!"

Edward spoke from the doorway. "A noble sentiment."

His words startled Victoria, her tea spilling over the edge of the pale yellow cup she held. He came forward, dressed in riding breeches and coat, a whip still in his hands. He flicked it against his palm as he studied her. "You look none the worse for yesterday. How do you feel?"

"Thank you, your grace, I am much better. I am quite well, I assure you, and ready to begin my duties."

"You are, are you?"

She took her courage in her hands, her eyes rising to meet his. She kept her gaze steady, her hands clasped together in her lap, fingers gripping each other as she spoke again. "Yes. I should very much like to begin."

He looked amused. He glanced over at Sylvia. "What are we to do with her, Sylvie? Toss her out or give her a chance?"

"Perhaps we could find employment for her."

"Oh thank you!" Victoria smiled gratefully at the woman.

"Just a minute," the duke said, "you're jumping the gun. Unless, that is, you wish to be away from here."

"No, sir! Your grace! I mean . . ." Victoria trailed off, confused.

"Yes, well, Sylvie means for us to find you a position as teacher to someone or another's children if we can drum someone up, something nice and safe and uncontroversial." He saw Victoria's expression fall, the light in her eyes draining away. He found himself feeling her distress and he did not like the feeling. Did not like the way she affected him.

"Since you're here, I shall use your services. And pay you of course. And we shall see what happens after a week or two. A trial basis. What do you say?"

"Oh yes, please . . . yes." She breathed the words, looking up at him gratefully. "I promise you'll not be sorry."

"Yes, well, we'll see about that. In the meantime, when you're finished, come along to the study. We shall see how you handle my dictation as opposed to Thomas's."

"But Edward—" Sylvia looked up at him doubtfully. "There is Judith to consider."

"Judith be hanged," he said, ending the discussion.

Sylvia returned her attention to her plate, looking up after Edward left to stare earnestly at the young girl. "You will have to be most dreadfully cautious. Aunt Judith is—well, she feels that any man and woman, left alone for even the briefest of time, will succumb to . . . temptation."

"Temptation?" Victoria said, and then blushed, realizing her meaning.

"Please don't take offense. You have led, as you said yourself, a very sheltered life. I understand from Sir Thomas that there were no men in Lady Ashbrook's establishment. Nor boy children."

"The doctor came, of course. And Sir Thomas, once the trouble over the will began. I have taken dictation from Sir Thomas and he has not found me lacking," she added quickly.

"I'm sure he did not." Sylvia rose from her chair. "Please, do not feel offended. It is merely that I wish to protect you, both of you, my brother-in-law as well, from any untoward gossip." She smiled. "And I shall ask friends about other employment since I feel certain you will be much happier in a more . . . conventional role once you have attempted this."

Victoria listened to Sylvia's step disappear out the door to the morning room, heard a door closing somewhere down the long hall, and still she sat where she was. It was easy enough to say that men would be difficult to work for, but there were none but men that she knew to ask for her position. Why did they train young women for positions they would not allow them to fill? A tiny doubt crept into her thoughts, a heavy suspicion that the values she had grown up thinking were normal—Mrs. Ashbrook's values —were, at the very least, unusual. At best frowned upon. At worst maligned and misunderstood.

Victoria stood up. She had been determined to have this chance and now she had it. She had wept and prayed and worried the entire trip out here yesterday, in truth for days beforehand, hoping against hope that somehow she would be given this chance. Now she had it. Not the way she had planned and certainly not with anyone's blessing, but she had it. The rest was up to her.

She left the morning room, resolutely determined that he should find no fault with her work. That she would make herself indispensable and secure her future.

A fleeting thought of his arms around her, combined with the memory of Lady Sylvia's words about men and women left alone together, brought a stain of deep color to her cheeks. She told herself that it had affected her so strongly because she had never been held in a man's arms before. It was merely the oddness of the sensation, of the experience, that kept the feeling stealing back over her, warming her heart and somehow making it ache at the same time.

It was of no account. Merely a little secret of her own she would keep to herself.

Chapter 4

IN THE STUDY THE duke looked up when Victoria entered and stopped a few feet in front of the desk. "Yes, well, come sit down."

She did as she was bid, the duke sitting back in his large armchair to gaze upon her. "You mentioned a book Sir Thomas had told you about. What did he tell you?"

She thought back, before answering carefully. "He said a book of history had been begun and that the present duke was determined to complete it."

"That was all?" He scowled at her.

She stared back at him. "Yes, your grace."

"There's more to it than that. The late duke's secretary quit his post rather than work with me on it." He seemed to be challenging her, as if awaiting some negative comment. But all that struck her about his words was that he called his father the late duke. Perhaps that was how the gentry addressed each other, she reasoned with herself. How much there was to learn.

"He did not approve." The duke spoke again, staring into her eyes. "You see the subject is Anglo-Irish history, from early times to the present." He watched her nod a little, looking at him still with earnest anticipation. "I intend to change nearly every word he wrote," the duke added flatly.

She was startled. "But why?"

"Because he held the popular view that England can do

no wrong and therefore all answers to all troubles reside on the other side of the Irish Sea."

"And you disagree?" she ventured quietly.

"I do. None are blameless in the present situation and I shall endeavor to show why."

She hesitated as he scrutinized her. She framed her words carefully. "That would seem a noble and brave goal."

"Not one that you would forsake your post in protest against?" he asked her ironically.

"No, your grace," she answered earnestly.

"This is not destined to be a popular position, I fear."

"It seems I have been brought up in a veritable hotbed of unpopular opinions, your grace. One more does not concern me."

A wide smile came to his features, lighting his dark eyes with sudden warmth. His features relaxed into the most handsome face she had ever seen. Victoria stared at the transformation. She heard him saying *capital!* Saying, *we may just get on with each other at that,* and still she stared at him. Staring into his eyes until she caught a flicker of something staring back at her. The sudden realization that she was gaping at him embarrassed her. She lowered her gaze but her disobedient eyes found wide, well-formed lips and would not leave them.

His manner became cooler, more distant. "Shall we take a look then at what's been done?" He moved a large sheaf of papers across his desk, waiting for her to stand beside him before continuing. "As you can see, he went to great lengths to prove his case. Here—" He stood up, carrying the papers to a long, narrow table situated in front of a wide window that was crisscrossed with narrow latticework, each pane of glass only a few inches square. "This will do nicely, I think, for your work."

Out beyond the tiny-paned window the rose gardens bloomed up against the house, stretching away toward an avenue of pleached lime trees.

The duke brought a narrow, straight-backed chair to the table, thrusting it toward her. She sat down upon it, watching him spread out the papers before her on the table. "This then is the first problem. We must have a list of all the facts and figures quoted, for example the timing of the Crown's letters to the Irish Parliament and vice-versa. Who received what first . . . do you see what I mean?"

"Yes. To ascertain what facts were available when decisions were reached."

"Precisely!" Well pleased, he divided the work into several piles upon the table, each division already held together by a ribbon whose color varied from pile to pile. "This then is the system he used. Red, for example, relates to the present situation. Blue here refers to the Georges, green for everything between James the First and Anne. Purple, most deservedly in my opinion, was allocated to Elizabeth—who may not have dealt well with the Irish but most assuredly made England what she is today, for good and for evil."

"Do you truly think so?" Victoria could not contain the note of happy agreement in her voice, her enthusiasm infectious and appealing. "You see, I too think she was the most illustrious of rulers, having come through so much to gain what she did and—" She saw his amusement now and stopped.

"No, please go on," the duke told her.

She bent her head to the paperwork. "Forgive my zeal. I am just so glad that I shall be working on something so important as this."

He found himself staring down at the top of her head, watching the sun's rays gleam through the russet and auburn and brown strands of softly curling hair. Bemused, his eyes followed the curve of her cheek. Her face was in profile to him, her head bent over the papers. She was truly shy, a quality he had had little experience of in the circles in which he moved. She had no knowledge of men, not even the most rudimentary. And therefore none of the skills of the accomplished flirt. Her eyelashes were long and curved upward gently; the smoothness of peach down held his gaze along the side of her cheek, her eyes turning to stare up at him as he bent over her. Their eyes met and held, each searching the other's, each unsure of what he or she saw.

The moment was interrupted by the door to the hall bursting open, Sylvia gripping the door's brass knob with one hand, her other crumpling a letter, squeezing it as if she were ready to fling it away. "Edward, it's happened! He's on his way!" Her eyes were large with fright, her entire body rigid.

Edward straightened up, moving around the desk toward his sister-in-law. "Calm yourself, Sylvia."

"Calm myself? *Calm myself!*" Her voice rose near hysteria. "Is that all you can say? You must *do* something!" She reached for him as he came near the door, grabbing his outstretched hand, beseeching him with her eyes. Edward glanced back toward the young girl who sat at the table, seeing her surprised eyes and the questions that lay behind them.

"I shall leave you to your work, Victoria. I believe you should be able to make a start at it." He was squeezing Sylvia's hands tightly, making her look up from him to the girl across the room. "When I return from London, we shall see what you've accomplished."

"From . . . London?" Victoria asked, her eyes still held by Sylvia's frightened expression.

"Yes. I leave for the city to attend the Queen, and will stay the night and possibly the morrow, if she requires."

Victoria watched the man upon whom her future depended. He left the room, leading the distraught Sylvia away, leaning in close to whisper words of encouragement as they left.

When the door closed behind them, Victoria stared at it for a full minute before returning to the pages at hand. At first she proceeded hesitantly, making small careful notes in the margins of the pages he had opened for her, going back over what she had read to ensure that she understood all that was there. But soon she gained confidence, alone now and undistracted. She turned the pages back to the very beginning, starting again, bending to her task with full concentration.

On the very first page of the foolscap sheets an inscription was scrawled, the writer identified as "Edward, eighth Duke of Bereshaven, by the Grace of God and Her Majesty." Beneath this the former duke had written: "In order to set forth fully the origins of the present troubles and to place the blame where it fully lies, upon the misguided and misbegotten Papists who incite riot and unrest against Her Most Gracious Majesty."

41

Victoria stared at the page. Before the reader would have begun to understand the circumstances, all blame would have been laid at the feet of one side, all honor at the feet of the other.

She pulled blank paper closer, raising the cap of the inkwell and dipping a pen into its black depths.

Determination furrowed her forehead as she began to annotate the manuscript before her, the injustice of the words, the lack of any fellow feeling at all in its tone pushing her pen faster and faster across the pages, caught up in the task before her as she copied out references to be checked.

The morning sped by, the day lengthening as Victoria sat at the narrow table, engrossed in her task. The sun climbed higher in the cloud-spattered blue sky out beyond the latticed windows; her back was to the spring day, her attention on the papers spread before her.

Soft sounds drew Victoria's attention away from those pages hours later, sound of movement and quiet conversation beyond the windows. Fresh air circulated through the study from the open window. Nearly unnoticed, Sylvia's words came floating in upon it. "I cannot bear it, Edward. I shall flee, I shall do something, anything, rather than face him . . ."

"Hush . . ."

The duke's one word caught Victoria's hand in midword. She stopped writing, straightening up, her back still to the windows.

"Sylvie . . . Sylvie . . ." The soft-voiced words, the gentle way in which he called Sylvia by a pet name, echoed through Victoria. She found herself turning toward the windows, curiosity driving her to see what was meant by the intimate tones she heard behind her.

The window directly behind the table was closed, the words and the fresh spring air coming in from its companion a few feet further away.

The couple stood between two rows of rosebushes, just beyond the window Victoria stared through. The duke's back was to the window, Sylvia's pleading face staring up at him, tears sliding down her cheeks. Edward reached to draw Sylvia nearer, his arms pulling her close. Victoria felt physical pain as she watched Sylvia lean into his embrace.

"Shhh . . ." he was saying softly, his lips near her forehead, his tone gentle.

"Stop this at once!" The sound of Judith's harsh voice broke them apart, the duke's expression turning grim. Judith was not visible from Victoria's position within the study. But her words continued as Sylvia stepped back and caught sight of Victoria through the latticed windowpanes. Judith spoke again, her words sharp. "How dare you?"

"Judith, be quiet," the duke said.

"Be quiet! Judith, be quiet! Do you seriously think you can carry on adventures such as this and have them neatly swept under the carpet! Have you *no* feeling for your own brother! He has been shot in the service of his country! He is coming home ill and in need of his family . . . I will not have him walk in to find licentious embraces between his wife and his own brother!"

Inside the study Victoria turned away from their voices, returning to her work, the duke's voice carrying into the room. "If you say as much as one more word, I shall send you packing."

There was a dead silence while Sylvia spoke. "Edward, please, don't make it all worse."

"Worse! How can any of it be worse, pray tell? Excuse me, I must leave for the palace, where I must appear quite normal in my interview with Her Majesty."

There was silence then outside. Victoria resolutely kept her back to the window. Her eyes studied the page before her but she made no progress, her whole attention pulled out beyond the windows where Sylvia's voice rose softly, placating her aunt by marriage.

"Please, Aunt Judith—"

"Don't 'Aunt Judith' me! You're no relation of mine! My poor dead brother was right. You were unstable as a child and have grown more so as the years continue. James should never have married you."

"He would not have, if he had not gotten me with child."

"How *dare* you speak so in front of me! In front of decent people! Then let me tell you that your miscarried girl-child could as easily be another's—as you *yourself* declared at the beginning of it all. Of course whether you accused Edward because it was true or because he was heir is a moot point, is it not? After your long 'association' with your husband's brother, it hardly matters!"

Sylvia's voice rose to match Judith's own. "Have a care that he does not hear you or you shall truly be cast out of his house!"

"His house! And that the result of calumny and intrigue! This is my dead brother's house and I have more right and reason to be here than you or that Irish witch's progeny!"

"Be careful, Aunt Judith." Sylvia's voice was silken now, as she regained control over herself. "Your precious James was the 'Irish witch's' progeny too."

There was no reply. Silence fell across the yard, Judith turning away from her nephew's wife, Sylvia herself turning once more to stare up toward the study windows. The window where she had spied Victoria's pale, surprised face was closed. But the window next to it was open.

Victoria did not see Judith leave. Nor did she see Sylvia look up toward the windows and then slowly turn away herself. The sounds of early spring birds calling to each other once more filled the grounds outside, human disruptions ended for the moment, nature herself the only occupant of the rose gardens as the two women disappeared inside the huge house.

There was a knock at the study door. Victoria looked up to see it opening, Sylvia framed in the doorway. "Would you like luncheon brought in to you, or do you prefer to have it in the dining room, Victoria?"

"Here, please." Victoria found it hard to look at the lovely woman who stood across the room, her deep blue eyes searching Victoria's expression for a clue as to her feelings. "I—that is, if that's all right. I have so much to do," Victoria finished lamely.

"Of course," Sylvia replied quietly. There was a moment in which nothing was said and then Sylvia continued. "I hope you can find time later to let me show you around the estate. There is much I would like to show you. And tell you."

Victoria tried to smile. "You are most kind."

"I would truly be grateful for a chance to talk," Sylvia said.

Victoria's eyes lowered. "I am, of course, at your disposal."

"Perhaps after dinner then."

Victoria looked up to see Sylvia closing the door, but before she could return to work, the door opened again. Judith walked in, almost slamming the door behind her as she strode across the room.

"What has she told you?" the older woman demanded, staring down at Victoria with fiery eyes.

"I beg your pardon?" Victoria saw the look of dislike that was revealed briefly and then hidden again within the woman's stern countenance.

"My dear girl, do you suppose you shall stay here for a moment longer than I shall allow?" Judith challenged, towering over the desk.

Victoria replied mildly, her tone deliberately noncommittal. "I understood that the duke himself made the decision whether to keep or let his employees go." Judith's gaze turned toward the open window, toward the rose gardens beyond. When she looked back, Victoria felt the full weight of the woman's dislike. And distrust.

"I assure you that much goes on within this house that the duke does not concern himself with. And that if he should return to find you gone, he would waste neither time nor energy trying to find you."

"Why do you find it necessary to threaten me?" Victoria asked the woman, amazed at her own fearlessness.

"Threaten? My dear girl, there is no reason, no need, to threaten the likes of you."

"The likes?"

Judith dismissed her with a glance. "Irish working class. A penchant for troublemaking, a sharp mind and a sharper tongue. No references, no breeding, no place in this world except that which others allow you."

"I thank you, Lady Judith," Victoria said. "No one at Mercy House knew from whence I came. My antecedents, my origins are unknown. It is sad that they did not have your perspicacity or they could have saved me wondering all these years and told me what you already know. Who and what I am and who and what I am not."

"Are you mocking me?" Judith asked.

"Surely you can tell if an Irish peasant is mocking you, Lady Judith."

Judith's eyes narrowed. "I don't know why he's brought you here, but I warn you, do not think you can mock me."

"Lady Judith, I would never presume such a thing."

Judith glared at her. "You have a pert tongue. It will cost you much."

Victoria's eyes lowered. "As you say, Lady Judith."

"Even in agreement you are insolent. A sure mark of the Irish."

"Did someone call?" Michael Flaherty's voice turned them both toward the doorway. He carried a tray of sandwiches and tea. "I was told to deliver this to the poor working girl who cannot leave her station long enough to keep her strength up." He came forward, past Judith. "As I told them, we can't be repeating yesterday's troubles."

"Thank you," Victoria said faintly, watching the Irishman look toward the duke's aunt.

Lady Judith swept out, her long gray silk gown rustling as she moved. When Flaherty turned back toward Victoria, he was smiling. "Was she giving you grief?"

Victoria found it impossible not to smile back. "I think she was trying to."

"Ah, well, you must understand the spinster's mentality. Finding no pleasure in life, and giving none, she is bound and determined that no others shall find pleasure either."

Victoria laughed as a broader grin lit the Irishman's face.

"And what has he got you doing, then?" Flaherty asked.

She took a deep breath, looking down at the papers before her. "He has me annotating his father's manuscript."

"In plain English, lass . . . in plain English."

She smiled. "I'm checking what is said here, finding out if it's right, wrong, or mere opinion."

Michael nodded. "Ah, and that's a challenge, is it not? I mean, what is all history, except one man's opinion of what happened against another's that's just as good?"

The duke's manservant moved to pull up a chair as he urged her to eat. "We can't have you fading away again, can we?" He stretched out his legs before him, relaxing back in the chair. "Can you make heads or tails of what's been done so far? The duke says it's a proper fright."

"I suppose it is. But then there's so much to be said. I mean, if the story is really to be told, then both sides must have their day in court."

Michael Flaherty stared at her, his honest blue eyes full of admiration and something else, something surprised. "You aren't one of them bluestockings, are you?"

"Would it be so bad if I was?" she asked him, earning a puzzled expression.

"But are you?"

"No," she told him. "At least I don't think so. I've never been told I was bluestocking, or anything else. Except by Lady Judith awhile ago, who knew that I am Irish working class just by looking at me."

Michael Flaherty harumphed, dismissing Judith's words with his tone. "Pay her no attention. She has no idea of what Irish is, working class or otherwise. She judges all by me and—" He stopped, closing his mouth firmly.

"And?" Victoria prompted. When she saw he did not mean to continue, she cajoled him. "I want to continue to work for his grace, if he'll let me, and the more I know about his household and its prejudices the better . . ." She trailed off, letting Mike think about it.

"Why?" he asked after a bit. "Why do you want to work for him?"

She hesitated, then answered honestly, feeling a rapport with this stranger that could not easily be explained. "He is trying to do something I believe in. He is trying to show the truth of something, whether anyone wants to hear it or not. And . . ."

"And?" Michael Flaherty prompted.

Victoria watched the duke's man and then changed the subject. "Why are you still here if he has left for the city?"

Michael grinned, recrossing his legs, propping his hands behind his head. "I am not welcome at Buckingham Palace, you see. I'm Irish and subject to subversive thoughts."

"But the duke himself is Irish."

"Half-Irish, it's true. But that doesn't count when the other half is of the blood royal. He's above suspicion. Or

47

nearly above it. Your namesake the Queen isn't altogether sure of him, but enough to feel she can divert any untoward tendencies he might harbor."

"Such as?"

Michael shrugged. "Joining the opposition. Lobbying for Home Rule."

"Publishing the truth?"

The Irishman smiled at the young woman, trying to put his finger on just who she reminded him of. "Aye, there's that. So now you know. You hold one of the keys to his future in your dainty little hands. Queen Vee would be most vexed if she knew he meant to publish the truth of all that's happened between Ireland and England."

"I wonder why he trusts me."

"I wonder too," Michael told her, smiling again when her eyes sought his across the cherrywood table. "He's not a trusting sort," he added, seeing her confusion.

Victoria saw the truth behind the man's words, saw his hesitancy to dismiss her out of hand, and realized it was because of the duke's decision to entrust her with the manuscript.

"I shall never disappoint him," she said.

Michael stared at her, searching her eyes. "That's a tall order you've taken on, if I might say so, Miss Leggett."

She blushed, looking down toward the papers strewn about the table before her. "Obviously I refer only to the work he expects."

"Obviously," Michael repeated. He unfolded himself from his chair, stretching a little as he stood up. "He's not an easy master, but he is a fair one. And more than that is hard to find." He started for the door. "Lady Sylvia said to mention that she would spare some time after dinner for you. She would like to welcome you. And talk a bit."

The man's soft Irish eyes were unreadable, his gaze polite but inpenetrable.

"She said as much earlier," Victoria replied.

"Did she?" he asked mildly. "It might have slipped her mind she'd already told you."

"It might have," Victoria said, knowing as well as he did that it had not.

"I'll leave you to your work, then."

She watched him cross the room, speaking out as he went through the doorway. "Thank you!"

He looked back. "I beg your pardon?"

She smiled. "I was told you put in a good word for me earlier. I appreciate it."

He grinned. "We Irish have to stick together."

"I don't know that I am Irish," she told him honestly.

"If you're not, you should be." He closed the door and left her to her work.

The pages swam before her eyes, her thoughts all on the tall, dark, handsome duke who was riding off to visit the Queen.

What did he truly think of her, what would his decision be when once he saw what she had accomplished. Or had not accomplished, she warned herself, pulling the pages near. If she were to stay, she had to impress him with her abilities. And stay she must, she told herself. Not only because she needed the position, needed the certainty of a place in life, a job to do, but also because she wanted to show him that she was as good or better than any other he could hire. That she could hold her own.

Deep inside a small voice nagged at her, telling her there was more to it than that. But she did not listen. She went back to her work, pushing all else away.

Chapter 5

THE PRIDE AND JOY of the Guelph family, Albert Edward, Prince of Wales, Duke of Cornwall, was surrounded by pimps, panderers, parasites, and blackguards, certain dishonor to any lady who was seen more than twice on his arm. At the moment he was in particularly bad odor with his mother, the good Queen Victoria, and so was seen leaving Buckingham Palace rather hurriedly. The Marquess of Hamilton, the Earl of Arran, and others followed him out to a string of waiting carriages.

The day was overcast and gray, the air hinting of rain. Edward Albert, Duke of Bereshaven, passed his namesake, nodding to the bloated prince but not stopping as he passed by. The Queen's red-suited guards opened the palace gates, their expressions impassive as they listened to the bantering of their debauched betters, the prince handing goods and girls up into the victorias and laudaus waiting for them.

Buckingham Palace was damp and cold and there was no help for it. The sumptuous hall the duke walked through was flanked by a double row of marble columns, each gilded at base and capital. One hundred fifty feet of them stretched away toward the grand staircase, itself made of purest marble. But with all its beauty, the Queen could not reside within this huge house, constantly catching cold from the chill dampness that pervaded it, escaping as often as she could, leaving behind library, council room, and sculpture gallery, no matter how splendid, for the health of the country palace at Windsor.

A beefeater, resplendent in red tunic and round flat hat, his legs encased in red hose, stood at attention in the magnificent hall near doors that led to a yellow drawing room.

One of the Queen's pages opened the doors for Edward, a series of paintings of the royal family meeting his eye as he stepped inside, the door closing silently behind him.

He was alone in the room. A full-length portrait of Her Majesty, looking very fat, with a heavy crown upon her small head, filled one panel of the room directly ahead of him, the late Prince Albert in his costume of Knight of the Garter portrayed beside her.

The Duke turned toward the sound of an opening door and saw a servant bringing a tray of sherry and biscuits before bowing low and leaving silently. Edward was left to stare at bust after bust of Prince Albert, as well as a host of pictures of the Queen's late consort. The room boasted a collection of small tables made of inlaid ivory, mother-of-pearl, and gold, each with its picture or bust of the Queen's late husband, each holding a volume of Shakespeare or other English poet, leather bound and looking unread. A current *London Times* was thrown across a petit-point chair, the only sign of recent human habitation in the large formal room.

A sound turned him toward an inner doorway. The Queen stood there, her short, plump figure encased in black, her face framed by a black veil. The duke bowed as the Queen glanced toward the *Times*. "Did you see what they say? The *Times* . . . they berate me for my continued seclusion. My maintaining my mourning for my dear heart, Albert. They say dressmakers are being forced out of business because the court does not call them to work. They even say I've developed a fondness for drink. And that my temper has become irascible. Ungovernable. My face inflamed with drink, my eyes swollen shut. An inebriate and all because of that scapegrace son of mine. You look shocked, Edward. Have you not heard them?" She settled herself onto a nearby chaise, motioning him to sit near her side.

"Your Majesty, I have neither heard such rot nor could any sensible person ever believe such folly."

"Are you quite sure? Can any of my people truly think me so weak of character, do you think? Or is this just political bombast?"

"Your people revere you, as you must know, Your Majesty. Scapegrace son or not, they shall continue so."

"Ah." She smiled, her round, pale face lighting up. "Now you sound very like my own dear Albert. He would have said the same. And with the same honesty regarding his eldest son . . . I suppose you've heard the latest tales of his boon companion, Charles, Lord Carrington. That wild, young rakehell and destroyer of women's virtue."

The duke watched the Queen. "You sound almost resigned to such activities, Your Majesty. Carrington is a member of your household brigade. You could threaten to dismiss him."

"A lieutenant no less. But you have no experience of sons if you think that threatening any such thing would end their association. Short of actually letting him go from my employ, I can do nothing. And having done so, he would presumably find work with my son, so where's the point?"

Her gaze wandered toward the huge portrait of her late husband, her eyes softening as she looked at it. "It's so very like him, don't you think? I look up at it sometimes and think he could almost step forward and tell us what should be done. With his brilliant mind he would find a way to make all work out successfully."

Edward watched the tiny woman who ruled much of the known world, perplexed as he had always been by her. "I'm sure he would have. But alas, he is not here."

"Alas," she agreed, sighing heavily. Then her attention returned to the young man before her. "Edward, I have heard many tales concerning your household. None of which bears repeating. Or needs denial." Her gaze hardened. "I feel sure that you would never indulge in behavior that would embarrass the Crown."

He almost asked her why she was so very sure. If her own son, the heir to the Crown, was such a ne'er-do-well, why should others have to toe the mark? But he knew he would not voice his objections. He would bow politely and acquiesce. And never mention the double standard she employed between her own son's activities and what she demanded of all others.

The Queen watched the fleeting emotions that crossed Edward's face, watched him bow submissively, and felt the power behind his bow, the lack of subservience that marked the very best of subjects and the very worst of enemies. Unsure which he was, she watched him closely. "I have always had a soft spot for you, you know, dear Edward. My own Albert held you as an infant, before your father decided to take you back to Ireland. An unwise course."

"We were not there long."

"Seven years. Long enough to forge false friendships, to influence the way in which one thinks about all else afterward." Her gaze was shrewd. "I hope such is not the truth in your case."

"I was very young, Your Majesty. Seven years, when they are the first years of your life, are not the same as seven years when reason rules the senses. I was too young to form more than impressions."

"Yes. One would hope you would be able to see that." She spoke more slowly. "You are aware that your father made an . . . unfortunate marriage. He lived to regret it, bless his memory, and I would be terribly concerned if I felt his mistakes had in some way . . . colored your own views." When the duke said nothing, she continued. "Nor do I hold much with kitchen gossip. But there is too much of it concerning you and your brother's wife. I hope there is a way to end it. Soon." She watched him carefully.

"There is, Your Majesty. My brother is returning from Africa; word has just come through. He should be in England straightaway."

"Ah! That is welcome news, is it not?"

The duke kept his opinion of the news to himself, lowering his eyes as she looked over at him.

"I have another thought," the Queen continued.

"Elizabeth Wyndham, the Earl of Suffolk's niece, is out this season and I would very much like to see the two of you get to know each other."

Edward stared at the Queen, stunned. "I beg your pardon?"

"A small dinner party would be quite correct. And before that she and her mother could visit you, so that you may become better acquainted. She is a lovely child, just eighteen and quite unspoiled by society. After all, Edward, you are getting to the age when you must think of an heir. You will be thirty-six this November. A man's duty to his family comes before all else, don't you think?"

He stared into the small eyes of the woman who controlled half the world and was now adroitly telling him what he must do. He could have behaved foolishly with his sister-in-law, she seemed to be saying, but it would now come to an end and he would do as he was bid. He would marry where told and dutifully produce heirs. Heirs that would be, in turn, dutiful to the Crown.

"Shall we say Wednesday next?"

"I beg your pardon?" he replied.

"I shall tell Lady Wyndham and Elizabeth that you wish to call Wednesday next so that you can tell them of your plans for a dinner party. I'm sure they will be most surprised and pleased."

Queen Victoria smiled benignly up at the handsome young duke.

Edward bowed his head, acquiescing silently, his thoughts far away. "If that is your pleasure, Your Majesty."

"It is," she told him, standing up, putting her hand out for him to kiss.

She swept from the room, the door to the next chamber opening before her as if by magic. Edward watched it close before he turned toward the outer doors.

Those doors, too, opened mysteriously before him, two guards outside coming to attention, their expressions impassive. Deliberately ignoring anything they might have heard except for his approaching bootsteps.

Unfortunate stories, she had said. Edward's mood blackened, his brow furrowing as he took the great stairs two at a time, his Wellingtons pounding across the floors and out to his waiting carriage.

Confound the woman, confound them all, he blasted away in his mind. How dare any of them tell him who and what he was to be. "Home!" he barked to the driver, brooking no further conversation as he threw himself back upon the carriage bench, glaring out at the surrounding landscape.

Dinner at The Willows that evening was a silent affair. The duke's aunt presided at one end of the long, dark table; the other end was vacant, the duke's chair empty. A small tight smile played around Judith's lips, but she spoke to no one, and the room remained shrouded in silence as the courses were presented, served, and cleared away. Soup from the large tureen, fish and roast and vegetables all came and left.

Victoria, seated across from Sylvia, picked at the food that was served, moving it about her plate, nibbling at the slice of bread before her. The atmosphere was too heavy in the dark room, the room itself too opulent for comfort. Dark green walls ended in dark wood floors, a Turkey carpet of varied dark patterns, blood red and darkest green and brown blending together into a swirl of darkly colored patterns beneath their chairs. A ruby glass chandelier hung above the table, candles set within it burning brightly down across the wide expanse of bowls and plates and food.

When finally Judith stood up, without a word placing her napkin beside her plate and leaving, Sylvia's sigh of relief was audible.

She looked across the table at Victoria. "Please don't take her silence to heart. She's like this no matter who is about." A cloud seemed to pass over Sylvia's face, and then her lips smoothed into a determined smile. "You look as though you have as little appetite as I, though you should have one, having nearly starved to death so recently."

"It was hardly to that point," Victoria protested.

"Come along." Sylvia stood up. "I should like to talk." Victoria hesitated only a moment before pushing her chair back and following the woman who waited in the doorway for her. "Edward says you are to stay. At least he will give you the chance of performing the duties you so recklessly pursued."

Watching the older woman, Victoria felt no animosity in her words. She spoke plainly, but with no malice. "I know you do not approve," she told her quietly.

"That is neither here nor there. I do not think it proper, but then you have already been trained and subjected to all that book learning, have you not? Thus the point is rather academic as to whether it has been bad for you. Only time will tell that. And as to my brother-in-law, he is a 'law' unto himself, so you shall have your chance to prove your worth."

"I am very grateful. Especially after my seizure yesterday."

Sylvia's laugh was merry. "Oh, my goodness, yes! What a drama. I swear you had both Sir Thomas and Edward all agog with wonder and worry!" She opened the door to a small parlor, motioning Victoria on inside. "I must admit you could not have done better if you tried. I fear if you had simply come and applied, he would not have considered your request."

"I didn't mean—I mean I hardly planned—that is—"

"Oh, I'm sure you did not. And I'm sure *he* knows that, which is more to the point. If he doubted that, he would have dismissed you out of hand. He does so hate to be maneuvered into anything."

"Of course."

Sylvia turned toward Victoria, her smile appealing now. The room surrounding them was cozy with the warmth of a fire, cut off by heavy drapes from the outside cold, filled with ornate tables that bore fringed cloths and all kinds of memorabilia and knick-knacks upon them. "I want to tell you about what you saw earlier."

"I saw nothing!" Victoria's cheeks flamed. "That is, it is none of my business, surely."

"Yes, of course, but I do not want you to think any the worse of Edward—or of me—than you must upon closer association."

Victoria sat down, her knees going weak. "Perhaps another time—"

"There may be no opportunity. Please." Sylvia drew a small hassock close to Victoria's chair, coming to sit upon it, staring earnestly into Victoria's widened eyes. "You see there is a long and dreadful association between myself and the Bereshavens." She looked down, then back up, resolutely continuing. "I was coerced into marriage with James when I was but sixteen years of age. A child. He treated me badly."

"Please, there is no need—" Victoria's discomfort made her try to stand up, but Sylvia caught at her hands.

"Victoria. Miss Leggett. There is a reason I tell you these things. Please listen."

Wishing herself away, unhappily aware that she could not very well walk out on the duke's sister-in-law, Victoria sank back upon the chair, staring at the blond woman stoically.

"Thank you," Sylvia said. "Because of his behavior in general, not just with me, James was given a career in the army. At first I tried to end the marriage, tried to flee, but between my parents and the duke, Edward's father, I was stopped at every turn. I have been a wife mostly in name only for as many years as you have been alive. Or nearly so." She twisted her handkerchief in her hands. "When he has come home, he has expected—demanded—his rights. And I have no recourse but to submit."

"But how horrible!" Victoria spoke out before thought. "I mean, in truth, the man is a stranger to you!"

"Yes. A stranger. But one I am tied to by bonds that cannot be broken on this earth." She squeezed Victoria's hand. "The reason I am telling you all this is so you will understand Edward's concern for me. You see, he has been . . . kind. And I have grown quite fond of him. But there is nothing more to it than that."

"Of course not," Victoria said.

Sylvia watched the young woman's eyes. "Do you mean that? Do you believe me?"

"Why should I not?"

Sylvia looked down. She let go of Victoria's hands. "Why not, indeed. Miss Leggett, Victoria . . . news has arrived that my husband is on his way home from Africa. He is not like you. He would not see any innocence in anything either I or his brother did. And so I would very much appreciate your discretion when he does arrive. I would be devastated if, while he is here, he should think—he should assume—"

"Of course," Victoria said quickly.

Sylvia looked back at her then. "Do you understand what I am trying to say?"

Victoria allowed herself a small, sad smile. "One of the

benefits, which others might call dubious, of being brought up by freethinkers was that I was fully educated about the relations between the sexes." Seeing Sylvia's raised brow, she added: "By lecture of course. And booklets. I know what you are speaking of."

"Good," Sylvia said slowly. "Then you understand my concern."

A knock at the door brought Nancy in. "There is a Mr. Ryan here, Lady Sylvia. He wishes to see the duke; he says it's most urgent. Or Mr. Flaherty, since the duke has left for the city."

"Yes?"

"Mr. Flaherty is nowhere to be found, your ladyship. I thought you might, instead of Lady Judith, I mean—"

Sylvia stood up, sighing. "Oh very well, although I can't imagine being of any help to the man. He shall just have to wait upon Michael if his errand is so urgent. Where is he?"

"In the front hall, your ladyship."

Sylvia stood up, Victoria following suit. "I think I shall retire early."

"The rest will probably do you good," Sylvia agreed, laying a hand on Victoria's arm. "Thank you for listening. And for understanding." She tried to smile, Victoria smiling encouragingly back at her.

Loud voices came from the front of the hall as they walked toward it, Judith's strident tones echoing back toward them. "How *dare* you set foot in my brother's house!"

A small man with a very large frown upon his face tried to stare down the angry woman. "I'm here to see the duke or Mr. Flaherty, not the likes of you." The man's voice had traces of an Irish brogue.

"I am Lady Judith Bereshaven and I am telling you that you are unwelcome here."

"I don't care if you're the Queen of Sheba. I was told to come here and come here I have. And I'll not be leaving until I've had my say."

"Aunt Judith." Sylvia came forward. "Perhaps I can help."

Judith and the man both turned toward Sylvia, glancing back at Victoria and then focusing on Sylvia's face—Judith in disgust, the man with obvious appreciation of the lovely creature now standing before him.

"There's nothing to help or discuss. This creature is to leave immediately."

Mike Flaherty walked in at that moment, giving one quick glance around, and then, ignoring the others, reached out a hand to the small man. "Well, Ryan, is it? You got here in good time."

"Yes!" The man glared at the grim-faced woman, who glowered back. "And who should I meet but this one here who tells me to get out good and quick!"

Michael Flaherty smiled easily at his employer's aunt, taking hold of Ryan's arm and turning him toward the doorway. "It's a quiet word I'd be liking with the man anyhow, your ladyship. Sorry you were bothered." He glanced at Sylvia and Victoria. "All of you," he added. "Well, now, let's be about it, then. I've saved a lovely pint of bitters for you after your long ride."

The mollified Ryan followed Mike outside, the door closing behind them. Judith turned toward the stairwell, her gaze resting upon the two women beyond. "I shall talk to Edward about Flaherty. Inviting his guests to use the front door!"

"I'm sure he meant no harm."

"Are you?" Judith asked Sylvia, and then paused, a small tight smile coming to her thin lips. "When I heard the door, I was so hopeful it was James. Wouldn't that have been a surprise?"

Sylvia did not answer. She watched Judith's smile broaden, saw her glance toward the new young amanuensis before she turned away from them both, mounting the stairs slowly, her long dress grazing the steps. The sound of the satin cloth sliding across the polished wood could be heard until a grandfather's clock began to chime the hour.

Sylvia smiled briefly at Victoria. "I'll say good night then too."

Victoria nodded. "Yes. Good night."

Sylvia started up the stairs, Judith having already disappeared above. The blond woman stopped once, turning back to look down at Victoria. "I forgot to ask how your work went today. Did you enjoy it?"

"Oh, yes," Victoria answered truthfully. "Most awfully."

"Good," Sylvia said, turning away.

Victoria hesitated, glancing back at the clock across the hall. It was just gone eight. At Mercy House she would have been at work mending by now, the day's chores over, the night chores just beginning.

She thought about the children, wondering where they were now, hoping none had been sent to the city orphanage. Terrible tales were told of what became of those who ended there.

A horse whinnied outside; the man Ryan was probably starting off again or taking his mount around to the stables to be watered and looked after while he lifted a pint with Mr. Flaherty.

She envied Flaherty's easy handling of Lady Judith. He did not kow-tow, he did not rebel, he simply said his piece and went his way, quietly getting on with whatever he wanted. There was a knack to that, a knack to managing people that she lacked, she told herself. She would have meekly done as she was bid. Or fought too hard and said too much.

A cloak was hanging on the hall tree beside the door, the sounds from outside gone now. All was quiet except for the slow ticking of the tall clock, its pendulum swinging gracefully to and fro.

She turned toward the door, reaching for the cloak and wrapping it about her shoulders. A good brisk walk in the night air would surely tire her out enough to sleep through until dawn. She would awaken refreshed and attack the book anew, astounding the duke with what all had been accomplished by the time he returned tomorrow, she told herself.

But she hesitated at the front door, finally turning around and walking back down the length of the hall to the French doors at the opposite end, walking out toward the gardens. She had no wish to run into Mr. Flaherty or anyone else. Just to be alone for a few minutes, to allow herself the luxury of breathing the fresh night air and coming to terms with the drastic change in her life, was all she wanted.

The night was cold. She was glad of the cloak, pulling it closer around herself, enfolding herself in its dark, heavy cloth. When she crossed the terrace and stepped down beneath the trees, hidden from the moon, her small figure blended in with the night, invisible from the house.

The river wound past the estate, gurgling down below the path she took toward it. A gazebo, painted white and shining in the moonlight, sat upon the riverbank at the end of the path, its open latticework sides giving a glimpse of its dark interior.

The moon's rays fell down across it, lighting narrow strips between the wood lattices, patterning across a wooden bench, a wicker rocking chair. Victoria paused near the gazebo, watching the silvery ripples of the river as it curved around rocks and flowed on toward the city and the sea beyond.

She never knew how long she stood there, watching the moon play across the moving water, listening to the small night noises. After a while she realized she was cold and glanced again toward the gazebo a few feet away. Walking toward it, she hesitated in the open arch and then stepped up, onto the wood flooring, her eyes becoming accustomed to the dark.

The latticework pattern was broken in two places by large square open windows, one of these directly in front of the rocking chair, looking out across the river toward the distant trees on the opposite bank. The view was serene and more beautiful than anything Victoria, growing up in the middle of grimy city streets and huge blackened buildings, had ever seen.

She sat down upon the rocker, relaxing back after a moment, watching a cloud play hide-and-seek with the moon. It would win and then lose, the moon blotted out and then coming back to shine down upon the landscape again and again. The moon looked bigger than it ever had in the city, and closer in the black sky, tiny pinpoints of winking stars all around it.

Her eyes began to close, tiredness and even contentment stealing over her so slowly she was caught unawares. One moment she was supremely content and the next she dozed.

Small night noises ebbed and flowed around her, the grounds silent except for the distant rustle of leaves and the scurrying of an animal, the water sometimes bubbling over a rock and gurgling a little louder before subsiding again.

Nothing woke her, nothing she could remember. But suddenly her heart was pounding fiercely and her eyes shot open to stare ahead of her.

Standing over her in the shadows was a man. Dressed in black, his face in shadows, he stared down at her. She gasped, sucking in breath quickly, ready to scream.

He heard her sudden intake of air and grabbed her before she could make a sound, one hand over her mouth, his other pulling her up, out of the chair, against him.

The moon fell across where they stood. Victoria found herself staring into the duke's eyes. "What are you doing here!" he demanded in a fierce whisper, as if she were spying upon him. She could not answer, his hand still over her mouth. The expression in her eyes changed as she recognized him. He felt her body relax under his grasp.

He began to let her go, his hand coming away from her mouth, his eyes still upon hers.

And then he reached for her, both arms engulfing her, his head bending to reach toward her mouth.

Shock coursed through her, her heart hammering. She watched, transfixed, as he bent closer. When his lips touched hers, she panicked, pushing against him, struggling to break free.

His lips were insistent, forcing hers apart, his tongue touching hers, something within her bursting, fire coursing through her veins as he caught her closer, ignoring her feeble struggles.

Her arms wound around his neck, her hands trembling as they caught in his thick dark hair. She forgot to breathe, forgot to think, forgot to fight as his tongue taught hers, his hands moving down her back. She curved even nearer, the length of her body longing to be close against his, trying to melt against his hard frame. Feeling his heat through all the layers of cloth between them.

He pulled her closer, becoming more insistent when he felt no resistance. Locking her in his arms, he pulled her down to the floor, hungrily searching her lips, both of them gasping for breath when he finally lifted his head to stare down into her eyes.

"Tell me to stop." His voice whispered at her harshly. "At least make a pretense of virtue."

The shock of his words was a physical pain. She pushed back away from him, feeling him tighten his grip. "That's more like it," he was saying as she slapped him hard across the cheek, stinging her fingers as well as his face. "What the—"

"How dare you?" She got no more out, his hand moving to her breast, making her gasp at the feelings he aroused. He saw the look of wonder in her eyes, his fingers moving to unhook the narrow row of buttons that ran down the front of her gown, from the high lace collar to the waist. The moonlight glowed and then dimmed. His hand stopped at her waist, her eyes closed, as an inner battle raged within her. She wanted to tell him to stop, but she did not want his hands to leave her. The breeze was coming up off the river, cold and damp. Victoria felt his hand reaching inside her dress, touching the bare skin above her thin petticoat, curving into the hollow of her throat. "What are you doing to me . . ." Her whispered words sent his lips to her collarbone, to the rise of her breast above the thin cotton. And then to cover her breast, his lips seeking out a nipple through the petticoat.

The bittersweet ache he caused within her brought her arms to cradle his head, caressing him.

She leaned in toward his bent head, holding him near. His weight upon her, his head moved away from her breast to take her mouth as she moaned softly, wanting his touch never to end.

"He said he'd be back." Michael Flaherty's voice boomed out nearby.

Edward sat up, reality washing over Victoria. Undressed, uninhibited, yielding to his every touch, she would be found here looking like a common wanton. Tears sprang to her eyes.

"You must find out and ride to let us know," a voice said.

"Mikeen, we're depending upon you to plead our case. There's none else."

"I'll do what I can. He's a stubborn man; he'll do naught but what he feels is right."

"Then you'd best convince him." The small man, Ryan, was talking to Mike, their voices fading away as they passed the gazebo, walking along a path that led to the water's edge.

As the voices faded the duke stood up, staring down at Victoria for a long moment before turning away. Without a word he disappeared into the darkness outside.

Victoria sat up, reaching with trembling fingers to rebutton her dress. She found two buttons missing, loosened by his urgent touch. She felt for them on the cold, straw-covered floor, shadows all around her. Finally she buttoned what she could, reaching up to her disheveled hair, pushing the loosened hairpins into curls that tumbled across her forehead and tangled into each other, falling completely loose at the back of her head. Bits of straw from the unswept floor were caught in her hair.

She tried to collect her wits, standing up finally and starting toward the archway, pulling the cloak tight around herself.

Tears were spilling over as she put her foot onto the path, starting toward the house with dread in her heart. He thought her a common whore. He must, what else could he think of her behavior? He had reached for her and she had clung to him, oblivious to all propriety. She tried to stop the thought, tried to wipe away the tears that would not stop flowing down her cheeks.

How could she simply have let him touch her, she asked herself over and over, a small voice inside reminding her that she had not only let him, she had pulled him nearer, had kissed him back, learning from his touch and wantonly encouraging him.

She had not meant to, she had tried to struggle—at first. He would send her packing immediately. Her thoughts all tumbled together, incoherent and confused.

Why had he come there? She stopped in her tracks. Unless he had followed her. Unless he thought she would repay his kindness with her body. Her cheeks burned at the thought. If he had expected all along for her to let him have his way, if he thought he could simply take her whenever he wished—the tears dried, her heart aching at the thought. What if he felt that was what she was? They had been warned when they first went to look for jobs, she and Edna Louise, warned that men thought poorly of freethinkers, thought women who pursued a trade were in truth still pursuing the oldest trade.

The enormity of her predicament rushed in upon her. If she left, she had nowhere to go. If she stayed, he might well feel he could have his way with her.

Her body pulsed at the thought. She swallowed hard, telling herself it was wrong, morally wrong, and she could not want him to hold her. To make love to her.

Her brain told her of all the pitfalls, all the reasons she could not allow him to touch her. All the reasons she must leave this house no matter where she must go.

But her body betrayed her, longing for his touch, her skin burning where his lips had set fires that would not die. At war with herself, she walked up the terrace steps, crossing to open the French doors and slip inside the house.

Voices came from an open doorway next to the study. She was almost past when the duke called out to her. "So there you are."

She stopped, her head down, her cheeks burning. She grasped the cloak tightly, turning to look up into his amused eyes. "Come along." He moved back inside the room, which was lined with books from floor to ceiling.

Sylvia stood near a blazing fire, and turned to stare at Victoria with bleak eyes. "It's too warm for that cloak," she began, and saw Victoria's face. "Are you quite all right? You look feverish."

"I'm fine." Victoria's voice was small. "But I am quite tired. If you don't mind—"

"But I do mind," Edward was saying, moving closer to stare down at her. "What on earth have you been up to?" His easy grin put her at a loss. She stared up into his eyes, seeing something strange there, something she'd not seen before.

"I see you've met my brother." The duke's voice came from the doorway, confusing her. She looked toward the door and then back at the man she had thought was the duke. "James, this is Miss Leggett, my new assistant." His words dropped coldly upon the room. "What on earth's the matter with you? You look a fright!" He stared down at her.

She swallowed.

"She's not been well," Sylvia reminded him. Then she turned away, staring hopelessly into the fire.

Only James seemed to be enjoying himself. He gave Victoria a conspiratorial wink. "I've just come in myself; there's quite a wind out tonight. It blows one's hair about if you're not careful. Right, my girl?"

Her cheeks burned even brighter, the duke staring at her oddly. "Employees wandering about the grounds in the dark, you arriving without warning in the middle of the night. It's lucky I arrived back tonight. I wasn't planning on it."

"Yes. I know I surprised you. You both looked so startled when I walked in," James told his wife and his brother.

Victoria could stand no more. Mumbling an apology, she turned away, walking out before anyone could stop her. She fled down the hall toward the stairs. Mike was coming down them as she moved quickly up.

"Miss Leggett." His words stopped her. She clutched the cloak tightly around herself, looking up to see the burly man smiling sympathetically down at her. "I think you lost these." His large hand reached to place two buttons in her own, closing her fist around them. "You didn't know they were twin brothers, did you, lass?"

She stared up at him, her eyes wide and full of pain.

"Don't you worry, old Mike's not given to telling tales."

She bit her lip, tears welling up again. He patted her shoulder and walked on, heading toward the library as she turned to face the long hall upstairs.

66

Chapter 6

VICTORIA HAD NO MORE than splashed cold water on her face from the bureau basin when a knock at the door made her stiffen. She turned around to face it. "Yes?"

Nancy opened the door, sketching a curtsy. "His grace says to tell you there will be a late supper in honor of his brother's return. You're asked to come join them in the dining room."

"Now?" Victoria searched for an excuse. "I—I'm rather tired, I thought I'd just turn in . . ."

"He most particularly said you were to come."

"He did." Victoria hesitated. "Thank you. I'll be a moment."

Nancy stared at Victoria's hair. "Would you like some help? I mean with your hair and all?" When Victoria hesitated, she added: "It might go faster."

"Yes," Victoria replied, defeated. "I suppose you're right." Nancy came inside, her eyes widening when she saw Victoria's bodice. Deliberately looking away from it, she reached for a brush.

"Won't take but an extra minute. Would you like to change first? I can have Emma sew up your dress for you."

Victoria found herself being managed out of her dress and into her best black, unprotesting as Nancy helped with the buttons and then sat her down, reaching for the brush and beginning in earnest on her tousled curls. "You have lovely thick hair, miss."

Victoria swallowed. "I took a long walk and fell asleep in the gazebo," she told the girl.

"Oh, yes. I can see the straw. It must have been cold out there. I wonder you could sleep."

"So do I," Victoria said bitterly, confusion turning to dread as she thought about the scene yet to come downstairs. She was too tired to fight any of it, her senses battered, her pride at low ebb.

Voices came from the library when Victoria descended a quarter of an hour later, her appearance neat, though she was pale, her hands balled into fists at her sides. She walked toward the sounds of their conversation as if walking to a chopping block.

Judith looked up to see her come through the doorway. "Really, Edward, it wasn't necessary to make the girl come down." Sounding more human than Victoria had yet heard her, Judith stood near James, her arm linked within his. She spoke to the duke as he poured sherry into small crystal glasses and handed one to Sylvia. In that moment Victoria realized she could tell the brothers apart. Something about James's stance, the look in his eyes, was different from his brother's.

"Good grief," James was saying to her, smiling. "The girl does clean up well, doesn't she?"

"James." Sylvia said only the one word.

Judith glanced over at her and then back at James, smiling. "I've sent your things up to be put away so that you can get a good long rest. Then you must tell me about all the places you've been to, all the things you've seen in the war."

Sylvia turned toward Judith. "Which room?" she asked, repeating the question when Judith merely looked over at her. "Which room did you put his things in, Aunt Judith?"

"Why yours, of course. James and yours."

"No." Sylvia put the glass of sherry down suddenly, shaking as she spoke. "No, I will not share the same room."

"But, Sylvie," James began, "is that any way to welcome your husband home?"

"I'll move to another room if you wish to have that one." She spoke stiffly, her back rigid. "I shall accommodate you by moving my things out, if it pleases you to take that room. But I shall not share a room this night. Years gone and suddenly walking in, just like that, expecting to share my bed. No. *No!"*

"Sylvia." The duke spoke quietly.

"No!" She told them all, then turned toward Edward. "No, Edward, please. I cannot do this."

"Sylvia, you're acting like an hysteric!" Judith told her coldly. "Really, I cannot understand you." Yet something about Judith's expression was pleased, as if she had expected this. Had planned it.

Victoria found James staring at her. She looked down, the outsider at this gathering, wishing herself anywhere but in this room.

Mike came to the door. "Supper is served, your grace." He spoke formally, his face impassive as he glanced past her at the duke.

"Shall we?" Judith said, smiling. She linked her arm with James's, leading the way to the dining room. "I want to hear absolutely everything, my dear boy. Everything."

He leaned to kiss her forehead. "At least you're glad to have me home, Aunt Judith."

"We all are, dear boy . . . it's just the shock of turning round and seeing you suddenly there. It's done poor Sylvia in for the moment, that's all. Her nerves never were strong, you know that. Always was too imaginative."

Their words floated back toward the others. Edward touched Sylvia's arm. She pulled away, then swept past Victoria and Mike to stalk toward the dining room alone.

The duke waited for Victoria to precede him out the door. As they moved, as he came near, she glanced at him and saw only a preoccupied frown. She walked on ahead, passing Mike and following the others with a slow step, almost stopping before she entered the dining room. The duke was close behind her, unprepared for her hesitation, stopping a bare inch behind her. She could feel his breath against her neck. "Sorry," he said, formally. "Is there something wrong?"

She shook her head, continuing on into the candlelit room, staring at the feast upon the table. The cook had pulled cold baked chicken from somewhere, had sliced a large cold roast, and surrounded it with asparagus and preserved apricots. Mulled wine sat upon the table, pears and trifle near it, tarts and brandy and cheese on the sideboard nearby.

"Aunt Judith, this must be your doing," James complimented her, holding her chair for her and then sitting down alongside her. "No one else could conjure up such a feast so quickly."

She smiled at him. "Ever since we received your letter we've been planning this little celebration."

Victoria slipped into the chair she had been given earlier, across the table from Sylvia and James. Edward moved behind her to throw himself into his large chair at the head of the table.

Victoria stiffened as he passed behind her and looked up to see Sylvia staring at her. Silent, her hands in her lap, Sylvia ate nothing. Her husband helped himself to food, answering Judith, calling questions down the table to his brother about who he had seen lately, who was up to what.

Edward answered in monosyllables, replying with stiff politeness when words were directed toward him, silent when they were not.

"I must say," James told Edward as he helped himself to more trifle, "you don't seem to have kept up with anyone."

"We've stayed here at The Willows," Judith told him. "It's quite a drive for just a social call. Now that you're home we shall have to plan a homecoming party." She looked up at the head of the table, catching Edward's eye. "We really must have people in, give James a chance to reacquaint himself with everyone. They'll all want to see him."

"Most assuredly," Edward said. "He was always most popular."

Victoria glanced toward the duke, hearing the irony in his words.

"As a matter of fact," Edward said suddenly, breaking his own silence, "I have decided to have a supper later this month. And a ball."

Sylvia stared at him. Judith put her fork down. Prepared to do battle for her idea, she was stunned when he so readily agreed. "A ball? You have not mentioned it before," Judith told him.

"I decided while I was in London. A Miss Elizabeth

Wyndham and her mother will be arriving Wednesday next. They will in all probability stay over, since it is rather a long journey, returning to London Thursday."

"What's this?" James grinned down the table at his brother. "Who is this Elizabeth and just what are you up to, old man?"

Edward stared at his brother. "The Queen feels I am past time for having an heir." He watched James's eyes flicker away and then back to watch him more closely.

"What are you saying?" Sylvia asked him, pain in her voice.

"Isn't this all rather sudden?" Judith asked him.

He shrugged, returning his attention to the mulled wine in his cup. When he looked up, it was to see Victoria's eyes, large and clouded, staring down the table at him. She looked quickly away, the cup of mulled wine she held shaking a little. She carefully put it down, avoiding all of them, her attention upon her plate until the meal was over.

When James had had his fill, leaning back in his chair and patting his stomach, he looked up the table toward Edward. "Let's not do the cigars and brandy, shall we? I'm not up to it really. It's been a long voyage home."

"Of course."

Sylvia stood up. "I shall see to my things."

James rose to stop her, catching her arm. "Sylvie, please, there's no need for you to do this."

She tried to get around him, but he would not move. Looking up at him, she spoke louder, calmness fleeing. "Don't touch me. Don't touch me!" She wrenched away from him.

"Sylvia! Really!" Judith stared up at her reprovingly. "What a scene you are making over nothing."

"Nothing?" Sylvia laughed, a small bitter little sound that stuck in her throat. *"Nothing?* How would you know? I won't sleep with him!" Her voice rose higher.

"Be quiet!" Judith told her more harshly. "The servants will hear you."

"Let them!"

"Sylvia—" Edward stood up, turning her toward him.

"Don't you start too," she told him, "I couldn't bear it!"

She looked around the room, finding Victoria. "Please, Victoria, will you come with me?"

"I'll—" James began, reaching out to take her arm.

"No!" She backed away from him, backing away from Judith as she stood up too, glaring down the length of the table at her. *"No!"*

Edward looked down at Victoria. "If you wouldn't mind . . ."

"Of course." Victoria stood up, watching Sylvia come around the table toward her, shaking. Her heart went out to the woman, though she was unsure why Sylvia felt so violently about her husband. "I'll help you move some things," Victoria told her softly.

"You'll do no such thing," Judith declared.

Edward interrupted. "Sylvia will do as she pleases tonight. Everything can be discussed tomorrow."

James suddenly sank to his chair, an oath escaping his lips, his hands reaching out to catch at the table. All eyes were upon him as he took a deep breath and looked up. "Sorry . . . it's not a very big wound, but they ordered me home because of it. Dirty Zulus are becoming frightfully accurate."

"You poor boy!" Judith bent to help him. "Now look what you've done," she told Sylvia.

"I'm fine, Aunt Judith, truly. I shall be fine." He looked over at his wife. "I'm just not up to arguments quite yet. I realize I've been gone a long time. It's natural for you to feel we're strangers. I don't mind, truly." He looked at Sylvia with utter sincerity.

"I mind," Judith told him. "It's completely unwifely and I shall not accept such behavior."

"Since she's not your wife," Edward spoke quietly, "it's really none of your business, Aunt Judith."

"I assure you none of this would have been tolerated under your father's roof. My brother knew his duty and he did it."

"And made others resign themselves to his duty too?"

"If necessary," she said repressively. "Come along, James, I shall get Michael to help you upstairs."

"I shall make it under my own steam," he said, standing

72

and then collapsing back against the chair. "Well . . . maybe just a bit of help."

Edward watched as Judith went into the hall, fetching Mike back. He watched as they led James out. But he did not offer to help, did not come forward to accompany them up the stairs.

Victoria followed Sylvia out, feeling the woman's hesitation as she saw her husband being helped up the steps. Then Sylvia reached back for her hand, grasping it hard, holding on to it as they climbed the stairs and went toward her room.

"I shall get a few things only," she told Victoria.

"Please—" James stopped ahead of them, looking back past Mike at them. Judith, beside him, glared at the two women. "I shall be content in any room. Leave your things there. Just let Mike get something for me for tonight."

Victoria stopped where she was, waiting while Judith turned toward a door across the hall, ignoring the others as she helped James through it, Mike stepping back.

"I'll just get his things," Mike said to them all, walking toward Sylvia's door and going inside. When he came back out and crossed the hall, Sylvia walked forward, still clutching Victoria's hand.

She did not let go until she was inside her own room. "Don't go . . ." Sylvia whispered. "Don't let him near me."

"He won't come tonight."

"You don't know him." Sylvia's eyes were hollow.

"Is there a lock to your door?"

"No."

Victoria looked around the room. "This chair." She reached for a narrow wood chair that stood in front of the vanity table. "If you prop it against the doorknob, it won't turn. And if he forces it, you'll hear the noise. And I'll come running."

Sylvia stared at her. "Do you promise?"

Victoria nodded. "I promise."

Sylvia stared at the chair and then took it from Victoria, following her to the door.

Once outside, Victoria hesitated. She heard wood scraping against wood and stared at the closed bedroom door. Sylvia had truly followed her suggestion.

Sounds of low-voiced conversation came from the bedroom across the hall. Victoria went on to her own door, closing it against them all. Inside there was no fire in her grate, and the room was chilly. She leaned against the door, unhappiness washing over her.

There were too many things she did not understand in this household. Too many secrets. Too much to take in all at once.

She caught her own reflection in the mirror, the one oil lamp she had left burning sitting on the bureau. In the darkness she stared into eyes that stared unhappily back. She thought of his hands, his lips upon hers, his arms around her, pulling her to the floor. It seemed ages ago instead of a few hours.

She looked the same. For one brief mad moment she wondered if she had dreamed it all, had fallen somehow from the rocking chair and dreamed his caresses.

But the two buttons torn from her gown were sitting on the bureau, her dress folded beside them, awaiting the seamstress in the morning.

Sounds of doors closing and people moving about came through the walls. She heard movement in the room beyond hers and stared toward it. Was that him . . . where was his room . . . she did not know.

He had acted as if nothing had happened between them. He had spoken calmly of an heir. Of a woman named Elizabeth. Her cheeks burned. He might grab her for a moment, but he would plan his life with one of his own kind.

Her heart breaking, she undressed and climbed beneath the covers, curling around her pillows and hugging them close. Damp tears splattered against the pillowcase until, exhausted, she finally drifted off into uneasy dreams.

She did not hear her door open, did not see the man who stood just outside, staring at her sleeping form, the moon outlining her body for a moment and then moving on to leave her in shadows.

Chapter 7

MORNING LIGHT BROUGHT MORE clouds, but no winds. The sun was lost high above the gray skies, a pale glow, the countryside's early greenery grayed over and dark.

When Nancy came in with a jug of hot water for the basin, Victoria begged off breakfast, asking for a tray in her room instead. The prospect of sitting through another meal in that dining room was too much to bear.

"Lady Judith did say they would be sitting down to breakfast in the dining room this morning. Like a family again, instead of picking food from trays." Nancy watched Victoria shiver. "Are you cold? Should I light the fire?"

"No, I'm fine. Thank you." Victoria sat down at the dressing table, staring at her drawn face in the glass. Behind her Nancy was staring too.

"It's not my business," Nancy told her, "but living here doesn't seem to be agreeing with your health. What with fainting fits and—whatever . . ." Nancy trailed off, still watching Victoria's pale face and red-rimmed eyes. "Did you not get any sleep?"

"Not much," Victoria admitted. Then, looking at the girl through the mirror, she smiled wanly. "If you could see to some tea and toast, I'll have a bite here and then go straight to my work."

"Yes, miss." Nancy turned away, closing the hall door

gently, Victoria watching its reflection in the mirror until she was alone.

Downstairs Judith's rasping voice came from the open doors to the large dining suite, Victoria hurrying by them, walking purposefully to the sanctuary of the study.

Inside a fire had been laid against the morning's chill. In preparation for the duke, Victoria told herself, her heart skipping a beat. He would soon walk in and the future would be decided. She must tell him she was leaving. There was no other course; she must be fearless and come right out with it.

Her head drooped at the thought. Gratefully she turned toward the pages she'd left behind yesterday, losing her worries in the task at hand.

When the door opened, she did not dare lift her head. Her heart hammered against her rib cage, the sound of his footsteps drawing nearer and then stopping beside the desk. "I shall be gone for a few days." The deep tones of his voice resounded within her, the mere fact of his walking into a room throwing her into confusion.

She looked up at him hesitantly, her eyes rising to meet his, her chin still bent a little down, as if afraid to meet his gaze squarely. "Would you prefer I left now?" The words were so soft he barely heard them.

"What are you talking about?" His face was expressionless.

"I—I assumed—"

"If you feel you cannot carry on your work without constant supervision, say so," he told her coldly. She stared up into oddly distant eyes, a subtle transformation going on within this man since his brother's return.

"I can carry on," she told him quietly. "If you wish me to."

"Why would I not?" He left the room, Victoria staring down at her own trembling hands. Slowly she reached for the pen, dipping it into the inkwell and forcing her attention back to the page at hand.

"The Poor Relief Bill," she read. "Lord William Henry Gregory's clauses: (1) gave assistance to 'surplus' Irish who wish to settle elsewhere; (2) added quarter-acre clause."

She saw Edward's note to look up exact provisions in bound volumes of Parliament Acts, 1840–1860. She pushed aside the rest of the papers, taking the one sheet with her as she walked to the library, searching the shelves for the volumes of Parliament Acts.

In a shadowy corner she came upon a row of political volumes, the light too dim to read their fading titles. She left them, reaching for the heavy crimson drapes that hung across the tall library windows, pulling on the braided cord that bound it, tugging it toward the edge of a row of built-in shelves, thus allowing more light into the room.

She moved past a large leather chair, trying again to read the titles. Suddenly a hand reached out and grabbed her. Her heart stopped as she saw the duke sitting there, in what had been the shadows of the room. Alone. "I—I thought you were departing."

"But I just arrived," James drawled, shocking Victoria. She pulled her hand back from his grasp, too shocked to see the small knowing smile he now graced her with, his eyes moving leisurely down her form and slowly back up it to see her near panic. "Judith told me you got here recently also. From a woman's academy of some sort. Have you so little knowledge of men that the merest touch of one sends you into shock?" He smiled. "You haven't been all that gently bred, have you, Miss Leggett?"

She took a step backward, his charming smile following her. "I assure you," he continued mildly, "you have no idea of the pleasures you are missing." His words became colder. "My wife could no doubt put you to rights about what a man's embrace feels like." He watched her. "Am I shocking you?"

"Yes, your grace. You are. Gentlemen do not speak thus to ladies."

"I am not your grace, nor anyone else's." His voice held bitterness that was quickly banished, replaced by a half-smile, a bantering tone. "My brother has inherited all titles in this family." He watched her. "Your attitude is most untutored. How old are you?"

"That is not a question a gentleman asks a lady . . . is it?"

"Oh ho! I'll wager you've given Edward a merry chase, my girl."

"I beg your pardon?"

"No need to beg. I would give you anything you asked. For a sweet smile and a loving caress I would do much." He watched her eyes widen at his familiarity. "James Henry Bereshaven, our ancestors giving their name to the lands which my dear, departing, brother is duke of. More's the pity, since the hint of Irishness haunts us in all the best circles."

"But you are English."

His smile twisted the sides of his mouth, but did not soften his expression. "Or Anglo-Irish, depending upon who you are talking to. You see our forefathers held land for over two hundred years on that godforsaken island . . . we stretch back to good Queen Bess in our hereditary rights. But thank God my father was determined to remain English. After his unfortunate marriage—to an Irish witch who beguiled him totally, they say—he realized that the heathen elements of that land were beginning to taint even him. And so he packed us up and brought us back to England, to grow up as proper Englishmen on good English soil. At last."

"At last?" she asked faintly.

"My father was born in Ireland, as were we and all our family for the last hundred years. We were evolving too far away from what we truly are. And so we came home to England."

She stared at him. "Home to a land that none of your family had been born in for one hundred years?"

"Sounds strange, yes, you're right. But my dear girl, you must realize that once an Englishman, always an Englishman. We may conquer the world. But we do not assimilate. We always remain true-blue English, through and through."

"You sound bitter."

"Do I?" He stared at her, some spark of real emotion coming through his carefully controlled manner. He shrugged. "They say, some say, I've been bitter since birth. After all, how many men miss their destiny, miss a dukedom, by but ten minutes?" He tried to smile.

She sat down in the chair across from him, for the first moment since they met feeling some fellow feeling for him, some glimpse of the man behind the mask. "Do you want to be English so very much?" she asked him softly, watching his eyes.

"Yes. Most dreadfully," he told her. "Edward has more ambivalent feelings, but mine are as my father's were. This is my land, my country, and I wish to fight for her, to work for her, to be a part of her."

"And are you not? Have you not?"

"Oh, I am. And I have. Of course." His eyes were on some distant vista far away from the room around them. "But you see I also know that we are accepted on suffrance by many of the people who truly count. They say nothing. After all, Edward *is* a duke, we *are* related by marriage to the Queen herself. But under the polite exterior the English are so very, very good at, one wonders at times if the taint of Ireland is not just a bit stronger than they can truly accept."

"The taint of Ireland?"

"Miss Leggett . . . Victoria, if I may so call you, you must remember before my father's realization of who and what he was, he had suffered a most serious setback. One that none of our ancestors, bless their English genes, had ever suffered. Whatever they did for fun, they married English, every single one of them. Not even Anglo-Irish, but English roses straight from England. Who sometimes wilted in the boggy Irish atmosphere, it's true. All except my father, who married Irish."

She watched the bitterness fill his face, his eyes, washing away as he saw her staring at him, his lopsided smile returning. "Ah, now, don't think I'm going too gloomy. That's an Irish trait, you know: emotionalism. Not quite the thing. Not quite the stiff upper lip. No. Not I. I am my father's son. I simply learned early, what he learned late."

"What is that?" Victoria asked quietly.

"That I am an Englishman—first, last, and always."

"And your mother?"

There was only a slight hesitation. "My mother had the good sense to see her mistake and die exceedingly young. And since I have had no knowledge of her since I was six years old, I do not fear any taint of Irish madness, no matter what our peers may think."

"Is it mad, then, to be Irish?" she asked the man seated across from her, his pain evident, his attempts to hide it merely exaggerating its depth.

"It does help," he said with a straight face, seeing her slow smile. And suddenly his expression lightened, his eyes taking in her red hair, her gray-green eyes and creamy skin. "Gosh, as they say in the East End these days . . ." He smiled at her. "I hope I've not hurt your feelings. You're not Irish by any chance, are you? If you are, I take back what I said and I'll never wonder at my father's folly again . . ."

Victoria smiled in spite of herself. "You must watch out for that, you know, for even I know it's called Irish blarney. As to myself, I cannot tell you. I was orphaned and left to fend for myself. There is no way of knowing what I am. Or am not, I fear. Which leaves me in the peculiar position of having to make myself up as I go along. I cannot rely upon ancestors to guide me as to what I should be."

"Aren't you the lucky one," James told her, smiling at her now. And then he stood up. "I am to sit in the fresh air and whatever sun there is, the doctors tell me. Won't you join me?"

"I cannot." She stood up. "I fear I have already been remiss in my duties."

He stared down upon her. "Will you consider another time? When your duties are performed? I should really like to talk. It's been so long, I fear I am quite rusty and I cannot make my renewed splash into London society with no preparation, now can I? You wouldn't want that, would you?"

She was smiling again, in spite of her best efforts to appear businesslike and professional. "I shall be honored to be practiced upon," she told him as seriously as she could, seeing his winning smile repay her.

"I don't know where Edward found you, but I must say for once he's outdone himself."

She dimpled, turning away, her smile turning into a wide grin she was determined to hide.

"I shall leave you to your ponderous tomes, then. Think of me, lolling away on the lawns, yearning for company."

"Get away with you!" She laughed, not turning around.

"Ah, now that's as Irish as they come! I fear I may soon be apologizing."

She fingered the political volumes along the lower shelf, reaching for one as he closed the door to the hall. Behind her the room was filled with silence, her hands holding a dusty book whose contents looked very dry at this moment. Resolutely she carried it back toward the study, finding herself sighing when she sat back at the narrow table and opened it, staring down at the neatly printed pages.

The pages swam before her in line after line of neat type, her thoughts far away and forlorn until what she was reading began to penetrate the fog of emotions that this family had released within her. The assistance Lord Gregory wrote into the Poor Relief Bill was the few mere shillings that would pay for the lowest order of fare to America. Not one farthing more. When these people, these "surplus" people, as the English lords were designating them, landed on a foreign shore, they would be destitute and homeless. She stared at the words, rereading them, beginning to make quick notes down the blank page of foolscap, noting the page of the old duke's manuscript, the page of the political volume, the actual words used. How could the old duke have made it sound as if the Queen's government was trying to help these people?

How could anyone force people out of their homeland with nothing but the clothes on their backs and the price of steerage to a foreign shore? It was inhuman, uncivilized. She paged quickly through the entire document, searching out the meanings of all the obscure passages, going over and over what these men had written.

According to the pages written by the late duke, if any wished help, any help at all, in keeping their children from starving during the dreadful famine, in gaining so much as one bowl of gruel, they must first relinquish all ownership of any lands they possessed beyond one quarter of a statute acre. If they kept one foot more there was no relief, no help available. No food. No medicine. It was *unlawful* for any to help until they'd surrendered title to all save that one quarter acre.

Victoria stared at the page. There was no provision for

families who had tilled their own land, buying it slowly over generations, gaining little by little against the barren rocks. Their grandfathers might have eked out a living that had brought enough to buy a tad more and their fathers might have spent their lives and their health building up their farm, but they must relinquish the family land or die of starvation. No quarter given except for the quarter-acre which would sustain no one in Ireland's rocky soil.

Her heart went out to these people she had never met, her soul raged against the injustices she read of. Her eye was caught by a Lord Bentinck's words, railing away at his fellows in the House of Lords, pushing for jobs for the destitute Irishmen whose livelihoods were wiped away by the blight that had fallen across their crops. Ireland sorely needed railroads, Lord Bentinck proclaimed, and these people could be put to work building them. "Never before has there been an instance of a so-called Christian government allowing so many to perish without interfering!" A hue and cry met his words, confusion and men crying out against him as the secretary to Parliament had taken down the proceedings. "Yes, you will groan," he told them, "but you *will* hear this!"

Victoria straightened up, staring down at the pages before her, at her own quickly scribbled notes on the papers she piled one on top of another beside the large leatherbound tome.

A knock at the door brought her head up. "Yes?"

Sylvia opened the door, standing with her hand on it still. Her eyes were red-rimmed, the expression within them so sad it seemed to press her downward, her shoulders curved, her movements tired. "I did not mean to intrude, but Edward said before he left that I should ask you to help with the invitations." She tried to smile. "We are to give a ball, it seems. He was not joking." There was no light in her eyes. "There is a list of people who must be invited. The Crown is sending it along . . . will you be available tomorrow?"

Victoria spoke quietly. "Of course." Watching Sylvia turn to leave, her heart lurched. "Lady Sylvia—" She stopped when Sylvia looked back toward her. "Is there anything else I can do to help?" she added softly.

Sylvia watched the younger woman, her face an enigma.

Finally she shook her head. "There is no help for me, if that is what you mean."

"Sometimes simply talking about what . . . ails helps."

Sylvia stared at Victoria. "Have you found that to be true?"

"Yes," Victoria told her. "Matron—the head mistress —always said it was so and often I unburdened myself to her. It did help."

"Unburdened yourself." Sylvia mused over the words. "Of what did you unburden yourself? No, don't answer. Let me guess . . . You worried about—what? Friendships? Your progress in your studies? The meaning of life, perhaps? Miss Leggett, my worries are somewhat more complex. You would be shocked to the core."

"You could try me," Victoria told the woman.

"Yes." She sighed. "I could . . . and perhaps I shall if this continues. But you will hear things you have no experience of, dear Miss Leggett . . . you will hear of rape. And murders. And of people who should not have been born. Yes? Were you going to say something?" Sylvia smiled. "I can see you are shocked. You see? I told you. Some things cannot be bettered by discussion. They are best left buried. As are the people they concern. And the rest of us, the ones who survived . . . we simply have to go on. And on . . . Excuse me." She turned away, ending the conversation.

Sylvia's words still filled the room, intruding when Victoria tried to return to her work. She could not mean, she could not have said . . . there must be some explanation, some overstatement of the case, something wrong with what she said.

And under all the rest, other words hammered away within Victoria: invitations, a ball to be given, a lady and her mother to be entertained.

A sudden vision of the life ahead of her filled Victoria.

Working away at books and papers, alone in the world, while in nearby chambers he and his bride would bring forth children. Would laugh and play and build their lives together as she looked on. Watching. Waiting for something that would never be.

She was not capable of accepting such a future. She looked across the middle distance and saw Edward, in her mind's eye, as he had been earlier. Cold. Indifferent. Aloof. There was no future with him. And scant days ago she had asked none, she told herself, none! She had wished a secure position and the ability to earn her livelihood. That was all. *All.* She had come to this house expecting no more than that and she had been given that.

At least for the moment. Even after her lapse, after last night. It seemed a hundred years ago, that moment when he had held her and reached down to take possession of her mouth. Her heart.

Her eyes closed. Her heart was not so easily won. She had what she had asked for and he was not so disgusted with her that he was dismissing her out of hand. Therefore she could continue in her position if she wished.

She did wish.

She wished to prove herself. The small voice deep within that nagged at her, that told her what she really wished was to stay close to him, was ignored.

Turning back to her work, she read down the pages she had covered, forcing her mind back to the task at hand.

Tomorrow she would have to deal with party invitations. Tomorrow would take care of itself.

Chapter 8

THE DAYS OF THAT long week followed one another, a succession of ever-brightening days, spring weather warming the countryside, opening the blossoms to soak up the sun's rays and spread their nectar across the fields of buttercups and daisies.

The roses poured forth, blossoms opening and quickly snipped for the cut-glass vases that sat upon table after table in the parlors of the great stone mansion. Tulips found their way to the tables, lilacs blossoming and calling to lazy bees that began to wake from winter's sleep and taste the fruits of early spring.

Victoria watched an uneasy routine settle over The Willows, watched Sylvia little by little accustom herself to the fact of her husband's return.

Sylvia would at least talk to James by midweek. Edward was still gone, Judith spending her days smiling and hovering about her "invalid boy," as she called James. She would fuss about, tucking in his lap robe, bringing him a special cup of Earl Grey tea, sitting on the lawns beside him with a huge-brimmed straw hat protecting her face from the sun, long lace gloves covering her hands and her arms. Judith would listen to tales of Africa, of exotic peoples and the far-off Zulu wars.

Sylvia sat with them one day. The sunlight beckoning, the house silent, all the light and laughter out on the lawns with Judith and James.

"I tell you they could!" James's laughing voice carried across the lawns to where Mike stood with the gardeners.

"No," Judith insisted. "Not possible."

"Forty miles in a single day. I swear it, Auntie, on my life. These Zulus are one fierce lot, let me tell you."

"Their leader—" Sylvia spoke, sitting a little distance away on a lawn chair, fanning herself, her eyes on the distant horizon. "I've heard his name I think somewhere."

"Cetywayo," her husband told her. "Their leader, their king. A cold brute."

"Of course," Judith put in.

"But brave?" Sylvia asked.

"Brave? Hard to say, in our terms. A very able leader, I'll give him that. But cruel. A great deal of selfish pride, and more untruthful than any of his predecessors, if you can credit that."

"How awful he sounds," Judith said, watching Sylvia's back as she rocked in the wicker lawn chair a few feet away.

"If you were to see him, you'd think worse. But then, you cannot expect more of a heathen."

"Tell us about him," Sylvia said suddenly.

"It's not a fit tale for feminine ears, my dear."

Across the lawns Michael Flaherty left the gardeners to their work, walking up toward the rose gardens and the study windows. Inside, Victoria could be seen, her slight form leaning over a great pile of books.

Michael turned back toward the Thames at the foot of the sloping lawns, shading his eyes. A fisherman stood across river, wading into the shallows, his line drifting with the current. When Michael pulled out his watch fob, no one was nearby. He turned the glass mirror within the ornate sterling silver case, catching the sunlight, reflecting it back. A flash of light hit the fisherman across the wide stream, making him look up and blink.

After another moment the fisherman turned away, returning to shore, reeling his line in. No fish was on it.

And after another moment Michael Flaherty returned his watch to his vest pocket, sauntering slowly toward the house, entering by the terrace doors.

* * *

The duke returned that afternoon, his boot heels echoing across the front hall as he strode into the study, pulling up short when he faced Victoria.

He watched her upturned face for a moment before he spoke. "How is our book progressing?"

He saw a tremulous smile look back at him, saw confusion and questions looking up at him. She looked unsure, tentative, but somehow trusting. His heart lurched within him. He looked away, his voice gruff when he spoke again. "Come along, have you done anything at all?" He waited for the sound of her voice, for the words that came tumbling out toward him before allowing himself to sit down, to turn back to watch her as she spoke.

"I've found all the references in the first chapters, up to page fifty of your father's work and—" Her voice rose with emotion. He could feel the surge of heartfelt reaction with her: "Some of it is too beastly to credit! I mean, forgive me, of course there are men, good and true, who tried to bring a voice of reason to the hearings, but in the period of which we speak, during the Great Famine and just after, I cannot tell you the vicious lies that Parliament perpetrated."

Edward watched the fire in her eyes, the self-forgetfulness as she expounded upon the injustices she was reading about.

"I thought the pursuit of equal rights was fraught with much rhetoric and bombast, but this! This is fratricide! I'm sorry!" She saw his expression and stopped for a moment. "I know this sounds excessive but it is so very dreadful —have you knowledge of what all transpired?" she asked him.

"Some," he replied mildly. "That was the reason for my initial interest in redoing my father's project."

"It *must* be redone!" She spoke with such vehemence she surprised herself. Subsiding, she felt at a loss, watching him shyly now, afraid he would think her a fool. "What I meant to say was that this work of yours is *vital*—there *is* no unbiased view of the events that have shaped the present predicament."

"What you meant to say," he told her, "was exactly what you did say. It *must* be redone." Before she could interject, he continued: "I, of course, agree wholeheartedly. And I am pleased that my cause has caught your enthusiasm."

"Why?" she asked him softly.

"Why?" He stared at her. "I should think that obvious."

"It's not to me," she told him. "I should very much like to know why you care about my opinion at all."

He studied her. Long experience with female wiles made him leery of her meanings, of what she was after with her words. "My work will progress much more rapidly if you share an enthusiasm for it. If you are to continue in my employ," he added.

She felt a stone hit the pit of her stomach. "And am I to continue in your employ?" she asked.

"Do you know of any reason you should not?" He watched her, his dark eyes unreadable.

"I have no wish to leave," she told him ambiguously, awaiting his reply.

He did not answer her immediately. "May I see what you have done?" he asked her, reaching out his hand.

She stared at the outstretched hand. She remembered that hand closing about her head, her neck, her breast. She looked down, picking up a sheaf of papers and handing them to him. "These are the notes I have made for you to go through."

His hand came near her own, taking the papers from her, a fraction of an inch separating their flesh. She swallowed, her eyes averted, her body turning away from him, trying to keep some equilibrium while his attention focused on her written words which he held in his hands now.

The silence in the study oppressed her. She stood up, his head coming up from the papers as she moved. "Where are you going?" he asked her.

"To—to allow you to read in peace," she replied after one heartbeat of hesitation.

"Stay," he told her. "I might have questions."

She looked down. "It is hard to sit while another reads your words."

He hesitated. "If you feel you must go—"

"I must!" she told him, fleeing toward the door before he could change his mind and order her back.

When she was gone, when the room was empty except for himself, Edward Albert, Duke of Bereshaven, stared around himself for a moment before he returned to the pages she had given him. The room was empty without her, a warmth stolen away by the mere fact of her leaving.

Just outside the study door Victoria ran headlong into Michael Flaherty. "Girl, girl . . . watch what you're about!" He reached out and stopped her headlong flight. "Where are you off to in such a rush?"

"Nowhere. I mean, I—the duke is within!" she told the man, confusing him further. She raced up the stairs while the Irishman stood below, staring after her.

Once she was out of sight he turned toward the closed study door, tapping it as he pushed it open. Across the cluttered room the duke glanced up, papers spread before him across the ornate desk that sat across the room from Victoria's narrow table by the windows.

"Have you a moment?" Michael was asking.

"Emmm? Oh . . . yes . . ." The man's dark head bent back toward the pages at hand, a bemused expression softening his angular features. After he closed the wrappings around the loose pages, trying the long silk ribbon, he spoke carefully. "I've just begun to go over Miss Leggett's work."

Michael watched him, curious. "And?"

Edward took a moment answering. His hands finished with the ribbon, still he held on to the manuscript, looking down at it and then back up at the man who was part and parcel of his childhood, the man who had raised him. "She has grasped the entire crux of the matter. The heart of it as much as I could have done myself." His eyes were upon Michael but his gaze was far away, seeing distant vistas that fled before his grasp; in trying to remember them they disappeared, fading into a vague remembrance of times past and people gone. "Yes?" The duke focused then upon the man before him, becoming businesslike, matter-of-fact. "Did you wish something, Michael?"

Michael Flaherty watched the grown man before him, seeing flashes of the boy who had once cried his heart out on the ship leaving Ireland. Burying himself in the burly Irishman's arms, he had sobbed for his mother who had been left behind, who was never to be mentioned again in his father's presence. "Why do you look so?" The unhappy boy who had grown into the ninth Duke of Bereshaven was asking now, drawing Michael's attention back to the present. Edward searched the older man's eyes.

"I was thinking of when we left Ireland," Michael answered. "It was a hard passage over. Your words, about the book, brought it back."

"I remember very little of it," Edward said. "Or of Ireland." He watched the man who stood before him. "Have you never thought of going back?"

"Every blessed day since I first clapped eyes on England's soil."

The duke stared at him. "Truly? Every day?"

"As true as I stand here before you."

Edward searched for clues in Michael's face, clues to his motives for leaving Ireland. "Why did you stay then?" he asked, waiting while Michael looked toward the rosebushes, taking his time with his answer.

"The truth of it is I promised someone I'd look out for you."

There was a heartbeat before Edward spoke: "Whom did you promise?" The words came softly toward Michael, belying the depth of their meaning, but some of the young boy's anguish still lurked behind the grown man's calm dark eyes.

Michael did not see the look in the duke's eyes. His gaze fastened upon the fragrant, still-forming blossoms out beyond the tiny-paned window.

"You have never mentioned her name. Not once in all these years," Edward said when Michael did not answer.

"The duke—" Michael turned to face Edward. "That is, your father, the late duke, said the only way I could come was if I never mentioned her, never spoke of her. And I haven't." A flash of anger sparked within him. "As God and you yourself are my witnesses, I have never spoken her name from that day to this." His voice strangled within his throat, emotion squeezing his larynx almost shut. "Siobhan . . ." The name came painfully, pushed out over the lump in his throat. "Siobhan . . ." Her name came floating into the air of the room, rising from some long-dead past to dredge up deeply buried memories in each of them. Michael stood in front of the desk, his shoulders slumping forward with the weight of his anguish.

Edward stared at him, forcing back the reality of her existence, the memory of what had happened, unable to face it all. Yet he kept on, picking at the healing scabs his mind had placed over the still-sore hurts, unable to let the subject rest. Something inside drove him on. He had to know, had to understand, had to hear the words. "She sent you." Edward's words came out flatly. "My—mother —sent you with us."

Michael's anger erupted into his voice: "He broke her heart, taking her boys away! You were her whole life! He left her to starve to death along with the rest of her people, along with her whole country while he just left. A proper Englishman, taking what he wanted and then going home to leave whoever's left to suffer for what he's caused. You asked why I came. I came because she begged me to, to look after you as if you were my own. I came because I loved her and I loved you, and she could not live with the thought of your being gone." His eyes clouded over. "I stayed because I had nothing to go back to. She was dead, my people were scattered to the four winds. I stayed because he and his kind had killed everything I had left behind."

"You hated him."

"Aye. I hated him." Michael looked the young duke straight in the eye. "I'll not deny it."

"And yet you care about his sons."

"Her sons." Michael's honest soul struggled with his words. "Her *son,"* he finally added flatly.

The room was silent, both men staring at each other. "Her son," Edward repeated carefully.

"I'll not lie. Your brother is more his than hers . . . but she lives on . . . inside you. God knows I've tried to love him . . ."

Edward looked away, unable to bear the raw pain in the other man's eyes. "We owe you more than I realized."

"You owe me nothing. And God forgive me, Jamie owes me less. Not that he needed me, he was always someone's darling."

"James is personable. Bright and witty and—all the things I am not." He spoke more slowly as he continued. "The wronged one. The one who should have been duke."

"Edward, don't do this to yourself. And don't listen to fools."

Edward shrugged. "They all say it behind my back."

"Not all."

"Ask Judith. The midwife herself told Judith a mistake had been made, that James had been firstborn . . . but my father would not change his will, would not admit the mistake out of pride. Even though he himself favored James."

"Bosh!" The word boomed out. Michael reached toward Edward, almost as if he would caress him, and then pulled back, self-conscious. "Your aunt Judith never even clapped eyes upon any Irish midwife! And such is what you had and good old Mary Megan would not have spoken to the likes of Judith if asked! Mary Megan spoke Gaelic and only such, and never left her own home village in her life except for her treks to Bereshaven House to look after your ma. And only that because of who your mother was, and how beloved she was to one and all. Your aunt Judith never stepped foot on Irish soil."

Edward found himself standing up. Unable to sit still, his innards roiling with emotions held in check for thirty years and more, he moved and stopped, his movements choppy, his thoughts in disarray. Michael watched him move from desk to window, from window to table and back again as Michael continued: "She's an evil busybody, your aunt Judith, and she had whatever she had from that puce-colored nanny your old dad saddled you boys with. She's the one who started all the tales and she's the one who gave little Jamie such airs and graces about himself that he's never been the same since. A witch of a woman and a liar to boot!"

Edward stood near his desk again, staring down at the papers, at the brass and crystal inkwell, the ornate French carriage clock that sat beside it, the green-shaded oil lamp that sat beside the brass letter scale. All of it his father's. When he looked up, his eyes were hollow. "I have inherited everything from a father who hated me. Who doted on my brother, whose heart was with my brother."

"Of course it was! Jamie took after him in spirit, if not in looks . . . Jamie's *English,* even though he's half-Irish, just as you are Irish at heart, even though you fight it and even though you're half-English."

Edward turned to stare at the man. "Fight it?"

"Of course you do . . . and why not, being who you are? Where you are. But the point is that you *are* your mother's son."

"And the very Englishness you so abhor is what forced my father to leave all he possessed to *me,* and not my brother. No matter where his heart lay."

"Which should prove to you that you have, and had, ample claim to it . . . your father would not have overlooked his coddled Jamie if he had had a *reason* to invest him with it all. That shows you the truth of who was born first, if still you need it."

"Oh, I need it . . ." Edward picked up the filigreed brass letter opener, fingering its delicate edges. "I need it."

"Mayhap one day we shall go back to Ireland. And find old Mary Megan. Would you believe her?"

Edward put the letter opener down. He gazed deep into his old retainer's eyes, beginning to smile. "If someone other than you translated for me, I would."

Michael grinned then. "And you don't trust this faithful old dog then . . ."

Edward grinned back. "As far as I can throw you."

"Good! Then I taught you well . . . Speaking of which, I have news of our friends."

Edward lost his smile. "Has something happened?"

"They're being pushed to their limits and they need a friend at court."

"I fear I am not the one they should seek."

"You are their only hope."

"The Queen is not happy with me to begin with, Michael. She has grave reservations because of my . . . background. She is determined I shall be . . . redeemed by a proper marriage. A rebel duke is not something she is willing to consider."

"And you?"

Edward chose his words carefully. "I have invited the Wyndhams here." He looked up. "Has their arrival been seen to?"

Michael nodded. "They've sent word they shall be here tomorrow night."

"Good." He hesitated. Then: "I shall do what I must."

"Including marrying someone you do not care for?"

"Many good marriages have begun with less in common. Who knows, we may be better suited than we know. The Queen is an able matchmaker."

"And what of . . . others?"

Edward watched Michael. "What others?"

Michael looked down, fingering the brass scale atop the desk. "How should I know?"

"If you are implying anything amiss between Sylvia and myself, anything at all—*you*—"

"Did I say that!" Michael answered heatedly. "I think of you and what's good for you, none else! God help the poor girl, I have nothing against Sylvia, I pity her . . ."

Edward changed the subject abruptly. "How has it gone for her—for them—while I've been away?"

"There's some sort of uneasy truce between them."

Edward grimaced. "She deserved far better than she got."

"So do many of us," Michael said quietly, bringing Edward's gaze back toward the burly, self-sufficient man who buried so much love—and hate, and pain—deep within his impassive exterior.

"And what of the rest of the household?" Edward asked obliquely.

Michael watched the man he had raised, watching for signs of his real feelings beneath the controlled exterior. "There's nothing to report. The girl who loses her buttons has been buried in her work." Michael watched unbidden emotions fade quickly across Edward's face.

"That is all?" he asked finally.

"As far as can be seen she has had little to do with him since the night he arrived."

"And did not know him before."

Michael shrugged. "As far as we know."

"Find out."

"I'll do all that can be done. It might lead to something to ask her about her . . . past."

"We know what she has chosen to tell."

"And if there's more?"

"If there's more—" Edward's words came slowly. "Then we should know of it."

"Why?" Michael asked, seeing Edward turn to stare hard at him. Michael stared back, meeting his duke's gaze.

"Why . . ." Edward repeated slowly, looking away finally from Michael's steady gaze. "Because I am entrusting her with much when I entrust her with the manuscript. Much could be made of it if it fell prematurely into the wrong hands." Edward returned his attention to Michael, examining the eyes that stared back at him. "I need to trust her—if she is to continue in my employ," he added, the words coming quickly, as if to explain the ones that had gone before.

"Yes. Well, I shall try." Michael observed the man before him, seeking out the truth behind his carefully constructed facade. "You are then, truly, considering this engagement to the Wyndham girl?"

"I am."

Michael hesitated. Finally he continued: "And what of Ireland?"

"What of her?"

"How do you feel about helping her people?"

"Her people are my people," Edward said simply. "But to do them help, to do them justice, I have to be in a position where I can do more than mere posturing."

"Ah, but even the posturing is helpful these days."

"Perhaps. But it's not enough to make a difference. That's the problem with the whole Irish movement, Michael. It's too fragmented . . . too precipitate. You don't move until you can defend your position, until you have some hope of achieving more than mere rhetoric. Most of the leaders of the Irish cause are in love with the sound of their own words. They're not thinking about the ultimate victory. They're thinking about the impression they're making at the time. It won't wash. More is needed. Or far less."

"Will you help?"

"Oh God . . . I don't know . . . I don't know what I can do."

"You can carry the banner."

"They're words, Michael. Pretty words. What do they mean?"

"You have the ear of the *Queen!"*

"I do not. I can attain an audience with Her Majesty. From there nothing is assured. And *nothing* is gained. Unless there is a specific purpose, a specific plan, and she is forced to see the efficacy of it. She is nothing if not practical. If a *practical* solution is presented to her . . . then . . . *then* we have a chance." Edward stopped. He saw Michael grinning at him. "Why the sudden smile? I have said nothing new. Nothing illuminating."

"Ah, but you have and you do not realize it." Michael beamed as he spoke. "You have said 'we'—" The burly man reached out to grab the younger man's shoulders, his grip hard and full of feeling. "You have said *we*—that means more to me than all else, including victory!"

Edward allowed himself a small smile. "You see how an Irishman is easily deflected from his main goal?"

"And don't you be about teasing me, your big and glorious dukedom! I tell you that what you've just said makes my life worthwhile—makes your mother's sacrifices worthwhile and you can tease me all you like—you're still the hope of us all!"

Edward groaned. "Don't be putting the weight of all of it on my shoulders. You'll be disappointed for a certain fact."

Michael grinned. "You see?" he said triumphantly. "You see! You even sound Irish when you let yourself."

"Be gone with you!"

"Gladly!" Michael replied, turning on his heel and starting toward the door.

Edward watched him leave. Watched the good and true man cross to the hall door and open it. "Wait!" he called out; the older man turned back. Edward took a moment, staring into the familiar face. "I owe you so very much," he said finally.

"You owe me nothing."

"I owe you so very much," Edward repeated. "For my

mother as well as for myself." He saw Michael's eyes cloud. "I will see whomever you want me to."

Michael watched Siobhan's son. "If you see them, you must do so because you want to. Because you believe in what you're doing. What they're doing. Not because of me or any misplaced loyalty."

Edward grinned then. "I cannot very well know if I agree before I hear what they say. Can I?"

Michael hesitated. And then, slowly, found himself grinning back. "Aye . . . 'twould be hard to do so."

"You tell them I shall talk. And listen. More than that I cannot guarantee."

"That's enough!" Michael told him. "More than enough. For a beginning," the Irishman added slyly.

"You're surely a devil, Michael Flaherty."

"Aren't we all, your grace?" Michael replied, grinning. He shut the door between them, his footsteps echoing away down the hallway.

Left alone in the study, Edward was slowly sobering as he turned back toward his desk—and the manuscript—with deliberate movements.

Could he trust her . . . could he not . . . and how could he know the truth of her feelings? Loyalties, he corrected himself, loyalties were what he was concerned with; nothing more.

Chapter 9

STORM CLOUDS COVERED THE sky all day Wednesday, keeping the household indoors. Victoria took breakfast in her room and then immersed herself in her work, bent over the narrow table in the study. By late afternoon she had need of the huge green-shaded oil lamp that stood at her elbow on the desk, the gloomy day darker and darker as the hours passed.

James sent word he was not quite feeling well and would rest until evening and the arrival of the guests. Sylvia took her sewing to the morning room and spoke to no one, content to be left alone with her thoughts.

Edward read in the library, receiving two villagers in the afternoon to discuss one of the estate's tenancy houses. The old farmer whose family had lived on the estate for over one hundred years had died, and his children had gone off to the city to find work, uninterested in the land. The old farmer's wife had left with her eldest son, tears streaming down her cheeks, fearful of what life in the city would bring. And now the house was vacant, both of the villagers proposing to purchase it.

Edward listened to their arguments and agreed to let them know his decision before the week was out, his eyes turning toward the closed study door once Mike led the two men out. He almost stood and then, thinking better of it, lapsed back into his chair, pulling the volume of parliamentary history close and bending over it again.

* * *

The sounds of the housekeeper and the maids polishing up the stairs, changing the linens in the guest rooms, resounded through the house, light footsteps running up and down the stairs, Judith's orders being carried out. The smell of beeswax and turpentine filtered through the rooms as Nancy polished up the furniture and directed the under-maids.

At every sound of a step coming near, Victoria found her heart racing, her concentration lost as she held her breath, listening to see if it was Edward. When the steps would pass by in the hall, she would find her heart calming down, a bittersweet disappointment stealing over her. Her thoughts kept stealing away, visions of Miss Elizabeth Wyndham rising before her eyes. Victoria pictured a young woman with stately grace and elegant beauty. Pale and golden much like Sylvia, but tall and regal, as slim as a wraith. He would love her at first sight, they would live happily ever after . . . he would loathe her at first sight . . . he would—she knew not what. Visions of the gazebo in the moonlight made her straighten up, turning back to look past the rosebushes out beyond the windows. To look back to where the white roof of the building was just visible past the dark shadows of the lime and plane trees between. She shivered, turning away from the cold view beyond the glass. Standing up, she walked to the fireplace and stirred the dying embers in the grate. She thought about throwing another log on, watching the fire blaze up, and staying on in this small, snug room, staying on through the evening. Never venturing forth to meet the mighty Wyndhams and see the fate that was held in store for Edward. For the duke, she corrected herself. She had no right to call him by name. Not even in her thoughts. The Queen had decreed that he was to like Miss Wyndham. The Queen of England was cousin and family as well as ruler and majesty to the house of Bereshaven; royalty married royalty and Miss Wyndham was niece to an earl. James had regaled them all with the news after hearing of the plans, telling amusing stories about her brother, George, an old friend of James it seemed. But Miss Elizabeth had been a child when last he'd seen the family; he had no idea of what she was like now. None of them did.

Victoria straightened up, deciding against the extra

log, allowing the fire to burn down. She was returning to her work, reaching for her pen, when the bells began to chime. First the grandfather clock began tolling the hour, and before it finished its five sonorous tones, the bells that heralded visitors began to peal, someone giving several good yanks to the bell pull by the front door.

Rooted to her spot, Victoria heard running feet, heard the heavier tread of Mike Flaherty as he walked quickly past the study door. As he moved, suddenly, so did Victoria, rising and almost running to the hall door. She wrenched it open and fled across the hall behind Mike, moving swiftly toward the green baize door. From the corner of her eye she could see Mike reaching toward the huge oak door before she closed the small green baize door behind herself, stopping in the safety of the back hall to catch her breath.

One of the undermaids looked up uncertainly as Victoria walked past a tiny room where the maid was cleaning lamps. Moving toward the back stairs, Victoria saw no others and soon she was halfway up to the next floor and the safety of her room. She opened the door to the front hall a moment later, looking down the expanse of closed bedroom doors and then heading for her own as sounds of greeting came up from the floor below, rising up the wide front stairs. Judith's loud clear voice answered another; lower, softer, the words indistinguishable.

Safety. Victoria opened the door to her room and stopped in the doorway, staring at the maid who was reaching into her wardrobe. "Nancy?" Victoria stared at the girl. "Do you need something?"

"Oh! No, miss . . . didn't Lady Judith find you? She was going to look for you."

"Find me? I've been in the study all day." Victoria watched the girl's discomfort. "Is something wrong?" As she spoke the words Victoria glanced across the room, something amiss with its contents.

And then a chill swept through her. None of her things were laid out as she'd left them. The room looked unused, the maid holding the last of the closet's contents in her arms. Staring at Victoria uncomfortably, Nancy started toward her. "Lady Judith told Mrs. Jasper that this room would be needed for the guests. It's the second-best guest room, and since Sir James is in the first guest room and all, she needs this room . . . and the blue room across . . ." Nancy looked away from Victoria's eyes, feeling the fear that welled up over Victoria.

"I see." Victoria managed to get the words out finally. "Where have you taken my things—where are you taking them?"

"To another room, miss." Nancy brightened visibly, glad the subject was closed. "If you'll follow me, I'll show you where it is. Lady Judith was going to tell you herself, but I guess she didn't get around to it."

Victoria did not reply. She stepped back into the hall, letting the girl out of the room. When Nancy turned back to close the door, her hands full, Victoria reached for the doorknob. "I'll get it."

"Thank you, miss," Nancy said as Victoria stared in toward the room that she had begun to feel was hers. Begun to feel safe in. All the uncertainties of her position here washed back over her now as she resolutely closed the door and turned to follow the maid.

There was nothing assured about her future, nothing she could count on to be permanent. Nancy was speaking and she tried to listen. ". . . and it's just down a bit from my own." The girl pushed the door to the back hall open, smiling at Victoria reassuringly. As they entered the servants' hall Victoria suddenly realized she was being put in the servants' quarters.

"It's just down here, miss. And a nice little view it has." Nancy reached a narrow doorway and fumbled for the knob, Victoria hanging back behind, silently watching.

The door opened onto a bare little room with a scrubbed wood dresser and a narrow single bed. One small window looked past the tops of the willows toward the other side of the river, part of the sloping farmlands behind the house visible from here.

Victoria walked to the small window, staring out at the landscape. Nancy deposited the clothes she held in a tall, scuffed cupboard that filled one side of the room. There was just enough room for Nancy to stand at the cupboard and Victoria to stand at the window, the bed taking up the rest of the narrow floor space. "You see how nice the view is?" Nancy asked.

"It's very nice," Victoria said quietly.

Nancy closed the cupboard door, glancing around the room. "It's not as big as the other one, but I'm sure this is just for while they're here—the guests I mean . . ." Nancy was trying to find something more to say, something to make Victoria feel better.

"Wherever they wish me is fine, Nancy." Victoria turned to smile at the young maid. "Truly. I was startled, that was all. Don't give it another thought."

Nancy nodded, reaching for the doorknob. "If there's nothing else you need, then—"

"There's nothing. Thank you." Victoria watched Nancy go, still standing by the window for a long moment after the door closed. Then she turned toward the bed, sitting down and staring at the clothes cupboard a few feet away.

The gulf between herself and this family suddenly seemed impassable. Without a single word Lady Judith Bereshaven had put the orphan from Mercy House in her place. Victoria looked down at her own clasped hands. This was a blessing in disguise, she told herself firmly.

There was no possibility of daydreaming about the duke from this narrow room, no way of ignoring the simple facts of birth and position.

Judith Bereshaven was saving Victoria from any possibility of folly and ruin. She should be grateful, Victoria told herself. She *was* grateful. This was reality, the first days here merely a dream. If she had not fainted, if she had been hired in the usual way, she would have been in this room or one like it from the very beginning.

A knock at her door startled her from her thoughts. "Yes?"

"It's only me," Nancy said, opening the door and peering around its edge. "His grace sent word you are expected at dinner at eight o'clock—so as to give the travelers a chance to rest and freshen up."

Victoria stared at the maid. "I am to join them for dinner?"

"Yes, miss." Nancy was closing the door. "Eight sharp, Mr. Mike said."

Victoria lay back upon the covers, staring up at the plain white ceiling. Her eyes closed of their own accord after a few minutes, her drifting thoughts a jumble of questions without answers.

The dining room was ablaze with light long before eight o'clock, the smells of roast duck and beef, of pork and fish all blending with the smells of onions and boiled vegetables and baking breads and sweets. The long table groaned with dressed lobster and a great round of roasted beef surrounded by biscuits and asparagus; crystal goblets caught the reflected light from hundreds of crystal prisms in the chandelier high above it. More candles in tall brass holders marched down the center of the table, casting their glow across ruby red wine in crystal decanters, across gleaming, ornately wrought silver and fine, pale china plates.

Kitchen helpers scurried in and out of the door that led to a narrow hall and the kitchens beyond, the cook and undercook keeping them busy piling up the table and sideboards, the kitchen alive with activity while evening shadows fell out beyond the steamed windows.

Across the wide front hall from the dining room people were gathering in the small parlor, Judith regal in a sweeping black dress that would have done Queen Victoria herself proud. She was talking to a dumpy little woman who wore diamonds at her throat and cuffs, more diamonds in her earlobes and the ample front of her bodice. Her gown was of a dark red velvet, ribbons and lace festooning the wide sleeves. Across from the two older women Sylvia sat quietly, looking as if she were politely listening to their desultory conversation. Judith had one eye to the doorway, waiting for someone else's appearance.

"And still to be in black, dear Judith?" the woman was saying.

Judith acknowledged the comment with eyes that lowered for one brief moment before being raised again to smile distantly at the woman and dart back toward the door now and again. "Yes," she told the woman. "It's been such a devastating year. It seems as if my brother was alive and walking into this very room just these few weeks past. You yourself Margaret have known what it is to lose the ones most precious to you."

Margaret Wyndham acknowledged the truth of the words and then brightened visibly, looking over toward Sylvia. "But we must go on, mustn't we, dear?"

Sylvia caught herself, almost staring at the woman, unsure what had been said. "Yes. Of course," Sylvia said quickly. "We're so glad to have you here," she added, earning a look of disapproval from Judith.

"And we are so glad to be here. And to see you dear people. Sylvia, I had quite forgotten how lovely you are, and I'm sure London society has too. Now that James is home you two must get about more. You are entirely too young to bury yourself out here year in and year out."

"I rather like the quiet life," Sylvia replied.

"That's all well and good, but there's more to life than sitting at home, my dear George used to say. I assure you, Judith"—Margaret Wyndham turned back toward the older woman—"when my little Elizabeth marries, she will spend a good portion of her year in the city. After all, I must be able to see my only girl, mustn't I? And as family comes, there will be need of a girl's mother at hand."

Judith nodded frostily, disliking the entire subject. James walked into the room, all three women looking up toward him.

He smiled disarmingly at Lady Wyndham, walking across the room to kiss her hand. "The enchanting Margaret Wyndham has arrived!" he told the room, seeing Margaret's girlish blush of pleasure as he leaned forward.

"Now I never do know which of you two boys I'm dealing with," she told him. "You're quite naughty to look so very much alike."

James straightened up, an easy grin in place. "It's quite easy to tell us apart, once you've gotten the hang of it. Isn't it, dear?" He glanced over toward Sylvia, who had stiffened in her chair. "The trick is,"—James turned back to tell Margaret—"that Edward is always serious and I am never so. Therefore, if you see a smile, you know it's me." He reached to kiss Judith's forehead and then walked near Sylvia, draping himself over the back of her chair.

Judith was smiling. "You scamp," she told him fondly.

Margaret was smiling too. "What a charming couple you two make! I'd quite forgotten. Now, James, I was just telling Sylvia that you must not be such a stranger to London. Everyone will want to invite you."

"I look forward to a round of socializing most eagerly, my dear Margaret. I have been recovering from war wounds and am not quite up to the mark yet. But I shall make sure you are the first to know of my recovery."

"Is it a promise?" she asked him.

"Made in blood."

"Oooh." She shivered a little, smiling. "How exotic."

"Where is my dear brother, Aunt Judith? Has he not come down to meet his charming guests yet?"

Margaret spoke before Judith could answer. "Elizabeth is among the missing too. I wonder if they're off somewhere getting acquainted?"

James reached to kiss his wife's cheek, Margaret seeing a quick frown cross Sylvia's features. Misinterpreting it, Margaret smiled at the younger woman. "Now don't think the worst of them, Sylvia. I know the current theory is that a man and woman cannot be left alone in each other's company without danger of intrigue but I have utmost trust in Elizabeth. And your brother-in-law, of course."

"So have I, dear Margaret." James drawled his words out, smiling lazily as he sank into a chair beside Sylvia's. "My brother is the soul of discretion. Isn't he, dear?" His eyes found Sylvia's and fastened upon them, something dangerous below the surface of his lazy good humor.

Sylvia stood up. "I shall see if all is well with dinner."

"It's quite unnecessary, Sylvia," Judith told her, but Sylvia was already disappearing into the hall.

"One would almost think her jealous," James said lightly, watching a flicker of unease cross Margaret's features. She studied James.

"James loves to tease," Judith told the smaller woman. "It's so good to have him home. I swear I shall be quite distraught if he decides to leave me to pine here at The Willows while he enjoys London's pleasures."

"Never fear, Aunt Judith. You shall come to town with us; what do you say?"

Judith didn't reply, her pleasure apparent in the warmth of the smile she gave him. "A touch more sherry, Margaret?" she asked.

"Yes, that would be nice. If you'll join me."

James stood up. "Of course she'll join you. And I shall do the honors." He reached for the decanter, walking toward them to pour as Sylvia reached the top of the stairs and stopped, looking down the length of the hall to where Victoria was coming from the servants' hall beyond. Sylvia waited until Victoria reached her side.

"Have you seen Edward? The duke, I mean?"

"No." Victoria stared at Sylvia, feeling herself blushing even as she spoke.

Sylvia stared at her. "Or Michael? It's almost time to eat and he's not put in an appearance."

"I haven't seen him," Victoria replied, her tone sounding defensive, as if she felt she were being accused of something.

Sylvia glanced toward the closed doors of the hall, and then shrugged. "Well, it's none of my concern." She turned around, walking down the steps a little ahead of Victoria. At the bottom she turned back to see Victoria lagging behind. "Aren't you coming?"

"I—I thought I might clear up some things I left in the study. I'll join you shortly."

Sylvia nodded. "The small parlor, then. And it's almost time for dinner, so don't dawdle or Judith will have your heart on a platter."

Sylvia turned away, Victoria watching the simple elegance of her blue satin gown as she walked away, her blond hair curled and coiffed high atop her head, a single strand of sapphires circling her slender throat, the largest of them falling into the hollow that lay between her breasts. Creamy skin fell away beneath smooth, shiny satin that was itself the color of sapphires.

Victoria glanced down at the plain black front of her best gown. With its ivory lace that Matron had so painstakingly stitched for the high collar and the wide cuffs at the end of the long, slender sleeves, she looked like nothing so much as an overdressed maid, she told herself. All she needed was a starched cap. She walked on, following the hall back toward the study, opening the door to find the lamp atop her table still lit. Behind her desk, near the windows, the duke turned to look at who had entered. A tall young woman stood near him.

She had hair the color of coal and eyes as blue as Sylvia's gown. She held something in her hands, and it wasn't until she put it down that Victoria realized it was part of the manuscript she was working on.

"Oh, there you are. I was talking about you," Edward said. "This is Elizabeth Wyndham—Victoria Leggett."

Elizabeth Wyndham smiled at Victoria, seemingly unaware of the wrongness of his introduction. Victoria found herself without words.

"Edward has been telling me the nicest things about your work, Miss Leggett," Elizabeth Wyndham said quietly, still smiling, but bringing the conversation back to the proper social channels.

"Thank you," Victoria replied finally. "How kind," she told him unnecessarily. Her eyes went back to the manuscript that now lay atop her table. The table she had been allowed to work at, Victoria corrected herself. Tied with green ribbons, it was the period between James I and Anne that Elizabeth Wyndham had been holding.

"Have they sent you to find us?" Edward asked Victoria.

She looked up into his dark eyes. "Yes," she told him quietly. "That is, Lady Sylvia was looking for you. She mentioned they were . . . looking. For you both."

"We'd best find Mama," Elizabeth told Edward, smiling up into his eyes. "She'll have quite the fit if she hears we've been wandering off without her."

He bowed slightly, giving her his arm before they started toward the door. She brushed her hand over his dark sleeve. The lightest of touches, it was also a little proprietary, as if she knew she had the right to touch him. "Come along," he was saying over his shoulder. "Don't bury yourself in here alone."

Victoria swallowed. "I shall be there directly."

She walked to the table and picked up a sheaf of papers while they left. It was the green-ribbon-enclosed era Elizabeth Wyndham had been looking through. Victoria put the pages down again, sitting down at the little table and simply staring at the green ribbons.

Finally she made herself stand up, walk to the door and on toward the small parlor where the others waited. She was only a few minutes behind the duke and Elizabeth, walking in while Margaret Wyndham was still teasing her daughter about already absorbing all of the duke's attention. "Now we can't have you making him forget his duties, my pet."

Elizabeth smiled up at Edward as he handed her into a narrow velvet chair. "I hardly think anyone could do that, Mama. Edward is quite the most serious of men about his duties."

"Here, here," James told her, smiling easily when she turned to stare at him. "Lord, you still look startled, Elizabeth." He saw Victoria edging toward a small settee across the room. "You should have seen Miss Leggett's first reaction upon seeing me. She thought I was Edward, and when he appeared in the same room, she fainted dead away."

Margaret turned curious eyes toward the girl. "Is that true, my dear?"

"No, ma'am."

"Tsk, tsk." James grinned at her. "Contradicting your employers, now what is the world coming to?"

"You're hardly her employer, James," Edward told his brother mildly. Movement at the door made him look toward it. Michael stood there, waiting for a lull in the conversation.

"Dinner is served."

Judith nodded. "Thank you, Michael." Slowly she stood up, drawing herself to her full height. "Shall we?" she asked the others, moving ahead before either of the men could offer for her arm. She passed by Victoria, glancing once at the girl's dress and then walking into the hall.

Edward gave his arm to Margaret and started toward Elizabeth, but James was already beside her, bowing slightly, helping her to her feet. "Edward has monopolized you until now; it is only fair that I should be allowed to escort you in to dinner." Margaret smiled back toward them. "Your aunt is right, James. You are a scamp."

"Ah, but an ingratiating one, I hope," James answered Elizabeth's mother, then smiled at Elizabeth herself: "I trust . . . ?"

Elizabeth smiled. "Only time will tell."

Sylvia stood where she was, waiting for James and Elizabeth to start after Edward and Margaret Wyndham. When they reached the hall, Sylvia walked toward Victoria. "I think we have been left to fend for ourselves."

Victoria nodded, biting the inside of her lower lip as they walked behind the others into the blazing light of the dining room.

Chapter 10

T HE STORM FINALLY POURED down a little after eight, the
clouds that had threatened all day unleashing a torrent
of wind and rain, thunder rolling out across the landscape
as soup was served, the steady rush of rain outside the
closed and heavily draped windows continuing through the
meal, raising the pitch of their voices to be heard over
nature's extravagances outside.

James was in top form, laughing and bantering with
Margaret Wyndham, an aside now and again thrown out
toward Elizabeth. Edward became more and more silent as
the meal progressed, as if James's words were stealing all his
own.

Judith kept up a steady questioning of the young Elizabeth and her life in London, her friends, her accomplish-
ments. Sylvia and Victoria replied only when spoken to,
Margaret beginning to notice their quietude.

"Are you feeling quite well, Sylvia?" Margaret asked
when plates were being taken away. Judith turned to stare at
Sylvia, her displeasure in her eyes.

"Yes, thank you, Margaret," Sylvia replied quietly.

Elizabeth spoke: "I'm afraid we've quite taken over the
conversation, Mama. We've not left room for a word in
edgewise."

"Nonsense," James told her. "My wife is never talkative.
Are you, my pet? She's simply enjoying the glimpses you
give us old fogies of life in the city."

"Old fogies!" Elizabeth's merry peal of laughter was infectious. "Edward, are you going to let him get away with that?"

The duke tried to smile. "James has a way of getting away with much."

James grinned first at his brother, then at Elizabeth. "You see, he'll not defend us. It's the truth. We are pining away for a little gaiety. For music and dancing and soft young beauties such as yourself."

"James!" Judith spoke more loudly than she intended, startling the others and lapsing into an uneasy laugh. "You will frighten Elizabeth with such talk."

James watched Elizabeth closely. "Oh, I'm sure the lovely Miss Wyndham has heard more improper nonsense than my small attempts at flirting."

Elizabeth seemed to be enjoying herself. She smiled coyly back at Edward's brother, enjoying the safety of flirtation with a married man. "In London such remarks are whispered behind fans at the edge of the dance floor. Not at the supper table."

James watched her, still smiling. "Only at the edge?" he asked softly.

Elizabeth found her eyes could not leave his. The clatter of silver broke her attention, causing her to glance toward Sylvia.

"Sorry," Sylvia said, retrieving her fork. "How clumsy of me."

"You can see," James continued smoothly to Margaret, "how badly we are in need of social practice."

"I hear you're going to have all you can want," Margaret told him. "I understand that your ball, Edward, is being attended by absolutely everybody."

Edward looked down the table toward her, his brow creasing slightly. "Really?" he asked mildly.

"Of course. How often does the Duke of Bereshaven throw open The Willows? I understand you are importing musicians from France."

"Am I?" he asked, looking past her to where Judith sat at the opposite end of the table. "Judith would know more about the details."

Judith smiled. "Yes, I would." She turned toward Elizabeth. "And I must tell you, running a duke's household is quite too much for someone my age. I look forward to being able to hand over the keys to his duchess one of these days and retiring quietly to my rooms."

"Nonsense, Judith." Margaret spoke with a great deal of spirit. "We are the same age, or very nearly, and I'm not ready to pass on the keys. Believe me, long after Edward finally decides to marry, the poor girl, whoever she may be, will need all the help you can give her." Margaret hesitated, then: "No matter how well she's been trained in the finer arts of household management," she added, looking across toward her daughter.

Elizabeth reached for her wine goblet, ignoring the conversation around her, finding her eyes wandering back to steal looks at James across the table. Each time she glanced his way his eyes sought hers out.

Victoria watched Elizabeth glance again and again at James, and looked down at her plate, trying to ignore them all. She sat between James and Edward, across from Elizabeth, and found each time she looked up that Elizabeth was again watching James.

Victoria did not look to her right, did not look to see if Edward was watching their interplay. The fact of his presence so near her at the table was suffocating her, her heart pounding so loudly she could hear only parts of the conversation around her.

Why had he wanted her at table? Why put her through all this, unless he was content with her work and truly committed to marrying Elizabeth? Even the word smote at Victoria's heart. He had been showing Elizabeth her work. He invited her to table. Was she to impress the future duchess so that she could retain her position once they were married? Did he want to prove to Victoria that there was nothing between them, that the night in the gazebo had never happened? She thought of the look of pain and anguish in his eyes that night, thought of the touch of him.

"Isn't that so, Miss Leggett?"

Victoria heard her name. She looked up to see Elizabeth looking at her expectantly, the others quiet. "I beg your pardon?" Her voice sounded strangulated to her own ears.

"I was telling my mother of the painstaking research you are embarked upon."

"Oh yes. I'm sorry . . ." She looked down the table, past James, at Lady Wyndham, who sat to Judith's right and was now staring at her. "It—there is much work to be done," she finished lamely.

Margaret Wyndham nodded. "Of course. Sounds terribly dull to me, however. Women and books weren't made for each other in my opinion."

"I beg your pardon?" Victoria said faintly.

"Oh, nothing against you, child. I'm sure it's quite different for one of—for you. But as the dear Queen has said, ladies are not to be overeducated. It only breeds trouble." She looked toward Edward, who was listening intently. "Don't you agree, dear Edward?"

The duke hesitated. "I've never met a lady who was overeducated," he answered finally. "So I have no way to judge."

"Bravo!" James grinned at his brother. "Spoken like a true diplomat."

"Diplomats!" Margaret grimaced. "I suppose when Parliament is in session, you have to be part of that beastly business of government." She still looked at Edward.

The duke shrugged slightly. "Duty decides," he told her. "But since Disraeli dissolved Parliament earlier this month, there is no need to concern ourselves with it at this point."

Judith interrupted them. "I will not have politics discussed at my table." She smiled. "There is no surer way to cause indigestion."

"Oh my, you are quite right, dear Judith." Margaret reached to pat Judith's hand. "I apologize."

"I think we shall have a walk about the long gallery before dessert in the large parlor. What do you say, Edward?" Judith looked toward him. "It's entirely too miserable to take a turn in the gardens, but I shall burst if I can't move a bit."

"Oh please—" Elizabeth turned to touch his hand, to cover it with hers. "I have heard you have the most wonderful paintings in your gallery."

Edward smiled a little. "If you like."

113

"Oh, yes—I like very much!"

Judith moved in her chair and a footman came up to help her with it. "Shall we, then?" she asked the room, waiting for Margaret before starting toward the door.

"What a good idea," Margaret said. "I swear I could not have eaten another morsel."

Sylvia's expression told of her disbelief, but Margaret had turned away and did not see. Only Victoria looked down the table, smiling at Sylvia when she caught her eye. James was helping Victoria with her chair as the duke stood to help Elizabeth.

The footman pulled Sylvia's chair back for her and then moved out of the way for the others to walk past. James waited at the doorway for his wife, who hesitated before letting him take her arm.

"Shall you walk with us, Miss Leggett?" Elizabeth was asking as Edward walked with her toward the door.

"I thought perhaps I'd—"

"Of course she shall," the duke cut in, turning to take Victoria's arm, escorting both of them out into the hall. He felt Victoria stiffen at his touch. He felt the warmth of her coming through the thin black fabric of her sleeve, his hand tucked around her elbow. The back of his hand grazed her side as they moved forward, Victoria's arm held stiffly to her side. Stiffening more when his fingers tightened around her arm and then slowly relaxed.

"Tell me about the paintings, Edward," Elizabeth cajoled, walking beside him, his hand around her elbow.

Victoria heard him talk of ancestors and painters, of styles and schools of painting. The words floated past her, the warmth of his hand melting into her side.

"Miss Leggett!" Judith was turned back toward them, waiting for them to reach her. "Would you do me a kindness and retrieve my shawl? I believe I left it in the small parlor and I shall be needing it."

Victoria felt the duke's hand leave her. She nodded mutely and then turned back toward the small parlor, letting the others walk on ahead. Her steps were carefully spaced and deliberate, her head held high. She could feel Judith's eye still upon her, watching her until she turned into the doorway of the small parlor and stopped, searching out the shawl. It lay across a small sofa, black lace with a long black fringe. She reached to pick it up and then stood where she was, clutching it to her for a long moment, closing her eyes and willing herself to be calm.

She turned around to find Judith in the doorway, watching her with cold eyes. "Just what is going on?" Judith demanded.

"I—I beg your pardon?"

Judith stared at the girl. "Why have you thrust yourself into the middle of a family dinner? And then into trotting along behind all evening?"

"I haven't!"

"Just what do you think you're about, young miss? Just what are you really after?"

Victoria stared at the woman. "I don't know what you mean."

"Answer me."

"I was told to come to dinner."

"By whom?" Judith demanded.

Steps came up the hall outside. Judith turned to see Mike standing behind her in the hallway. He glanced from Judith to Victoria, then spoke to Victoria. "His grace is asking for you, Miss Leggett."

Victoria started toward Mike and then stopped, Judith still blocking the doorway. She did not move until Victoria looked up to meet her gaze. Finally the older woman stepped back into the hall, letting Victoria pass.

Casting a swift glance up at Michael, Victoria tried to smile.

"I'll show you where they are," Judith said.

Mike saw the look of fear that crossed Victoria's face. "Along here, Miss Leggett." He walked with them past the library and study to double doors that opened onto a huge ballroom.

To one end of the hundred-foot room gracefully curved arches opened onto a promenade that ran the length of the room. The walls of the promenade were hung with huge paintings, some of them visible from where Victoria stood, more visible as she hurried across the hardwood floor toward the arches, leaving both Judith and Michael to come behind her.

Not until she had reached the promenade, not until she was standing behind the duke, looking down the long rows of paintings to each side of them, did she realize she still held Judith's shawl.

"There you are." The duke turned toward her. "I had meant to tell you before that there are pictures along here of some of the people you are researching for me. It might be of aid to take a good look at them in daylight." He waved toward the wall sconces that were lit at the moment, throwing soft light across the scene. "This is very pretty, but in daylight you can get more of a feeling about what they really looked like. Mayhap you shall find a secret or two hidden behind their eyes."

She found herself staring up into his eyes as he spoke, trying to see what lay behind the dark irises that gazed down upon her enigmatically.

Elizabeth was slowly walking the length of the promenade, James at her elbow pointing out various paintings while Sylvia walked along beside, his hand still at her elbow.

The duke was reaching for Victoria's arm when Judith reached them. "Ah, my shawl. Thank you, dear girl," Judith said smoothly, taking the black lace garment from Victoria and turning toward Edward. "Help me with this, will you, Edward? My arms are too arthritic to be of much use in this weather."

Edward did as she bid, reaching to wrap the shawl about her shoulders. When he was done, she took his arm, standing between him and Victoria. "Now, let's go down the rows here and you shall tell the girl why you make her walk up and down when she'd rather be about other things."

"Would you?" he asked Victoria.

She shook her head, not trusting speech.

"Good . . . Along this wall are the Dukes of Bereshaven; across from each of them is their duchess. You can see the changing styles of fashion—can you not?—as the years march forward. Here's my great-great-great-grandfather Edward, the one my father and I were both named after. A real devil he was, they say. Do you know the expression *full of old Ned?*"

He stopped walking, turning to look down at her. Victoria felt his eyes upon her. And Judith's. "Yes," she told him. "I have."

"Well, it was supposedly this notorious bandit for whom it was first coined." He looked up at the dark portrait. "My father was called Ned too," he added after a moment.

"Edward," James was calling out from further down the promenade. "Which great-grandmother was it who killed her husband?"

"James!" Sylvia spoke sharply, Judith echoing his name. Judith continued: "You are forever trying to shock, you scamp! You shall frighten the poor Wyndhams."

"Oh, I'm sure we've enough scapegraces of our own," Margaret said stoutly, smiling at Sylvia now, turning away from the painting before her to look toward the one James was looking at.

"Elizabeth says it must have been this one. She looks the part," James continued. "Is it?"

Edward reached them, Victoria and Judith still beside him. He glanced at the painting James stood before. "That, my dear brother, was Agatha Percy Bereshaven. After her husband died, she became a nun."

"Good grief, you mean he drove her into the arms of the church?"

Elizabeth laughed, Edward smiling a little as Margaret joined her daughter. "Do tell, Edward," Elizabeth was saying. "Was it she?"

"The gossips at the time said she had been a secret Roman Catholic for years; when he died they accused her of much."

"Good lord, an R.C. in the family!" James looked about him in mock shock. "How shall we live it down?"

"A murderous R.C.," Elizabeth told him merrily.

"Aren't they all?" James teased her.

"I fail to see the joke," Edward said coldly, as both James and Elizabeth turning to face him. Elizabeth lost her smile but James's grin returned.

"Don't be such a stick, Edward."

Margaret looked from one to the other. "Your mother, I believe, was Catholic, wasn't she?"

Judith spoke quickly: "The boys were raised Church of England! They were raised in this house. By my brother and myself. There are no Roman Catholics here."

"Whatever difference does it make?" Elizabeth said lightly. "It's hardly a capital offense these days, is it?"

"Now, where were we?" James turned back toward the paintings.

Margaret called Judith over and Victoria felt the duke's eyes watching James and Elizabeth moving away. Sylvia looked back toward Edward, a look of sad knowledge in her eyes. When she turned to walk on, Victoria started forward and then felt the duke's hand on her sleeve. She stopped. His hand dropped to his side.

Victoria looked up to see him watching her. "There's no painting across from the end," she told him quietly.

"What?" He looked up toward the others and then back down at her. "Yes," he said then. "I know."

"Whose portrait is that?"

"My father's."

She hesitated. "And . . . your mother's?"

"It's not hung here." The words came slowly.

"You have none?" she asked him.

"My father wanted nothing that reminded him of his . . . unfortunate youthful lapse."

"I see."

"Do you?" He searched her eyes for something. She stared back, not knowing what he searched for.

"Edward . . ." Elizabeth came toward them, smiling. "You have to tell me about the rest of these. Your brother is simply not interested in history. He fabricates whatever suits his fancy."

"I resent that," James called out. "I have only fabricated where fabrication is needed. On the whole we are the most deplorably boring of families."

"You, on the other hand, dear Edward, will tell me the truth," Elizabeth said. "Won't you?"

He stared down at her. "Do you wish it?"

"Why yes. Of course." She tucked her hand into his arm. "Come along and acquaint me with them all."

He glanced at Victoria. "If you wish, you can go," he told her.

Victoria watched them move off together, watched Judith turn toward Margaret, easier now, listening more carefully to what was being said around her.

The sounds of her footsteps echoed across the grand ballroom as Victoria left the others behind, walking slowly out toward the hall and the stairwell beyond. As she came into the front hall Mike was opening the door. A man stood there, surprising Victoria. She had heard no bell.

Mike turned and saw her. His face darkened, a mask falling into place. She nodded to him, turning toward the stairs and starting up. It wasn't until she had reached the second floor that she realized she had used the wrong stairs. Her bedroom was now off the back stairs. The servants' stairs.

She was halfway to the back hallway before Mike and the man he had let in moved from the bottom of the front stairs, heading back toward the study.

Chapter 11

VICTORIA CLOSED THE DOOR to the small room off the back stairs and walked to the tiny nightstand, raising the wick of the lamp.

The shadows in the corners of the room shortened, the lamp burning brighter as she began to change out of the black gown, putting it carefully away.

The room was chilly. She reached for her night robe, pulling it around herself as she reached for nightclothes and slippers. Shivering, she looked toward the small window and the violent storm. Sheets of rain washed down the glass, nothing but blackness and water to be seen outside.

Gathering her things, she opened the door to the hall, stepping out and looking for a bathroom. Hesitating by closed doors, she tried two and then looked toward the door to the front hall. No one had said she was not to use the bathroom. No one was upstairs in any event. Not yet.

The front hall was silent, sounds from downstairs muted, the rooms all around her empty. Victoria moved to the large bathroom near the room that had been hers and went quickly inside.

It was warm and cozy, the large room laid out with fresh towels, the WC in its own separate little room. She changed quickly, glad of the warmth, moving as fast as she could for fear of running into the others. The sound of someone outside brought her up short. Standing still, hardly breathing, she waited for them to pass on by. After a moment more steps came behind.

"Edward!" Judith called out. "Edward, just what do you think you're doing? And what should I tell them?"

Victoria did not breathe. She stood near the door, leaning against it for support, her eyes closed, praying not to be discovered.

"Tell them an unexpected visitor arrived." His voice was cool. And very close.

"Just like that."

"Yes. I'm sure they themselves have had unexpected visitors."

"Just who is this that is so important you walk out on the Wyndhams?"

"That's not your concern, Aunt Judith."

"It's that man, isn't it?"

There was a long pause. When Edward spoke, his words came slowly. And very carefully. "Just what do you mean, 'that' man?"

"That Irishman!" She spit out. "That friend of your Michael Flaherty's who's always coming round and sidling about looking as if he'd as soon murder us all!"

"You're being fanciful, Aunt Judith. I'm surprised at you."

"I tell you, I won't have people like that in this house!"

There was no reply.

"Edward. Edward! Where do you think you're going?"

"I'm going to my room, Aunt Judith. And from there I shall return to my visitor. I am sure you can see to our guests until morning. I am sure James will enjoy the opportunity."

"Just what does that mean?"

"The opportunity to brush up on his social skills." Edward's voice was farther away, his steps echoing away.

After a few moments Victoria could hear Judith on the stairs. She waited until she could hear no more movement and then carefully opened the door. Moving swiftly, she reached the back hall, opening the door. As she opened it someone grabbed her, a hand clapped over her mouth in expectation of her crying out. She fought against whoever held her from behind, struggling in the doorway and trying to kick out with her slippered feet.

Twisting around within his grasp, she stared up at Edward. Or the image of Edward. She stopped fighting, staring with wide eyes up into the face that haunted her dreams. He was staring down at her. Just as she realized that she felt nothing, that it could not be Edward, a door was opening behind her and James reached quickly to cover her lips with his own.

Mike and the man who had been in the front hall came out of Edward's door, Edward just behind. All three of them stopped in their tracks, staring at James and the girl in night robe and gown that he held in his arms. He looked up, slowly letting her go, smiling a little sheepishly when he saw the other men staring at him. "Oh my . . . I do seem to have put my foot in it. Don't blame her. All my idea really." He spoke easily. Victoria stared up at him still. And then looked toward the others. She saw only Edward's eyes, as cold as black ice staring back at her.

Mike Flaherty looked at her as if she had disappointed him mightily. Only the little man smiled. He looked from her to James.

"Ah, the war hero . . . Did you enjoy your last tour of duty, then?"

"Tim, we have to go," Mike said.

Edward saw James whiten at the man's words. Edward turned away, heading down the hall with the others, leaving James to watch them go. James turned back toward Victoria, looking down at her curiously.

"And what were you about, my dear Victoria—I hope I may call you that at this point."

"I was readying for bed."

"You were not listening at doors, by any chance?"

"No!" Her cheeks flamed red, remembering herself in the bathroom, her ear pressed against the cold wood of the door. "No!"

"A pity . . ." James smiled. "I'd give much to know what that little conversation was all about." He looked toward where the three men had stood, then back at Victoria. "If you can find out, I shall make it worth your while. Very worth your while, my dear." He touched her cheek. "You have a lovely mouth. Don't let it go to waste." She watched him walk away, toward the front stairs. "Excuse me, my dear Victoria . . . one of us must see to our guests." He stopped once to look back toward her. "Perhaps we'll get to know each other better."

Victoria shivered in the draft from the back stairs. She closed the door, reaching the little room and sinking down onto the narrow bed, her heart pounding. All she could see was the look in Edward's eyes.

She thought of James' kiss . . . he had used her. He had come up the back stairs, and when caught by his brother, he had pretended they had had an assignation. When he was truly spying on his brother.

Victoria stood up, ready to find Edward, ready to tell him what had happened. And then she sat back down. She was undressed. He would not believe her. James would say she was not telling the truth. The others would hear of all of it. She stood up, wearily putting her underclothes away, reaching to pull back the blankets on the narrow bed, climbing inside them and pulling them up around herself.

A great hollow opened up within her, an empty ache gnawing at her. When she closed her eyes, she saw Edward's expression again, accusing her without words. It didn't matter, she told herself over and over again, it did not matter. He did not care one way or the other. He had felt a moment's passion, had indulged in a moment's dalliance one night in the gazebo. Nothing more.

Nothing more. Tears began to fill her eyes, softly seeping out and down her cheeks. It was much more than that for her. No matter how little it meant to him. And she could not bear to have him think she would willingly sneak off to an assignation with his brother. Would willingly kiss James.

The rain pounded against her window, the winds shrieking around the corners of the house, the sky crying along with her as Victoria curled toward her pillows and sobbed.

Outside the windows the storm poured down across the countryside, mud puddles deepening along the riverbank, the weight of the water bending the willows even farther toward the ground beneath them. Gusting winds whipped through the trees, the thick rain drenching the lawns, obliterating the far side of the river from view. All that could be seen were sheets of water that brought distant rolls of thunder and poured on, drowning the grounds, filling the river and washing on downstream.

Something woke Victoria. She lay in the darkness of the small hours of the morning, listening. Someone was opening and closing doors. She sat up, preparing to throw off the covers. The door burst open, a man's large outline filling the narrow door. She stared up at him.

And Edward stared in at Victoria's slender shoulders and tousled hair, backlit by the tiny glow of the night-dimmed oil lamp she had never extinguished.

She was dreaming, she told herself. Time stopped as each of them stared at the other. Neither moved. Until he slowly walked forward, dwarfing the little room, looming over her bed.

"What the bloody hell are you doing in here!?" he demanded in a fierce whisper.

"Someone will hear . . ." she told him.

"Answer me!" His voice became louder. He took another step nearer and stopped. He stood over her now, staring down at her.

"Judith needed the other room for your guests."

"Damn and blast the woman, she had no more need of your room than I have of that—that lamp! There are ten guest rooms!"

"She said I was to be here."

He reached for her, grabbing her hand. "You are *not* to be here!"

"What are you doing?" she gasped. He was dragging her out of bed. "I'm not dressed!" she whispered fiercely, trying to pull away from him. "You're frightening me!"

"I wish I knew how to frighten Judith! Come *along* —here!" He reached for her robe, throwing it toward her and lifting her off the bed in one swift movement.

She felt his arms pulling her up, felt the strength of him. He was wearing his breeches still, and boots, his coat and vest pulled off, his thin white cotton shirt pulled halfway out of his trousers and gaping open at the throat as if he had stopped in the middle of undressing to start banging open doors along the corridor. He looked like a pirate with his open shirt and wild tousled hair.

He was carrying her out into the hall, her robe across her lap, her thin gown the only material between his hands and her skin. "How did you find me?" she asked him.

"By opening every door in the bloody house!"

She felt the draft of the back stairs. "Where are you taking me? Edward, why did you find me? How did you know I was not in my room?"

Neither of them seemed to notice that she had called him by name. "I am taking you to see something you asked about," he told her. He stopped by a doorway at the end of the hall, opening it to start up a flight of stairs that rose above the floor they were on.

"I can walk."

His arms held her tighter, as if she were going to pull away and set herself upright. "This is quicker," he told her, and carried her up the stairs. Blackness was all around them, no light from the night outside, no lamps in the stairwell. A draft came down toward them. She shivered and he held her closer. "Are you cold? Put your robe around yourself."

She reached to do as he said, one hand pulling the robe toward her throat. Her other arm was around his neck, her hand holding on to his shoulder. She pulled the robe closer and then reached to lace both hands around his shoulder. Telling herself it was perfectly all right, that anything was possible in dreams, she let him carry her upward, her body feeling again the sensations she had first felt the day she had fainted and he had carried her upstairs. She closed her eyes, darkness all around them, the smell of him clean and leathery as they climbed.

They reached an upper floor, his steps slower now, his arms curved close around her as if never to let her go. She floated in the feeling until suddenly he was putting her down, her bare feet hitting a cold wood floor, her body turned away.

"What are you doing? Where are you going?"

"For this." He struck a match, and as it flared she saw an attic surrounding them, saw dust and cobwebs and a lantern which he now lit. As lamplight flared up she watched him turn back toward her, his eyes, his face in shadows as he held the lamp. "Look." He held out the lamp.

She turned to see what he was pointing at and stared at herself. Her intake of breath pleased him. She could hear him chuckle. "Ah, you do see it, then, don't you? Mike felt it was nowhere near like. But I could see what you do."

Victoria moved toward the painting, Edward lighting the way, shining the lantern up and down the length of the age-darkened oils. A full-length portrait of a woman stood before them. With auburn curls in a different style, with green eyes that stared quietly back at them, Victoria saw the face of someone who at first glance was very like herself. The woman wore a low-cut gown, jewels at her throat and in her hair.

"With more light the resemblance fades to something not quite as breathtaking," Edward was saying. "But at night, in moonlight, or by the light of a lamp such as this, you could be sisters." He hesitated, then spoke again quietly. "You asked me earlier about my mother's portrait. This is my mother."

Victoria turned to try and see his eyes. "This is why you have befriended me?"

"No." His eyes clouded. "Perhaps." He paused. "I don't know." He turned away, finding a box and sitting down upon it heavily, leaning forward to rest the lamp on the floor near his feet.

Victoria watched him bend forward, studying the floor before him, his face in the shadows. Slowly she came back to sink to the floor beside him.

"It is cold for you," he said.

She shook her head a little. "No. Truly . . . is that what you saw in the gazebo?"

He didn't answer. Instead, after a moment he told her something else. "I looked in upon you. That first night. To make sure you were all right. In your sleep . . . in the moonlight . . ." He stopped. "You are very like her."

"You haven't seen her since you were a child," Victoria said.

"Since I was seven years old. Almost seven."

"What happened tonight?" she asked him after a long pause.

The rain beat down upon the eaves over their heads, the sound loud up this high within the mansion. "You asked about the empty space. And I realized that there was no reason it should be empty any longer. That he was dead. The house is mine now, to do with as I please. And if it pleases me to have a picture of my mother about, then there is nothing to stop me."

"Your father kept it," Victoria told him gently.

"My father would not let her name be mentioned! Would not let us go back to see her when she was ill! She died with no one there. Don't talk to me of my father; he hated her and he hated me for reminding him of her." He looked down into her upturned eyes. "You see I am like her. So they say. I have no way of knowing. As you have no knowledge of your parents, I have none of my mother. Except childhood memories that are perhaps all wishful dreams. And nightmares," he added after a moment.

"He did not destroy her picture. He banished it, but he did not harm it." Victoria spoke quietly.

"Whatever his reasons, believe me, they had nothing to do with affection. He was beyond affection."

They sat quietly listening to the rain hammer down upon the room. "I looked in upon you. I wanted to ask you— " He stopped, his words coming more slowly. "You weren't there. I went to James's room and the door was locked."

"James!" Startled, she reached for his hands. They were clasped together before him and she covered them with her own. "You did not believe him earlier, you could not have thought that I—" She watched him lift his eyes to meet hers again.

"I was not thinking. I started back to my room, started to undress, and then decided to—to find you."

"Opening and closing doors up and down the hall."

He watched her, a small smile forming around his lips. "Halls," he corrected her.

She smiled back at him. "I had changed in the bath when you came up—you and Judith. I thought perhaps I should not have been using that bath—after she had—"

"Changed your room," he finished for her, his voice hardening.

"I waited for you both to leave and tried to slip back to my room. James was in the back hall, coming toward your rooms.

Edward stared at her now. "Why?" he asked her, searching her face in the shadowy light.

She hesitated. "He asked if I'd heard anything you had been discussing. With the other man . . ."

He looked down. "You made a good alibi. I did not think him eavesdropping." Edward looked back up. "Mike thought you both were eavesdropping. He told me you had come upon him downstairs. By stealth."

"Stealth! You told me to leave."

"I!" He stopped. "The ballroom."

"Yes. I was coming upstairs."

Edward stood up. "Come along."

She looked up at him. He reached down to help her to her feet. "It's cold up here," he told her.

He reached for the lamp, extinguishing it before reaching to take her hand. "Better wait a moment," he continued, "until our eyes adjust to the darkness."

She stood beside him, her hand within his larger one, the darkness surrounding them. A chill rose up her back, her movement turning him toward her. "Are you all right?" He asked her. "Are you cold?"

"No . . ." She whispered. "No . . . I'm not cold."

His hand closed around hers, squeezing it tight. She felt his muscles hardening, felt the strength of him as he slowly pulled her nearer. "Are you afraid of the dark?" he whispered, bending his head near hers.

She shook her head, the movement bringing his lips close to her forehead. "No. I'm not alone." Her voice trembled, her body alive to the nearness of his.

"What is it?" he asked her softly.

She swallowed. "Nothing. I'm fine."

"Are you sure?" His lips came nearer her forehead, brushing against her hair as he spoke. He felt her stiffen, felt her trembling.

"We must go downstairs," she told him.

"Yes," he replied, his lips still against the curls that caressed her forehead. And then he scooped her up in his arms. "It's safer this way."

"No," she said softly. "It's not."

His arms tightened. He started down the stairs slowly, the warmth of her filling his arms, the scent of lilies and lavender strong in his nostrils.

Chapter 12

THE SOUNDS OF THE rain softened once they reached the servants' hall, the elements farther away and locked out for the night. Edward did not slow his step as he passed the room his aunt had assigned to Victoria.

"I must go back." Her words came from beside his ear.

"Why?"

Victoria found no answer. She leaned her forehead against his cheek, feeling the harsh stubble of his beard, closing her eyes against reality. Let this be a dream and all will be well, she told herself, willing herself to believe that it was just a dream.

But her senses knew better. The sharpened sense of touch she felt was part of no dream, nor was the roughness of his face where his beard darkened the sides of his cheeks. "Put me down," she told him softly. "Please . . . your grace . . . please."

"I shall." He went through the door to the wide front hall, carrying her toward his own suite of rooms. He felt her stiffen, tightening his grip on her with one long powerful arm as he reached to open his door, carrying her on inside.

The room they entered was a small parlor, the fire dead in the grate, one lamp burning on a table beside the fireplace. He walked on through to his bedroom. Victoria caught a glimpse of a huge mahogany bed before finding herself thrown upon it.

She gasped, staring up at the man who towered over

her. "You see?" he was saying. "I promised to put you down."

She turned toward the edge of the bed. "I must get back to my room."

"You shall never set foot in that room again." His words rang out in the silence, his anger welling up again. She watched him, unsure how to leave, afraid to stay in this room, in this bed, feeling herself melting when she looked up at him. She wanted to reach out and touch his hand, to draw him near. "I can't stay here, your grace."

"My name is Edward." His dark eyes did not leave her face. "You called me that earlier . . ." He watched her duck her head, avoiding his eyes. "You shall never sleep in that room again. It is a servant's room and you are not a servant."

She looked up then, uncertainty, even fear, in her eyes. "What am I then?"

"You are in my employ." His voice softened. "Perhaps you will even become a . . . friend . . ." His voice strengthened. "But you are not a servant and I will not see you treated as a scullery maid."

"I could have been," she told him quietly. "If I'd not paid attention to my studies, if I'd been in a London orphanage instead of Mercy House, I could have been Nancy or any of the girls you employ . . ." She trailed off, staring up at him. "What are you going to do with me?" she asked him quietly.

He watched her. "I don't know," he told her slowly. "I know what I would like to do." He hesitated, his eyes liquid black seas. "Tell me you do not wish it."

Her breath caught in her throat, suffocating all thought. She could feel the warmth of his body, she could feel the touch of his hands, her heart beginning to race as she stared up at him.

"Have you ever made love?" he asked her softly. "Do you know what I am speaking of?"

"Yes . . ."

His eyes flickered. "You have."

"In the gazebo . . . was that not . . ." She could not find the words, could not ask him.

He answered her. "That was the beginning of lovemaking. There is more."

She faltered over her words. "You speak of love, but I am not sure that is what you mean."

He reached for her, bringing her to her knees on the bed, bringing her closer, his hands under her arms, his gaze trying to read her expression. "It is an overused word, you are quite right . . . Victoria . . ." He spoke her name for the very first time, his lips caressing it. Feelings were welling up within her, unbidden and unknown. She felt carried away as she had the night in the gazebo, as she did whenever he touched her. Her eyes closed, her body acquiescent beneath his touch.

He stared down at her, his blood pounding now, her closed eyes an invitation. His gaze fell to her thin white nightgown, to the soft curves that welled up toward him, that lay between his hands as he held her there. He pulled her up, his arms lifting her higher, his head bending to kiss the hollow of her neck. Her moan resounded through his body, his hands shaking now, his mouth against the thin fabric that lay around her neck. He heard her say his name, her arms tightening around his neck. He reached to cover her breast, his lips searching out the hard nipple that strained against the thin cotton bodice, her arms clutching him when he pulled at her flesh.

They were falling toward the bed, their arms entwined, his dark head to her breast, her hands reaching to cradle him, to pull him nearer, to keep him with her. Her blood was singing through her veins, needs and emotions welling up within her, the world the width of his hands as he reached to pull her gown off, down to her waist, his mouth hungrily reaching back for her breast.

The length of his body fell across her, his left leg pinning her body to the bed, his hands reaching to cup her breasts as he moved from one nipple to the other, caressing, suckling, and then kissing the hollow between her firm young breasts, moans escaping her when his mouth reclaimed a taut nipple, covering its dark pink aureole with his hungry lips.

The sensations that coursed through her body, the liquid melting of her limbs that responded to his slightest touch, were new and strange, were too sweet to dismiss. She could no more have pushed him away now than she could have run from his touch. One word, one outstretched hand, and she would come flying back. Would beg him to hold her again, to make her feel this way.

He could feel her each and every reaction, could feel her surprise as he touched her, her soft acceptance as her body curved to meet whatever he did to it. His hands caressed the length of her. He moved back a little, seeing her eyes fly open to search his. He watched the trust in her eyes as he leaned closer, his lips covering hers, his tongue probing against her lips. Her lips parted, his tongue invading her mouth, sending diamonds down her spine, pinpoints of light bursting within her, waves of them washing up and over her as he invaded her mouth, as he took possession of her body with his hands.

Her hands reached to open his shirt, to its hem, and pulled on it, tugging it up toward his head. He moved a little, letting her pull it, his arms coming up to let her slip it off them. When she had it off, she stared at his chest, at the soft dark hair that matted his body, at the flat nipples. She reached up, shyly touching one, her eyes moving up to stare into his. "Do you feel the same," she was asking, her voice a whisper, "when I do this?" Her fingers rubbed his nipple. She turned, reaching up to touch her tongue gently against his flesh, to feel the hardness of his nipple with her lips, her tongue. He reached down to pull her head up, his hand beneath her chin as he pulled her near, bare flesh against bare flesh now, her arms reaching to cling even closer, tremors coursing through her that drew him nearer, his arms tightening around her slender back, his mouth searching out hers.

When he laid her back, she stared up at him, watching his eyes fall to her breast, to her waist, to the gown that still clung to her hips. He stared down at her, reason and rushing blood at war within him. He felt his flesh throbbing, painfully hard, stretching against his dark breeches. His eyes moved to stare into hers. And then he pulled away, feeling her hands unwilling to let him go, watching her search his eyes, uncertain, unsure.

He stood up, looking down at the fullness of her breast, sloping away to the narrowness of her waist. He could feel her eyes upon him. When he reached to unbutton his breeches his eyes found hers. He saw her eyes follow his hand, saw her watch him unbutton the first button and then turn back up to look at his eyes. He bent the toe of one black boot against the heel of the other, getting leverage to pull his foot out of the long smooth leather, reaching with his hand to get the other boot off. Kicking them away along with his stockings.

When he reached for his breeches, he waited for her eyes to follow his movements, watching her as he pulled them off and sprang free of their constraint. Her eyes widened, her intake of breath involuntary. She stared at his body, and realizing she was staring, she began to blush, her face suffused with her shame.

He spoke softly. "Many women prefer total darkness . . . they feel embarrassment at any nakedness . . . if you prefer—"

"Yes! . . . no . . ."

His hands were reaching for her gown. They were at her waist, pulling her gown toward her hips. He stopped, his hands against her belly. "Do you wish me to stop?"

"No."

With one swift movement he had the white cotton slip of a gown down, letting it fall to the floor as he stood above her, watching her closed eyes, her trembling legs. An exquisite agony tortured him; he wanted to reach for her, to devour her. Now. This moment before he exploded with the force of the urges that were pulsing within him, pushing him on.

He wanted to prolong the moment, to watch her reactions as she lay there, new to all of it and wanting him.

Victoria lay naked and open to him, her eyes squeezed shut, her heart hammering at her. Her body was tensed, awaiting his touch, awaiting what he would do to her. In her mind all she could see was his firm, solid body, his strong arms and long, strong legs. And the flesh that stood stiff and straight, rising from his loins.

Long moments passed, the feeling of total nakedness bringing a pale blush to her entire body, her body rigid with the waiting. Fear filled her, vying with the liquid wanting that called out to him. The unknown loomed large, the tremors that went through her at the sight of his naked body compounded of fright as well as desire. She wanted his arms

134

around her again. She wanted his hands, his lips . . . but nothing more . . . Surely not that huge, hard shaft of flesh . . . memories flooded her, memories of the girls at school, of the giggling stories of what all happened between men and women, jokes about animals in the fields . . . she felt tears welling at the corners of her eyes and still he did not come near.

She was afraid to open her eyes. Afraid that the onslaught would begin, that she would be caught in a web she could not free herself from.

He did not move. He did not speak.

She blinked back tears, opening her eyes finally to look up to where he had stood. He was not there. Sudden shock raced through her. He was not there! She turned her head. Beside the huge bed, a large arm chair, covered with a dark tapestry pattern, sat beside a low table. The chair, like the bed, was built for someone of great size. He sat upon it, staring at her. His nakedness accosted her senses again, her eyes drawn toward his legs, toward the power that his body held leashed within itself. She could feel his strength across the room, could remember the feeling of his flesh. Could see the excitement that he was deliberately leashing, the desire that sprang hard and engorged no matter what his reason would have liked.

His eyes, slowly, were traveling from her crown of auburn curls, tousled and undone, to her eyes. Dropping to her mouth, her breast, traveling on down toward her belly, her body reacting to the direction of his gaze, flushing within and without.

"I have never taken advantage of anyone in my entire life." His voice was very soft, the words so low she almost did not hear them. "Never. I have never taken advantage of anyone's position in my employ." His eyes burned into hers, a fierce light pouring out at her. His body ached but his control was regained. At least for the moment. "I will not begin this night."

She stared at him, stared into harsh resolve. The storm was softening outside the windows, a vague light beginning to color the countryside. She could not move. Nor did he.

"You will not—" She did not know what words to use.

"I will not," he told her firmly.

She sat up, reaching to look for her gown. "I should—"

"No!" The sharpness of the word startled her. She stared toward him. "Please—" He swallowed. "What has happened has—happened. There is no way to undo it." His eyes held unhappy lights and something more, something she did not understand. "There is no need for you to go."

"But I must."

"You will stay here this night. And your room will be made ready for you tomorrow. Your own room. I never want to see you in the servants' wing again. And if anyone, anyone at all, gives such an order, you are to tell me immediately. Do you understand?"

She swallowed. "I cannot stay here."

"I want you to."

"But you have said—"

"I shall sleep elsewhere. I give you my word you shall sleep unmolested." He hesitated, the rest of his words coming more slowly. "But . . . please . . . stay the night . . . stay as you are."

Her arms were folded before her, the corner of the sheets they had disturbed rising around her hips. She stared into his eyes, seeing something she could not name. The enormity of what he was doing suddenly came to her, an empathy for what this was costing him. Gratitude flooded her. Her fears for what would happen on the morrow, her memories of what the days following their meeting in the gazebo had been like, ebbed away, leaving now only the longing that had first filled her at his touch.

She wanted to cross to where he sat, to reach for him and draw him to her and let him know every part of her. If he had at that moment asked, she would have given him anything, everything, gladly.

But she did not move, she did not speak, some wisdom inside her telling her to be still, to let him make this decision and wait.

The same bone-deep wisdom was speaking through her veins, telling her that something more was happening between them, something very special that was binding them together in ways neither of them could imagine yet as they lived through this night.

She hesitated. She watched his tension as he waited for

her reply, waited for her to do what she would. And she knew he would not stop her, would not interfere no matter what she did. She looked down at the floor, seeing the small heap of white cloth her nightgown made beside the bed. And then she looked up toward him, not smiling, not even speaking.

He watched her as she lay back against the pillows, letting his breath out as she moved. He watched her as she slowly unclasped her arms, her nipples stiff and taut, her body facing him as she lay on her side, staring into his eyes.

Slowly she kicked the bedding away from her hips, stretching out her legs and then lying still, watching his eyes travel the length of her.

The rain was pattering softly now, the moonlight pale beyond the window, the only light in the room the oil lamp that burned on the table between the chair and the bed.

They were a few feet apart, his body throbbing, watching her, watching her eyes as they began to droop closed. Trusting. He could see her breathing deepen, her breast rising and falling with the air she took in, her belly a rounded ivory form in the half-light. Shadows caught at her hips, auburn curls of soft hair tendriling up toward her belly from between the smooth rounded thighs that tapered away below.

. . . I love you . . . he heard a whisper on the air, his brain telling him he had heard nothing. He found himself watching her eyes. Which were closed in sleep, he told himself, she had said nothing . . . or had he . . .

His self-respect restored, his body throbbing, his heart full within him, only one thing was truly clear to him: he had never felt so close to anyone in his entire life. Had never felt so trusted. Everything else seemed of much less importance.

Chapter 13

MORNING LIGHT BROUGHT NANCY with the duke's tray
of early tea and toast. She had passed the large bed
and placed the tray on the table before she realized that
Victoria lay tangled in its sheets.

Nancy stood stock-still, her eyes large with surprise.
"Miss . . . *Miss!*" Nancy reached to tug at the covers and
looked down at naked skin which she quickly re-covered.
Victoria's sleepy eyes opened. She yawned and started to
turn over before realization hit her. She sat up, the covers
falling around her. As she looked down at her naked body
the night came flooding back to her. She reached to pull
them back around her, a feeling of peace calming her from
within, glowing out her eyes as she looked up to see Nancy's
consternation.

"You've got to get back to your room before she finds
out!" Nancy was telling Victoria in a harsh whisper. "Before
any find out!"

"It's all right," Victoria was telling her, "it's not as it
seems."

"All right!" Nancy was struck dumb by Victoria's calm
smile. Footsteps sounded behind the maid and she whirled
around to confront the duke, dressed and staring at
her.

"Is that my tea?" was all he said.

The girl watched him walk forward, around the bed, and
started out the door, stopped by his voice: "Nancy, please
bring Miss Victoria something to put on—and help her

with it, will you? Then see to it that her things are put back to rights in her own room."

The girl stared at him. "Her . . . own room, your grace?"

"The one across the hall."

The girl stared at him still. And then dropped a quick curtsy before speeding away. "Yes, sir." Her words came back toward the two of them as they watched her go.

The duke turned toward Victoria to see her blushing furiously, the covers held tightly around her. He reached for the tray. "If you'll excuse me, I shall take this and leave you to—" He stopped, watching her. "Are you all right?" he asked.

She swallowed, nodding a little, afraid to trust her voice until he started away. "Where did you sleep?" she asked, watching him stop and turn back toward her. A faint smile played around the corners of the mouth that had taught her body so much in the wee small hours of this morning.

"You might tell Nancy that the attic needs to be straightened up a bit," he said ambiguously, his eyes reaching within hers to read what she was feeling. Trust shone back toward him. And a new softness that melted something inside his breast. He had to look away before he could turn away, walking out into the sitting room with the tray.

Victoria sat where she was, hearing his movements in the next room, listening for the small sounds he made. Nancy came back through to the bedroom, clothing in her arms, her face full of questions. She closed the door to the sitting room and came toward Victoria.

"Here you are, but where are you, then? What's happened?"

Victoria took the chemise Nancy was holding out. "Nothing has happened, Nancy. Things are not as they seem."

"Oh, and aren't they just!"

"No," Victoria replied mildly. "They're not. His grace asked that you straighten up the attic; he says it needs some doing."

Nancy's eyes became even rounder. "And what were you doing up *there*, then?"

Victoria found herself smiling, found herself feeling such liking for the girl, for the whole world this cloud-covered morning. "Looking at a picture," she said.

"I'll just bet."

Victoria lifted the chemise above her head, slipping into it before standing up and taking the dress from Nancy.

Nancy watched her every move. "I'll get fresh water in the basin," she told Victoria, but Victoria shook her head.

"No, thank you. I think I'll have a proper bath later. And do my hair. What do you think?"

"I'm sure I don't know," Nancy replied.

Victoria smiled at the girl, reaching out her hands to her. "It would be a great favor if you did not speak of any of this."

"I'll not speak of it!" Nancy said, indignant. "But if you think none will know, you're wrong. Why, they're all up and about. They'll see you leave here. And Lady Judith—" She stopped, unwilling to think of Judith Bereshaven's reactions when she was told the duke's orders.

"Hush now," Victoria said. "You go on before me, out into the hall. If none are there, I shall come out and then we shall just be two girls walking down the hall. That's all."

"All . . ." Nancy's tone told of her disbelief, but she moved forward anyway, opening the door to the sitting room.

The duke glanced up from a letter he was reading, the fire high in the grate beside him. He watched Nancy head straight for the door, determined not to look his way. Victoria smiled at him, a little uncertainly, until he smiled back. Nancy had the hall door open and was stepping outside. Victoria followed, hesitating until Nancy motioned her forward.

"Victoria," the duke called out, turning her back toward him as she stood in the doorway. "Were you telling me the truth about James?"

She stared at him. "Yes." Her heart hammered. He nodded and went back to his letter as Judith's voice rang out from the hall: "Nancy, where were you going with those—"

Victoria closed the door to the duke's sitting room and turned to see Judith staring at her. And her dress.

"—clothes." Judith finished the sentence, her expression hardening as she stared at Victoria. Then the older woman strode toward her, reaching for the door and flinging it open. Nancy retreated down the hall, Victoria standing still, feeling the woman's wrath.

The duke looked up to see his aunt in the doorway, her eyes blazing. "Edward! Was this . . . this *person* in your rooms last night!"

"Are you attempting to talk to me or to the world at large, Aunt Judith?" He spoke quietly, having the satisfaction of seeing her glance momentarily toward the closed doors across the hall. When she spoke again, her voice was lower, but no more friendly.

"I expect an answer."

"I can't see why it should concern you, but the answer is yes."

She could not speak for a moment. When she finally did, the effort showed. "I cannot believe you're telling me this."

"I cannot believe you moved Victoria out of her room and into a scullery maid's quarters," he snapped.

"Victoria is it now?"

"Miss Leggett's name is not the issue. What is the issue is that she is to have her room back and she is not to be disturbed further."

"Disturbed!" The woman was beyond words. "If you think I'll have that . . . that strumpet under the same roof—"

"Be careful, Aunt Judith."

"*I!* I'm not subjecting this house to gossip and ridicule! She had set her cap for you from the very first. I saw through her then and I see through her now."

"That's enough."

"It's nowhere near enough! I shall not permit this!"

"There is nothing for you to permit. If you continue, you shall have to apologize to Miss Leggett."

"Apologize!" Her scandalized voice rose louder.

A door opened across the hall, James looking out. "Aunt Judith?" His eyes were puffy with sleep, his hand reaching to rub them, looking out toward the noise that had awakened him.

She glanced back toward him, saw Victoria, and turned back to glare at Edward. "This is not the end of it!" she snapped. "She shall leave or I shall!"

Victoria took one step toward her. "Please, Lady Judith—"

"Don't even speak to me!" Judith pulled away and walked past James, retreating into her own room down the long hall as Victoria watched her go.

James smiled when Victoria looked his way. "Now just what has been going on, dear girl? Hmmm?"

She turned her back on him, walking toward the back hall and her things. James watched her leave and then looked in on his brother, who sat reading as if nothing had happened.

When James turned toward his room, his eyes had come awake along with the rest of him. He reached to pull lose his robe, staring across toward his bed once he stood inside, thinking about what he had just witnessed. Then he dressed and went in search of Judith.

Later that morning Victoria was sitting at her table in the study, working, when a knock at the door brought Sylvia in to stare at her. Realizing what she was doing, Sylvia looked away, embarrassed. Only to look back again as she walked hesitantly forward. "Do you have a moment?" she was asking as Victoria put down her pen and watched the duke's sister-in-law approach.

"Of course."

"We have received replies from a great many concerning the ball. The names need to be checked off so that we know who have sent word they will attend. Rooms will have to be made up in case of inclement weather; the third floor can be aired and readied."

"Would you like me to cross them off?"

Sylvia reached the small envelopes toward Victoria. "Yes," she said, and stopped. She looked uneasy. Victoria waited, watching the woman's unease. Finally Sylvia said more. "I should like to talk to you about something."

"Yes?" Victoria folded her hands, waiting.

"You were not at breakfast this morning."

"I was not hungry."

"Yes. Well, it seems certain . . . sounds awoke Lady Wyndham in the night." Sylvia looked up when Victoria said nothing. "When she mentioned them, Aunt Judith spoke of seeing to the 'problem' and Edward . . . I mean, the duke . . . walked out. Leaving the rest of us at table. Including Lady Elizabeth."

Victoria wondered what Sylvia wanted her to say.

"What I am saying is that, after that, James suggested Lady Wyndham ask . . . you about the . . . disturbance."

"I see."

Sylvia watched the younger woman. "Is there any more you wish to say?"

Victoria spoke softly. "There is nothing more to say."

"I see." Sylvia walked toward the windows then, her hands clasped together. "Aunt Judith said as much."

"I beg your pardon?"

"Aunt Judith said you would have to leave." Sylvia turned around to face the girl. "I could not believe . . . I mean I felt she was—must be misinterpreting—oh, I don't know! I simply didn't believe her!" Sylvia turned away. "She has a most unforgiving nature."

"I have done nothing to her. Nothing she must forgive."

"Have you not?" Sylvia stared at Victoria. "Did you not spend the night with him in his rooms?"

"I spent the night in his rooms. But not with him." Victoria saw Sylvia look down and then back up, trying to understand her words.

"I don't understand."

"Lady Judith had moved my things to the servants' quarters and he was determined I should not remain there. He asked that I sleep in his room. I did. Alone." She blushed, thinking of how nearly that had not been true.

"I see," Sylvia said slowly. "That is, I don't really see at all. I mean how did he know where you were?"

"He found me; he searched through the rooms."

"But why was he searching for you?"

Victoria started to reply and then stopped, looking away from Sylvia toward the vista outside the windows. "I am not quite sure. You would have to ask him."

"It won't end here," Sylvia told her. "Judith won't let it."

Victoria nodded slowly. "I . . . and you?" She searched the blond woman's face for understanding. She found pain there.

Sylvia twisted a small lace handkerchief in her hands. "I can tell you that the greatest good I can do you is to see you safe from the . . . temptation of doing something you'll regret." She looked up. "If you already have not."

Victoria watched her. "And if I had already done it?" she asked the woman quietly.

Sylvia's words were very soft. "Then I would pity you mightily. For there would be nothing but shame for the rest of your life. And pain. I know." Sylvia stared at Victoria. "Believe me. I know."

"What are you saying?" Victoria asked faintly.

Sylvia shook her head. She stood up, expressions fleeing across her face. "It is not of any moment now. All that is important is that appearances be kept up for Edward's, for the duke's, sake, until the Wyndhams leave. On that head we shall expect you at luncheon."

"Oh!" Victoria's eyes pleaded with the other woman. "I would truly rather not—"

"You must. For his sake." Sylvia stared at her. "For the *duke's* sake." She emphasized the word, underscoring his position, his relationship to the rest of them. "The Queen wishes him to arrive at an understanding with Elizabeth. Elizabeth must not know of . . . last night. If you care for him at all."

Victoria felt tears welling up behind her eyes. She closed them, barely whispering, "I shall be at luncheon."

Sylvia nodded and turned away. "At one o'clock then. The rest can be handled later."

The sound of the door closing brought Victoria's eyes open, to stare ahead of herself. She felt a painful constriction at her heart. None of them would understand. Could understand. Nor would they believe anything but the worst of her. She was not one of them. She was an outsider and as such must fulfill a certain role. Keep a certain distance. And never, never step over the bounds of that role, that distance, to touch one of them.

He was not like that. But he had obligations. Duties. And he would live up to them. Just as he lived up to his own self-respect. He would do what he had to, no matter how much it hurt him. *If* it hurt him.

She looked down at the papers before her. They seemed meaningless words scribbled across paper about people who were dead and gone now. Did it hurt him? Did he feel what she did? Could anyone know what his touch meant to her, what his kindness, the sound of his voice, the strength of his arms, meant to her without having been alone themselves . . . ? They had grown up with love and affection, with hugs and embraces and kind words . . . could they understand someone who had never been held in her life until the night she arrived here? She had fainted from hunger and awakened to find all the warmth and strength in the world holding her close and carrying her upward. Safe within those arms, she found something that she had lacked and desperately wanted. Would the words even have meaning to people who had never known loneliness . . . never been thrust away from all that they had known and loved?

The clock on his desk said eleven o'clock. In two hours it would be time to sit down with them, to try to pretend normalcy while sitting at the table with him so near and all the others staring at her. Wondering.

Nine hours ago he had awakened her from her sleep . . . her sleep of over twenty years. She now knew what she was lacking. What she wanted and needed. And she was told at the same time that it could never be hers.

The injustice of it rose within her. If they were to blame her, if they were to think the worst, then she should have gone to him, she should have reached for his naked flesh and brought him to her and been allowed at least one night of love before her world collapsed around her.

She looked out toward the gardens. He had been wrong to stop. Or wrong to let her decide. Somewhere within this house he was living and breathing. Her heart swelled with the thought. He was here; at least she would be able to see him. To sit near him. To have him near.

For how long she did not know . . . but today. Today she had. Last night. This morning. Luncheon. She stopped her thoughts there, unwilling to look into the future, afraid of what she would find there.

Today she was near him. Tomorrow she would face when it came. And whatever it brought it could not take the memory of his arms away. It could not stop her from loving him. She hugged her arms tightly around herself, holding in the wonderful warmth that filled her when she thought of him now. She could close her eyes and relive his kisses.

Edward opened the door between the library and the study, watching her until her eyes opened, finding him there.

She smiled softly. "I knew you were there."

"You did, did you?" His own voice surprised him with its gentleness. He hesitated and then came forward, his eyes falling to the front of her plain gray gown and then rising to look into hers. "You need a new wardrobe."

"I am content," she said quietly.

He searched for answers in her face, finding an expression in her eyes that warmed him. Being in her presence, he felt calmer and yet strangely on edge. He tried to see if she felt the same things and could not see past the gray-green depths of her eyes, the small fine nose, the lips that opened so willingly to him. "I . . . wanted to see how you were progressing. With the manuscript," he added, earning a small smile.

She bit her lip, looking down at the papers strewn across the table. "I'm afraid my mind is not on my work this morning."

"Truly?" He leaned over the desk, looking down at the papers. "I can't imagine why not."

"Yes . . ." She smiled, reaching for the papers she had been annotating. Pulling them nearer, she rested her hand upon the edge of the folder. Edward reached to see the page better, touching her hand, cupping it within his as he studied the manuscript. Her warmth reached through him, exhilarating him. He looked down at the top of her head, seeing the soft smile that played about her mouth. "You look happy," he told her quietly.

"I have never felt so happy in my entire life."

"Such a long life, to date," he chided her gently.

"It would seem long to you if you'd lived it. Alone."

"Yes, I suppose you're right." He still held her hand within his, steadying the paper. "But I'm afraid all will not be well as this day wears on."

"It's all right, your grace."

"Don't call me that!" His voice took on urgency. "Don't do that. Victoria, do you hear me? Not now."

"Shhh." She reached to cover the hand that held her own. "It's all right . . . Edward . . . truly."

A knock at the door pulled her hand back, the duke still leaning over the table, leaning over her as she sat at the table. "Yes?" he called out.

The door opened, Mike standing there, Judith behind him. Mike grinned at them. "Lady Judith was looking for you, your grace," he said smoothly, ignoring the expression on the woman's face.

"I have no need of your help!" Judith told Flaherty, seething as he shrugged and left. She turned toward the two at the table. "Elizabeth wanted to see more of your manuscript." She hissed out the words. "I thought I should precede her in case of what I just found!"

"And what's that, dear Aunt?" Edward's face was impassive.

She did not reply. "I shall fetch her," Judith said before leaving, the door to the hall deliberately left ajar.

Edward straightened up. "I fear I have made life intolerable for you. I did not mean to."

"I would do it all again . . . and more," she added softly.

He stared down at her. "More?"

Her expression was answer enough. And still he stared at her. "I want you," he told her, his voice husky. "I was a fool to stop."

"I could not have faced them if you had not."

"Truly?"

Her love was in her eyes. "Truly."

"But they think the worst."

"And we know the truth."

He grimaced. "The truth is I wish they were right in their assumptions." Her eyes were merry; he looked into them and could not keep himself from smiling back. "What a pair of fools we are."

She laughed and he found himself laughing too as Elizabeth and Judith walked into the room. "So there you are, Edward." Elizabeth walked forward, smiling. "How wonderful to hear such happy sounds early in the day." Her eyes swept past Victoria. "Miss Leggett, you must enjoy your work to be so cheerful about it."

"I do. Very much so, thank you."

"Now you must tell me all about it." Elizabeth perched upon a nearby chair, smiling up at Edward. "All Edward has thus far said is that it is a history and rather controversial at that. Would you agree, Miss Leggett?" Elizabeth's eyes slid to study Victoria.

"It is all of that, I daresay, to some. I do not find it controversial."

"Ah, you do not? Why not then?"

"Because I agree with what it states."

"I see." Elizabeth spoke slowly now. "And what is that?"

Judith watched the three of them from halfway across the room. "Wouldn't you rather take a turn in the garden, dear Elizabeth, than discuss books on such a day? The clouds have gone, the sun's warming the roses . . . surely you'd rather see nature at work than be weighted down with history, controversial or no."

Elizabeth still sought out Victoria. "The garden sounds delightful." She turned her gaze toward Edward. "Can I convince you to leave your work behind for a bit? We have to leave this afternoon and shall not see each other again until the night of the ball." She smiled prettily, Victoria envying her the smooth black hair that was curved into a high chignon, the easy grace with which she stood up. Each movement was as perfect as if it had been studied in a mirror.

Edward bowed slightly. "How could a gentleman resist such a pretty entreaty?"

Judith looked relieved, standing where she was until they had walked past her. Once they had gone, she looked back toward Victoria. "I'm told your things are to be moved back into the front bedroom." She waited for Victoria to reply. When no reply came, she continued. "You shall not be here long enough to enjoy what you mistakenly think is a victory."

Chapter 14

LUNCHEON WAS SERVED AT precisely one o'clock. The grandfather clock in the front hall bonged the hour, the Wyndhams' baggage piled in front of it as the driver and the maid they had brought with them carried packages out to the waiting coach in anticipation of their departure.

The small group in the dining room sat down to cold chicken and curried rice, preserved fruits and custard tarts awaiting their turn on the sideboard.

Margaret Wyndham was quiet, her eyes continually wandering toward the red-haired girl who was employed as the duke's assistant. She sat to his left, as she had at dinner the night before. Quietly eating her food. Or picking at it, as Judith made conversation with Elizabeth and the others joined in.

She looked different than she had last night. Something about her was more self-possessed than she had seemed before, as if she had secrets.

"Don't you agree, Margaret?" Judith was looking at her, smiling.

"I beg your pardon, I lost the train of conversation, my dear. What were you saying?"

"I was saying that it is always difficult to sleep when one is not in one's own bed."

"Yes," Margaret agreed, her gaze going back toward Victoria, who looked up and caught her eye. "Yes, I've always found it so."

149

"I too. That is why I quite dislike traveling. The Continent and all, you know. I am skin and bones when I return." Judith spoke as if she made periodic visits to foreign shores.

"Yes," Margaret said again, a little distracted. She looked up toward Edward at the head of the table. "I trust the business that called you away from table last evening has been . . . settled?"

Edward hesitated. "Thank you," he replied.

"I am to have tea with the Queen the day after next," Margaret was saying. "It will be a pleasure to tell her of your plans."

"I beg your pardon?" Edward said, waiting.

"For the ball."

"Oh. Yes, of course."

"And that you and Elizabeth seem to get on just as well as the Queen had imagined you would."

"Mother." Elizabeth laughed. "For pity's sake . . . you'd think you were trying to push me upon Edward."

James grinned at her. "I wish someone would push you on me."

Her laugh and Judith's remonstrance came at the same moment. "Really, James." Judith was glaring at him. "You must learn a little propriety."

"Oh, but I have, Auntie—a very little . . ." He grinned at Elizabeth again. But his hand reached under the table to touch Victoria's leg beside him.

She jumped, the others staring at her.

"Is something wrong, Miss Leggett?" James asked smoothly.

Her eyes blazed but she shook her head. "No."

"You're quite sure?" He sounded solicitous.

"I assure you," Victoria told him quietly. "I am quite all right. I felt a sudden chill, that is all."

"Oh. A chill."

Sylvia stared at her husband across the table. "James, will you pass me the wine, please?"

A footman stepped near to take the decanter, walking around the table toward Sylvia.

"How long have you worked for the duke, Miss Leggett?" Margaret Wyndham was watching Victoria again.

Edward answered: "She has recently begun."

"It is a temporary position," Judith said quickly. "The research on the book is quite nearly finished."

"My dear Aunt." Edward stared down the table at her. "How could you possibly know that?"

"I am sure I am correct in my assumption," Judith told him. She then turned toward Margaret. "I shall look forward to seeing you at the ball. May we hope you and your lovely daughter will stay the night? Or longer if you prefer. It would be so much more enjoyable for us all."

"I doubt we can get away again for very long. So soon, you know. There are so many details about Wyndham House that do not get seen to if one is not around. I'm sure you understand."

"Yes, of course."

"But you should come to the city. Open up your town house and let us see more of you," Margaret told Judith.

James was looking at Margaret, perplexed. "Dear Margaret, did you say Wyndham House?"

Margaret looked up toward him. "Yes. Elizabeth is of course taking over more and more since it will one day be hers alone."

"But forgive me, I thought George . . . ."

Margaret stared at him. Elizabeth spoke first. "Darling James, you have been gone a long time. My brother was killed in India. I am sole heir to our family's estate."

James digested this. "I'm—I'm so sorry . . . I didn't know."

Margaret had recovered, smiling faintly now. "It's been four years . . . but it's still hard to accept. One's own child, you know." She paused again. "One should not outlive one's children."

"Nor shall you," Elizabeth told her briskly. "I shall marry and hand you more grandchildren than you know what to do with!"

Margaret shook her head a little. "That is not a proper remark for a lady to make in mixed company, Elizabeth. Well intended as it was."

Elizabeth looked toward Edward. "Do you think it was not a proper remark?"

He shook his head. "Nothing you could say would be improper."

She looked disappointed at his words. James grinned. "I'd venture Elizabeth could say much that would be most improper indeed, if she put her mind to it."

Elizabeth smiled at him, dimpling. "You make me sound quite naughty."

"He does indeed," Margaret said reprovingly.

"Ah, do not dismiss me from your lists, kind Margaret; I am a poor old married man, carried away by your daughter's beauty and charm. Quite enthralled," James told Lady Wyndham.

"Are you really?" Elizabeth smiled at him. "That sounds quite delightful." She looked toward Edward. "And you, dear Edward? What is your opinion of me?"

"Elizabeth!" Her mother was scandalized.

"Yes, Edward, dear brother. You'd best watch out or I shall steal this beauty's heart quite away. Or at least attempt to."

Edward saw Judith watching him, and Sylvia staring at her husband. Sylvia stood up. "If you'll excuse me," she said stiffly, walking out before anyone could stop her.

"Oh, my dear child . . ." Margaret said to her as she left. "Please don't go." She looked up the table toward her daughter. "Now, see how you two have made poor Sylvia feel—there's an end to it this very minute."

Elizabeth looked as if she would rebel. And then merely sat back in her chair, watching Edward. "Edward, you never replied," she told him. "Have you no opinion?"

His eyes were solemn when he looked into hers. "I am not the witty gallant that my brother is. Repartee quite eludes me. I fear if you treasure James's quick speech, you will find his brother quite boring."

Elizabeth turned her attention toward Victoria. "And you, Miss Leggett?"

"I beg your pardon?"

"Do you find the duke boring?"

"I—"

Margaret called out to her daughter. "Elizabeth, you'll quite put the girl on the spot. If she tells you yes, her employer will be quite rightly put out with her, and if she tells you no, she will sound overfamiliar."

"You did not let her finish, Mother." Elizabeth waited.

Victoria could feel Edward stiffen to her right, his face a mask as she looked past him at the woman who sat to his right. "No, Miss Wyndham. If I must answer your question, I must in truth say that I could never find his grace boring."

"Of course you hardly know him," James said, smiling. "It's early times, dear Miss Leggett . . . give him time."

"Elizabeth, I think we should be going. It is a long and tedious drive back to town." Margaret stood up. Judith followed suit, the perfect hostess, smoothing over their words, leaving James, Victoria, Elizabeth, and Edward at table as the two older woman walked out of the room.

James reached for his wine, draining it. Victoria put her napkin beside her plate. Folding her hands in her lap, she waited for the duke to stand.

"Shall we?" Edward was asking Elizabeth.

She nodded, letting a footman help with her chair. Edward stood up, glancing at Victoria and James. James pushed his own chair back, rising beside Victoria and reaching to help her as the footman came around the table. "I have it, Tim," James was telling the young boy.

Victoria slipped out of the chair, following Edward around the table, not waiting for James to move back. James watched her round the table away from him, hanging back enough to allow Edward and Elizabeth to walk into the hall before following them.

"Victoria . . ." James called out softly.

She turned toward him, surprised. She saw him smile.

"You'd best be careful . . . you need a friend if you wish to continue here."

Her cheeks burned. "What are you saying?"

He shrugged. "Judith is quite determined and she usually gets her way. In the end. She's used to it."

Victoria left him behind, hurrying out the doorway as he watched her go.

The Wyndhams were seen into their carriage, a snack prepared and boxed in a small wicker case in case they should become hungry or thirsty along the road.

And the afternoon wore on, the sun occasionally shining out from behind clouds, then disappearing for a while behind gray banks of slow-moving fog, and then breaking through again to shine down upon the damp ground, warming the day.

James found Victoria taking a turn in the garden, a dark cloak pulled around her shoulders, her head bent forward as if in thought. She did not see him until he stopped in her path.

"Oh! You startled me."

"Did I?" He spoke quietly, an earnest expression in his eyes. "I'm sorry. I didn't mean to."

He sounded so unlike himself Victoria found herself staring at him. "Are you quite all right?" she asked.

"Better for being near you." There was no banter in his voice. He sounded like Edward. She stared up at him, surprised. "What's the matter?" he asked her. "You seem strange."

"I?" She swallowed, watching him carefully.

He looked off, across the lawns to where the grounds sloped away. "You can see the gazebo from here."

It was not Edward. She stared at him. She could feel the difference between them. They looked alike and yet they did not. Their expressions were different. The way each carried himself. The feeling that Edward engendered in her was missing with James.

"Meet me there. I must talk to you alone. Before James and the others come back."

"Back?" His words were ricocheting around within her head.

"They went for a turn along the river. Please say you'll come." His eyes searched hers.

"James, why are you doing this?" she asked him.

"James!" He looked startled. His eyes clouded. "You think I am James? Can you not tell the difference between us, then?"

She stared at him.

He reached for her, pulling her closer. "Have you tasted his mouth, then?" He was reaching to kiss her. She pushed away from him, stumbling back. He caught at her. *"No!"* she shouted at him. "Stop it! Please!"

Edward and Sylvia walked out from the terrace doors, stopping at the sound of Victoria's sharp pleas. Edward walked forward, reaching for James, pulling him back, away from her.

James smiled at his brother. "I was only trying to help dear Miss Leggett. She stumbled."

Edward looked to Victoria, who was shaking. Sylvia came close, touching Edward's arm. "Be careful . . ."

James watched her. "You should be telling *me* that, as my wife, should you not? Your solicitous nature should be concerned for your husband. Should it not?"

She stared into James's eyes, something ugly rising within them. Something snapped within her. "I married you thinking you were Edward, James. That should tell it all."

He smiled still, a mean edge to his lips. "You mean you went to bed with me thinking I was Edward. And then had to marry me, dear girl." James glanced at Victoria. "A distinction Miss Leggett seems in some wise to be able to make." He looked toward his brother. "Congratulations, Edward. I disbelieved Judith until now but obviously she's right. The little baggage has got her claws into you."

"Leave this house." Edward's voice was cold, the words flat.

"I beg your pardon?"

"I said you are to leave this house. Now."

James stared at his brother. "My dear chap, what will they all say—I'm hardly recovered from battle and you are to kick me out? After all, you are duke by the grace of ten minutes, dear brother. If that."

"You will leave this house today. You may use the London house if you wish until you make other arrangements. But I do not want to see your face."

"And I?" Sylvia asked quietly.

"You." Edward stared down at her. "You are welcome here as long as you wish to stay."

"Dear Miss Leggett." James looked over toward her and then back toward his brother. "It would seem you have competition. Are you collecting a harem, Edward?"

Edward's first shot out, hitting James squarely in the jaw, knocking him back. His left connected with James's midsection, sending him to the ground, James's hand crashing through the ruby-red roses beside him, thorns scraping at his flesh as he hit the ground at Edward's feet. Edward stared down at him. "If I were you, I would learn to watch my words." Edward turned away, Sylvia staring after him and then turning to look down at her husband.

James stared up at her, pure hatred in his eyes. "He will pay for this. He will pay dearly."

James grabbed at Victoria's skirt as she started past him, stopping her. "Help me up," he commanded. Victoria stared at him and then felt him grab at her hand. Her eyes went to Sylvia, who stood watching as he pulled himself erect.

He twisted away from them both once he was on his feet, stalking into the house after Edward, leaving Sylvia to droop against Victoria. "I'm sorry," Sylvia was saying. "I'm so sorry. I don't seem able to stand up."

"Let me help you to the bench." Victoria did as she said, helping until Sylvia sank back upon the wrought-iron bench to one side of the rose-garden path. "Would you like some water?" Victoria asked her.

Sylvia shook her head. "I just need a minute. That's all." She took a deep breath and then another. "You see, if I do not go with him, the break will be apparent to all. And the gossip will be worse." She looked up at Victoria. "There has been gossip for years about my being here. You see what James said was true."

"True."

"Yes. I was sixteen and James was home from school before Edward. He'd been sent down, but I didn't know it. He knew I'd always preferred Edward. So he . . . pretended. And I—I—James and Edward were twenty-one that year. He was twenty when I let him make love to me. And I became pregnant." She saw the look in Victoria's eyes. "My dear girl, when I said I could warn you, I meant it. As you can now see. I lost the child. But not before my parents had gone to the old duke, demanding Edward marry me. After what he'd done to me. You see I still thought it was Edward."

"How did you find out—I mean . . ."

Sylvia's laugh was bitter. "That was one of the best parts, my dear. You see the duke was suspicious, since he knew James had been home first. And Edward told James that if he married me, our child would be his heir. That James's son might inherit, but never James himself. Our children would come between. Since James has lived his life coveting what his brother has, he of course was not to be done out of the possibility by a brat of his own making. He married me. I miscarried a girl and he has felt that I deceived him into it ever since."

"How can you stand to be near him?"

"My dear, I don't do it very well, as you have seen. But I have had the protection of his being gone and my being able to live here. Judith does not approve of me, of course, but that is because I kept trying to run away when we were first married. James is her favorite."

Victoria's compassion showed. She sank to the bench beside Sylvia. "I should have done more than run away, I fear."

Sylvia nodded. "Life has become tolerable, with James away. But now—now I must face it all. And I am a weak person, Miss Leggett . . . I would not do well with society's disapproval. I fear I shall be forced to live out my life with a man I cannot abide."

"You cannot!"

Sylvia gripped Victoria's hands, staring hard into her eyes. "Do what you must for yourself, Miss Leggett. And do not let Edward hurt you. He will marry his own kind. Do not allow yourself to forget that."

Victoria swallowed, Sylvia's grip painful. Sylvia looked down, releasing her hands. "I'm sorry. It's none of my business, of course." She stood up, looking back at Victoria sadly. "You should be grateful that he will not be able to marry you."

"I beg your pardon?"

"He was married, you know."

Victoria stared at Sylvia. "Edwa—, the duke?"

"Yes. But she made the fatal mistake of becoming pregnant."

"I don't understand."

Sylvia spoke slowly. "James killed her." Victoria's eyes widened. "He tried to kill us both. We were riding together. He thought to be rid of the heir presumptive and the extra baggage of a wife at the same time. But I survived. And he was sent to the army. He should have died in one of those desert places. It would have made life so much easier."

The woman turned away, walking slowly toward the house, oblivious to Victoria's shocked eyes following her every movement. Before she reached the end of the path, she turned back, shading her eyes against the sudden sunlight that came flowing out from between the clouds. "It would be very dangerous to be Edward's wife. Think yourself lucky and leave here before it's too late."

She moved toward the house then, moved with the slow, deliberate pace of a sleepwalker, her tiny footsteps echoing away until she was up the shallow stone steps and inside the terrace doors.

Voices were coming from the library, loud and angry. Victoria closed her eyes against the sound, too tired to think coherently. Too much had happened, too little rest in between, to be able to sort it all out.

The voices were louder. Alarmingly louder now. She stared toward the windows and then hurried toward the door, worried for Edward.

"I'll not stay under this roof if James leaves!" Judith's voice rose even louder once Victoria was inside. Mike Flaherty stood near the study door, beside the wall. Unseen from inside, but ready to help if help were needed. He looked up to see Victoria coming toward him and held up his hand, shaking his head.

Sylvia's voice came out toward them. "You cannot consider leaving. The ball is only two weeks away."

"Do you think I care?"

Edward's voice was lower, softer. "You must do what you feel you must, Aunt Judith. I shall not stop you."

There was a long pause. "Are you telling me I must leave too?"

"I am saying that James is leaving. You are free to follow your conscience."

"And you!" Judith's voice rang out.

"I shall leave with my husband," Sylvia said woodenly.

"Well! For once, you're showing some sense."

"No," Sylvia replied. "Only cowardice . . . I'm sorry,

Edward. But if he leaves, I cannot stay without tongues wagging so loudly we'd hear them all the way out here."

"You must do what you feel is right," he said quietly.

"I am sorry. You know that, don't you?" Her voice was almost breaking.

"Sylvia, don't concern yourself," Edward told her.

"A fine scene! Why should you apologize to the man who is throwing your husband out of his rightful home?"

"Aunt Judith, if you are leaving with James, you'd best pack."

"I assure you I shall stay no longer than necessary."

"If you take what you shall immediately need, I shall see the rest of your things are delivered to the town house before the week is out."

"How thoughtful!" She spoke caustically. "Come along, Sylvia.

Judith came through the door, stopping face-to-face with Victoria. "Of course." Judith turned back to look into the room toward Edward. "Sylvia, are you coming? He wants all of us gone so that he can fornicate to his heart's content with this little trollop he's found!"

"Edward—no!" Sylvia spoke quickly, coming through the door toward Judith, giving Victoria not so much as a glance. "Come along, Judith. James has already called for a carriage."

They moved toward the stairs. Mike looked down sadly at the woebegone girl beside him. "Well," he said. "It's been quite an eventful day so far, wouldn't you say?"

She stared at him, then looked toward the library. Mike saw the direction of her glance. "I'll be seeing to him. Why don't you find a quiet corner to hide in until they've left . . . it'll be easier. On him as well as yourself."

She nodded, turning away and walking to the study door. Before she closed it, she looked back toward him. He was watching her, his curiosity apparent.

Chapter 15

EDWARD CALLED HER INTO the library after a solitary dinner. She had eaten in the study while working on the manuscript, trying to escape the weight of all the rest of it by losing herself in her work. Nancy told her Edward had eaten in his rooms, had spoken to no one since the others had left.

And still Nancy lingered, fingering a book, picking at a piece of fringe, straightening a tablecloth. Victoria watched her. "Is there something else?"

Nancy hesitated. "Yes, miss . . . it's Mr. James."

"Mr. James?" Victoria stared at her.

Nancy nodded. "Before he left, he told one of the footmen, who told Cook, that they were all leaving because of you and his grace."

Nancy saw Victoria's shock. "Cook—she can't keep her mouth shut, you know, miss . . ."

"You mean they think—they all think—"

"Yes, miss. I—I thought you ought to know. And I wanted you to know it wasn't me that done it!" she said in a rush. "I didn't say a thing!"

"Oh God . . . I'm sure you didn't. Thank you . . . for telling me."

Nancy stood where she was, awkward, unsure, and then finally turned and left the room, not knowing what else to say.

When Edward's summons had come, she had gone toward the library, dreading every step. For she would have to tell him. His good name was being ruined, his reputation bandied about.

He stood near the fireplace, his back to her when she came in. Mike had left and they were alone, the silence in the room heavy until Edward finally spoke. "It has been a very trying day," he began.

"Yes." She swallowed. "And I fear I have more . . . trying news."

He turned to see her then. "Yes?" His frown etched deep furrows into his brow.

"Nancy tells me that James has let them think he—they —left because of . . . me . . . of us."

"I know."

"You know!"

He nodded. "Mike . . . he has long ears." He threw himself into a chair by the fire. "Sit; we have to talk."

She came forward, sitting on a chair across from his, watching him as he stared into the fire, speaking slowly. "I am afraid I did not foresee such results as seem to have transpired."

"You could not expect—I mean, James has told untruths."

"He has simply enlarged upon what he has seen. And I could have—should have expected that." Edward sighed. "He has been gone for a great many years. I had forgotten the extent of his hatred. Anything that has meaning to me, he will destroy. Or try to."

Her eyes filled with pity. "I am so very sorry."

"Yes. Well, neither of us can change the facts. I shall, of course, give you the very best of references." He spoke briskly now.

"References . . ." she repeated.

"Although you must realize that they will be in doubt since they come from me. You can be sure that he will waste no time enlarging upon the story he has begun. It will give him great pleasure to discredit me." He stared at her then. "I shall see to it that you are provided for, financially, until you have succeeded in acquiring the position that you wish. However long that may take."

"You can't do this," she told him softly.

"I assure you, I will hear of nothing less. I could not bear

to think of you—without—I want to insure your future."
He stopped.

She was standing up, coming toward him to sink to the
floor at his feet. "You cannot send me away. Not now," she
told him.

"My dear girl, I—" He stopped again, his voice becoming
more anguished. "Victoria, I have to do this. For you.
Whatever else they say, people must not be able to say you
have stayed on under my roof. Unchaperoned."

"Is there any way to stop them talking about you?" She
reached for his hands, feeling him tense at her touch. "Is
there?"

"I am afraid that's out of the question." A wry smile
turned his lips upward, his eyes unhappy. "My brother will
ensure that his damage to me is done. But I can save you
from becoming a drawing-room topic."

"How?" she asked him gently, seeing his stricken look. "I
already am." She pressed his hands close.

"If you're not here—"

"They shall still talk."

"It will end if you are not here."

"And so will I."

He stared at her. "You cannot mean that."

"There is nowhere else I wish to be."

"I can't let you do this."

"I couldn't care less about the opinions of people I do not
know."

He hesitated. In the midst of it all, he could feel himself
responding to her, could feel the bittersweet ache she
brought to him, the closeness they had shared filling his
senses. He stared at her. "I have never felt so close to anyone
in my life as I do to you. Not even James, to whom everyone
says I should feel thus."

"There is no 'should' with feelings. You feel them or you
don't. That's all." She watched him. "Please don't send me
away too."

"Oh God, Victoria . . . this won't end here. James won't
let it. The Queen herself won't let it."

Victoria bit her lip, hearing the truth of what he said. "Let
me stay until they force you to make me go."

"No one can force me to make you go! Except you yourself. And what's good for you. That is my main concern."

Her hands were gentle upon his. "Don't make me leave. Not yet."

"Then when . . . ?"

She shook her head, rising on her knees, her face coming closer to his. Her words were whispered when she spoke: "Not yet . . ."

A strangled sound escaped his throat. He started to bend toward her and then straightened up, using every ounce of strength he could muster. His voice came out harshly: "If you are to stay, you must keep away from me."

She fell back, her hands falling away from his as he stood up. He looked down at the pain he had caused.

"If you stay . . . if I let you stay for now, we both must know that what they say is a lie." His face hardened. "That we are not as they suggest. No matter how much . . ." He stopped. "That is to be understood or you *must* go. I will not take advantage of this—of you. Do you understand?"

"No," she told him quietly.

"I have to be able to live with myself. Without that I am useless to anyone, including myself."

"May I stay?" she asked him softly.

He stared down at her. "Are you sure you want to?"

She nodded. "I want to stay as long as you'll let me. Whatever conditions you set."

"You'll regret it. If you don't already."

"Never," she told him.

He turned away. "I hope you are right." These were his last words as he left the room.

Victoria stood up and then, slowly, then sank to the chair he had just left, leaning against its arm and staring into the fire.

Rain began again outside, falling gently past the windows and pattering against the glass. The sounds were muffled by heavy drapes and curtains, the fire spitting out now and again, the grandfather clock bonging a slow procession of hours as the fire burned low.

Mike came in to wake her much later, touching her shoulder. She jumped, her eyes blinking open and staring at him. "What is it? What's wrong?" she asked.

He shook his head. "Nothing, girl . . . nothing. It's time to go bed." She swallowed, letting him help her to her feet, moving a little unsteadily across the floor beside him. "Have you eaten today?" he asked her.

"I had lunch and supper."

"Not by the looks of the plates you left is what I heard."

She smiled tiredly. "Is there nothing that isn't known by all in this house?"

"Not much." When they reached the hall, he hesitated. "Are you up to a little walk?"

"What? It's raining—"

"Not outside. I want to show you a little something."

She hesitated and then nodded, letting him lead her down the hall toward the grand ballroom.

He reached for a lamp that sat on a hall table, lighting their way across the dark and chilly room. "It's over here," he told her, leading her toward the promenade they had paced the night before.

James and Elizabeth, Margaret and Judith. Sylvia. All of them gone this night.

Mike moved to the end and flashed the light on the wall. "Do you see what this is?"

She stared at the portrait from the attic, at Edward's mother.

"That's Siobhan . . . did you know that?"

"It's his mother."

"Aye, she's that, all right, and more as well." He turned toward the slender young woman. "And she's here, where she belongs, because of you."

"I don't understand," she told the man.

He looked down upon her in the flickering light, shadows falling between and around them as he held it high. "Nor do I, girl, but I want to thank you anyway."

Victoria stared up at the portrait. "I'm glad she's here."

Mike nodded. "I thought you might like to see it. After all else that's happened today."

"Michael, you must not think badly of him."

"Nor could I ever, Miss Victoria . . . no more than you."

"Thank you . . ." Her voice was husky. She turned away.

"We'd best get you to bed . . . you've had a long day."

"Yes," she said quietly.

The house was silent around them as they walked back toward the main hall and the upper floors. They did not speak, each lost in his or her own thoughts, both thinking of the man who was in his rooms above. Discontent and alone.

Victoria closed her door finally, turning to look around the room that the duke had so dearly bought back for her. A fire was laid in the grate, her night robe and a fresh gown laid out across the bed. Nancy had done that, she was sure. No one else would have bothered. Tired, moving slowly, Victoria undressed, letting her clothing fall toward the chaise longue beside her, too tired to hang it up.

She reached for her robe finally, curling up atop the blankets that lay neatly folded back upon the bed, her head turned toward the window.

A waning moon cast silvery light across the black hulks of the trees beyond her window, clouds slowly covering it as she watched, its light fading behind the layers of black and gray.

She listened for movement, waiting for him to come to her. Waiting for him to open the door and beckon her. She fell asleep waiting.

And in the morning he was gone.

Chapter 16

"I DON'T UNDERSTAND." VICTORIA found Michael in the duke's room, laying out clothing. "Why did he go without a word?"

The Irishman continued with his work, moving from a huge mahogany armoire, closing its breakfront doors. "And since when does a duke have to explain his actions to his hirelings?"

The enormity of what he was saying to her turned her away. He watched her drooping shoulders turn toward the hall. "Lass, what he's doing has to be done."

The man spoke kindly. Victoria did not turn back but she stopped for a moment, nodding her head a little before she left his bedroom.

Victoria walked slowly toward the study. A maid coming along the hall toward her dropped her eyes, avoiding her. The girl moved closer to the wall as they passed. Feeling her cheeks beginning to burn, Victoria held her head higher, a determined thrust to her chin. They could call her names behind her back. They could avoid her. They could laugh at her. But they could not know the truth and they could never share, never know, what she had found in his arms.

The house seemed hollow around her, the maids' work done in whispers this day, stories of what had transpired, of what would happen now, filling the ears of all who would listen. Even the village had now found out about the exodus from The Willows, had heard tales of libertine behavior and terrible quarrels.

Alone in the study, Victoria crossed to the narrow table he had sat her down at a few short weeks ago, opening a sheaf of papers to—

She stared at the desk.

The manuscript was gone.

It couldn't be gone. She turned to his desk, its clock and scales, its letter opener awaiting his use. There were no papers upon it. She stared at her feet, at the floor, knowing that none of the maids would have knocked it off, would have left it if they had.

The library was cold, no fire laid in the grate, the night air still trapped in the cavernous room, chilling it. She ran to the drapes, tugging at them to pull them aside, letting light stream across the thick Turkey carpet toward the shelves of books.

Her eyes searched out the tables, the chairs, the mantel, the library table with its globe of the world . . . there were no papers, no manuscript bound in colored ribbons.

A large leatherbound volume lay on a round table near the cold fireplace, a marker set within it. Victoria reached for it, opening it to the marker. Parliamentary speeches from the past two years were bound within, Disraeli's name and Gladstone's, Isaac Butt's and Charles Stewart Parnell's met her eye, their words marked.

She stared at the pages and then lifted the heavy book into her arms, carrying it back to her table in the next room. Sitting down with it, she pulled blank paper toward her, beginning to copy out material about the Irish Question, as so many of the speeches called it, immersing herself in the work he had been doing. Trying to help. Trying to feel the closeness that bound them when she could look into his eyes.

In the distant city she had left behind, warm spring breezes mingled the scents of primrose and crocus, yellow and purple and white flowers springing up all over Hyde Park, spreading down toward Green Park and Buckingham Palace itself.

The diminutive lady who was Queen of England and Scotland, Queen of Ireland, Empress of India, and all else she surveyed, was seated in her own apartments talking with John Brown.

The room in which they sat boasted a magnificent bed filling one corner. Hung with red velvet and yellow silk, the arms of Great Britain were emblazoned upon the heavy red velvet, lions and unicorns disporting playfully all over the large room. The bed was large enough for three the size of the Queen and faced a wall of large oil portraits: George IV, the Duke of Kent, and the Prince of Wales as a colonel in the British army.

Elegant lounges were arranged around the large apartment, each of them covered in damask and satin. On one of them the Queen was sitting, a faint delicious odor of patchouli rising from carpet and counterpane.

Near Her Majesty, standing in front of an intricately carved sideboard and filling a green Venetian glass with sherry, stood the Queen's longtime body-servant. The raw-boned, robust Highlander had come to the end of his comments. Outside the deep bay windows the morning sun warmed the robin's-egg-blue satin drapes, sentinels tramping past on the battlement. The hoarse cry of a warder rang out as they went their rounds, the sounds of their feet receding in the distance as John Brown turned back toward his Queen.

The sixty-one-year-old monarch sat sipping coffee from a porcelain cup the color of a summer sky; beside her a tiny table of ivory, inlaid with gold and lapis lazuli held a silver teapot, the table itself supported by a tripod elegantly worked in solid silver.

"The fact remains," she told her most trusted confidant, "that there is talk already. And now this latest gossip. I must confess I will be glad to leave for Windsor and be away from all of it. Poor cousin Ned is in his grave and this young son of his seems determined to put me in mine."

"Nonsense."

The Queen did not react to his familiar tone. She had clung to this man since Albert had died almost twenty years ago, clung to his servant with a warmth and a fierce tenacity missing from her other relationships, even those with her own children.

"You are the only one I can unburden myself to, truly unburden, John . . . what should I do with him?"

"There's always gossip; there's no need to put such weight to it."

"You're speaking of Bertie . . . I know most of what they say. And most of it is true, as you well know. My son is such a disappointment. If only he'd been more like his father . . ."

"Even closer to home. They still whisper about me, about the two of us . . . I see no reason to worry more about what they say about Bereshaven than what they say about your continued seclusion and how I'm to blame for it."

She drew herself even more erect in her chair, her eyes blazing with imperial displeasure. "Nevertheless I shall *not* have my relatives and my court held up to ridicule. Edward Bereshaven is cousin to the Crown and he shall behave accordingly."

"You expect more of him than you do of your own son."

"Yes," she told him. "I do. I cannot stop the talk about you, for I will not do without your services, and that is that. It seems I cannot affect that scapegrace of a son of mine, nor save him from his libertine friends. But I can and shall use all at my disposal to ensure that Edward does not contribute to my problems!"

"Have you sent for him?"

"As a matter of fact, he's sent to ask if we might speak. As has his brother James. Not together, I might add."

John Brown's expression changed when she mentioned the younger Bereshaven.

"What is it?" she asked him.

"Your Majesty, if I were to go into battle, I should think twice about going into it with your cousin James."

Queen Victoria's displeasure showed on her round little face. "What do you mean? He is quite charming, and as I remember I was always fond of him. He has been in our army for years now, defending our territories. In our service."

"Has he?" John asked enigmatically.

The Queen of England's round little figure was encased in black satin. She stood up, waving away the six-foot giant who moved to help her. "I am all right as I am. And you must needs explain yourself."

"I never shared your fondness for him."

"I suppose *you* prefer his solemn-faced brother!"

"Your Majesty, in a great many ways men are like your racehorses. James may have the flash, but Edward is the winner over the long haul. On that I would bet money."

"Yes, well, we shall soon see, shall we not? Let us see if Edward is intent upon his duty. Or if he has inherited his father's penchant for undesirable liaisons."

"Ned married but once."

"Once was quite enough!"

She moved toward the huge doors to the hall. As if by magic they opened, a red-tunicked beefeater standing at attention on either side of the opening as she passed through it.

On the next floor of the palace, Edward paced the length of the apartment he'd been shown into. His hands behind his back, his brow furrowed, he heard the doors opening and swung around to see Her Majesty walking through them, one of her ladies-in-waiting at her side. He unclasped his hands from behind his back, bowing low as the Queen spoke.

"Edward, you know Lady Diane, I'm sure. Come here, let me see you." She gazed up at him and then turned toward a couch. "Let us sit or I shall have a fearful neckache from peering up at you." Lady Diane came near to arrange pillows on a couch for the Queen, Edward bowing slightly to the woman as she passed. Her smile full with subtle innuendos, Lady Diane plumped pillows and then sat nearby, her face all innocence as the Queen glanced at her and back at Edward's deepening frown. "Are you ill?" the Queen asked him.

"No, Your Majesty, thank you for asking. I am in perfect health."

"Ah, good. That is always good news." She watched him seat himself across from her. "James is coming to tea with

Lady Wyndham this afternoon. I believe he is escorting both Margaret and Elizabeth."

Edward nodded pleasantly, his teeth gritted within his mouth. Consciously relaxing his gaze, he caught a glimpse of Lady Diane's amused expression—at his expense. He ignored it. "I wished to make known to Your Majesty immediately how very grateful I am that you suggested that Lady Wyndham, dear Margaret, might entertain the possibility of allowing her daughter and myself to become . . . better acquainted."

"You are?" The Queen gazed into his calm, dark eyes. "I mean, of course. I knew you would hit it off."

"She is most charming. Taking after her mother a very great deal. And a more charming mother-in-law would be impossible to find."

"I must say, Edward, you are taking this in exactly the spirit in which I hoped. I do feel very strongly, very strongly indeed"—she stressed her words—"that it is important for you to assume the role of father and husband as soon as possible."

"Yes, I quite see that."

"I am glad. Especially in the light of these latest . . . unfortunate stories."

His gaze was bland, mildly curious. "I beg your pardon, Your Majesty?"

She glanced at Lady Diane, who lowered her eyes to her own lap. The Queen turned her gaze back toward her cousin. "We talked at our last meeting of certain . . . comments about your household. About Sylvia, to be specific. Which I am happy to say are firmly put to rest now that her husband is home and she is with him. As for the most current stories . . ." She searched for the right words.

"Your Majesty, I hesitate to interrupt, but I am at a complete loss." His voice, his face, showed his lack of understanding quite clearly. "To what are you referring."

"Why, to the reasons that James and his wife—and Lady Judith for that matter—find themselves in the city."

His perplexed expression deepened the furrows in his brow. "The coming party?" he asked.

"I beg your pardon?" the Queen of England replied.

"You mention the reason my family is in the city. They have come to help with the preparations for the ball which we are to give next week. At Your Majesty's suggestion, if Your Majesty remembers . . . the last time we talked?" He smiled at her.

"Of course I remember," she told him. "Edward, I fear we are talking at cross-purposes." She hesitated. "Lady Diane, would you please excuse us for a moment?"

Lady Diane stood up, curtsying slowly, her eyes upon Edward as she rose. Murmuring her good-byes, she left the room. The Queen turned her full attention upon Edward. "Now, let us speak plainly. Why are you here?"

"As I said, Your Majesty—the ball. You see, I realized with the weather being so uncertain these last weeks, and the distance to The Willows, that the only practical alternative was to prepare Bereshaven House and hold the ball here in the city. In that manner many who could not attend because of the distance would be able to come, and in case of any untoward weather, all would still be able to travel home. And so Aunt Judith felt she should come as soon as possible to see to the details; you see we had not discussed the impracticality until the Wyndhams were forced to stay overnight at The Willows due to the weather on Wednesday. After they left, the topic came up and James and Sylvia kindly volunteered to aid Judith. I myself, of course, was unable to drop everything at a moment's notice since there have been estate problems these past weeks. Then, as it happened, I had to consult with the estate solicitors. So I followed the others to town."

She watched him carefully. "You spent the night in town?"

"At my club, yes. Why do you ask, Your Majesty?"

"There is conversation about a young woman in your employ. And rather . . . radical ideas."

"I beg your pardon?"

"Do you or do you not employ a young woman who has emancipation leanings—who, to put it bluntly, believes in women's vote, free love, and Irish Home Rule?"

The duke stared at his queen. His consternation was very real and most obvious. He recovered his composure quickly, the Queen now doubting the stories she had heard. "Your Majesty, I have several young women in my employ, as maids and whatnot. And I have not the slightest knowledge of their politics. However, I can hardly credit anyone who is so . . . so radical . . . willing to work for a member of the aristocracy. The only other young woman I employ is an orphan from Mercy House that Sir Thomas Poysner asked me to engage as a personal favor."

The Queen's expression was slowly dissolving into understanding. "Just one moment, I begin to see some light on this subject. If a servant heard discussion about such a young lady's background, there could be room for misinterpretation. Lady Ashbrook, although having the highest of morals and intentions, did have an unfortunately liberal bent to her philosophies. Perhaps the girl has spoken to someone and they have repeated her words to her disadvantage."

"Her words, Your Majesty?" The duke's tone was mild, belying the roiling within his stomach.

The Queen was studying him more kindly. "I fear, what with your father's example and your measure of wild Irish blood, I may have assumed there was more veracity than there truly was to these accusations."

"If Your Majesty would enlighten me—I am at a complete loss. Who has said what against my household?"

"Lady Diane heard from Lady Mortimer, who in all probability heard from her maids, a rather farfetched tale of libertine activities within your household. And outlandish philosophies."

"As to the outlandish philosophies, I have no knowledge, but as to the libertine activities, you yourself, Your Majesty, were good enough to mention to me the stories concerning my sister-in-law and myself."

"Yes, yes . . . I know. This was not about that. It concerned this young woman in your employ."

"Your Majesty!" The ninth Duke of Bereshaven rose to his feet, the picture of indignation. "Who has *dared* to accuse me of yet another scandalous adventure!"

"Calm yourself, Edward. It is not important."

"If it came to your ears, Your Majesty, it most certainly is! Who all has been told this tale? And why?"

173

"I tell you it is not important." The Queen thought about the matter for a moment. "Where is the girl now?"

"If we are speaking of the girl Sir Thomas asked me to hire, her name is Miss Leggett. Miss Victoria Leggett, by the by, Your Majesty, named after yourself." He saw her eyes flicker with this new information. "Miss Leggett was trained at Mercy House in secretarial duties and is at the moment engaged in helping me finish the manuscript that my father was working on when he died."

"Truly?" The Queen smiled then. "That is very good of you, Edward; that is a mark of true filial devotion." A cloud passed over her expression, her thoughts turned inward for a moment. "Something that is sadly lacking in our family, I fear." She roused herself from her momentary reverie. "Sit down, Edward, you shall give me the neck ache. You are much too tall to hover above one so. Especially your monarch."

A fleeting smile crossed her lips and he responded, sitting across from her and leaning forward, "Your Majesty is most kind. And understanding."

"Well, as you tell me nothing has transpired, there is no reason for me to be otherwise, is there?" She watched him carefully. "From your comments earlier, am I to assume that you will press your case with Miss Wyndham?"

"It is what you desire, is it not?" he replied.

"Good! Now . . . I shall look forward to hearing of your ball. And of your engagement."

"These things take time," he said slowly.

She read his hesitation as diffidence. "Nonsense, you must trust your own special . . . charms." She smiled at him. "I am sure young Elizabeth is wise enough to see your worth and value you in kind." The Queen stood up. "I shall look forward to news of you."

He stood as she did, bowing low when she dismissed him. As he left she called after him, "You must never forget your duties."

He stopped. And slowly bowed again. "Your Majesty."

Lady Diane waited nearby in the hall. She came forward as the duke came out of the room, beefeaters closing the doors behind him. She saw his expression when he saw her

174

and smiled her gayest smile. "I trust all is well between yourself and Her Majesty," Diane said sweetly.

He sketched a bow, a wide smile forming across his face. "Thank you, it most certainly is." He saw the lady-in-waiting's surprise and the question in her eyes. "Please tell my brother when he arrives that we will not hold dinner for him. I am sure he will find cause to stay late at his club."

"I beg your pardon?"

"Isn't my brother expected? Her Majesty mentioned it."

"Yes . . . but . . . dinner, did you say? You will not be at The Willows?"

"Whatever for? We are staying in town until after the ball."

She stared at him and then realized she was staring.

"Is something the matter?" he asked her.

"No . . . no . . ." She dipped a small curtsy and turned away. "If you'll excuse me, I should return to Her Majesty."

"Of course," Edward said blandly, watching the woman walk quickly away. When he turned toward the marble stairs, his expression was grim.

And very very determined.

Chapter 17

EDWARD'S COACH, WITH HIS coat of arms emblazoned in gilt against the shiny black paint of the side, pulled up to the front steps of Bereshaven House, his driver leaping down to open the coach door and race up the steps to open the house door.

The duke stepped across the threshold of his London establishment, flinging off his black cape and throwing it to the under-butler, who stood just inside, staring at him.

"Hullo, Jasper . . . are things in order at this end?"

"What, your grace? I mean, yes, of course, your grace. We—we were not expecting you."

"Why not?" The duke watched the man.

"I was told that you were . . . staying on at The Willows."

"And were you told to ready Bereshaven House for a fancy-dress ball Friday next?"

"Your grace! No!"

"No?" The duke spoke mildly, pulling off his gloves and looking at the man as he handed them over. "Well, I suggest that first you remind Lady Judith—she *has* arrived, has she not?"

"Yes, your grace." The man's eyes were round with surprise.

"Good. Please tell her that I am here and that I wish to go over all plans with her and Lady Sylvia first thing in the morning. Now come along, I want a message sent to The Willows immediately and then I shall dine alone in the dining room. The ladies will find they have much to do in order to be ready for our morning conversation—shall we say ten o'clock?—and therefore will find it easier to dine in their rooms."

Jasper's eyes barely flickered. "And Sir James, your grace?"

"I believe my brother is dining out at his club this evening. He has been away so long, I am sure he wishes to renew old acquaintances as soon as possible, since he will now be home for good."

Jasper bowed. "Yes sir. I shall see to all the messages."

"Good." The duke walked toward the library, Jasper following him.

"Is Mr. Flaherty with you, my lord?"

"He will be arriving with my assistant and my work. Please see that one of the guest rooms is readied for my assistant, Miss Leggett, and that whatever is needed for Michael is ready before Monday next. Oh, and send me a footman immediately."

"Yes, your grace."

Ten minutes later Judith Bereshaven came down the wide circular stairwell, stopping at the sight of a footman stationed at the door to the library. "Is my nephew within?" she asked the young man imperiously.

"Yes, milady." The footman tensed as she moved toward him.

"Let me by," She commanded.

"I'm sorry, milady, the duke does not wish to be disturbed."

"Does not wish! That is for visitors, you fool! I am his aunt and I wish to see him at once!"

"I'm sorry, milady." The young man held his ground. "My orders are that he not be disturbed, by anyone, until he is through with his work."

"And what 'work' is that?"

"I cannot tell you, milady. I do not know."

"He certainly did not tell you that that order included me!"

"He said as how it included everyone, milady . . . even family."

Judith stared at the closed door. "I am in charge of this household," she said almost absently. "What is your name?"

"I am Charles, milady."

"If you wish to continue working in this household, Charles, you had best learn that *I* hire. And fire." She eyed him now, challenging him.

He looked a little afraid when next he spoke. "His grace also said as how I was to tell him if any threatened me or my job, milady . . ."

Anger blazed within her. She turned her back on the footman, starting for the stairs and Sylvia's room, not even knocking when she reached it.

Sylvia was at her dressing table, looking into the mirror to see Judith's wrathful face framed in the doorway. "Did you receive a message from him too?" Judith was asking.

Sylvia's attention went back to her hair, which she was brushing out with a long-handled chased silver brush, its bristles of boar combing through her long, blond hair. A small smile played about her lips. "Yes, I did."

"I suppose *you* were told in person."

"By Jasper," Sylvia replied. "I was told it would be convenient for me to sup in my rooms and to ready myself for a morning meeting with the duke." She turned around on the vanity stool, looking directly at Judith. "And that you were being given the same message."

"And James? What of James when he walks in and is told of this turn of events?"

"I rather think he must already know, since Jasper also told me that the duke informed him that my husband would be supping at his club tonight."

"What has happened?" Judith demanded.

Sylvia shrugged. "I do not know, Aunt Judith. But I fear egg may be all over James's face if he's been . . . repeating tales."

"I will not put up with this!"

"Yes." Sylvia smiled sympathetically at the woman. "It is rather a pity that we women don't have private clubs to repair to, isn't it? But then again, how should we pay for one? I'm beginning to see the value of all this talk of women's freedoms and such . . . I mean, after all, look at

178

our plight. I am bound to a husband who does not want me and you are bound to a nephew you dislike."

"I shall not suffer this! James will see to it that I do not have to stay under Edward's roof one more day!"

"I rather doubt it. He has never paid his own way, or mine, let alone anyone else's . . . and you have no money in your own right, do you?" Sylvia asked her sweetly. "The only women James has ever bothered himself with were ones who had money. To help him out with his little . . . excesses, in gambling and the like."

"He is high-spirited! Nothing more."

"Oh my, yes. High-spirited." Sylvia turned back to her mirror and her brushes. "I quite agree."

Judith stood across the room, eyeing Sylvia carefully. "Just what do you expect to tell him when you see him. *If* you see him."

"James?"

"No! Edward!"

"Oh . . . Edward. I expect I shall tell him that he must be a very good chess player, Aunt Judith."

"You are mocking me," Judith said coldly.

"No. Truly." Sylvia put down the brush, looking at Judith again through the mirror. "But I think things have changed. I think you may have to assess your treatment of Edward. You've made no bones about his not being your favorite. Or of your dislike of much of what he is and does, if not even of him, himself. You had best face the fact that he may no longer put up with that. He may have been stopped from . . . from doing something he wished to do, but in the stopping you may find that he is no longer willing to allow others any leeway either. Any leeway at all."

"Are you saying he will throw me out on the street?"

"I am saying that you would not be happy pensioned off to a cottage somewhere in the country. Alone."

Judith looked horrified, the idea new to her, the thought appalling. "He would not do that."

"Why would he not? If he is unhappy, and we are the cause of his unhappiness, why should he wish any of us around? Particularily if we are the least bit unpleasant to him . . . hmmm?"

Judith turned away, reaching for the door. "I find I am

exceedingly tired. I think I shall retire to my rooms for the night."

Sylvia nodded. "We shall need all our strength for our morning meeting, I fear."

When she was alone, Sylvia put down her brush and stared at herself in the mirror. Slowly she began to smile. She stood up, reaching for her bell pull and walking toward a table near the windows. When the maid knocked at the door, Sylvia called out for her to enter.

"Will you please see that his grace gets this?" Sylvia put a sealed note in the girl's hands. "And have a light supper sent up to me . . . I am quite tired and will retire early this evening."

The maid took the envelope while Sylvia replaced her pen and papers within the drawer of the table.

When the footman gave the note to the duke, he stared at the sealed envelope until the man had left and then slowly opened it.

It contained a single piece of paper with two words on it: *Bravo . . . Sylvia.* Edward stared at it, his eyes softening a little before he crumpled it up and threw it onto the fire. He watched the flames lick at it and then devour it, his thoughts far away. Restlessness was ruining his evening, a black cloud settling about his eyes, the thought of the future bleak and barren. Visions of Victoria rose in the flames, her eyes staring out at him, haunting him with their sadness, their plea for kindness, at least kindness. He shut his eyes so as not to see her and found her naked body awaiting him in the darkness behind his eyes, filling his senses, a physical longing washing over him that was so intense he felt his body responding.

His eyes snapped open. He was never to have her. He could not have her; he would not demean her. He was forced upon a journey that led him away from everything he longed for. The reality of what was happening burst forth within him, bowing his head as the ache grew larger. He sat in the small room, surrounded by books, not lighting the lamp as daylight faded away outside. The only light in the room danced from the flames in the hearth. He laid his head back against one wing of the chair and gave himself over to the visions in his mind. For this one night he would let himself hold her, let himself make love to her, if only in his dreams. Tomorrow's light would bring the beginning of a charade that was to last a lifetime. He would have to get used to it; he would have to face the challenge of her nearness by Monday. He would have to break her heart and become so cold she would beg to leave his employ. He would have to lie to the one person he cared about, lie about the one truth in his life. And he would do it. A hardness within him told him he had lost love before and survived. He would do so now.

But for this one night he would have her. She would be his. And unharmed.

His eyes closed, her naked body coming slowly toward him. He let her approach, reaching out to her when she stopped and drawing her nearer. . . .

Jasper had to rouse him to warn him of dinner being ready in a quarter hour's time, a mantel clock above the fireplace chiming a quarter to eight.

"Thank you," the duke said tiredly, standing up to see the look of disquiet on the butler's face. The duke saw the man glancing toward the unused lamp. "Don't worry, Jasper. I've not gone completely round the bend. That will come later." He strode past the man toward the stairs. "I shall freshen up and be ready to eat by quarter past. Please inform Cook."

As the duke was striding up the circular stairwell in London's posh Mayfair, Mike Flaherty was reading the message the duke had sent to The Willows. When he finished reading it, he nodded to the rider who had brought it and hesitated before starting back toward the study where the girl still sat working.

She looked up when he entered, her eyes wide, her body tense, as if expecting bad news. "What is it?" she asked him, half rising in her chair. "Is he well? Has something happened?"

Mike shook his head. "Damn me if I know. Begging your pardon, miss, but . . . here, you read it." He handed over the letter.

Victoria took it with an unsteady hand, bringing it toward her, still looking into Mike's puzzled eyes. Then she bent

181

her head, drawing the oil lamp nearer as she read: *Will hold ball in London, advise Miss Leggett to pack, as well as yourself, all that you will need for the next several weeks or more. Plan to arrive Monday and inform others of our location. Repeat, plan to arrive Monday. Not before.* Victoria looked up at Mike. "I'm not sure I understand."

"Neither am I." He sat down on a chair near her table. "And the part I do understand I don't like." She waited for him to continue, and after a moment he did. "He's planning on staying in London for a while, that much is clear. And he wants us there."

"He wants my things packed and wants me to come to London. It does not say I am to . . . stay in his employ."

Michael shook his head. "It doesn't say you're to be sent packing either, so I wouldn't borrow the trouble until it's upon you."

"What's this about location?"

Michael frowned. "If he means what I think he does, it's dangerous. It's one thing to meet the boys out here but another matter altogether in the middle of nosy London."

Victoria looked back down at the paper. "He says nothing about what has happened, what *is* happening. Why we are to stay in London when . . . when the others have repaired there."

"I'd say that was to squelch all the talking and it's smart too. But as of the rest . . . it's not smart to meet with Tim Ryan and them all in London town. I can't imagine what he's thinking about."

"Why should we not come until Monday? This is only Friday." She stared at the paper again, her voice lower when next she spoke. "He says nothing of himself . . ."

"Well, he's not shot James, nor gotten shot, or we'd have heard."

"Shot!"

"A manner of speaking, Miss Victoria, just a manner of speaking." He stood up, watching her look back down at the note she still held in her hands. "If you'd like to keep it . . ."

She looked up. "Yes. May I?"

He nodded. "I'd best see to how to get hold of—" He stopped. "That is, I'd best see to doing as he asks."

Victoria was staring at the paper when he left the room,

her hands holding it carefully, touching what he had so recently touched. And held.

Monday . . . on Monday she would see him. And know her fate. She looked up to ensure that Mike was gone and then tucked the note into the pocket of her gown, holding it clasped in her hand.

She stared down at the book she had before her and realized she had forgotten to ask Mike if he knew why the duke had taken the manuscript with him.

Nancy came to ask if she wished her supper in here or in her room.

"My room, I think," Victoria said, standing up. "And I shall have to pack. It seems everyone is to stay in London for the ball."

Nancy stared at her. "It's still to be? The party, I mean? I thought it was canceled what with all the . . . everything."

"It's to be held in London and it seems all is well."

Nancy walked beside Victoria. "I did so look forward to the party. Do you think I could come to London too?"

Victoria hesitated. "Oh Nancy, I don't know . . . But I can tell you I'd dearly love it if you could."

Nancy looked more hopeful. "I could help you with your things, getting ready for the ball and all."

Victoria almost laughed. "I doubt I shall have need of a lady's maid no matter what is happening." She saw Nancy's face fall, glum at the thought of being left behind. "It's been ever so long since I've been to London," Nancy told Victoria.

"I didn't know you had ever been," Victoria replied.

Nancy grinned. "I haven't. You see how long it's been!"

Victoria found herself smiling in spite of herself. "We could ask Michael to send to town and ask. They might need an extra pair of hands what with all they'll have to do to get ready for the party."

Hope came into Nancy's eyes. "Oh, would you ask? Please? It would be ever so kind if you would."

Victoria smiled again. "It would be a kindness for me too. To have you there."

Nancy nodded. "Yes, miss. What with all the others around and the talk and all, you could do with someone of your own about."

Victoria reached an arm around the girl's shoulders. "Thank you, Nancy."

"I haven't done anything yet, miss."

"Oh, yes you have. You've just told me you're a friend. And I need one badly."

Nancy looked uncomfortable at the praise. "You don't need the likes of me."

"Well, I can't imagine a better friend to have," Victoria told the girl.

Nancy stared at Victoria. "You know, I think you mean that, miss."

"Of course I mean it!"

Nancy took a moment to put it all together. And then she smiled, turning away to go through the green baize door to the back of the house as Victoria hesitated beside it. "You go on up. I'll just see to what's about that I can nip for your dinner."

Victoria started toward the stairs.

"Miss . . ." Nancy called out to her softly.

"Yes?" Victoria turned back to look at the black and white uniformed girl who stood a few feet away.

"Did you truly—I mean you and the master—was all that . . ." Nancy blundered with the words, her face twisted with the attempt to find the right ones.

"No," Victoria told her, staring her directly in the eye. "No. We did not." Victoria saw the relief and the doubt in the maid's eyes. "I would have, Nancy. If he had wished. But we did not."

Nancy smiled then, relief overshadowing the doubt. "I would too, miss." Nancy grinned then. "I believe you."

Victoria watched the girl until she was out of sight, her body full of a bittersweet longing that would not go away. Climbing the stairs, Victoria stopped halfway up, turning around and skipping back down them quickly. Reaching for the lamp on the hall table, she made her way to the ballroom, to the promenade, and the oil paintings that hung one after another along the hundred-foot-long expanse.

She raised the lamp upward, shining it on duke after duke until she reached the eighth Duke of Bereshaven, Edward, called Ned by his friends. She stared at the hard, uncompromising lines of his face, at the haughty expression about his eyes that gave a hint of pain mixed in with all the pride. When she turned away, she walked across the aisle to shine the lamp upon his wife.

Siobhan Bereshaven, eighth Duchess of Bereshaven, had eyes that spoke of love and trust. She did not look as if she expected the fate that awaited her. Victoria stood for a long time staring up at the face of Edward's mother, trying to find something in her face that would help.

All she could see was beauty unawares.

Chapter 18

SATURDAY MORNING BROUGHT JUDITH and Sylvia to the library at precisely ten o'clock to find the duke seated at his desk beside a man they did not know. The man was taking notes.

Judith gave Sylvia a triumphant smile and sailed to a chair in front of the desk. "Good morning, Edward. I trust your journey was pleasant and that you slept well."

"Thank you." He looked up at her and then smiled toward Sylvia. "Wouldn't you rather sit? This may take awhile."

Sylvia nodded, sinking to a chair across the room. "James, it seems, has not returned," she told her brother-in-law.

"Oh?" He looked entirely disinterested. "When he does, please tell him I would like to see him. If he is to leave the army, we must discuss his future plans."

"Yes," Sylvia said faintly, "I will." She stared at Edward. He could have been a stranger across the desk from them.

"Now, then; Mr. Phipps handles the books for household expenditures for Bereshaven House and works directly with the shopkeepers and such. He has made a tentative proposal of what all must be arranged. I suggest we listen to his ideas and then decide who shall do what and when. Understood?" The duke glanced at the two ladies across from him.

"Understood," Sylvia said quietly.

"Agreed," Judith amended. "Shall we begin?"

"You may wish to take notes," Mr. Phipps told her.

She looked affronted. "I assure you, there is nothing wrong with my memory."

The duke motioned to the man. "You can have copies made of any reminders needed and I shall see that Lady Judith and Lady Sylvia get them. Shall we begin?"

The man bent to his notes, his pince-nez perched upon the thin bridge of his nose. He spoke with a nasal twang, the duke sitting back and idly playing with a worked silver letter opener as the man discussed the orderly transformation of the barely used town house into the home of a gala ball.

The door to the hall burst open a few minutes later, James standing in the doorway, flushed, still dressed for the evening, his clothes in disarray. "So you *are* here!" he shouted.

"We are busy, James. I shall see you later," the duke said mildly, Mr. Phipps looking up from under lowered eyes to stare at the inebriate across the room. The man was the spitting image of the duke.

"Now!" James bellowed.

Judith looked at him with distaste. "James! Stop making a spectacle of yourself and go upstairs and change! You look as if you've slept in your clothes!"

James stared at his aunt, surprised by her tone. And the distaste he saw in her eyes. He hesitated, seeing the little man beside the duke outright staring at him now. "What are you staring at?" James challenged the man, watching him duck his head to look down at the pad he held on his lap. When no one spoke, James finally drew himself up to his full height and turned away, slamming the door behind. The duke smiled at Mr. Phipps. "He drinks a bit. Pay no attention. I should hate for it to get around."

Mr. Phipps looked down at his notes, mentally dismissing the look-alike brother of the duke. He cleared his throat and began again where he had left off.

Only Sylvia stared at the duke, wondering at the pleased expression that lurked in his eyes.

Upstairs Jasper came out of the room James had chosen the night they arrived. "What the devil are you doing in my room?" James demanded.

Jasper had James's shaving accessories in his hands. "The

duke has arrived, Sir James, and wishes his father's room for himself. He has had you moved to the first guest room."

"Guest room! I don't want the blasted first guest room!"

Jasper kept his opinions to himself as he waited for the unkempt-looking gentleman to quiet himself. "His grace has said since Lady Judith has the duchess's rooms and Lady Sylvia your old rooms that the first guest bedroom would be best. It has a lovely view of the square."

"Damn and blast the square!" James roared.

Jasper moved down the hall to the first guest bedroom. "I am sure you will be most comfortable."

James found himself standing alone in the upstairs hall, Jasper within the bedroom, putting his things away. With bad grace he finally followed, pulling off his clothes as he moved.

Later the duke sent for James and was told he was sleeping. Word was given to awaken him and have him come to the back parlor as soon as possible.

James awoke with a raging headache and swore continuously at the footman who had been commandeered for the job of gentleman's gentleman—a position at which he was inept—helping James to dress. When he was half dressed, James stood up, pulling the cravat out of the man's hands and stalking out of the room toward the stairwell. He took the stairs two at a time, bounding toward the small parlor, swearing to himself about being treated as a bloody servant at Edward's beck and call.

Still swearing, he opened the door to the small room and started in. "Edward, what the devil do you want?" He was crossing toward his brother when he saw the two men seated with their backs to the door. He stopped in his tracks, suddenly aware of his unshaven stubble of a beard, his open shirt, the cravat in his hand. He looked a bloody mess and he was staring at Lord Carrington and Commander Sir Gerald Everston-Martin.

Carrington looked him up and down with a pitiless eye. "Good grief, James, what on earth have you been doing to yourself?"

James turned toward his brother. "I was not told we had visitors or I would have dressed more properly."

"Do you mean you usually go about the house like that at five in the afternoon? Dear boy," Sir Gerald was saying, "you'll give the army a bad name. Must keep up appearances you know. For the servants and all."

"If you'll excuse me . . ." James bowed slightly. "I shall repair my disarray and join you shortly."

"They'd like to hear about Africa, James," Edward was saying, watching James go.

"Yes. You were with Chelmsford in Zululand last year, weren't you?"

James hesitated by the door. "In January. Yes."

"Ah, well, you must tell us all about Cetywayo and the Twenty-fourth Regiment then."

"Yes," James said through tight lips. "I shall be most happy to." He shot Edward a look as he closed the door. He could hear Carrington as he spoke to Edward: "I say, dear chap, you really must do something about James . . . can't have him falling apart now, can we? Royal house and all."

James stood in the hall, his fists clenched. Cold anger began to replace the hot-tempered response he had felt before, a cold implacable anger that he nursed as he started back for his rooms. For the guest room, he corrected himself, anger twisting tighter within him. Carrington telling him about the royal house and its duties. James's expression hardened as he thought about the Prince of Wales's boon companion. Carrington himself had visited the club last night, had gambled till late and whored until dawn. How dare he talk . . . His father's words spun into his mind . . . *A gentleman may do many things he would not admit in polite company and still remain a gentleman—as long as he behaves like a gentleman, as long as he keeps up appearances* . . . Edward, it seemed, had learned that lesson well . . . For all the good it would do him.

James smiled to himself. Let him think he had won. He would soon find out how wrong he was. Once in the room he rang for help, and waiting for hot water, he began to compose a note, his brain full of it when the footman arrived to do his bidding.

"I need paper and pen and ink," he told the man when he had brought in the hot water. It wasn't until the man had left that James remembered the questions about Africa.

Edward had brought the subject up. Something twisted within James. Edward had said they wanted to talk about Africa.

James stared at his own reflection in the shaving glass, turning over his brother's words one by one.

Downstairs Carrington was eyeing Edward while Sir Gerald held forth on Africa: "It wasn't Cetywayo in the end, you know, it was our own man that caused the worst of it. Wolseley's damnable meddling did the mess up proud."

"I don't see what you mean," Carrington drawled.

"Wasn't he sent down to oversee?" Edward asked the naval commander.

"He oversaw us into worse trouble than before he went. He divided the land into thirteen tribal units. Arbitrarily, I might add. Ones that no tribe ever laid a claim to in the first place. Then he picks a resident who doesn't know his arse from a teakettle; made it all worse, the poor devil."

Carrington yawned. "Sounds a complete cock-up."

"They parted brass rags, I can tell you." Sir Gerald grinned toward Edward. "The brass hats that inherited the mess call it Wolseley's Kilkenny cats, all those chieftains plunging into civil war over land they'd never seen!" Sir Gerald stopped. "You're awfully quiet, Edward."

The duke roused himself. "Sorry . . . isn't there a Paul Kruger mixed up in things down there?"

"In Zululand? You mean the Transvaal and the Boers and all that . . . don't know the name. Why?"

Edward shrugged. "Heard something in Parliament these last months. Pushing for independence or something."

"From us!" Sir Gerald laughed. "Hadn't heard that —some ingrates, after you save their bloody necks to turn on you. Can't say why they'd want to be left alone down there . . . outnumbered, you know."

Carrington yawned again. "Military matters are all so distastefully boring, don't you think?" He earned a look of disapproval from the commander. "Unless one is there, of course."

"Have you ever been on the field of battle, Lord Carrington?" Sir Gerald asked stiffly.

"Lord, don't go all pomp and circumstance on me . . . can't we talk about something else?"

"Reform?" Edward said helpfully, his wry smile almost invisible.

"Good grief! Government will be utterly impossible if they have their way!" Carrington stared at Edward. "How can you speak so casually about it? Do you realize what it really *means?* I say, we shall have intriguing country attorneys, hungry soldiers of fortune, *bankrupts in trade and character* messing up the system. Every kind of street orator and itinerant haranguing the mob would have the franchise! Venal writers for the press would be voting on matters of government and law, every kind of glib talker over the age of twenty-one would have a vote and a say!"

Sir Gerald nodded his head, finally in agreement with something Carrington said. "It's true, you know. It would be the first step toward anarchy and doom. Mark my words."

"I do," Edward said quietly. "I do, indeed."

Carrington caught Edward's tone. "Don't tell me that you of all people are *for* reform!"

"Do you wish us to end as the French did?" Edward asked the two men quietly. "If you'd rather save your necks, you'd better have a care and think about it all again."

"The English people would never run amuck as the French did. We're entirely different stock," Carrington said stoutly. "Agreed, Commander?" He looked over toward the naval officer for support.

But Sir Gerald was staring at Edward. "Different stock, yes. But mobs are not unknown in London, for God's sake . . . one reading of history will tell you that."

"A military man must have the courage to fight for his convictions!" Carrington told Sir Gerald.

Sir Gerald's pale blue eyes focused on the court dandy, the boon companion to the Prince of Wales. "I am not in need of a lesson on duty, my dear sir . . . and as a 'military man,' as you put it, I might add something a *non*military man should consider: going into battle with an enemy is far different than going into battle *against your own people."*

Carrington stood up. "I can see I have fallen in with

subversives and cutthroats." He walked to a carved oak sideboard, reaching for a cameo-glass claret jug. A scene of birds in flight was etched in clear crystal against the ruby glass. "Anyone else?" he asked pleasantly.

"Edward," Sir Gerald was saying, "you've been a recluse for years . . . why this sudden interest in London socializing?"

Edward shrugged, watching Carrington cross to the tall, leaded glass windows that looked out across the back lawns. "My father was ill for many years, I had much to do on our estates. And once he passed away the paperwork became more difficult. Many things happened at once. Now . . . now things are more settled. And James is back; he needs to find his niche in life."

"Yes." Sir Gerald sounded unenthusiastic. "I wonder about the capital, though, for someone of his . . . temperament. He might do better in the country."

Edward shrugged. "He never seemed to wish an active role in the estate's . . . management."

"I daresay," Sir Gerald replied darkly.

Carrington threw himself into his chair again, crossing one elegantly clad leg across the other knee. "I fear you would prescribe the same medicine for me, Commander, had you the opportunity. Two parts fresh country air to every one part of Crockford's night revelry." Carrington looked toward Edward. "From what I hear our Gracious Majesty has had some influence upon your coming to town."

"Really?" Edward smiled. "I wasn't aware Her Majesty confided in her illustrious heir about such minor matters."

"Touché. But there are other sources than dear Bertie."

Edward hesitated. "It is true that there has been some conversation about securing an heir."

"Here, here!" Sir Gerald stood up, reaching for the claret jug.

"He hasn't done the deed yet, Commander." Carrington smiled back at Edward. "Have you, dear chap?"

Edward saw amused knowledge in the other man's eyes. Sir Gerald sat back down, waving his hand toward Carrington. "Of course not; you know what I meant." He saluted Edward with his full glass. "My dear boy, here's to happy hunting in the marriage mart—by Jove, I hear there are good pickings this season. You shall enjoy your stay in London!"

"He may already be enjoying the favors of some young Aphrodite and thus disinterested in the chase, Commander." Lord Carrington smiled at Edward's obvious displeasure.

"Have a care about whom you speak," Edward told the man.

"Oh, ho! Methinks I've hit a nerve!" Carrington grinned.

Edward stood up. "I shall not have Miss Wyndham's name bandied about so!"

"Miss Wyndham's!" Carrington lost his smile, staring at Edward.

"Quite so!" Sir Gerald told Carrington. "Very bad form, my boy. Girl of impeccable family and all . . . not like some light o'love found in the back pantry."

Carrington looked confused. Edward's back was to the room, his eyes focusing on a hummingbird that hovered near a tall row of tulips planted near the library windows. The roofs of Mayfair rose beyond the yellow brick walls that marked the far end of the land behind the town house. Sir Gerald and Carrington were yammering away behind him, Edward's entire concentration on calming himself, on not letting them see his true feelings. On not turning around and hitting each of them squarely in the jaw.

They understood his wrath at Carrington or thought they did. They would be incredulous at the same wrath on behalf of an orphan from Mercy House. She had no right to such delicacy of treatment. He thought of his arrogant comments the day of her arrival, his rebuke about her lack of sensibility. His eyes closed. He could not imagine why she had not left there and then, going back with Sir Thomas and finding employment with some lesser fool.

But of course she could not. She had been prostrated. The men behind him would accuse her of deception. Of entrapment. Of immodesty and lack of morals.

"Come along, Edward. I meant no harm to the lady," Carrington called out to him.

The sound of James's voice turned Edward back to see him as he continued speaking: "What lady, Carrington?

What harm?" James glanced at his brother's sober face as he came forward to join them.

"It seems I put my foot in it, James. About Elizabeth Wyndham." The tone of rebuke, and question, in Carrington's voice did not escape Edward. He stared at his brother, knowing who it had been who had spread tales to Carrington's ears. Carrington confirmed Edward's suspicions a moment later. "Last night at Crockford's, you did not mention Elizabeth."

Edward walked slowly toward the others, speaking before James could reply. "My brother enjoys a strange sense of humor. I fear he was setting you up for a practical joke. I hope you didn't fall for repeating it." Edward reached for the claret. "James?" he offered, watching his brother's eyes harden.

"Joke!" Carrington did not sound amused.

Edward shrugged. "Come along, have another glass." He walked toward Carrington. "James has kept his penchant for fun within the family so far, but now it seems you all had best watch out."

Sir Gerald stood up, shaking his head. "No more for me. I am expected for tea. At Lady Wyndham's by the by."

"For Lord's sake, don't repeat my folly!" Carrington exclaimed, looking over toward James. "I shall not believe a word you tell me, James, I swear it, if you insist on such pranks."

James stared at the glass Edward was now holding out to him. When he took it, he watched the ruby-colored wine fill the small glass. "I assure you I shall not make the same mistake again."

"I should hope not," Carrington said. "In the meantime . . ." He stood up. "I shall be most cautious. My carriage is here, Commander, and I shall be going straight past Wyndham House. Would you care for a lift?" Sir Gerald nodded, the men starting out.

Edward said his good-byes, taking the men as far as the front door. When Jasper closed the door, Edward turned around to find James standing in the library doorway, staring across the hall at him.

Edward walked toward his twin. Jasper had disappeared into the back regions of the house when Edward spoke.

"Keep as much out of my sight as possible, and unless you wish to be on the street, keep far removed from Miss Leggett when she arrives."

"You need have no concern on that head. I shall not go near your whore." James flinched involuntarily as Edward's arm rose toward him. But the blow never came. Edward held his arm where it was and then, slowly, deliberately, relaxed it. Returning it to his side.

"I suggest you re-consider your army commission," Edward told his brother coldly. "We do not suit for living together. Or even near each other, it would seem."

Hatred shone from James's eyes. "You can't force me to leave England."

"No," Edward agreed, "I cannot."

"You owe me."

"I owe you nothing," Edward replied.

"I am your brother! I am your flesh and blood, I have rights to my father's estate!"

Edward moved past his twin. "You have no legal rights to any of it. What you had rights to you had on sufferance. On moral principles."

James watched Edward walk away from him. "You cannot disown me—and my *wife*—because of some . . . some jealousy over a girl you barely know!"

"Nor would I." Edward sat down, reaching for the book he had been reading before Carrington had arrived unannounced.

"Then you admit you owe me at the very least a living."

"No. I do not."

"And what of your much-vaunted moral principles then?"

"You lost all moral right when you sped to London to undermine my position, my title, and our family name."

"It's that cut and dried, is it?" James challenged. "No feelings, no human emotion. Merely cold logic."

"Be grateful for cold logic, it saved your life." Edward spoke with a ferocity that took James visibly back. He stared at his brother, at the coal-black eyes that seared soul-deep. Fear began to edge into James's consciousness.

"I don't know what you mean." James sounded unconvincing to his own ears.

"I *mean* that I should have killed you when you murdered my wife and my child." Edward started to rise from his chair, James backing away from him into the hall.

"You're crazy!"

"Or when you tried to poison me when we were children. Do you remember, James? Do you think I did not *know?* The single reason you are alive is that father spirited you away to the army before I returned. He knew, as did I, what really happened."

"You lie!"

"As you know what really happened," Edward told his twin, his voice relentless. James pulled farther back and then turned away. Edward watched him until he was out of sight. Then the morass of pain deep within him sucked him downward. He slumped into the chair, fighting to push back the raw pain that threatened to engulf him. He could feel control slipping away, could feel the downward spiraling anguish that pulled him toward black pain. And anger that knew no release.

The loss of his mother, of the wife he had barely known, and the child who had not yet been born, the threat of the loss of his reputation, the reality of the loss of one whom he had barely come close to . . . his mother gone before he was old enough to fight his way back to her. His wife and child gone before he knew what had happened. He opened his eyes, staring grimly ahead. No more. He would stand for no more. He would do whatever was necessary to protect his reputation. He would never again open himself up to pain. To loss. To love.

The pain was too sharp, the price too high.

Monday would bring the greatest challenge. If he could get through Monday he would get through the week. And once through the week he would be able to map out a safe course for the future.

Life would not allow him to love but it could not take away his pride.

He stared down at the book he had been reading. Very carefully he closed it. Pride was a very cold companion.

Chapter 19

M ONDAY MORNING MICHAEL ARRIVED with Victoria and Nancy in tow, so early that they had their breakfast at Bereshaven House after they arrived.

Victoria was shown to the family dining room, the others eating in the kitchen. Her pleas to just have a bite with them was met with stern disapproval and the reminder that the duke would not hear of it.

And so Victoria was staring down at eggs and deviled kidneys when Sylvia walked into the room.

"Victoria!" Sylvia smiled in surprise. "I mean, Miss Leggett it's good to see you."

"Please—please, call me Victoria. I should so much prefer it," Victoria told the duke's sister-in-law over crumpets oozing with melting butter. The smell of sizzling bacon filled the room, a maid bringing in a platter from the kitchen.

Sylvia sat down beside Victoria, letting the maid fill her plate. She saw dark circles under Victoria's eyes and a pallor that had not been present last week. "Victoria then," Sylvia replied when the maid had left. "He has averted the worst. So far." Sylvia spoke quietly, watching for the others as she quietly tried to lighten the burden Victoria obviously felt.

She was rewarded with a look of gratitude, Victoria smiling faintly when she looked up. "Thank you for telling me."

"Has he said anything to you? As to the future?"

Victoria lowered her eyes. "I have not spoken with him since the day you left."

"I see," Sylvia said slowly. "My dear child, I wonder if it is best for you to continue on here."

"Oh, please!" Victoria pleaded now, her eyes bright with fear. "Please do not suggest that I leave."

"I think only of you. Of your, I can't say happiness, but at least . . . serenity, perhaps. This cannot be easy for you." Sylvia saw the misery in the other woman's eyes and her heart went out to her. She reached to cover Victoria's hand with her own. "No one knows better than I what you must be going through, what you must be feeling. That is why I dare to mention it. For your sake. Not his. Or anyone else's."

They heard footsteps nearing them, Judith appearing in the doorway and stopping short. She stared at Victoria, who averted her eyes. Judith looked from Victoria to Sylvia. Finally she walked forward, seating herself as far from Victoria as possible. When she began to speak, she ignored the girl, addressing herself to Sylvia as if they were alone in the room.

Escaping as soon as she could, Victoria went in search of Nancy to find where her things had been taken. Fairly dancing with excitement, Nancy talked the whole way up the stairs of the plans for the ball. *"Every*one will be here; did you know the royal family is to put in an appearance? The Prince of Wales and his wife are to come and Lord Carrington and the Duchess of Athole and Jersey and just, oh, everyone you have ever heard of!" They headed down the upstairs hall, Nancy casting a sideways glance toward the silent Victoria. "Are you feeling all right, miss?"

Victoria nodded, not trusting her voice. Nancy's enthusiasm was dampened by the expression in Victoria's eyes. She opened the door to the room that had been chosen for Victoria. "They said as how your things were to—oh!" She stopped in midsentence. The duke stood across the room, near the windows, his hands behind his back as if he had been standing there for a long time. He turned toward the door as it opened, staring at Victoria as Nancy quietly withdrew.

When she was gone, there was silence in the room. He

pulled his eyes away from Victoria, glancing around the room, his voice calm and cool when he spoke. "I trust this room will prove satisfactory."

Victoria nodded, barely seeing it. "I am sure it will." She choked over her words, her throat filling. She cleared her throat, seeing him look quickly toward her.

"Are you coming down with something?"

"No! No, I—it's just . . . I'm fine, your grace."

His gaze flickered at hearing his title. He said nothing. Finally he came toward the door. And Victoria. "Good. When you are settled in, I would like to see you in the library to discuss your work."

She swallowed. "I shall be there directly."

He hesitated, looking around the room, memorizing its dimensions, its furnishings. When he pictured her at night, he would know what the room looked like, how if she turned her head on her pillow she could see the plane trees that lined the far yellow brick wall. "I shall expect you then," he told her as he left.

The door closed. She stared at it. Her whole life had become a series of closing doors, it seemed to her at that moment. Each of them, all of them, closed away behind separate doors. Unable to truly come close. To know each other. She reached into the oak wardrobe, pulling out her best black dress, changing out of her traveling costume. Freshening herself before she went back downstairs.

She entered the library to find Mike there, grinning up at her and leaving as she walked forward. The duke's eyes held no smile. He seemed to be gauging her, studying her face intently. "Are you sure you are quite well?" he asked her again, as he had in her bedroom.

"Yes," she said faintly. "I am quite well, your grace."

He nodded. "Sit down, please . . ." He watched her as she sat. "There are certain things I must tell you and then I shall consider the subject closed." His eyes searched hers. "Do you understand?"

"I am not sure," she told him, looking into the eyes that had devoured her body, had looked at her with such need, such longing. All she could see at this moment was a guarded wall behind which he had locked away all else.

"Let me explain," he was saying. "The . . . events that transpired last week—the unfortunate events—have been to some degree righted." He watched her. "That is to say that I believe I have averted any damage to your reputation. Or mine."

She swallowed, ducking her head. "I see."

"Yes. Well, there may still be whispers but they shall soon subside." He took a deep breath. "I will be speaking to Lady Wyndham this week and—"

"Your grace, that's none of my concern!" Victoria interrupted him, her hands twisting the lace handkerchief she held within them.

"Please allow me to continue," he said quietly, watching her eyes. He could see her pain. It stabbed at his heart. "I shall in all likelihood be announcing my engagement to Miss Wyndham immediately after the ball." He went relentlessly on: "I have also decided to discontinue work on the revision of my father's manuscript." A look of comprehension came into her eyes. He stared at it. "Yes?" he asked her.

She stared at him. "I see. I wondered at the time."

He stared back at her. "I beg your pardon? You wondered what at what time?"

"It was just that you had said nothing about discontinuing work on the manuscript, so I was confused about why you had taken it with you."

"Taken it where?"

"When you left. When I found it gone, I wasn't sure what you wanted me to do. If anything. So I began to annotate the speeches you were working on—Gladstone's and Disraeli's and the others."

He was watching her closely. "Are you telling me you do not have the manuscript with you?"

She stared at him, her eyes widening, her voice faint. "Why no . . . didn't you take it when you left?"

"No."

They stared at each other, each confused, each worried, Victoria concerned about who had taken it and why, Edward only too sure of who *would* have taken it and why. "When did you notice it gone?"

"When I went to begin work the morning after you left."

"And you said nothing?"

"To whom?"

He hesitated. "Yes, of course. And so you worked on the speeches." He let out a long breath, his eyes falling to a small pile of letters upon his desk. "In any event work will stop on it."

"Yes, your grace."

"You do not ask why," he told her.

"I assume you have other things to occupy your time at this . . . juncture." She fought to keep her voice steady.

"Victoria—" He leaned forward across the desk, her name wrenched out of him. "I am fighting for our *lives,* for our reputations *are* our lives. Do you understand that? Anything, *any*thing that endangers one endangers the other. The Queen was told tales of radical politics and libertine behavior. There must be no proof of either or I'll not be able to protect you. Do you understand?"

"Why would the Queen care about me?"

"Because I am her cousin. Because she has a sixth sense about people and she distrusts what I tell her. She is aware of my Irish blood and my father's indiscretion, and she has heard stories about me and a young woman in my employ."

"But how—so soon, I mean—"

"The court is a very small circle. When one has access to that circle and wishes to cause trouble, a rumor given to one, an innuendo passed on to another . . . and human nature does the rest."

Victoria stared at the man who leaned toward her, his eyes full of concern now, his mask slipping from place. She wanted to reach out, to touch his hand, to make contact. She was afraid to move. When she spoke, her voice was a whisper: "I do not care what any say about us."

He looked down. And then pulled back, straightening up. "Then I must." He spoke coldly, pain filling his chest at the look in her eyes. "If you do not care what is said, if I cannot rely upon your discretion, then I must make other arrangements for you."

She could not control her voice enough to answer immediately. She took a great deal of time, Edward watching her in silence, before she could reply. "And if you can rely upon my . . . discretion?"

His voice dropped, his own words almost inaudible. "Then I can keep you near."

Her eyes flew to his. "I don't understand!"

"Then listen to me: I shall begin work on a history of Parliament." He began to speak faster, the whole plan he had been conceiving tumbling out toward her. "I shall need a great deal of help with my research. And I shall need you to accompany me when Parliament is in session, to take notes and to transcribe my remarks as well as others I shall have you pay particular attention to—we shall work on this history exactly as I have outlined. And publish it. And meanwhile we shall continue to work on the Irish history —not immediately, but soon, and we shall not publish it . . . at least as long as I am alive . . . but it shall be finished."

Her eyes met his. "Do you know where it is?"

"I think I know who has it."

"Is there harm that can come from it?"

He almost laughed. "Only downfall and ruin . . . you see, alone, I could have gone forward and been named an eccentric after it was out and people had news of it. But now, with the Queen having heard of it in advance, I cannot publish it without deliberately disobeying her, without being thought at the least disloyal. At worst traitorous."

"Edward . . . I mean, forgive me, your—"

"Don't say it!" He realized how loud he spoke, stopping to listen for footsteps. For people too near. He was more cautious when next he spoke. "Not when we're alone."

She shook her head. "How can I not? You are saying I can only stay near you if we have nothing to do with each other. How can I do that unless I erect barriers?"

"It would be easier if I sent you away."

Her voice was small. "Yes."

"And it will destroy me when I have to."

"Yes . . ." She lost herself within his eyes, feeling the pain and the desire she found there, their eyes telling of the memory of touch and tongue.

A knock at the door dragged them apart, Edward speaking softly as the door opened. "This won't work."

Michael came toward them. "I have some news." He did not continue.

Edward nodded, looking at Victoria again, his eyes opaque. "I shall try to determine the whereabouts of the material. In the meantime you might like to set up a worktable in the blue parlor. Jasper will show you which one it is. I mentioned to him we would have to make some changes. He is awaiting instructions."

She stood up, her head bent forward as she left the room. Michael watched the duke's eyes follow her. When Edward looked back, he saw Michael watching him. "The Irish manuscript is missing. Has been since James left."

Michael's eyes clouded. "I don't like this a bit. It's too dangerous by half the way things have come about. I want to tell Ryan that it will have to wait."

"He said it could not."

Michael looked determined. "It will have to. You'll do them no good in the Tower!"

"I doubt the Queen would go to that extreme."

"Do you? And what of the book, then? What if it's put in the wrong hands?"

Edward stared at the Irishman. "There is nothing I can do about the manuscript until it turns up. We shall have to face whatever that brings when it happens. As to the other, the message I received said there is important information that I should have and it must be given in person." He paused. "You don't suppose they could somehow know something about the book, do you? I mean, about its whereabouts?"

"I can't see how. But then again I can't be telling you what I don't know. What I *do* know is that I don't like your meeting with them here."

"You set it up."

"Not here! At The Willows is one thing, here is another."

"Yes. Well, thanks to James, we are here and here we shall have to stay for the time being . . ." He stared down at one of the letters on his desk, picking it up and staring at the envelope that held it, making his decision. "Tell Ryan to pick a place I can meet him tomorrow night. There is a supper I am to attend. Our meeting will have to be late."

Michael started to demur and then thought better of it, seeing the determination in the duke's gaze. He shrugged with rather bad grace and turned around. "If you won't be listening to my advice, I shall have to be looking out for you more carefully. For sure as you're sitting there, there's going to be trouble."

"There seems to be plenty of that no matter what I do. Or don't do, Michael. There seems no help for it."

"Aye . . ." Michael hesitated. "And the lass?" He watched the duke's expression change, the planes of his face sharpening. Hardening.

"Yes?" His tone was like ice.

"Is she to stay or to go?"

"Stay. For the moment. Why?"

Michael shook his head. "You always were one for playing with fire . . ."

The duke watched the man leave, feeling the doubts the other man was suffused with, feeling the worry that colored Michael's thoughts.

"Are you saying I'm a fool?" the duke asked. But his man was already gone and did not hear. The duke looked back down at the correspondence on his desk. He needed no answer to the question, he knew the answer well enough himself.

Chapter 20

DELICACIES OF ALL KINDS were spread out on the tables that lined one wall of the Everston-Martins' huge front parlor. Sweets and savories filled with meats, puddings and pastries, fruit ices and cakes plain.

The sound of chamber music came from the end of the room, a piano and a violin listened to raptly by most of the assembled guests. Here and there an older guest, dressed in dinner clothes and boredom, stifled a yawn. Behind one or two of the low-backed settees a young gentleman in full dress black leaned a bit closer to the bare shoulders of a young beauty who seemed not to notice.

The music ended, a brief smattering of applause greeting the two gentlemen who now stood bowing to the group, others drifting off toward the food, the hum of conversation growing louder by the minute.

A frail-looking old man peered up at the dark-haired giant beside him near the punch bowl. "Well, bless my soul, is that Edward finally coming among us, or are you James, back from the wars, I hear, heh?"

Edward smiled. "It is Edward, Colonel. You are looking well."

"Well? Well, is it? When one is eighty-five, merely to look *alive* is a blessing, heh?"

"Yes sir, you're quite right."

"Don't patronize me, young Bereshaven, I'm still all that I was."

205

"I wouldn't dream of it, Colonel." Edward spoke quietly.

"Or at least all that I was since you were born. In my youth I could outshoot, outhunt, and outdance any of you. Can't say that anymore. At least about the dancing."

"Edward!" Lady Wyndham bore down upon them. *"There* you are, you naughty boy—come along. You were late and Elizabeth is pining away to have a look at you."

Edward put his punch glass down. "If you'll excuse me," he said to the colonel.

The old man shrugged, turning toward the punch bowl. "Duty calls," he told the young duke as he dismissed him, addressing himself to the food.

Edward walked across the large bright room, lit with hundreds of tapers, their warmth making the room close. Edward took a deep breath, feeling suffocated in the midst of all the noise and people.

"You have been missed, dear Edward, all these years. Why, I can't remember the last time you were at a London fête. Can you?"

"Only too well," he replied, earning a sidelong glance from Elizabeth's mother.

"I admire a sensible man. It seems many of the younger men have become such, how do they call them? Party animals, isn't that the new way? Yes, it is and I think it less than the best form. A little too self-indulgent, don't you think? But how would you know, you have nothing to do with that crowd, now do you? I must say I am rather glad you've stayed away while Elizabeth was growing up. This is her first year, you know, and I should have been devastated if you had already been married and unable to call upon my darling child. You two will find you are made for each other, mark my words."

"I was married." Edward spoke with no inflection.

"Yes, of course . . . such a loss . . ." She brightened then. "But it was a very long time ago."

"Ten years next month."

She was at a loss for a moment. "Imagine," she finally continued, "Elizabeth was only nine years old . . . ten years ago. That was when we lost sight of you, my dear boy. And not only you! Your charming brother went off to war . . . you must have been quite devastated."

"I was," he replied shortly. Victoria would have been what that year, thirteen . . . and he had been twenty-five. Turning twenty-six. The gulf between them stretched out even further.

Edward heard Margaret Wyndham calling out greetings to those they passed as they entered the hall and walked toward a large terrace, the doors thrown open to the spring night. "It's a tad chilly out here, don't you think?" she asked him.

"It's delightful," he told her, drinking in the cool air.

She shook her head, smiling, glancing about at the few couples who were standing to the edges of the semicircular terrace. "You and Elizabeth . . . she is a positive fiend for fresh air! Now, where is the girl? She had come to get away from the noise, she told me, and I told her to wait right here."

"Perhaps she took a turn in the gardens?" He looked off toward the grounds, disinterested.

"Alone! She would not do so. If you'll excuse me, Edward, I'll just look in the cloak room. She may have felt the cold, after all, and gone for her wrap." He nodded and she turned away, turning back a moment later to smile at him brightly: "Now, don't you disappear. I shall expect you to be precisely here when I return."

He attempted a faint smile. "I shall look about the lower level for a moment and then return." He pointed off to where shallow steps led down to a graveled semicircle on the edge of the terrace. Tall hedges threw shadows across it, a couple walking toward the steps from beneath the shadows.

"She must be inside," her mother decided, and went in search as Edward started for the steps and the freedom of the dark walkway below.

Music was again being played inside, the sounds drifting out across the lawns, the moon a pale, dim sliver. Rosebushes and hedges crowded near the graveled path, the sounds of conversation floating over the terrace's stone railing. Edward caught a word here and there, a whispered plea for a meeting, a hint of a seduction already accomplished behind the anguished words of a female voice, another younger female playing the coquette a few steps beyond where he walked.

The path was empty. He rounded the far edge of the terrace and turned to start back, feeling better for the air and the exercise. He walked in the shadows of the tall hedges, relishing the quiet moments in which he did not have to find polite conversation.

"Do say you will." James voice came from behind the hedge, stopping Edward in midstride.

A giggle met the words and then James whispered something inaudible. "James, you go too far!" Elizabeth's husky voice spoke out softly.

"Too far or too soon?"

"You must let go of me this instant. I must find Mama."

"If she sees us, she'll think it's Edward and be quite content. After all you are to marry a duke, my dear. Certain dispensations are made in such cases."

She giggled again. "For his brothers?"

"Only one . . ."

The sound of a kiss, of her dress crushing against the front of James's dinner jacket came through the bushes. Edward looked up toward the terrace to see Margaret at the edge, peering over the side in the other direction. "Elizabeth?" Margaret's voice came out into the night. "Elizabeth, where are you?"

A whispered exclamation came from behind the bushes. The sound of feet rustling in the grass and leaves. "Come along!" Elizabeth whispered. "And brazen this out!" They moved quickly now, rounding the hedge six feet ahead of where Edward still stood in the shadows. "Mother?" Elizabeth called gaily, her mother turning at the sound of her voice, her expression changing when she saw the man beside her daughter.

"I see you found each other," Margaret Wyndham was saying, staring down at the couple intently.

"Of course," Elizabeth replied. "But we do so want a few moments alone. To talk. Must we go in already?"

Margaret Wyndham watched her daughter, her eyes moving after a moment to the man beside her. "Well . . . if Edward agrees to see you safely inside. In a very *few* minutes."

"I do, my dear Margaret." James smiled up at her.

Margaret hesitated. And finally smiled down at them.

208

"You are certainly different around my daughter. I told you that just yesterday and it is the absolute truth, Edward. You positively glow. I swear it's love."

"Mother . . ." Elizabeth began to move down the path, away from Edward, Margaret watching the couple move off before slowly turning back toward the interior of the house.

Edward stood where he was, watching the couple walk to the end and then move across a narrower path, following it around the bushes again. He hesitated. And then turned away, cutting across the lawns toward a narrow side door that led to the mews that marked the end of the property. He opened the door in the tall stone wall and cautiously glanced about.

A horse and carriage was pulling around the corner at the far end, the cobbled mews silent in the night but for the faint sounds that came from the house.

Edward walked quickly toward the far street, not stopping for his own carriage with its crest emblazoned upon the doors. He struck out across the square and waved down a hackney carriage, pulling himself quickly up and in. "The Three Trees," Edward told the driver. "How long will it take?"

The driver leaned down to glance at the dark interior of his carriage, seeing only a man in shadows. "About ten minutes, guv'nor."

"An extra shilling for each minute you shave off that."

The man grinned toothlessly. "How's about a quid instead and I get you there in five?"

Edward smiled in the darkness, unseen. "A quid if in five."

The hired carriage sped east, leaving the posh houses and wide avenues behind. Traffic became crowded as the driver urged his horse past slower-moving vehicles once they left Oxford Street and wound around into Soho Square. The quiet of the square was somehow sad. Shabby gentility surrounded the carriage until the quiet gave way to the sounds of revelry, a group of men coming out of a pot house the better for their wine and meat.

"Drop me here," Edward told the driver, reaching for his money. He handed the driver his quid, the man grinning.

"Need me again, don't you, guv'nor? You won't be the type to stay about here long, now will you?" The man leered at Edward.

Edward hesitated. "If you're here in twenty minutes, there'll be another quid in it for you."

The driver beamed toothlessly. "Right you are, guv'nor. I won't move from the spot!" He threw the reins over the brake and sat back to watch the tall man in the expensive clothes head toward a small public house down a bit on Carlisle Street across the Square. He would give the nag some oats and dream of his newfound riches while the gent sullied his new clothes against whatever bohemian pleasure he was seeking out.

Twenty minutes. The driver shook his head, removing his cap to scratch his head. He didn't believe in dallying long with them, that's for sure. Probably had to get back to the posh party in the West End before his wife caught him out.

Edward walked into the dingy little building, passing the bar as he had been directed. A low passage dipped down into a back room about twelve feet wide by fifteen feet long, the ceiling low, the only ornament a steel engraving of the Duke of Wellington on horseback. Tobacco smoke filled the air around the plain wood tables, dandies in heavy scarfs and pins near where Edward stood, speaking French to each other. Others, more English looking, sat here and there, their clothes showing wear, their faces closed and sullen.

The small man that had come to see Michael at The Willows stood up across the room when he saw the duke. Edward caught his eye and moved forward.

"Good evening, your—" Edward's upraised hand stopped the man, who nodded and sat back down. "You're right," he said as Edward took the bench across from him. "Tim Ryan at your service." The man leaned across the table, the smell of beer and gin about his breath. "We'd best look natural like." Tim Ryan reached for a bell behind a narrow door and the pot boy came out from a dingy room to eye the two men balefully. His cheeks were red with the heat of the kitchen, where chicken was being cooked, by the smell. "Quarter fowl for ninepence, three for a bottle of

Marsala and olives." The boy spoke and the smells of macaroni and oils accosted Edward's nostrils.

"Just two pints and be about it, me customer don't want waiting on the likes of you!" Tim told the boy, who gave Edward a malevolent glance and turned back toward the kitchen.

When the boy had gone, Tim leaned closer. "He's to leave within the week. But Mike says as how he's not to come to you here in London."

Edward hesitated. "The message spoke of urgency. Why?"

Tim Ryan shrugged. "It's not for me to be asking Charles Stewart Parnell what he's about. He's an angel from heaven is all I know or care to, the hope of Ireland and that's a fact." Tim studied the man across from him. "I don't suppose you'd be knowing him."

"We've met, in chambers, once or twice. Not to speak of."

Tim nodded. "Aye, I've been to visitors' gallery and seen the great men in Parliament flying at each other's throats—"

"That's Commons," Edward said carelessly.

Tim stared at the duke. "And it's different, is it, where you sit?"

Edward stared back, watching the sharp blue eyes that followed his every word. "If he is to leave within the week, he will have to postpone his departure. I cannot leave London before at least the next fortnight."

Tim Ryan shook his head. "He's not leaving because he wants. He's leaving because he's *asked*. Something's afoot, some troublemakers whispering in the Queen's ear about us heathens across the channel. There's no waiting a fortnight."

Edward hesitated, and then spoke quickly, the boy heading toward them with their ale. "I have a plan. Tell him if it's truly urgent, I shall expect him."

"When?"

The boy arrived, shoving the mugs of ale toward them, standing and waiting for the coin to be put in his hand before he left.

* * *

Outside the hackney driver was just settling himself down for a short nap when he heard the gentleman's boots striking hard against the pavement, coming nearer. He straightened up, opening the door for the gent. "Quicker than you thought, guv'nor. Wasn't all she was cracked up to be, aye? It happens." The driver was climbing to his post. "If you want, I know of others, some right pretty even."

"No."

The driver waited, and when the toff said no more, he turned his attention on his horse, starting out toward Mayfair. "You want as quick as we come, guv?"

"There's no need." Edward sat far back on the bench, thinking about what he was doing. And of Ryan's words as he left. Be careful of that brother, your—be careful. He's with Charley Carrington and that lot, fell right in amongst 'em and he talks too much.

"There's no way of stopping him I'm afraid," Edward had replied, off guard in the strange circumstances, the night seeming more dream than reality.

"Oh, there's ways . . . bring up his soldiering and he'll quiet down a bit."

Edward had stared at the man. Hard. "That was said once before. What are you referring to?"

Tim Ryan looked surprised. "You didn't know? He was booted a year ago. Some trouble over money and some foreign woman . . . he's been cashiered and that's something his friend from the Queen's household brigade wouldn't be fast to cotton to, as me wife would say."

Edward had stared hard at the Irishman. "How do you know this?"

"I have a mate who was with him in Zululand. Before he got booted."

"And now you're sent as messenger to his brother."

"That's not happenstance, your grace. I was chosen for this because I knew what he looked like, my mate told me, so I'd know you were you when we met."

Edward almost smiled. "And in case I was of the same caliber as my brother?"

Tim Ryan did not speak right away, and when he did, his tone was cautious. "There's talk your family hasn't been on our side. But your mother's people are amongst those who've suffered the most. And helped the most where they could." Tim hesitated. "And then Mike's my first cousin and he says you're cut of a finer cloth than your brother and the rest."

They had reached the bar, had pushed through the men along it to reach the door to the narrow street. Edward thought about what the man had told him. "You set store by what Mike says."

"I do. Great store. As do all who know him," Tim said stoutly.

The duke nodded. "As do I."

As the streets became wider, the traffic lighter in this late evening hour, Edward stared straight ahead, his thoughts upon his brother. And the future.

The brightly lit Mayfair mansion came into view across the wide green of the square. Edward told the driver to stop and stepped down in the shade of the plane trees that lined the square. A tall stone statue of an ancient prince stood sentinel in the middle of the green, paths leading across from it to the other side of the square. Across the street hundreds of candles still burned within the tall narrow windows of the gray stone house, carriages still lined up and waiting for their owners.

Edward walked toward where his own driver waited, coming out of the shadows behind the carriage and taking the driver unawares. "Home, Harry . . ."

Harry straightened up, bobbing his cap toward his lordship and reaching to open the door for him. Hopping onto his perch, he pulled the carriage out of the waiting line and headed west as the hackney trotted slowly away in the opposite direction, a damp fog rolling in between them as they moved.

At Bereshaven House Mike sat dozing in a chair by the fire in Edward's bedroom, his legs stretched out toward the dying fire. A cold draft hit him, Edward throwing off his coat as he walked in, stopping when he saw Mike opening his eyes.

"You needn't have waited up for me."

"And what else would I be doing? Sure and you think I'd go happily off to the land of Nod with you still out God knows where?" Edward was pulling at his cravat, loosening his coats and shirt. "Well?" Mike asked, standing up to look him over carefully. "And how did it go? When's it to be . . . or is it?"

"It's to be here, this week's end."

"The saints preserve us, you've gone daft! *Here!* It's asking for trouble and well you know it! What are you thinking of?"

"My mother." Edward's words came out softly, Mike straining to hear him. Mike stopped himself from replying, staring at the boy who'd grown up in his charge into the man who faced him now: dark, distant, and even dangerous, given the right circumstances. He remembered holding Edward back, using all his strength to pin him down after Martha's accident. Pulling him away from the bloodied bed where the child had tried to be born, holding him down when his father's words came toward them: *James is gone and that's the end of it.*

It hadn't been the end of it. Any more than never mentioning her name had been the end of Siobhan. But the old duke would brook no argument. Then or ever.

"What are you staring at?" Edward was asking the man who had raised him.

Mike took a moment to answer: "Why are you doing this?"

"I'm not sure."

"You have to be sure. Listen to me, you *must* know exactly why, for it's too dangerous to do for naught. Especially with all else that's happened and your brother prattling on about you at court."

Edward thought about what Mike did not yet know. "The Irish manuscript is unknown to Tim Ryan . . . nor has he heard anything other than my brother's claims to be able to prove I am a traitor and should no longer be duke."

Mike groaned. "Isn't that enough for you?"

Edward sat down to pull off his boots, Mike coming near to help. "James has it. He must. He's the only one who would take it."

"And the girl . . ." Mike replied.

"I trust her."

"Oh, you do, do you? She came into the household out of the blue, with pretty strange timing if you ask me."

Edward stared down at Mike's head as he pulled the last boot off. "Do you say you distrust her?"

Mike straightened up. "I'm not saying I do not trust her. But as sure as I'm standing here, if he's got it, it will cause you grief before long and you'll know why." Mike shook his head. "Edward, you can't do this now. There's too much at risk and too little to be gained. Just because Parnell wants to meet doesn't mean you have to. He can write, you can meet later—something, anything other than this!"

"I've given that very message. That if it can be done later, or by hand, to do so. The decision is up to him. If he feels it important enough, he will come the night of the ball." He watched Mike's eyes widen. He smiled back. "What better cover than all of London being in the house?"

Michael shook his head again. Before he left, he spoke again. "I hope I've not been the cause of bringing you grief by bringing their messages."

"We do what we must."

"I still don't understand why you are doing this. Risking this."

Edward flung himself into the chair that Michael had dozed in, staring moodily into the flames before him. "I wish I could tell you."

Mike watched the side of Edward's face, speaking slowly. "Perhaps it's for the same reasons as my own."

Edward glanced toward him. "Which are?"

"I think of your mother and what happened to her."

Edward still looked into Mike's round and reddened face. Slowly he nodded his head. "Yes," he said, his voice low, "I think you are right."

"She would never want you hurt."

Edward turned back toward the fire. "We do not always get what we want." He heard something outside. "See if that is James."

Michael did as he was bid, coming back a moment later. "It is. Do you want to speak to him?"

"No." Edward stared back at the fire. "Good night."

Mike Flaherty stared at the lonely man across the room. If he was hurt by all this Irish politics, there would be no one to blame in the end but Mike Flaherty, he told himself. When he left, Edward was still staring moodily into the fire.

Chapter 21

THE NEXT MORNING VICTORIA found Sylvia on a far bench in the garden, a pile of material at her side, a thimble and threads in her lap. She looked up at Victoria's approach, her pale blond hair as white as wheat in the sunshine. Victoria shaded her eyes with her hand, stopping in front of the bench.

"You look quite serious," Sylvia told the younger woman.

Not knowing how to begin, Victoria sank to the bench beside the duke's sister-in-law, choosing her words with care. "May I ask you something quite . . . personal?"

Sylvia's smooth forehead puckered. She watched Victoria with care. "Why do you ask?"

"There is something that concerns the duke."

"Yes?" Sylvia put her sewing down, waiting.

"My question is"—Victoria searched the other woman's face as she spoke, trying to find some hint of her loyalties —"if you knew that something existed . . . something harmful to the duke. Or something that could be harmful to him . . . and you knew it had fallen into his enemy's hands, would you try to help him?"

"Of course. What do you take me for?" Sylvia stared at her. "He has been nothing but good to me, he has supported me for years, he has—" Her eyes narrowed. "What are you speaking of?"

"If . . . the enemy were to be his own . . . your husband?"

217

Sylvia's eyes widened. "What do you know? What has happened? Tell me quickly."

Victoria shook her head. "I cannot tell you what I do not know. But there is something missing. Something that could be harmful to the duke's position with the Queen."

"And James has it? What is it?"

Victoria looked down, her eyes on the brown earth beneath the bench. "I do not know if he has it. But I can imagine no other who would have taken it—who had the opportunity to take it. It is the manuscript the duke has been working on."

Puzzled eyes watched Victoria. "His father's manuscript? Why would that harm Edward . . . or anyone?"

"He has been researching many happenings that led to the Irish troubles . . . and the famine which forced him, them, from Ireland."

"I do not understand. Who would care about a history of times gone by? Why would that be harmful to Edward? Why would he be working on something harmful to himself?"

"Whether you understand or not, if I tell you that he feels it dangerous for it to be in the wrong hands, can you, could you, help me to find it?"

Sylvia reached for her sewing, carefully folding it, carefully weighing her words. "You ask me to search my husband's things?"

"I ask you to . . . help find something of the duke's that is . . . misplaced."

"I see. And if it is not James who has it, what then?"

Victoria's troubled face was answer enough. Sylvia reached for the bag that held the rest of her sewing, putting her things away.

"Will you help?" Victoria asked again, watching as the other woman stood up.

Sylvia stared down at the girl. "When did you—or whomever—find it gone?"

"The morning after you left The Willows."

"And you are just asking now! It could be anywhere by now. Why did you wait?"

Victoria's misery was in her voice. "I thought the duke himself had taken it with him. I did not know until my arrival here that he had not. That it was missing."

"You realize if James did take it, he would hardly have brought it here."

"Where else?" Victoria stared up into the other woman's eyes, pleading for help.

Sylvia spoke slowly. "I would venture to say the obvious place would be his club. Or wherever he spends his days. And nights." Sylvia started up the walk toward the rear of the house. "I shall look." The words came back toward Victoria. "But I would not hold out much hope of success if I were you."

The sounds of traffic in the square beyond the high yellow brick walls came toward Victoria from the distance, her eyes on a tiny bird who fluttered near the flower bed. The sun's rays were warming the garden, the scent of lilies and roses filling the yard.

Judith walked very close before Victoria heard her steps and looked up to see the tall, thin woman, "Are you employed to sit daydreaming in the gardens?"

Her dislike soured her expression. She watched Victoria spring to her feet. "No, your ladyship, I am not. If you'll excuse me . . ." Victoria sped past the duke's austere aunt, the woman watching her go. When she was alone, Judith surveyed the grounds about her, walking along the path among the rosebushes, her thoughts kept to herself.

Upstairs Sylvia put her sewing away, turning toward the hall and stopping Nancy as she walked toward the duke's rooms. "Is my husband up yet?"

Nancy looked startled. "Oh, your ladyship . . . I, I didn't know he was in."

"I see. Thank you." Sylvia waited until the maid closed the door to the duke's rooms before walking across the hall to the room James had been given. It was dark inside, the curtains and drapes still drawn shut against the daylight. Sylvia crossed to the windows.

The room brightened as the drapes were slowly opened. She went to the other window, repeating the procedure until the sun streamed into all four corners of the room. Then she turned to survey the scene around her, moving first to a desk against the wall.

She opened drawers and closed them, moved on to a

small bedside table and its one drawer. On impulse she reached to feel under the pillows and then under the mattress, to no avail. The door to the hall was still open, Sylvia straightening up quickly when Nancy crossed outside, glancing in, curious.

Sylvia moved to the door, gently latching it and then looking toward the tall, carved walnut wardrobe. She opened one side, riffling through the shelves and drawers, pushing underclothing and socks out of the way, finding a military bag and opening it, feeling inside. Empty.

She reached for the other wardrobe door, opening it and seeing James at the same moment. He stared at her from his hiding place, seeing her eyes widen as he came at her, his hand over her mouth before she could scream. "Don't be a silly twit, my love . . . come along." He dragged her toward the bed. "It's been a long while since you willingly came into my bedchambers. It must be an important mission."

She struggled against him, fighting as he forced her down onto the bed, his body pinning her down. The look she saw in his eyes as he hovered above her, his hand still over her mouth, stopped her struggles. She could feel his enjoyment. She went limp, her eyes dulling over.

"Now . . ." He spoke very quietly. "Suppose you tell me what you were after, my dearest wife. Just what has brought you to me?"

He released his hand from her mouth.

"Let me up," she said quickly.

"Not quite so fast, dearest Sylvia. First you shall tell me what I ask."

"I'll scream."

"Now? And make yourself look silly? Why should a woman scream to be on her husband's bed? And which of the maids shall rescue you? Speak quickly or I may find myself forcing my attentions upon you. Surely you can feel my . . . growing affection?"

She gasped as he let his weight fall against her legs. "Let me up!"

"What were you looking for?"

"You know what I was looking for!"

He hesitated. "Do I?" He pressed himself against her, feeling her body stiffen against his touch. "Do I?"

"Not that!"

"No? I thought not. You can imagine my surprise when you opened the door to my room. I thought I was dreaming. And when you walked to the window instead of to my bed, I was, of course, devastated." As he spoke he thrust himself harder against her legs, her belly, relaxing a bit and then pushing forward again. "When you went to open yet a second set of drapes, I felt I should give you the opportunity to do whatever you wished in privacy. I must admit my curiosity knew no bounds."

"And so you hid in the wardrobe." She spoke contemptuously.

"Rather silly position to be found in, I admit. But not as silly as a thief."

"Thief!"

He smiled at her. "Isn't that what this was all about?" His grip on her arms grew harsher. "What were you searching for, my sweet?"

"The manuscript, and you know it! They know you have it. It will do you no good."

He straightened up, staring down at her. "What are you saying?" he asked, letting go of her arms, losing interest in the game he was playing against her body.

She rolled away, scrambling off the bed and to her feet. He grabbed at her but missed, Sylvia already at the door. "Don't come near me!"

He was quiet, studying her. "Who sent you to find a manuscript here?"

Sylvia was out the door, James watching it close, his face closed off within itself, his thoughts walled away.

Sylvia raced down the front stairwell, running into Michael in her mad flight. She pulled away, excusing herself, twisting away from him and running toward the small back parlor, through the hordes of servants who were transforming Bereshaven House into garlanded splendor for the ball.

Mike stared after her, his eyes following her and then rising to the top of the stairs as James appeared there, looking down at him. And smiling.

"Ah . . . so it was you, was it?"

Mike stared up at the boy he had promised to help. To protect. "It was I who did what?"

James still smiled. "Whatever would my brother do without you . . . and whatever will you do one day without my brother?"

"James, why are you home?"

"Home? Home is it you call it? I have no home and well you know it. Your favorite, your charge who can do no wrong, has seen to that. I have nothing. Nothing, do you hear me? But my wits. And I intend to use them."

"What are you threatening?"

"Threatening? Me? My dear Michael, how can you even think such a thing?" James pulled away from the head of the stairs, lost from view on the upper floor. Mike hesitated, trying to decide whom to go after, James or Sylvia, and finally turned toward neither. He turned back toward the library, knocking before he entered.

In the back parlor Sylvia interrupted Victoria's work, slamming the door behind her and stopping in the middle of the floor. "He knows!"

Victoria stared up at the woman, startled. "Knows what?"

"He found me! Don't you understand? I was looking for it and he found me. He knows I was looking for the manuscript. It will never be found now. Never. Until he wants to use it." Sylvia watched Victoria's expression change, worry filling her now, the feeling transmitting itself to Sylvia, who sank to a chair, forgetting her posture, forgetting all poise. "Oh, Victoria, what shall we do?" She stared into Victoria's eyes. "It's bad, isn't it? I have made things worse, haven't I?"

"No—no, truly, he would have to know it would be missed. There is nothing different than before."

A little hope gleamed in Sylvia. "Truly? You're not just saying that?"

"Truly." Victoria made herself sound positive. And definite.

Sylvia let out a long sigh. "Oh, I am so glad . . . I was afraid . . . I don't think I could bear making things worse for Edward." She hesitated. "He cares for you, you know."

Victoria blushed, bright color suffusing her cheeks. "I—I don't know what you mean." Her heart ached. She wanted to ask, Are you sure, how do you know, has he said something, tell me, tell me please, for I love him, I love him. "He thinks well of my work, I believe," was all she finally said out loud, but Sylvia watched the girl, knowing more of heartache than Victoria could imagine.

"When I was forced to come to The Willows, I ran away." She watched Victoria look up, surprised. "Yes. Forced. When I found it was James that was to be my husband, they had to force me to go through with it. He too. They let me stay with my family until the baby was born, but she was stillborn and I would still not leave my mother's side. My father took me there. To The Willows. And I ran away, trying to get back home. It did not succeed, my little attempt. I was only sixteen, after all, and I had no friends. Except one . . ." Her expression softened, a faraway look turning her toward the sunlit windows. Her voice was softer when she continued: "His name was Nigel and we had thought . . . had planned, when he was through school . . . but of course I made this ghastly mistake and all was lost . . ." She trailed off into a little pool of silence, Victoria watching her as she relived a time long gone.

"All was lost?" Victoria repeated softly after long moments of silence.

"What? Oh . . . yes. Well, not quite, we thought. You see James went ahead with his career plans, or his father's for him, if the truth were known. James never went against his father's wishes. For all the good it did him." She smiled, her eyes sad above her curving mouth. "He always said his father liked him best. That his father would find a way to leave it all to him. That it should have been his anyway and his father would make it all right. But of course he didn't. If he ever planned to, he did not in the end do it. So there was James, following his father's every suggestion, and there was I, living at The Willows with the old duke and his horrid sister Judith . . . and Edward, of course. Who felt so sorry for me and on whom I had had such a devilish crush . . . in any event, Nigel got word to me."

Victoria waited while Sylvia paused again. A soft light came into Sylvia's eyes when she thought of Nigel. "He was only two years older than I. We hatched a plan . . . we were going to ship out to America and find our own fortune in the New World." Her eyes clouded over. "We got as far as Dover."

"They found you," Victoria said gently.

"Found and gagged and beat—my father, of course, for the shame I had heaped upon my family name . . . I was brought back to The Willows and virtually locked in my room for two years."

"Oh, Sylvia—I mean, your ladyship."

Sylvia smiled sadly at Victoria. "I hardly think it necessary for you to call me a title I hardly deserve in the first place. I like to be called Sylvia. It makes me think I am still me. And not the creature James has made me into."

Victoria's eyes were wide with pity. "And yet you've stayed. All these years."

"My dear, I've learned life's bitter truths. Nigel married a burgher's daughter and has a houseful of children I am told, having easily forgotten his passionate youth. I have no family left, my estates of course devolving upon my husband when my parents passed away. My husband has gone through every penny they had, sold off what Edward's father did not buy of the land, and generally left me destitute and dependent upon his brother while he has followed his army career until this very month. Quite happily away from the sight of all of us." She stared at Victoria. "And here I sit today, middle-aged and penniless, married to a man I cannot abide and dependent upon a man I suppose I have loved all my life. And more so now, after all the years in which he has provided for me what my husband should have . . . can you blame me if I am a little in love with Edward too?"

"Too . . ."

"My dear child, do not think you can hide such feelings from one who has felt them. Why do you think I warned you so heartily before we left? You will live to regret any folly you do. He is to marry as the Queen likes, and he has never shirked his duty. As you can see by my little story. Nor will he. Not ever."

Victoria looked away, tears brimming in her eyes. "I would not ask him to do so."

"Poor child, you would and so would I and all the others on this planet who have ever felt love. We wish it to know no bounds, to conquer all and do so just for us. But that is only our dream . . . it is not even a hope . . . and it can never be reality, for if he were to do as you wish, you would not respect him and love would end. There is no way out of your maze, my dear. Except the least painful all round."

"To leave." Victoria's words were so quiet they almost sounded whispered.

Sylvia stood up. "I cannot advise anyone; I have done nothing but the wrong things my entire life long. But as a friend—and I hope you consider me one—I can tell you my own sad tale. If you profit by it, perhaps it won't have been entirely wasted."

"Thank you." Victoria forced tears back, struggling to maintain some shred of composure. "I cannot leave until the manuscript is found and things are put right. I cannot leave while he is in danger. But I shall leave as soon as things are as he wishes them."

"My dear child, he will be in danger as long as James lives."

The two women stared at each other for a long time. Each hearing the words Sylvia had said, Sylvia surprised she had voiced them out loud, Victoria shaken by the knowledge deep within her that every word Sylvia said was true.

Chapter 22

THE NIGHT OF THE ball Bereshaven House glowed. Hundreds and hundreds of candles flickered in their sconces, in candelabra and chandeliers, casting a soft light out across the square, the drapes pulled back as if daylight reigned within, the tall narrow windows open to the night air. Violins tuned up, playing a soft accompaniment to each other as the final touches were put upon the decorations, Mr. Phipps rushing from kitchen to ballroom, Jasper in close pursuit. Even Michael had been commandeered into helping with last minute chores, the family upstairs in their rooms, finishing their toilets, adjusting their finery as maids fussed about them.

Victoria stood in the middle of her room, staring at the gown in Nancy's outstretched arms. "Come along or you shall be late," Nancy was telling her, grinning at the expression on Victoria's face.

Victoria was staring at a ball gown of emerald-green satin, paler green ribbons laced through the low-cut bodice and into the puffed sleeves, pearls encrusted across the length and breadth of the bodice. "I—I cannot possibly put that on."

"Don't be daft!" Nancy told Victoria, sternness in her tone. "He wants you to wear it and wear it you shall. Why you shall look exactly as Cinderella did, coming to the ball!"

"It's too—it's beautiful . . ." Victoria's eyes could not

leave the gown. The lamplight caressed the shiny satin, burnishing the depths of the deep Irish green.

"It was his mother's. Now that's a compliment not to be taken lightly. He says it will fit you and I hope he's right. Although what men know of women's sizes could be put in a thimble and still not fill it up. Come along. You have to at least try it on."

"It will never fit."

"Well, come along and find it out then! Then you truly have a reason not to wear it."

Carefully Victoria touched the material, feeling its richness, succumbing to its beauty. She let Nancy drape it over the bed, let Nancy help her with her fastenings, hearing the sounds of music from below and the first carriages that came around the square, clip-clopping to a halt by the wide stone portico.

Despite herself, Victoria stared into the pier glass once Nancy had the gown upon her. Turning a little this way and that, she caught a glimpse of Nancy's look of triumph reflected in the mirror. "I can't wear this."

"And why not?" Nancy asked practically.

"It's too good for me." Victoria was again staring at herself in the mirror.

"I've heard of every kind of an excuse from ladies as to what they would and would not wear, but that beats all." Nancy came nearer, coaxing now, touching the sleeves, reaching to pull a ribbon straight. "He wants you to wear it. You can't very well go down dressed in your old gray, now can you?"

"That's just the point." Victoria turned unhappy eyes toward the girl. "I should not go down. I am *not* one of the ladies who you spoke of, I am an employee and, and, all will think I am above my station if I . . . they will talk," Victoria ended.

Nancy eyed Victoria shrewdly. "It's true they'll talk. And it's true he wants you there. Now, which is more important to you? The idle words of people you've never met or his wishes?"

Victoria hung her head. "I will be frozen with embarrassment."

"Why?" Nancy asked. "I should feel proud, if it were me. I would hold my head twice as tall as anyone else, and if I heard them whispering"—Nancy saw Victoria's quick look —"oh yes, I know they will and I would not care. I would remember one thing: *he* wanted me there. Their jealousy would only make it all the more sweet!" The ring of honest truth was in Nancy's plain speech.

"I wish I were you," Victoria told the maid. "I wish I could feel as you do."

"Even if I did not, I would *act* as if I felt I was in my place and *they* the intruders. After all, it's not the likes of them he searches out in the middle of the night, now is it?"

Victoria stared at the girl. "Nancy!"

"Well." Nancy eyed the auburn-haired beauty before her. "Is it not the truth?"

"It . . . it was."

"Is, was, if he felt any different you would not be invited this night, now would you?"

Victoria stared at Nancy, the simple words whirling around within her. "He must have a reason for inviting me," Victoria said after a long pause when Nancy just stood nearby, her hands on her hips, waiting for Victoria to make up her mind.

"Yes! Now, let's see about your hair."

Victoria found herself plunked down onto the stool in front of the vanity, Nancy taking over and moving with practiced speed as the sound of more and more arrivals came from downstairs.

Downstairs white-gloved servants awaited, handing over drinks and ices to the earliest arrivals under the watchful eye of Mr. Phipps. The hall was crowding with guests and noise, the sounds of music rising over the conversations and the laughter.

The duke stood near the ballroom doors, greeting people with a distracted smile upon his face, watching the crowds that began to fill the floor and move to the music. Across the gigantic room along the wall beneath the windows were a line of dowagers' chairs, filling already with older women dressed in elegant finery. Younger women drifted around them, seeing to their wishes and making themselves useful, shyly glancing toward the men who approached or boldly making conversation with those already known to them.

In the large parlor that opened off the ballroom, tables were spread with pheasant and wild rice, cold roasts and asparagus, caviar and delicacies from around the world, laid out in row upon row across the length of the long tables that marched across the center of the room. Champagne and punch and stronger liquid refreshments for the gentlemen were outside in the wide hallway that led back around to the huge double doors that gave entrance to the ballroom itself.

Above the bustling scene Victoria hesitated at the top of the curved stairwell, colors swirling together under the masses of flickering candles as she swayed a little, grabbing hold of the banister. A small group came closer to the bottom of the stairs, Victoria shrinking back into the shadows as some of their words carried toward her.

A sound behind her in the hallway made her glance back. The door to the duke's room was closing. Her heart skipped a beat. She was already turning toward it, to tell him of the impossibility of what he asked of her, when his name, spoken below, stopped her.

She looked down at the small group of men who stood drinking at the foot of the steps. "What did he say?" one was asking the one who had just spoken.

"Edward said he had no interest in the subject."

"Oh, I say, he could not have meant that!"

"Go over and ask him, he's just inside."

Victoria stared toward the men, thinking of the door closing behind her. Someone was in his rooms. She started down the steps, thinking only of warning him, her heart tripping quickly under the bodice of the low-cut gown.

"Good grief, is it Sylvia?" An elderly man stared up at Victoria as she descended the stairs, others turning toward the sound of his voice. "How could James ever have left one like you at home alone, my dear?" The gray-haired man reached out a hand toward Victoria as she came nearer.

"No—sir, I mean I am not Sylvia."

"Of course not." A contemporary of the gray-haired man stared at Victoria. "Sylvia was blond, Henry, don't you remember?"

Henry shrugged. "It's been a very long time." His hand

still held Victoria's. He smiled at her encouragingly. "Your family has been gone from our midst for such a beastly long time and it is not fair to hide such lights under bushels. Which one are you, my dear?"

Victoria swallowed. "I am not of the family, sir. I am Victoria Leggett."

"Not of the family?" He stared at her.

Judith appeared from within the room, seeing Victoria and coming forward to hear the end of the conversation. "Family! My dear, Henry, this is one of Edward's employees; she works for us."

Henry's hand fell away from Victoria's, his face closing over. "Sorry," he said quickly, turning away toward Judith and walking on down the hall.

Victoria found herself alone on the bottom step, men all around her eyeing her now, a knowing look in their eyes. A smile here and there did nothing to encourage her, the look in the men's eyes answer enough to what they thought they knew. She straightened up, pride and anger bringing a high flush to her cheeks as she started forward. Nancy's words came back as she headed toward the doors to the ballroom, ignoring the looks she received as she moved. Appraising stares followed her as she moved across the hall and on into the room, eyes meeting behind her back to raise a brow and voice unspoken comments.

A waltz was in progress in the room beyond the hall, its dulcet strains filling the room. The warm glow from huge crystal chandeliers shimmered across the movements of the dance. Victoria saw a blur of movement around her, her heart pounding as she walked steadily forward, her ears, her cheeks burning.

He was standing before her, staring at her with eyes that widened slightly and then simply focused on her. She stopped, seeing only his face, all else around them lost from view. "I must tell you something," she whispered urgently, Edward hearing only half the words.

He reached for her, his arm coming around her as others stared at them. He cupped his hand against the small of her back. "I—I don't know how . . ." she whispered fiercely.

He began to smile, pulling her toward him. "Then you shall learn this night."

People around them began to whisper, their comments rippling through the crowded room, others hearing tidbits and turning to watch surreptitiously as the duke led the unknown girl across the floor.

Here and there were people who whispered of who she was, of the stories they had heard this past week . . . and of his liaison with Elizabeth Wyndham, who had not yet arrived.

Edward was staring into eyes that had never looked so green, the room spinning with them as he held her in his arms, moving with the music, her feet following his as if they were one.

His voice was choked when he found it. "You are beautiful. Have I ever told you that?"

"No." Her own voice was small, her body responding to his, swaying with him, her senses sharpened. Her body was melting against his, their dance ever closer. She could feel the hardness of chest, the muscles of his legs as they grazed against her in the dance. Her eyes closed, her body flowing with him.

"You were made to wear such dresses," he told her, his voice close to her ear. They danced scandalously close, his breast against the low-cut bodice of her gown, his breath hot and irregular, chilling through her as he spoke into her ear. "I will never let you go," he was saying, chills racing down her spine, down her legs and arms as if his breath itself coursed through her blood. One, two, three, around and around, one, two, three, the slow strains of the waltz caressed them. "I should carry you up to my rooms and leave all of blasted London to itself."

His words cut through the music, reminding her of her mission. "I swear I shall," he was saying. "I swear—"

"Someone is in your rooms." Victoria spoke softly, quickly, interrupting him. "When I came down, I saw the door closing."

He missed a step, their movements stopping for one brief moment, then continuing the dance. Registering her words, he did not reply, his mind racing over the possibilities. As he took them one by one he danced nearer the terrace doors, nearer an exit, his body intoxicated with the touch of her, his mind racing over the meaning of what she had told him.

231

Her arm rested against him, her hand reaching to his shoulder, the length of her arm against the length of his. Her other hand was palm to palm, blending with his, his fingers part of her own hand, her own fingers reaching inside his to become part of him.

They had moved close to the doors that led to a brick terrace, night breezes caressing them, the music muted as they danced out onto the bricks. A few other couples were on the terrace, a dozen pairs of eyes following them as they moved outside.

Couples that were not dancing stood near the edge of the terrace, drinking in the cool night air along with the champagne that was being served from a small table near the doors.

He stopped dancing, still holding her, hand within hand, arm against arm, his legs pressed against the silk skirts that spread out around her. She could feel the heat of his body through all the layers of their clothing.

He was stepping back, away from her, as his name was called out. "Edward—Edward, the Wyndhams are arriving." Judith's clear, harsh voice broke into their thoughts.

Edward still stared down at Victoria's emerald eyes. "I shall find out who it was," he told her, turning away, turning toward his aunt and walking back into the ballroom.

Victoria stood alone on the terrace, eyes that had stared curiously at her now turning quickly away, avoiding her gaze.

Michael Flaherty came up the terrace steps from the grounds below, in formal attire and looking uncomfortable. He stopped for a moment beside her. "Girl, are you all right?"

She stared up at him, too much happening too fast. "I—yes. Someone was in his room." She saw Mike's expression change. Saw it harden.

"I'll tell him."

"I have," she told Mike. "Can—" She blinked back tears. "Can you please see me out of here?"

He stared down at her, his expression softening a little. "When you're dressed so pretty? Don't you want to be staying and having a little fun?"

She swallowed. "Please . . ."

232

He saw the pleading eyes, caught a glimpse of curious eyes nearby, and reached for her arm. "Of course I'll do it. But I won't be dancing with you. Not here."

She tried to smile, summoning the courage to stand straight as they entered the room and started across the wide expanse toward the hall doors she had come through. As they moved she stopped suddenly, surprising Mike. He glanced toward where she was looking, seeing Elizabeth and Margaret Wyndham with the duke near the doors to the hall.

"This way, then," he said, moving toward the large parlor and the doors out from there.

Victoria squeezed his arm gratefully, walking beside him toward the tables of food in the room beyond. Far across the ballroom Edward looked up to see her leaving, his eyes following her.

"Edward, did you hear me?" Judith shook his arm the least bit. "Elizabeth has not had her first dance yet."

Edward's eyes returned to the group surrounding him. Bowing slightly, he held out a hand to Elizabeth. She took it, smiling, walking easily beside him toward the dance floor. Margaret stared after them, standing beside Judith. "He's quite changeable, isn't he?" Margaret was saying.

"I beg your pardon?" Judith turned from watching her nephew to look closely at Elizabeth's mother. "Why do you say that?"

"My dear, only the other night he was so determined to be alone with her that, to tell you the truth, I was quite worried. Until I remembered who he was. He would never do anything . . . unseemly, I realize. Not with Elizabeth. He is too much the gentleman. But tonight he seems a thousand miles from here, his attitude entirely changed."

Unease rose within Judith, her gaze wandering about the room, looking for Sylvia and James. "I assure you, he has spoken of nothing but his affection for her since first they met."

Margaret smiled. "I do believe it was love at first sight, Judith. They do make such a pretty pair, don't you think?"

Judith followed Margaret's maternal eye, staring hard at her nephew as he moved across the floor, his polite expression as distanced from Elizabeth as if they were speaking across a table. "Yes, very pretty," Judith said after a moment of watching. "If you'll excuse me for a moment . . ." she continued, "I must see to the food."

"Of course, my dear. I shall exercise a mother's prerogative and simply bask in my daughter's reflected happiness."

Judith left the plump little woman, her face a polite mask of smiles as she moved through the crowds and crossed to the stairwell and the upper hall.

The sounds of the party were muffled in the upper hall, the music mixing with laughter and voices into a dull din. Judith pushed open the door to Sylvia's room and stared.

Sylvia turned toward the woman in the doorway from her chair near the window. A crystal decanter sat on a tiny table beside her. And in her hand was a ruby-colored goblet. She raised it, toasting Judith. "Here's to you, dear almost-auntie —here's to the family that ruined my life!"

Judith closed the door quickly, glaring at the woman across the room. Her blond hair was disheveled, as if she had been lying down, her silk gown creased and wrinkled. "What do you think you are doing? You are expected downstairs."

"Me?" Sylvia laughed. "Now? Don't tell me, please . . . after all these years, suddenly I should smile sweetly to people who know all about my wandering husband? Who have talked behind my back for years? I hardly think so!"

Judith walked forward. "Which is precisely why you must put in an appearance! You have caused enough talk!"

"Like this?" Sylvia raised one languid hand to indicate her gown. "Do you really wish me to attend now? If you say it, I shall, of course." She rose unsteadily to her feet, glass still in hand. "As always, I am your obedient servant, *dear* Judith."

"You are drunk!" Judith accused.

"Oh I don't think so. Not quite yet. One is supposed to feel good when one is drunk."

Judith watched the swaying figure in front of her. "Sit down before you fall!"

"Yes, Auntie." Sylvia collapsed back into the chair, spilling some of the port she was drinking down the front of her gown. She stared at it. "Oh dear . . ." When she looked up, Judith was already gone. Moving carefully, Sylvia reached for the decanter, refilling her goblet before falling back against the chair, her eyes closing.

The sounds of the party could be heard as faint eddies of distant pleasures, making the echoing silence of her own room less and less bearable. She swallowed more port, escaping them all while Judith stood beyond her closed door, staring across the hall and hesitating.

Finally Judith moved toward James's door, tapping softly before opening it. It was empty. She closed the door, worry creasing her forehead, sending her toward the back stairs down to the kitchens and beyond.

Chapter 23

VICTORIA STEPPED DOWN ONTO the damp grass far away from the sounds of the party, walking along the far edge of the grounds, tracing her way next to the yellow brick walls that rose ten feet high, protecting the grounds from the city beyond them.

The moon fled through branches overhead, a light fog reflecting across its face. At the nearest corner of the wall she hesitated, staring back toward the house and the lights that blazed out from the ballroom far across the lawns. People moved within and without, couples wandering outside in pairs, while inside, larger groups congregated around the edges of the dance floor, talking and eating and drinking and watching the dancers move to the music.

Sounds of running feet came nearer, Victoria standing where she was. Two couples were nearby, heading far from the watchful eyes behind, laughing softly as a young woman's voice pleaded for rest, still laughing. "I can't move another inch. Come along you two."

Elizabeth's voice came toward Victoria, her tone gay. "We didn't ask you to follow, Gwendolyn, we have things to discuss."

"Things, is it?" A young man's voice laughed. "Edward, my friend, you'd best be careful about your 'things' out here in the dark. People will talk."

"Not if you don't tell them, Lionel." Edward's voice was lower than the others. Victoria could pick out the four dark shapes in the shadows under the plane trees. Edward stood taller than the others. Reaching out his hand, he took possession of Elizabeth's waist, pulling her back to rest against him, her back against his chest, as they told the other couple to leave.

Gwendolyn sounded unsure. "Are you positive, Bethie? I mean, your mother would never approve—"

"Oh, bother Mother! Go along!"

"If you're sure . . ." Gwendolyn was being pulled back by the young man beside her. He whispered something into her ear that made her giggle. As they turned away Edward's voice came back toward Victoria. "Bethie, is it?"

Elizabeth's laugh was throaty. "And what if it is?"

She was leaning back, craning her neck to look up at his face. He reached with one hand to cup her chin, lowering his head toward her mouth.

Something within Victoria screamed out, her body going rigid. Jealousy coursed through her, constricting her heart. The pain she felt was physical, her breath caught as she stared at the couple who stood a few bare feet away, a few low bushes between where she stood and where they stood entwined.

Elizabeth's voice was breathless when she pulled away from his lips. "What about your wife?"

"What about her?" His voice came back, husky and demanding. "Come here."

James. James, not Edward. The relief that washed over Victoria almost buckled her knees. And chasing behind it came shock. This was James, and Elizabeth knew it was James. Confused, Victoria took a step back, the sound of twigs breaking pulling his head up, turning him toward the sound.

Victoria turned and ran, hearing him swear behind her, hearing part of a frightened question from Elizabeth before there was too much distance between to hear anything more. Victoria ran as if pursued, not looking back to see if he followed.

She made the safety of the back door, stopping her headlong flight when she reached the kitchen hallway, servants glancing toward the emerald satin gown, the lovely face that was flushed with exertion and panting from her headlong flight. She took a deep breath, walking more sedately toward the green baize door at the end of the hall, the sounds of the party growing louder.

Her heart in her mouth, she shoved at the door, walking back out into the crowds that milled about the drink tables. A flurry of activity turned Victoria and the others toward the front of the hall where a stout man walked between two others, his glance regal as he looked about himself, nodding when he saw a face he knew and continuing on into the ballroom.

"It's the prince . . . it's Bertie . . ." Voices were rising around Victoria. "Wales is here and he's with Carrington, my dear, not Alix."

The words meant nothing to Victoria. She moved forward through the sea of evening-clothed people, searching out Edward. Mike appeared at her elbow. "Have you seen the duke? The Prince of Wales is arriving."

She shook her head. "I was just looking for him."

He glanced about the throngs that surrounded them and pushed on past, leaving Victoria to float with the force of the crowd around her, forward toward the ballroom.

The heir to the throne of England was speaking to an old woman whose white-haired head bent at an angle to look into his eyes.

Elizabeth Wyndham came through the doors from the terrace, James beside her. Elizabeth drifted off toward her mother as if by accident drifting away from James, who circled around the room and saw the prince. He stopped and then strode forward, bowing slightly and speaking.

Victoria saw James glance about, his eyes falling on her and resting there for a long moment. Then he turned back to answer the prince, Victoria pushing against the people that surrounded her, forcing her way back into the hall and toward the stairs.

She reached the bottom of the stairs as James pushed through the crowds, coming out toward the hall and spying her rising toward the next floor.

He came after her, stopped momentarily by someone who thought he was Edward and made to turn back to talk.

Victoria glanced back and headed quickly down the hall. The door to Sylvia's room opened, Sylvia standing unsteadily and peering out at Victoria. "I thought someone knocked," she said, the words ever so slightly slurred.

Victoria hurried toward her, helping her back inside, closing the door. "Come along, you don't want them to see you like this. Your hair is undone."

Sylvia let Victoria lead her toward the bed, sitting obediently. Her pale blue eyes stared up into Victoria's. Sea-green concern watched Sylvia. "I'm all right," Sylvia assured Victoria. "All I need is a little something to drink."

"I think you've had quite enough," Victoria told her. "You shall have the most beastly head tomorrow and you shall wish you had never been born."

"How do you know?" Sylvia asked innocently, letting Victoria help her unbutton her gown.

"I was raised in a home where many of our warders had the habit. And miserable they were to be around, the day after they'd taken too much. Now lie back and close your eyes."

Sylvia did as she was told, her eyes reopening quickly. "I cannot. The room spins round when I close my eyes." She struggled to sit up. Victoria pushed her back.

"It will not help to sit. Or to stand. Lie still and I shall get you some strong tea." Victoria watched Sylvia hesitate and then fall back toward her pillows, too tired to argue.

"I wonder who knocked," Sylvia was saying as Victoria walked back toward the door.

"Knocked?"

"It wasn't you, was it?" Sylvia's eyes were closed, her voice trailing off.

"No . . . rest for now. I shall be back." Victoria left Sylvia on the bed, stepping out into the hall and looking carefully back toward the farther reaches. No one had come past her on the stairs. Nor had anyone come to the near doors or she would have seen them. Victoria was about to dismiss the thoughts when her eye fell on the closed door to Judith's room. The next one past Sylvia's—a knock upon it could have sounded closer than it was. But no one was upstairs except herself and Sylvia. Her step slowed as she passed by the door, making her lag a moment, and then she remembered Sylvia's condition and hurried toward the back stairs and the kitchen. Tea as strong as possible and a bit of fresh air were all the remedies she knew for the unhappy condition Sylvia would soon find herself experiencing.

As she walked she realized she had felt no surprise upon seeing Sylvia's condition.

James came up the front stairs as Victoria hurried toward the back. He watched her go, walking more slowly, glancing toward Sylvia's door and then his own. He quickly crossed to his own, opening it wide and staring at its contents.

Nothing looked disturbed, things strewn where he had left them. He considered the room, hearing steps behind himself as he stood there. He whirled around to see Judith. "Where have you been?" she asked. The words came out sounding urgent.

He watched her. "Downstairs. Where else?" He smiled a little, still watching her worried expression.

"You haven't been doing anything . . . you shouldn't?" She looked at the boy she had raised, the boy she loved as her own, not seeing the grown man before her, but the child he had once been, thin and hurting, with dark eyes large with fear, reaching out for her affection, grabbing at it hungrily, binding her to him as surely as if he were her own.

"Aunt Judith . . . what do you mean?"

She hesitated, watching him, wanting to believe him. But knowing him so well. Too well not to hear something behind his words. "I want to talk to you for a moment." She spoke the words as if resolving something finally within herself.

"Of course."

"Not here." She reached for his hand, taking it into her own, clinging to its warmth as she started toward her own room. James followed along. Curious, he watched her until they were inside, alone. She turned to stare into his eyes. Almost as tall as he was, she looked at that moment older than he had ever realized. "I have decided to take matters into my own hands. And I want, I need, your help."

"Yes?" His eyes coaxed her confidence, his face showing nothing but willingness to help her in whatever she chose.

She relaxed a little, sitting down and motioning him to follow suit. "This family has been through too much. Too much since your father's wild younger days and his mistaken marriage." She saw something flicker in his eyes and she reached out her hand. "Not that I don't love you, you know I do. But he was wrong in what he did."

"I know." James's voice was harsher than he intended.

She nodded her head a little. "You understand me. You are the only one who feels as I do. Who cares about what I do." She hesitated. "Your brother cannot be allowed to make the same kind of mistake his father did before him."

James watched his aunt's face. "You mean with the girl."

"I mean with the conniving little baggage who has foisted herself upon us and is determined to lead us to ruin. As you well know. As tonight she has shown her true colors. Brazen as a tart!" He hesitated, letting her go on. She took a moment, watching him, gauging She took a moment, watching him, gauging her words, before she continued: "My words are harsh, but they are a measure of the disgrace our name will suffer if he is allowed to let his passions overcome his common sense."

"I don't understand why you say this, Aunt Judith. To me, I mean. You know I agree . . . you know we both left rather than have to condone it."

"Yes, yes . . . and now look what has happened. Well —well, I have an answer. A solution. I have taken steps to ensure that she would not be kept on." Her eyes clouded. "She should not be here even now."

"I agree. But there is nothing we can do. As he reminds us all so often, all is his."

Her chin jutted out, her resolve hardening with his words. "Not quite all if he is in bad odor with the Queen."

James watched his aunt. "He seems to have convinced her that there is nothing amiss."

"I heard him talking to the Irishman." Judith leaned forward and James found himself straining nearer, listening more intently as she continued. "The Queen is upset that the rumors she has heard are true. She has already heard of the girl."

James's expression did not change. "There is always someone at court who will gossip," he told his aunt blandly. "And no doubt they will gossip more after this night and her . . . appearance."

"Do you think so?" His aunt stared at him, indecision written large across her face. "Possibly that is enough then?"

"Enough?"

"The Queen was not pleased about the girl because she had heard more than just that the girl and he were—that they had—were close. She asked him about radical leanings, about dangerous politics. About where the girl came from and what all she might lead him into."

"Yes?" James spoke softly. "And you?" he prompted her cautiously.

"I—I saw an opportunity to ensure the girl's departure and I took it. Only, he has not sent her away. She is still here and I am not sure what is to be done now."

"An opportunity?" James watched his aunt carefully, "You . . . took . . . something, is that it?"

Judith stared at him. "Have they told you? Have they mentioned it to you? About the manuscript?"

"Only that it was gone," he said blandly. "They had no idea where."

"Or who?" she added, staring at him.

"I believe I was suspected," he told her, smiling a little. "But I am used to being misjudged."

"My poor boy, I know it. I remember even your father, after Martha's accident—" She shook her head, clearing it. "Now is now and I am not sure what to do."

"What if they search for it?" He saw her eyes widen. "There has been some talk," he told her smoothly, his face taking on a look of concern. "I do not want you to suffer the consequences of his wrath. We know he is capable of anything."

Her eyes widened. "Do you think he would dare to ask me to leave?" Fear tinged her words, the enormity of what she had done, of what might be the consequences, rising before her.

James took his aunt's hands within his own. "I think you must hand over the manuscript to me. For safekeeping."

"But if they find you with it—"

"I shall take it to my club." He smiled reassuringly. "There it will be safe until you wish to use it. Or give it back.

Or let him know what you have done with it. I shall stand beside you no matter what. You know that."

She was touched. Withdrawing one hand from his grasp, she reached to push an unruly lock of his dark hair back from his forehead. "You have always been my favorite, you know that, my dear James. I was heartbroken when I realized your father was to let the succession stand . . . you should have been duke. You *are* duke. In my heart."

He almost laughed, exercising iron control to keep his face from showing the bitter levity he felt. "Thank you, Aunt Judith. I do not know what I should have done without you."

She patted his hands and stood up, walking toward her wardrobe. He watched her, keeping his face expressionless, keeping his hands relaxed.

"I think you are right. The safest place is with you." She turned back before she opened the wardrobe. "I thought it would be so simple. If she had nothing to work upon, he would have to let her go."

"And instead he has kept her on."

"Yes." She reached into the wardrobe, pulling out her sewing bag. "It is in here," she told him, turning back toward him.

"Let's leave it so. I shall take it to my room and put it in my cloak, ready to leave with me as soon as possible."

He stood up, taking the bag when she did not bring it forward. One small doubt lurked in her mind, making her watch James carefully. "You will be careful with it? It was your father's, after all, and we should preserve it."

He nodded. "Have you read it?" he asked casually, as if the subject were of no importance.

"No, there was no point, was there?"

He wasn't sure he believed her. He smiled. "None that I am aware of." He reached to kiss her forehead. "I must get back before I am missed. And you must too."

She nodded, her face grim when next she spoke. "Yes, we must. Particularly since Sylvia is unavailable. Have you seen her?"

"No."

Judith shook her head. "Your father should never have

forced you to marry her . . . it wasn't fair to you. She's no wife for you." That thought brought another back. "James, you haven't been seeing Elizabeth, have you?"

"Elizabeth Wyndham?" His tone spoke volumes of surprise at the question. "Whatever for?"

Judith smiled at him. "There would be no reason, would there? Dismiss the question. It is just that it is very important that Edward make that match. Make that match and send this chit away. There is nothing more important than the family name. And an heir, of course."

"Of course," James agreed. "I shall see you downstairs then."

"I shall be there directly," she told him.

He left her with a smile warming her stern features, his own fading as he turned away and headed toward his room and the privacy it would afford him.

Chapter 24

Victoria was stopped when she started back up the back stairs by Mike, who blocked her path. She stared at him, a pot of tea and a cup on the tray she held.

"Sylvia is waiting for some tea."

"She can wait longer," Mike told her.

Victoria stared at him. "What's happened? What's wrong?"

"Nothing's happening and nothing's wrong," he answered, still blocking her way. "You just go on down and enjoy the party."

"Michael, I cannot. I was going to give this to Sylvia and go on to my room. This evening has been longer and harder than you can know."

"It would be better if you left these stairs," Mike told her, "and stayed downstairs until I tell you to come up."

She stared at him. "What are you saying?"

"If you don't like the party, miss, you might want to work in your back parlor until I come get you."

Still she stared at the man. "Are you telling me I cannot go upstairs?"

"I am telling you it would be best if you left here. Now."

She watched his expressionless face. With bad grace she finally turned around, going back down the stairs. When she reached bottom and turned to look back at him, he was gone. She hesitated, almost turned back toward the upper hall, and then thought better of it, retracing her steps to the kitchen.

There, Cook looked up at her. "I thought you were taking that tea up."

"So did I," Victoria told the woman, putting the tray down and walking out toward the small back parlor where her desk and her work awaited.

The cook was watching the young woman's pale ivory shoulders as she walked away, the emerald-green satin gown swishing with each step. When Cook looked away, she saw Jasper watching the door the girl had gone through. Cook shook her head. "She's too pretty by half to be working for an unwed toff. Lord knows what all is true about what they say."

Jasper glanced at the fat woman. "What do they say?" he asked, seeing Cook light up as she settled back to tell him of the stories she had heard.

"What do they say?" a dowager, sitting on a chair by the windows in the ballroom, was asking behind her fan at the same moment. She watched the dancers and beyond them, the Prince of Wales with his boon companions.

The lady she asked the question of leaned nearer. "They say that the dear princess has accepted her lock, stock, and barrel. Can you imagine? Alix and the Jersey Lily, as they call her, sitting at tea in Marlborough House, with the prince there between them . . . I wonder who he places on his right."

"My dear, I wonder if it matters . . ."

They smiled to themselves, watching the prince move about the edge of the floor, the duke introducing him to someone across the way.

"Isn't that Margaret Wyndham?"

"Oh my, yes . . . the Queen has determined that our bachelor duke shall settle down with Elizabeth Wyndham."

"Truly?" The dowager stared at the duke through her opera glasses. "He is the handsomest of the lot, isn't he?"

"Next to poor pudgie Bertie, I'm afraid anyone would look the better . . . and Alix, still so exquisite . . . do you know she is as young looking and lovely as any of their daughters."

"Who must have taken after her, I presume," the dowager retorted, earning a laugh.

"Olive, you are too droll!" her friend told her, their conversation ceasing as the prince and his party came closer. For all their familiarity there was awe in the women's eyes as they stood up, curtsying low as the prince stopped near them. He was, after all, heir to the throne.

The evening wore on, the horses in the street outside stamping their feet, their drivers gossiping among themselves or snoozing in their seats, a bottle close by some to guard against the nip in the night air. Here and there early arrivers were already leaving, the sound of trotting hooves fading away around the square, while others still waited patiently, the moon climbing higher as the night grew later.

Victoria sat in a chair by the cold fireplace in the small parlor at the back of the house. Her work sat undisturbed on her desk across the room.

These past weeks filled her thoughts. Her precipitous arrival at The Willows and the disapproval in his eyes when he first heard of her purpose in being there. The feeling of his arms when he carried her upstairs. His insistence upon her having the guest room, his ransacking of the house the night she was not in that room. Their idyll in the attics while he spoke of his mother and his decision to hang her portrait where it belonged. His body as he leaned over her . . . She shivered, standing up to shake off the memory of the night he had carried her to his bed.

He had left without word. He had called for her to come to London. He had said no more about any of what transpired that night and yet he had said he wanted her near, wanted her to stay. He had told her of his interview with the Queen, of his duty to follow her dictates, and then had led her into the dance tonight, had sent his mother's dress for her to wear.

She could still feel his arms around her, could see the look in his eyes as he gazed down at her, her thoughts tumbling past each other, rolling around in her brain, demanding reasons, a thread of understanding.

When Mike entered the room, she stared at him as if he were a ghost, so startled was she by his sudden appearance beside her. "I—I didn't hear you!" she told him, her eyes wide.

He stared at her. "You said you wished to go up . . ." He hesitated and then said no more.

She stared at the burly man who had by turns been friend and guarded servant, kind and laughing one time, distrustful the next. "What is happening?" she asked him plainly, watching his expression become guarded.

"Nothing that concerns you," he told her.

"Everything that concerns him concerns me." She spoke the words before thought, only realizing as she said them how true they were.

Mike stared at her. "He did not mean to cause you harm. You must believe that."

"I do believe that," she replied.

"He needed a decoy this night and the fact of all of them looking at you and speculating about the two of you kept them busy so they did not see more than they should."

She stared at the man, her face pale, her eyes wide as she watched him, as she heard the words he uttered. "He asked me to dance," she said, and stopped.

Mike was nodding. "Yes, and a great help you were, as I told him myself not moments ago."

She spoke slowly. "And his mother's dress—I could not very well appear at the ball—to help—without being properly clothes."

"Well, I don't know about the dress, but it's sure enough that you haven't the kind of clothing that fits in with the likes of them, no more than I."

She swallowed. "No," she said. "No more than you . . . So how goes it?"

He sank to a chair opposite her, mopping his brow with the back of his hand. "I'll not say I'm pleased until the night is over. But at least so far nothing has gone amiss."

"And James?"

Mike stared at her. "What of James?"

"Does he know of . . . anything?"

"Good Lord above, I hope not!" Mike's face clouded over. "He seems to be finding comfort in the wrong arms."

"Then you know," Victoria said quietly, earning a quick look from the duke's man.

"You saw them?"

She nodded, turning away as he watched her movements. "You do not trust her?" When she turned back to stare at him, he added: "I mean, you think she knows which is which?"

"I heard her talking of his wife," Victoria said.

Mike took this in. "I'll tell him."

"You mean, he knows? Of . . . James and Elizabeth?"

Mike nodded. "He's seen them before." He watched her closely. "You care about my boy, don't you? Do you love him, then?"

She faltered. "I—I care . . . of course. I mean he has allowed me this position, and I have the utmost respect —and admiration—"

Mike brushed aside her words. "You love him or you don't, and all the fancy words you can find from all your books won't change the one into the other." He stared at her. "Answer carefully, my girl, for he is in need of those he can trust these days."

She stared at Mike. "Whatever else I feel, he can always trust me."

"Good. For you may be seeing more than you should before this night is over. Or hearing it. And he'll be needing to trust you and all else in this house." Mike stood up.

"Can he trust—all else?" she asked as he turned away.

"We shall soon be finding out, I fear," he told her. Quick tears were springing to her eyes. She did not want him to see them. She looked down at the dress he had sent to her, fingering its fine fabric. He had sent it so that she could be of use tonight. He had danced with her to avert suspicion from whatever Mike was doing. She told herself the plain truth over and over, but a tiny rebellious voice inside her insisted that there was more to it than that. The way he held her, the eyes that had looked into hers, his very words . . . he had not simply been playing a part . . . he had been as affected as she had been.

The sounds from the public rooms were softer, more of the guests calling an end to their evening, saying their good nights to their host, and calling for their carriages. Victoria could hear carriages pulling away outside. She thought of Sylvia, still waiting upstairs. And Judith. And James. All within this house. And the servants. And the guests. How many pairs of eyes had seen whatever Michael thought he was hiding?

A sound outside the window caught her attention. She started to reach for a lamp and then thought better of it, moving toward the window to stand in darkness next to the closed drapes, listening.

She heard nothing more. Reaching for the edge of the heavy velour drape, she lifted it away from the window, edging closer to see outside. A figure startled her, moving in the bushes near the window as if hiding from someone. Others were coming nearer, a couple in the shadows, stopping and leaning together.

The moon broke out from a passing cloud, the fog swirling across the lawns making it hard to see clearly. The figure near the window stood straighter, and Victoria recognized the little man who had visited Michael at The Willows. He moved back around the house, toward the rear. Victoria dropped the deep green velour drape. Turning to warn Michael, she ran headlong into Edward. "Oh!" Her heart raced as she looked up into his eyes in the darkness near the windows. "You frightened me."

"Did I?"

She stared at him. "Someone is going round the back."

"Why are you spying?"

"What?" She tried to pull back and still he held her. "I heard something and—please, you're hurting me . . ."

Michael appeared from the hallway. "Her mother is looking for the girl" was all he said, Edward still staring down at Victoria.

"She's in the garden," Victoria said. "She's walking with someone near the rosebushes."

"Why are you spying?" he repeated, his hands still holding her arms tight. He stared into her eyes, trying to see through the shadows into what she was thinking.

"I heard noises. I was worried and I heard noises and I saw the man who visits Michael sneaking around the house. Then I saw them and turned to find you. To warn you." She saw pain in his eyes. And distrust. "You can believe me or not."

He turned away, heading toward Michael. "Find Margaret" was all he told Michael, walking on past him. Michael started off, Victoria left standing where she had been. The realization that he was unconcerned about Michael's friend sent her after him. If he was not dangerous, he was part of what Michael was trying to protect.

The back door that led to the hall was open, the air turning chill in the late-night hours. She raced to close it, seeing Michael and Edward stopping a little way across the grounds, Margaret and Judith beside them.

"What is the meaning of this?" Margaret was asking her daughter. Elizabeth looked shocked, staring at her mother and then at Edward.

"I—I don't know what you mean," Elizabeth was saying.

James stood beside her, one arm still around her. He pulled away from the embrace in which they had been caught. "I rather doubt they'll believe you, Bethie . . . although you can try."

He smiled easily at her mother, Judith staring at him as if she had never seen him before. "Why would you do this?" she asked him. "James, why would you do this to us? To me?"

"My dear aunt Judith, it has nothing to do with you, believe me."

Edward was turning away. He saw Victoria by the door to the rear and walked toward her across the grass. Judith called after him. "Edward, what shall we do?"

"Nothing, Aunt Judith." His words carried back to them. "I believe it's time for Elizabeth and her mother to go home."

Margaret grabbed her daughter's arm, wrenching her away from James. "You—you blackguard!" she spat the words at him.

He smiled. "Careful, dear Margaret . . . you could very well be speaking to the next Duke of Bereshaven."

"What are you saying?" Judith stared at him in horror. "James, what has possessed you to do something like this?" Her voice rose. "How could you?"

Edward passed by Victoria. "Would you mind closing the door? It's becoming rather chill," he said evenly, heading toward the front hall where Mr. Phipps's minions were clearing away the debris of the food and drink from the special tables laid out for the occasion.

Victoria closed the door against the loud voices issuing from the lawns. The sounds died away as she walked toward the front rooms, staring at the candles that were still burning brightly along the hallway. At the servants whose uniforms were no longer fresh as they tidied and cleaned up the leavings from the guests. Edward was disappearing up the stairs, Margaret and Elizabeth coming through the doors from the ballroom, Judith rushing a little ahead and seeing Victoria. "Their coats!" she called out, turning back to see James coming in behind them. "Their coats!" she said again as she turned back toward Victoria, her hands pressed together as if in prayer. Margaret's lips were a thin, firm line. Elizabeth looked almost sullen as she was half dragged forward.

Victoria turned away and found Jasper coming toward her, their wraps in hand. She reached for one as he held the other out to Mrs. Wyndham. Elizabeth stared at Victoria and then grabbed her cloak from Victoria's hands. "I saw you!" she told Victoria furiously. "Don't think I didn't. Or that I'll forget! I know why you caused this, but you shall live to regret it . . . do you hear me? You will rue this night and your tattling!"

Victoria stared at the girl, too taken aback to reply. She saw James grinning behind Elizabeth. "Bethie," he was saying, "don't work yourself up so. Before this night is over they both will regret more than you know."

Judith stood back, watching the Wyndhams leave, watching James move to open the door for them, wishing them a pleasant good night. Which Margaret ignored, as she did his presence. He looked back toward Judith and Victoria. "Don't worry, my dears, I shall return sooner than you imagine." And with that he was gone.

Judith sank to the bench behind her, her hands still clenched, her rigid back bent forward as if she were in pain. Victoria hesitated and then came forward. "Can I help?" she asked, seeing Judith stiffen at her words.

Judith looked up, as if to reprimand her, and then seemed

to crumble, her voice breaking when she spoke: "I fear for what I have done."

"Why?" Something in the woman's tone chilled Victoria more than the night air that still blew in around them from the open terrace doors. "What have you done?"

The eyes that looked up at Victoria had lost their hardness. They almost beseeched as they stared into Victoria's, looking for some kind of help. "I gave him the manuscript."

The words echoed across the hall. A servant's footsteps behind them seemed loud in the silence that followed. "You did what?"

"To James. He asked for it and I gave it to him."

"You took it?" Victoria stared at the woman.

Judith spoke as if they were discussing someone they both knew. "I wanted you gone, and I thought if there was nothing for you to be working on, he would let you go. Then I was going to give it back to him. I—I read some of it . . . after we arrived here and I realized that—what he was doing. I was worried to death because you knew too . . . for fear of what you would do."

"I?"

"James asked for it tonight and I gave it to him. I wasn't worried about him. He is family and he might know how to dissuade Edward. Edward never listened to me . . . to what I said. And that Michael would be no help. I never thought that James would do anything with it . . . would—"

"What harm can he do? What is he planning?" Victoria spoke urgently now, staring at the woman, fear filling her voice.

"I don't know." The woman sounded broken. "I do not know. But in the garden he spoke of becoming duke, and he cannot do that unless—unless something happens to Edward . . ." Judith stared up at Victoria. "He cannot mean to harm his brother . . ."

"Has he not done so before?" Victoria asked quietly.

Judith came alive. She stood up, anger flaring: *"No! That is a lie. Lies! Gossip!"* She saw a maid stop in her tracks, staring toward her, and she turned away, heading for the stairs. "A lie," she said again, more quietly.

"And his behavior in the garden?" Victoria asked, watching Judith grab the banister, supporting herself with its help.

"He is not a bad boy. He is misunderstood, misused . . . he has been through much and has been gone far too long . . . he has been hurt in the wars . . . upset by it all."

Victoria followed Judith up the stairs. When they reached the upper hall, Judith turned back to stare at Victoria. "He is not a bad boy at heart," she told Victoria.

"He is not a boy at all, your ladyship."

Judith finally turned away, walking heavily toward her room. "You'd best tell Edward what I've done."

Victoria hesitated, staring across the hall at the door to the duke's rooms. The sounds of cleaning up came up the stairs, a footman walking across the front hall below with a long-handled candle snuffer, reaching it high to douse the candles, one by one. Shadows began to fill the hall below, Victoria still hesitating by the stairwell. She thought of going after Michael, of finding him to tell him. Of not going near the door to his rooms. She thought of his rooms at The Willows. And of waking up in his bed.

And she walked forward, tapping softly on the door and calling out his name.

Chapter 25

THE DOOR DID NOT open immediately. She had time to think of what she was doing and had turned away when he opened it, staring out at her. She heard the door opening. Heard him speak. "Yes?"

Her back was to him, her back trembling a little as she slowly turned to face him. He held a candle, the light flickering up toward his face, outlining the sharp planes, the angular nose, the straight lips. "Yes?" he said again.

She swallowed. "Your aunt has just told me that it was she who took the manuscript."

He stared at Victoria, digesting the information, puzzled. "Judith took it?"

Victoria nodded. "She wished to be rid of me and thought it a way to have me leave."

He took another moment before answering. "I see," he said at last. He was watching her closely.

"There's more," she told him. "Earlier tonight she gave the manuscript to James."

His expression hardened but he did not speak. He watched her turn away. Taking one long step forward, he reached for her arm, stopping her, turning her back around. He searched her eyes. "Why did you not tell me earlier?"

"Oh, Edward, do you have to ask that? Judith just told me, downstairs a few moments ago. I came directly up." She moved as if to leave and he held her fast.

"Come inside," he said.

She felt his hand pulling her toward the doorway. She hesitated, walking slowly behind him as he led her toward it. "If you do not trust me—" she began.

"Shhh. Not now," was all he replied.

The room was in darkness except for the candle he carried, no fire laid in the sitting-room grate. He moved around her, closing the door and reaching to light a lamp. "It's all right," he said.

"What is all right?" she asked.

"What do you mean, all right?" another male voice asked from the darkness, startling her. She jumped, Edward reaching toward her as the lamp flared higher, a man visible now across the room near the bedroom door.

"I would trust her with my life," Edward said simply from beside Victoria.

The man moved closer, sitting in a chair across from a dark blue settee. "Would you, now? Since you already are trusting her with mine, I suppose that's encouraging."

Victoria stared at the man. He was of rather slight build, his face pale white in the lamp glow, his eyes as dark as Edward's. His expression was impassive at the moment, belying his words. He had a romantic good looks but an air of icy reserve and a cold, clear voice. "Do you know who I am?" he was asking her as she stared at him.

"No, I do not," she replied.

"And if I tell you my name is Parnell—what then?"

"Charles Stewart?" she responded, seeing his eyes acknowledge her question. "Ireland is not a geographical fragment of England, she is a nation," Victoria quoted, watching the man's surprise. "From your maiden speech in Parliament if I am not mistaken."

He stared at her. "Nor are you misquoting."

Edward was handing Victoria toward the settee, a small smile playing about his features as he sat down beside her. "Victoria Leggett—she has been working with me on my history of Ireland."

"I see," he replied, still watching her. "An unusual occupation for a young Englishwoman."

"You sound very English yourself, sir," Victoria told the

man boldly, watching him as if he had come to life off the pages she had studied.

He grimaced. "The result of an English education. My mother taught me to hate England. And sent me here at every opportunity. I suppose feeling that the more I saw, the more of her opinion I would share."

"And do you?" Victoria heard herself asking out loud.

He glanced at Edward before answering. "Do you know who Wolfe Tone was Miss . . . Leggett?"

"No, I do not."

"No matter. He was an Irish patriot, not someone you would have learned much about. He confessed in his autobiography that his hatred of England was so deep-rooted in his nature that it had become instinct rather than principle."

Edward stiffened beside Victoria. "I do not share your feelings, if such be your feelings, Mr. Parnell."

"You are as Irish as you are English." Parnell spoke in a clear, cool voice as if he knew nothing of the danger to himself of what he was saying to a peer of the realm.

"I am as English as I am Irish," Edward told the man. "And I owe allegiance to my Queen. As you yourself do. In attempting to help Ireland, I have no intention of hurting England. If help Ireland I can."

"Oh you can, your grace. You are in a singular position for helping poor Ireland, since you are not only Irish by birth and mother but also an English peer. You sit in the House of Lords, where we desperately need support for what we are trying to do in Commons. And you have the ear of the Queen herself. It is hard for me to imagine any way in which Ireland could hurt England, except in the pocketbook of the English absentee landowners—which includes, in truth, you yourself, although you would lose nothing, since your rights to your land come down through your mother's family as well. We cannot harm your interests, your grace. But you can immeasurably aid our cause and the land of your birth by speaking out in our behalf."

"Speaking out," Edward repeated.

The man was brilliant, this much Victoria knew from all the speeches and information she had been dutifully accumulating on his work and that of the rest of Parliament concerning the Irish Question. But he was cold. He was speaking still to Edward: "If you do not already know it, I shall repeat my position most firmly. I will not be a party to bloodshed. I have made that plain to all my followers. I am attempting to bring about change—and justice—through the processes of the existing government. Not, as the Queen seems to fear, attempting to overthrow it."

"I doubt that the Queen fears any—" Edward's words caught in his throat as the door to his sitting room burst open, James standing wild-eyed in the opening, his army revolver in his hand. "What are you doing?" Edward asked his twin, seeing the others in the room converging toward the man in the doorway.

"Stay where you are!" James brought the revolver up, aiming the Enfield directly at his brother. "All of you."

Mike was coming up behind James, Victoria's eyes widening as she saw him move quietly toward James's back. James saw her eyes flicker, saw Edward begin to walk toward him. In that moment Mike grabbed for the gun.

It went off, Parnell reaching to shield Victoria as Edward buckled forward onto the settee.

"Edward!" Victoria pushed Parnell away, reaching for Edward as Mike wrestled James to the floor, the gun flung loose. Parnell grabbed for it, Edward sitting up straighter with Victoria's help. Pain turned his complexion stark white, his voice strained when he spoke: "I'm all right."

"All right! You've been shot!" She stared down at the hand with which he was clutching his own thigh, blood seeping through his fingers.

Mike's fist connected with James's jaw, the younger man going limp. Mike turned James over, pinioning his arms behind his back and yanking him to his feet while Parnell covered them both with the gun.

"I rather doubt you've met my brother James before this night," Edward was saying to Parnell through gritted teeth.

"Your twin," Parnell said. "I see." His eyes turned back toward the mirror image of the duke as James wrestled against Mike's grip, his angry voice rising as he struggled: "You'll pay for this, all of you! Treasonous writings and Fenians in it with you!"

"There is no treason in this house!" Edward barked the words out, grimacing at the pain that shot through his leg when he moved. Victoria pulled on her petticoat, tearing off cloth to bind his wound.

"He came upon me unawares." Mike sounded disgusted with himself. "I must be getting too old to be any use."

The sound of someone approaching turned them all toward the door, the little Irishman stopping to stare at the scene before him. "It's trouble outside too, soldiers coming up quiet toward the back."

James's laughter barked out at them. "They'll find out your true position now—Fenians and your own words!"

"I do wish you would stop calling me a Fenian." Parnell stared at the duke's twin brother. "You have no idea what I am."

"I know who you are and that's enough!"

Victoria stared at James, something he had said echoing within her. Edward moved as if to stand and she helped him try, feeling his pain as she saw its marks cross his face. As they moved she realized what James had just said. "Edward, he said they would find your words. The manuscript must still be here."

Each of the men stared at her. James felt Mike's grip slacken. He jabbed his elbow into Mike's midsection and wrenched away, forcing the little Irishman aside. The little man regained his feet as Mike lumbered past him. He turned to follow the burly man toward James and the door he was running toward.

Edward hobbled toward the hall, reaching it in time to see James stop stock-still at the threshold, staring straight ahead. *"No!"* James was shouting, the sound of knocking coming up the stairs from the front hall.

"See . . ." Edward leaned against the doorjamb. "Go see . . ." he told Victoria. She released him unwillingly, speeding down the hall to where she could see Judith kneeling by the fireplace in James's rooms, feeding the last of the papers she held into the fire. *"No!"* James took one step toward her, his rigid back to Victoria. She heard footsteps below and looked down the stairwell. Jasper was heading toward the front door, carrying a lamp, his night robe floating about him.

"No!" Victoria shouted out to him. "Jasper, do not open that door!"

Jasper stared up at her in amazement. Edward hobbled across to where he could see Jasper. "Do as she says," he told the man, almost falling as Victoria rushed to help him.

"You must get back to your rooms," she told him. "They cannot see you like this!"

James came out of his room, his eyes wild. He stared at them all, pushing past the group at the top of the stairs as Sylvia opened the door to her room, staring out at her husband. "What's happened?" she asked.

No one replied. Mike wrestled with James to stop him from going near the door where the pounding was now louder. Parnell stood in the doorway to the duke's sitting room, his expression mildly amused. "It seems we have a problem." He reached the gun out toward Edward.

"Get inside!" Judith's voice rang out, startling the others. "Get inside!" she cried as she moved toward them. The little Irishman moved toward Parnell, motioning him back inside the duke's room as Judith spoke: "He is a peer of the realm. They cannot search uninvited!"

Victoria was half dragging Edward toward the same rooms. "She is right. And they cannot see you like this." Victoria faltered with his weight, Sylvia coming forward to help her half drag, half carry the wounded duke into his sitting room and the bedroom beyond.

"Come with us!" Victoria told the two Irishmen, turning toward Sylvia as they reached the huge mahogany bed in Edward's room. "Sylvia, try and stop James if you can!"

Sylvia stared at her. Then she left the room. "I must—" Edward tried to get up, only to be pushed back.

Victoria reached for his jacket. "You—" she called to Parnell and the other man. "Here, quickly; help me get him undressed and into bed!"

Parnell did not hesitate, moving around the bed to her side, speaking to his companion as he did so: "I hear the voice of authority, Tim Ryan. I think we'd best do as the lady requests."

"It's not proper . . ." Ryan was coming slowly around the bed. "Her being here and all." He spoke his doubts but he moved to help with the duke's trousers, pulling the bloodstained cloth off the duke's long legs. When he straightened up, he gasped. Victoria was quickly unfastening the fancy emerald satin gown, her fingers fumbling with the speed of her movements.

"Girl! What are you doing?"

"Shhh!" She watched them lay Edward back in the bed, saw his eyes turn toward her at Ryan's words, his shock as great as theirs when she dropped the satin gown to the thick Turkey carpet, stepping out of it and coming toward the bed in her thin cotton chemise and knickers.

Only Parnell seemed to realize what she was doing, his eyes alight as he pulled the bedding back beside the duke. "A diversion, my dear?" he asked.

"Victoria, you cannot do this—" Edward began to sit up.

She was next to him, moving swiftly to lie beside him and pull the covers up over them. "The wall hangings at the head of the bed," she said to Parnell. He looked to where she directed, seeing thick velvet hangings draped from the high ceiling to the top of the huge four-poster bed. The voluminous material hung draped around the top of the bed.

"Ryan—" Parnell moved toward the hangings, slipping between the wall and the hangings, a bare foot between the high back of the bed and the wall behind him. Ryan followed suit, his eyes wide still as he tried to keep from looking at the brazen baggage who had just jumped into his lordship's bed.

Edward stared at her. "They dare not search—"

Voices, loud and male, came through the walls, Judith's own rising over the others, coming nearer, telling them they had no right.

"In here!" It was James who called out from the sitting-room doorway, turning the knob to find it locked. "Break it! They are inside!"

"You have no authority! How *dare* you . . ." Judith's voice was lost in the melee outside as Victoria turned to face Edward.

"Is the pain very bad?" she asked him softly, her lips a few bare inches from his. She was moving beneath the covers, struggling with her clothing.

"What pain?" he asked in a whisper, his eyes on her lips,

his ears full of the sounds from the outer room as men surged against the door, forcing it open.

"You must kiss me," she told him. "They must think us so . . . involved, we did not hear all that ruckus."

"We would have to be very involved."

She lay back against the high pillows, the sheet falling a little to show her bare shoulders and the top of her breast. He stared at her. She reached up to touch the hair of his chest, his hand pulling the sheet up to stare down at her nakedness. "What have you done!" he asked her, his eyes traveling down her body as she reached for him, pulling him nearer.

Her words fell against his mouth: "Given them something to stop them long enough for you to think of something." His lips were against hers.

"Think . . ." He groaned, his hands reaching to cup the breasts beneath him, to draw her nearer.

When the door to the bedroom was forced open, his tongue had found hers and for one brief moment all else was lost. Sudden silence filled the room, his wound, Parnell's presence, and all else meaningless next to the rocketing explosions going on within him.

"What the bloody hell—" The sound of James's voice snapped Edward out of it, bringing his head up to stare at two soldiers who stood at the side of his bed, James beside them, Judith in the doorway between the sitting room and the bedroom. Beyond Judith, Sylvia and Mike stared at him from farther across the outer room.

Edward's voice thundered out, taking the men aback: *"How dare You!"*

They shrank a bit, staring at the creamy pale skin of Victoria's breast before she reached to draw the covers up higher.

The duke rose on one elbow, naked as far as they could see, as naked as the girl. One of the soldiers looked uncomfortably at the other as Edward continued: *"What is the meaning of this?"*

"I—I tried to stop them," Mike called from behind.

"I tell you there are Fenians here!" James yelled at the men. "You must search!"

"And I told you the duke had retired!" Judith spoke

quickly. "You have trespassed and now look what you've done!" She sounded genuinely shocked, as well she was when she stared across the men at Victoria's naked arms crossed over the thin sheet and reaching to pull the covers up higher about her.

"We—we had reason to believe that dangerous criminals were within," the senior soldier began.

"What reason?" Edward demanded. "Do you know the law of the land? *None* can trespass upon the property of a peer of the realm without direct orders from the Queen herself!"

"We have those orders, your grace."

"Show me!"

The soldier looked uncomfortable. "We do not have it in writing, but—"

"The law states it must be in writing and *signed* by Her Majesty! Show me her signature!"

"Don't listen to him," James was saying, imploring them. He started around the bed, one of the soldiers stopping him and looking toward the other. "This man is a member of the family and has invited us within, has invited us to search this house—"

"This man has no right to invite *any* into this house," Edward told the soldier coldly. "He is a deserter from Her Majesty's African forces and as such is disowned by myself and my family!"

"Deserter?" The soldier holding James's arms stiffened his grip, the other soldier staring at James. "Is this true?"

"Don't listen to him! I tell you, he is a traitor, he should not be duke! He should be sent to the Tower!" James was shouting at them.

"You didn't answer the question," the senior officer told James coldly. "It is easy enough to verify." He watched James's expression become defensive and turned away from him, disgusted.

James pulled away from the soldier. "I'll show you!" He raced to the cupboard across the room, wrenching it open to show rows of clothing neatly hung away.

"I shall give you this one moment to leave my room before I request your names and ranks—you shall be cashiered along with my errant brother if you do not leave my private quarters this instant! If you wish to discuss anything at all, I shall receive you in the sitting room. *Not here!*"

The two soldiers looked at each other and then turned back toward the door. James came toward them. "Don't listen to him! I tell you, they are here! *Here!*"

One of the soldiers spoke quietly. "There is no door out from this room save the one we came through. None can escape while we wait for his grace to dress." The soldier's eyes slid to Victoria—who turned away, blushing, from the frank look he gave her.

"They are deceiving you!" James shouted.

Sylvia came through the doorway, touching Judith to let her pass. Judith hesitated, unsure, and then stepped back a little to let Sylvia through. When she passed the soldier nearest the door, she smiled at him pleasantly. "Will you please help me take my husband to his rooms? He has been off his head for days, threatening the duke and even threatening me." She pulled on the sleeve of her dressing gown, pushing it back to show an ugly bruise. "As you can see, he has no compunctions about attacking even his own wife."

The man stared at Sylvia's arm, Edward seeing it for the first time. "Sylvia, you said nothing!"

She shrugged. "He wishes to be rid of his brother," she told the soldiers. "He wishes to have him out of the way and to inherit the dukedom for himself. If you allow yourselves to become party to his schemes, you are sure to be caught up in the consequences."

The quiet way she spoke, the utter honesty in her words, drew the soldiers toward James, ready to help her.

"Where do you wish him, your ladyship?"

"Locked in his room until you can ascertain all you need to put an end to this night, gentlemen. After that we are thrust upon the mercy of his grace. If he can find any left after this appalling scene."

The soldiers came at James, Sylvia carefully, and unobtrusively, moving between James and the bed. He pulled back but they had hold of him, dragging him forward as he protested. "Don't you see what they are doing? They are all in it together! Stop this! I shall have your heads if you do not let me go! *Let me go, I say!*" They dragged him toward the door, Judith stepping back out of the way, her agony plain upon her face as she saw him struggle with the soldiers. He was being held in their grip as they led him past her.

"You!" He looked at her accusingly. "Why did you destroy the manuscript? *Why?*"

Her eyes were bleak, her voice near breaking as she turned away. "What manuscript?" she asked softly, the soldiers shaking their heads, the man obviously off his head.

"You can't go around accusing everyone, your lordship," one of the soldiers told him as they moved, earning a harsh laugh from James. "I am not a lordship, gentlemen! *You* have seen to that!"

"How about deserter?" the older soldier asked harshly. "Does that strike your fancy, then?" His grip tightened on James's arm.

They had him in the sitting room, Sylvia leading the way to the hall beyond. Judith looked back toward the bed and then reached for the bedroom door, closing it behind her as she spoke. "We shall await you in the next room."

The words came toward the bed as the door closed. Victoria huddled beneath the bedding, shaking, her eyes closed. When she heard nothing but silence for long moments, she opened her eyes to see Edward staring down at her.

Still propped on his elbow, he watched her eyes as conflicting emotions fled through them: worry, relief, shame, love . . . he saw each in turn as she looked up at him, trying to manage a smile. "So far, so good . . . but they'll see you are wounded and have more questions." She lost all trace of a smile, her worry rising high again.

He reached beneath the sheets, reaching to caress one perfect breast, watching her as her breath caught in her throat at his touch. "I can stave them off . . . now. Thanks to you." He leaned forward to kiss her and stopped, remembering the men behind the wall hangings. "Stay," he whispered. "Please . . . stay here." She watched his eyes, slowly nodding. "Say it," he told her. "Promise me."

"I shall stay . . . here . . . now."

"Until I come back."

"Until you come back . . ."

He brushed her forehead with his lips and then pushed

himself away, sitting up and leaning over to retrieve the shirt that had been thrown to the floor beside her ballgown. He spoke very softly as he buttoned it. "Can you hear me?"

"Yes." A whispered voice came back toward him from the head of the bed.

"It might be best to stay as you are until I ensure they have left. And James has been . . . taken care of."

Edward stood up, holding on to the bedpost for support, taking one step toward a high-backed chair and reaching for it to help take his weight. "No, stay!" he told Victoria as she began to rise. "I have to do this." He reached the wardrobe, pulling open a door and reaching for the first pair of trousers he could find. Wrenching them out of the cupboard, he sank to a nearby chair, pulling them on, taking several deep breaths before he stood up and fastened them in place.

He reached for the back of chairs as he went, but he walked straight to the sitting-room door. Upon opening it, he saw the soldiers walking back inside. They watched the duke, taking his grimaces for anger as he closed the door behind him and slowly walked toward the nearest chair. "I shall expect this interview to be brief. I have had a long night and wish to return to my bed."

He stared at them belligerently, watching their expressions as they glanced toward the closed door and thought of the lovely redhead reclining within; they could understand his impatience.

The senior officer spoke slowly. "Your brother contacted the palace, telling of dangerous associations with the Fenian movement and a seditious paper or papers in your possession. Written by you yourself, your grace."

"Not too bloody likely, is it?" He glared at the soldier. "First and foremost, I am an English duke, not some malcontent foreigner bent upon intrigue! Secondly, the papers you speak of are a history of England and Ireland which my father, the late duke, had been working on at the time of his death. I had told the Queen that it was my intention to complete his work."

"She—you told the Queen of these papers?"

"Last week!"

The officer swallowed. "Upon arrival—"

"Upon forcing your way into my household!" the duke corrected.

"Upon being *invited* in by your brother," the soldier said quickly, "your brother then announced that seditious Fenians were on the premises and he wished protection from them."

"Which you, of course, took at face value."

"I beg your pardon?" The officer drew himself up straighter.

"And well you should beg my pardon! Tell me, now that you have seen my brother, have seen my household, have talked to his wife—doesn't it begin to dawn on you just how outrageous these accusations are? How wildly fanciful at the very least?" Edward stood up, his size, his position, his wrath intimidating the Queen's men. "I would suggest you first ascertain from your superiors the truth of my brother's desertion under Zulu fire. Then I would suggest someone mention this outrage to the Queen and hear what *she* has to say about this! And lastly, I would suggest that before you undertake a commission such as this again, you look a little more fully into *who* is accusing *whom* of what!" He turned away, reaching for the door, stopping as he had hold of it. "That is, of course, unless you wish to go forward and reinvestigate my cupboards for traitors and Fenians!"

The senior officer glared at his sergeant. "Well?"

The sergeant stared back as if the officer was demented. "Well, what, sir?"

"Have you seen enough?"

"Sir, he said he was the duke at first—that was the message we received—and needed assistance—"

"Enough!" The officer bowed toward the duke, not glancing at Mike and Judith, who stood in the room, watching. "We shall see ourselves out, your grace."

"*I'll* see you out," Mike said, coming around the settee. "And lock up for the night," he told the duke.

Edward nodded. "Please. And see that my rest is undisturbed for what little there is left of the night."

"Yes, your grace," Mike said meekly, standing and waiting for the soldiers to precede him out.

When they had gone, only Judith remained in the sitting

room, staring at Edward as he collapsed back against the door. "Are you unwell?" she asked him.

"James shot me," he told her quietly, seeing her shock. She took one step closer and then stopped. He tried to see into what she was feeling. "Aunt Judith—thank you . . ."

She spoke slowly. "It is our name, your father's name and title I was protecting."

"I understand."

"Do you?" She eyed him strangely. "I—I burned your papers," she told him.

"I know."

"Oh." She looked down. "I don't suppose that girl is going to leave."

"No."

"This will not be kept a secret. Not with those men involved. And the servants and what all they must have heard. And seen. She—Victoria—she has done much for you this night. At her own expense." The words were hard for Judith.

"Yes," Edward replied quietly. "I am aware of that."

"Do you love her?" Judith looked up then, staring at him.

"Yes," Edward told his aunt. "I think I do."

"No good will come of it. For her or for you."

"We shall see," was all he replied.

Judith looked toward the door he leaned against, her thoughts on what lay beyond it. "Do you wish me to stay while she dresses?" She hesitated. "I assume she is leaving now."

"Not just yet."

Judith watched him. "I see. And are there Fenians here?"

"No."

"Is there—someone . . . ?"

Edward watched her. "If so, they will be long gone before morning."

She nodded, turning away. "Good night then."

"Good night, Aunt Judith." He watched her walk away, her thin shoulders curving forward, her posture bent as if with the weight of her head. Or of the evening's events.

"Aunt Judith—" he called out to her, his leg throbbing, his head feeling lighter and lighter. She slowly turned to glance back at him. "I thank you again. For all of us."

She shook her head a little, turning away again. "Don't thank me . . . please . . . don't thank me."

He watched her walk away before he turned to open the door, fighting back an attack of nausea as he turned, the pain shooting up the nerves in his leg now as he moved into the bedroom.

He reached the bed before he collapsed.

She stood by them a little longer, staring again. "Don't think up . . . Stay . . . close to me."

He watched her walk away; waited for her to reach the door, looking past the diminishing figure of the woman. Then the curtains that he saw dimly before her disappeared into the distance.

He closed his eyes and remembered . . .

Chapter 26

HE CAME TO A few minutes later, Victoria leaning over him, the shirt that he had worn now wrapped about her, Parnell peering down at him from behind her shoulder.

"He's back with us," Parnell said, his voice sounding a long way off. Tim Ryan floated into view and then swam away as Edward closed his eyes. "Or almost back with us," Parnell was saying.

"Have to"—Edward forced his eyes open—"have to get them out of here."

"I know . . . I know. Stay still now; a doctor has been sent for." She pressed a cool cloth to his forehead. Its dampness felt good against his hot and clammy flesh. He tried to smile. "This isn't what I planned," he told her. "For our next . . . meeting."

"Have you been planning it, then?"

"Yes." His eyes closed.

"We've got to get out of here," Ryan was saying. "And that's a fact."

"The question is whether the good soldiers completely believed the story they were told. Or whether for good measure they have stationed men near enough to see who comes and goes." Parnell spoke as if he were discussing a point of parliamentary procedure, not his freedom.

"I don't understand what has happened. As a member of the House of Commons, surely you have the right to visit any you wish."

"Ah, but you see, my dear lady, Parliament was dissolved and Her Majesty has ordered me for the time being to depart England's shores. I am to be arrested if I am found here."

"But why?" Victoria asked, bathing the duke's fevered forehead as she spoke.

"The Queen has no sympathy for the Irish cause. Which is to say she is actively opposed to it and distrusts all Irishmen on sight. She sees Fenians ready to blow her and her country to kingdom come at every turn."

"But that—that's preposterous! No civilized people would permit such things!"

"The order, however, still stands. I was to have left England by last week. Any who harbor me would be harboring a fugitive from the Queen's justice."

A quick rap at the closed bedroom door startled them. Mike's voice came through: "It's me and I've bad news."

Ryan reached for the door, unlocking it. "What more could go wrong?"

"James has climbed out his window and is gone."

Victoria caught her breath, thinking quickly. "Mike, rouse the stables and have them ready a carriage. Quickly. And find some footmen's clothing that will fit these two." She looked over at Parnell. "I know of no other way, do you? They shall hardly think to look twice at one of our footmen."

"Dear lady, a brave idea. And I hope you are correct in your assumption."

"Can you think of better?"

"Aye," Mike said. "I shall ready two carriages. The first shall start out at a merry trot and let them follow if they choose. It will make its way to the doctor, to find what's keeping him. The second will head for The Willows, where there is a skiff left by our Tim here himself and a boat on down the river."

Ryan nodded. "I'd forgotten, but we did plan for the meeting to take place there. You left all as it was?"

Mike shrugged. "I saw no reason to change it. I still hoped this would not come off in London. I knew there'd be trouble."

"You don't know when James left," Victoria said.

Mike turned toward the door. "You're right. I'll see to the horses and the clothing."

Parnell saw Edward's eyes opening. "How are you feeling?"

"I'm all right," Edward said. "We must get you away."

"It's in the works, your grace." Parnell studied the man who lay stretched out against snow-white pillows. "You are willing to help, still and all?"

Edward nodded his head a little against the pillows. "Yes. More so than ever. This is not the way government should be run."

"I quite agree. But then you know that." Parnell hesitated. "I am very curious about your reasoning."

Edward focused on the man. "I beg your pardon?"

"If you are as concerned about Ireland as you seem—as you obviously are—I would think you would have made an effort to at least see your lands there. Your people there."

Edward's face closed over. "I have no wish to see Ireland."

Parnell's eyes clouded. "That is what puzzles me. One would think you would at least want to see your mother and her people. After all—"

"My mother is dead."

Parnell stared at Edward. "I beg your pardon?"

"My mother died when I was a child. When we were children," he amended, thinking of his brother. "James—"

"James has gotten away," Parnell told Edward.

Edward struggled to sit up. "He must be stopped."

"We can't stop him, Edward. He is gone from the house." Victoria spoke quietly, urging him back toward the pillows.

"You must leave—"

"We are leaving, your grace . . ." Parnell hesitated. "I do not mean to intrude . . . but who told you your mother was dead?"

"What?" Edward's voice was weak from pain.

"Your mother is as alive as I am."

Edward heard the words. His eyes widened, staring up at the Irish leader. "Say that again," he told Parnell.

"I assure you, your mother is as alive as I am. Or she was when I left Ireland three months ago. She was against my coming to you, by the by. Felt that you had no sympathy with our cause."

Edward forced himself to sit up, his eyes raking across the other's man face. "You cannot be serious! She cannot be—I was seven years old when we were told . . ." The words stopped, Edward staring at Parnell's pale face. "You have . . . seen her?"

"I have. I understand that she was left well provided for by your father—on the provision that she never make herself known to her sons. She had thought that when you were old enough, you would come looking for her, would want to know her side of what had happened . . . at least so my sister tells me; your mother has not confided in me directly. But she was assured by your father's agents that neither of her sons wished any contact with her."

"Oh my god . . ." Edward's head swam with the news. The knowledge that she was alive, that she had been alive all these years, hit him like a physical blow to his already weakened body. He felt himself falling back toward the bed, felt Victoria's arms cushioning him, cradling him, heard movement around the bed as Mike came back to the room.

"Is he all right?" Mike was asking, coming near to stare down with worried eyes. Edward looked up at him.

"My mother—"

"Aye, boy, you rest—"

"My mother—"

"He is trying to tell you that his mother is alive," Victoria told Mike.

"What are you saying?" Mike stared at her as if she were crazed.

"It's true." Parnell took the clothing from Mike's arms. "I have met her myself. Are these the clothes I am to wear?"

Parnell pulled pieces of clothing up to himself, thrusting some at Ryan and keeping others for himself. Mike was still staring at Parnell, his disbelief written large across his features. "Siobhan . . . alive . . ." He leaned against the bed, staring down at Edward, tears forming in his blue eyes.

Victoria watched the large man raise his arm to brush the back of his hand against his eyes, wiping the water that fell unbidden, shoving it away as the shock of Parnell's announcement wore away, a dull ache of knowledge filling him. Even as the words were said, somewhere within him he knew them to be true.

Edward's hand closed around Victoria's; she looked down to see his gaze intent upon her. "Parnell and Ryan—"

"Are to dress as footmen and drive away with the carriage; in case any are watching."

"We are to go too."

"What?" She faltered, trying to push him back as he rose toward her. "No, you must rest until the doctor comes—"

"Get my clothing," Edward told Mike. "And pack a light bag. We shall leave for Ireland directly."

"Ireland!" Parnell, Mike, Victoria, even Tim Ryan stared at the wounded man on the bed.

"You cannot possibly take that trip in your condition! The Irish Sea alone is—it's not to be thought of!" Parnell spoke first and quickly.

"I can, I will, and I must." Edward spoke to Mike. "You can come or stay as you please."

Mike stared at the duke. "Stay? Are you daft?" He turned toward the door.

Tim Ryan scowled at Mike as he left. "No one answered the question; it is daft to try this!"

"You shall go aboard ship as my retainers. Once on board you can do as you please. You'll be off English soil and therefore free." He could feel Victoria's eyes upon him. When he looked toward her, she spoke slowly.

"And what am I to do?"

"I cannot ask you to come with me. Unless you . . . you must do as you wish."

"Is there any way I can stop you from going until you are recovered from this?" She motioned toward his leg.

"No."

"We cannot possibly travel together; it will be too obvious." Parnell spoke at last, watching the duke.

Edward looked toward Tim Ryan. "We can leave here in my carriage. When we reach my doctor's house, you can go on as you would have, if you prefer. But I will need your help, Tim Ryan. I will travel in secret until I reach the ship. Just in case."

"In case?"

"In case the Queen has questions she would like to ask me. They will have to wait until I have seen my mother."

"That is what this is all about, then."

Edward stared at Parnell. "I learned last week, from Tim here, that my brother had left his post. Had been cashiered from the army, had wandered about Europe, been wounded in a duel, and arrived home as if he had come from the battlefield. That was . . . unsettling. Now you tell me that the mother I have mourned for almost thirty years not only is alive, but thinks I do not care enough to seek her out." Edward turned toward Michael as he walked back in. "And Michael: either you get my clothes or I'll get them myself. Twenty-five years is long enough to wait. I shall not take the chance of the Queen detaining me. By morning's light those soldiers will have more questions . . . and our story will not hold up under too much questioning. If the Queen wishes to see the manuscript, for example."

"There's no use arguing with him," Mike told the others as he went toward the mahogany wardrobe. "There never has been since he was a child."

Parnell turned toward Mike. "Where can we change?"

Mike handed Edward's clothing to Victoria and turned toward the others. "Follow me and I'll show you."

Edward reached for Victoria's hand, holding it as the others left. When they were alone, he watched her closely. "I must do this."

She bit her lip, finally lowering her head to his shoulder. "I know."

"Will you come with me?" he asked her softly.

She kissed his cheek. "Do you think in your weakened condition you could stop me?"

His arm tightened around her. "I can dress myself. You had best see to a bag. And only tell Sylvia that we are going to the doctor instead of having him come here. The less others know, the better—should James come back."

She stood up quickly, thinking of James. "Can he cause more trouble tonight?"

"I don't know. But in the morning, when the Queen is wakened, we had best already be away."

She nodded and left, looking back once to see him bending forward and pulling his shirt around him. "I shall be back straightaway."

"Quickly now."

Victoria threw a few things into the bag she had brought to The Willows from Mercy House, thinking of all that had happened since she took that fateful ride. She tried to move quietly, most of the servants in their beds, Mike sending others to ready the horses and hitch up the carriages before going back to their own warm beds.

The fog had become thicker as the hour grew later, the thin wisps of the earlier hours replaced by a low-hanging gray miasma that smothered the moon and blanketed the night in pitch blackness.

A muffled cough came from somewhere across the square, a horse's steady clip-clop across the wet cobblestones echoing through the silence as the first carriage came around to the front portico.

A footman came out of the house beside the duke, helping him down the stairs and into the carriage, Victoria at his side. The driver called to the horse and they started out, the sounds bringing a man who stood in the shadows across the square to attention. He watched the carriage and moved hurriedly off, jumping up into a waiting cab and calling to the driver to waken.

Moments after the duke's carriage disappeared around the block, the waiting cab started out after it.

A few moments later a figure in dark clothing slipped out of the back of Bereshaven House, heading for a narrow door in the thick back wall and hesitating, listening carefully before opening it. After a moment he opened the wooden door, stepping out into the mews and walking away, whistling softly. If any looked on, the figure appeared none the better for a night of drinking, listing to one side as he walked across the mews to the shadows along the opposite side, heading toward Piccadilly and a night of more fun.

In the carriage Parnell sat across from the duke, the footman's clothing ill-fitting, binding him at elbow and knee. Victoria sat mopping the duke's brow, her worry apparent in her every movement.

"Can you hear me?" Mike's voice came from the driver's box, just discernible over the sounds of the carriage.

"Yes," Victoria called back softly.

"It's followed we are, just so you know. I shan't try to lose them."

"I'm all right," Edward was telling Victoria, pulling her hand away. "Save yourself. We don't know what all we will have to survive this night. Tim Ryan will be in Soho, where we met before?" Edward was looking at Parnell, who nodded. "Good." Edward relaxed as best he could.

The carriage pulled up to the house in Bloomsbury, Mike jumping down and running to the door. It opened almost immediately, the doctor staring out to them. "I was ready to come when your man came, telling me to stay here. Are you sure he should have been moved, Michael? What all happened?"

"See him first and then we'll be answering the rest." Mike turned back to the carriage, staring up the road, trying to see through the fog. "One thing's for sure," he told Edward as he leaned inside to help him out and down. "If we can't see them, they can't see us."

"Hurry," Edward said. "I don't want them to see me like this; it will bring more questions. And trouble to the doctor."

The old doctor heard the last of his words as Mike helped him up the steps. Parnell had moved quietly to take Mike's place in the driver's seat.

"I thank you for worrying," the doctor told Edward as he moved back into his own hall. "But I know Mike well and he would not ask something that wasn't necessary."

Victoria came behind them, the doctor shutting the door as Parnell turned the horse around, starting back down the street the way they had come. He passed the hired cab, hearing someone hail him.

"Halt!"

A man came near in the fog. Parnell peered down. "Yes, guv?" he said in a muffled voice through his scarf and cloak.

"Where are you headed then?"

"Why, to Bereshaven House. Who's asking?"

"Where's the duke then?"

"At home in bed, I suppose. His brother has been poorly

all night. Off his head you know. They had him sent down to the doctor to see if there was any help for him this side of Bedlam."

The man digested this. The fog swirled around the lamp that hung beside Parnell, soft yellow light arcing down toward the man who stood undecided in the street.

"You're not to come back then?"

"Not till I'm called. They say it will be morning."

The man nodded. "Away with you then. And no need to mention the questions. It's the Queen's business we're on."

"You don't say!" Parnell leaned a little forward. "What's going on then, guv?"

"Get on with you. That's for the likes of us to know. Not you. Get along now!"

Parnell pulled himself back up in the driver's seat slowly, as if reluctant to leave. He gave the horse his head, starting off again toward Bereshaven House.

He continued west for two more blocks, listening for the sound of anyone following. When nothing moved behind him, he finally turned off the road, circling around to the narrow mews that angled toward the back of the doctor's house, pulling the carriage up and handing it over to Mike when he stepped down.

Their conversation was whispered. "You'll take this back yourself?"

"Aye," Mike told him. "Tim Ryan will be here to take the duke and the girl on by themselves. It'll be safer this way. I'll go back for the bags and head out toward The Willows."

"We'll meet at Holyhead?"

"God willing."

"If not, you'll wait there for them. I can manage alone. I've been this way before."

Mike grinned. "Aye, it's a new experience for his grace and that's a fact."

"How's his leg?"

"Should be all right if he doesn't infect it. Lost some blood but he seems to be himself. A little weak."

Parnell hesitated. "He's very strange for an Englishman."

"Do you think so truly?"

Parnell smiled, his features softening for the first time all night. "Of course he's half-Irish."

"Aye. That he is."

The intense young man started away, slipping through the fog as Mike watched him go. Then Mike slipped into the driver's seat, heading off at a good clip back toward the duke's house.

Inside the doctor's house Victoria watched the old man bandage the duke's leg, listening carefully as he gave her ointments and directions, stuffing them into a narrow black bag for her and handing it over. "You should wait, but since you won't, this will have to be changed every few hours. If he infects, you will not reach Ireland. Or anywhere else. Do you understand me?" he asked the girl who was staring wide-eyed at him.

"Don't speak of me as if I were not present!" the duke said irritably.

"That's the only way to talk to a patient who won't listen to the medical advice he seeks."

"I have listened."

"You're still attempting to travel."

"And how did you know it was to be Ireland?" the duke asked.

The old doctor shook his head. "And where else would it be with Mike Flaherty involved?" A knock at the door interrupted him. "Unless the whole city's gone mad, this must be your people." He stood up, going to unlatch the back door. The room he left was a tiny parlor, cluttered with overstuffed chairs and a sofa much too big for the rest of the room. Tables heavily draped, portraits and miniatures and statuary from Bristol spilled across mantel and tables, every square inch of the room filled with some small trinket. The duke's eyes were closed, resting while he could, storing up what little energy he could muster.

Victoria rested her hand on his arm, listening to the sounds of movement and quiet conversation that were coming toward them. After a moment a man's head appeared around the door, staring in at them. The man took off his cap when he saw Victoria, holding it between his hands when the duke's eyes opened. "It's Tim Ryan who's sent me, guv'nor . . . says as how he's arranging your things

279

and how we're to meet him down along . . . if you're ready."

Edward rose to his feet. Victoria looked from the doctor to the man she had never before seen. "Do you know this man?" she asked the old doctor.

He nodded, smiling a little. "This is Davy Muldoon, a good man and right quick in getting things done, if you know what I mean."

"Yes," the duke said. "The quicker we leave, the better for all. Thank you."

The doctor nodded. "I hope I see you back here. And well."

The duke smiled. "So do I, doctor." Victoria came alongside, taking his right arm as Davy Muldoon took his left, helping him down the hall toward the back steps and a waiting hired carriage.

When the doctor closed his back door, the fog had already swallowed them up, only the faint clip-clop of the horse telling of their existence.

Chapter 27

THE STREETS THEY DROVE through were shrouded in fog, total silence around them until they reached Aldgate and wound through zigzagging lanes, as if in a maze, between Whitechapel and Bethnal Green.

The lanes they drove down now were only two or three hundred feet long, the odors rising from the cellars and the lodging houses fetid. Shouts and drunken curses began to pierce the night air around them, Victoria leaning closer against Edward inside the hired cab.

When the cab stopped, she stared out into the black fog, hearing sounds of revelry from somewhere nearby. Davy Muldoon appeared beside her, reaching to help the duke.

"I can manage," Edward said. Gritting his teeth, he stood up, letting Victoria step out beside Davy before he reached to brace himself and follow suit.

He almost fell. Victoria turned quickly, catching him, helped by Davy and then shrugged away. Edward righted himself. "I can walk," he told them.

"There's no reason you can't lean on me," Victoria told him softly, afraid to be overheard, chills turning her spine to jelly as the strange sounds around them continued.

"She's right, guv," Davy was telling him. "It'll look more like usual, you know? Like you're off to somewheres together after a night out. Not too good to look formal-like around here."

Edward succumbed, letting Victoria take his left arm around her shoulders. "You could never hold me up for long," he told her.

"I've done it this far," she answered back. "And I can do it as long as necessary. Davy, do we stand here in the street?"

"No, ma'am . . . this way . . ." He moved forward, showing the way, and soon they found themselves in a narrow court between three-story, tumbling-down, dirty brick buildings. The yard was about a hundred feet square with barrows and handcarts and a few empty barrels piled about. The stink of cabbage leaves and fishbones mixed with other stenches, garbage strewn all around.

Davy reached into a corner and brought forth a lantern, which seemed to be waiting for him. "This is a rum spot, best to be careful, guv—and missus . . ." He walked toward stairs that led to a cellar straight ahead of them. Slowly they followed him toward the opening in the ground from whose bowels a stream of light was issuing. Shouts of laughter and the yelling they had heard from the street came louder to their ears now.

The opening itself was about six feet wide by five feet long, a haphazard set of broken wooden stairs leading fifteen steps down to the bottom. Victoria counted each one, ending at a door that was latched from the inside, a dirty pane of glass sending out light from inside. A round red face appeared at the watch hole, staring out at them. "Wot does you want?"

Davy answered, shoving close to the glass. "It's for Tim."

"Davy, is it? Why didn't you say so!" The door opened, pitted faces, and disheveled hair above the faces, all around. A huge fireplace lit the room, thirty or forty people of all ages looking toward the newcomers, the corners of the room buried in darkness. From one of the corners Tim came toward them, leading them into the gloom to a broken chair and two three-legged stools. "Thought you got lost," Tim said loudly. "Foreigners often do in these parts." The other lodgers went back to their pewter pots and dirty places.

Victoria stared at a heap of dirty straw near the fire where a bunch of children were piled together, sleeping. The odor of stew from a large black pot hanging over the fire from a big hook mixed with the odors of dirty bodies and foul breath. The floor was dry and hardened near the fire, damp farther back. As their eyes became adjusted they could see more and more people on the floor, on ragged pieces of matting and logs of wood. Bundles of rags were being used as pillows.

Tim leaned close to the duke as they sat down. "You're to say nothing. I've got it about that you're Belgian and had your things stolen by thieves just off the boat. If I get you safe to the coast, there's money in it for me, 'cause you've naught with you until you meet up with your own. That's to save you being bothered in the night."

"Are you saying we're to stay here?"

"Shhh. Upstairs there's a place to have some privacy until it's time to go. And a sack or so to make it look more like you're traveling." He glanced at the black bag Victoria carried. "You need more than that before you reach the station."

"Station?"

"The safest way is to take the train north. It's quick, and in with all the others none will think to look for the likes of you. They'll be checking the post houses if they want you back. Figuring you'll use your own equipage and head to the coast or north."

Edward stared at Victoria in the dim light. "My god, what have I gotten you into?"

She squeezed his hand. "An adventure."

"Keep your thoughts to yourselves or others'll hear you," Tim Ryan told them, Davy Muldoon coming near with two beakers of ale. He handed one to the duke and one to Tim.

Edward took a long draft and then held it out to Victoria, who let the liquid burn down her throat. A pockmarked and dirty-faced woman came toward them from a stairwell across the room. Bloated with gin, she stared into the gloom at Tim. "It's you that wants the room, then?"

"Aye, it's us." Tim drained his ale and stood up. "Come along me foreign friends, Davy and Tim'll show ye a good time." A short laugh came from nearby, someone shouting something at Tim, who grinned and answered back in a strange tongue. As they mounted the steps he leaned close to the duke, taking his weight and whispering, "They think you're drunk and soon to be done in for your money and your missus. Stagger a bit, good . . . looks good."

"I assure you, at the moment it's quite the easiest request you could ask of me." The duke's voice was weak, carrying no farther than Tim's ear.

The room upstairs was narrow and bare, one paltry cot with none too clean a blanket thrown across it stood against the wall, a tiny window at its head. Edward sank down onto the cot.

"You'll not be here long. Rest while you can."

Tim and Davy left, Edward struggling to sit up. "You must rest," he said to Victoria.

She pushed him back to the cot, sinking to her knees beside it. "Rest as much as you can. I shall be fine right where I am."

His eyes closed as he lay back, too weak to argue. His voice when he spoke came drifting out toward her. "This isn't how I imagined our next night together."

"Shhh . . ." Her eyes closed and then opened, looking toward the unlocked door. She sat up upon her knees, reaching toward it across the tiny space of the room. A rusted key was in the lock. She turned it.

"What are you doing?" he asked, his eyes closed, the room in darkness except for the lantern Davy had left with them.

"Locking the door. When they come for us, they can knock."

He thought he told her of his agreement but she heard nothing but a murmur as she laid her head back against his arm, draping her arms over the side of the cot, sitting on the floor beside him and closing her eyes.

Sometime later there were stealthy steps outside. And the turning of the handle. Victoria heard the movement, waking from a troubled sleep to hear the rattle and then silence. And then steps going back away. She yawned and leaned back to gain what sleep she could.

A dirty gray light was coming through the narrow window when next she woke. Edward was moaning, as if in pain. She came wide-awake, sitting up straighter to see his face in the pale gray light. He was murmuring in his sleep, his head moving from side to side, more and more agitated.

She spoke to him, reaching to cradle his head, crooning to him that all was well. And still he turned and tossed, bits of words coming toward her.

"Edward . . . Edward are you all right? Edward . . ." She shook him, terrified until his eyes opened to stare at her, unfocused and fuzzy with sleep. He stared at her, his expression strange. "Edward, are you all right?"

He shook his head a little, trying to clear it. "Yes," he said finally, her sigh loud enough for him to hear. "Sorry."

"Are you in pain?"

"No." He turned away from her, facing the wall, lying now on his side. "It's nothing."

"Edward, don't turn away . . . please."

His back was still to her when he finally replied: "I have dreams. About the famine . . . Dead bodies walking the land, babies . . ." He shuddered. "It's all right. This place must have brought it back. It's nothing."

She stared at his back. "You were there . . . in the famine? In Ireland?"

"I was six when we left. The winter of fifty . . ." He turned back, lying on his back again, closing his eyes. "They were drawing blood from the cows and their horses. A little at a time and boiling it with milk and tree bark . . . trying to feed their children on it . . ." He shuddered. "We left. While the rest just starved."

She reached to hold him, his head turning toward her when she did. She could feel his tears against her cheek. "It's all right. It's all right now," she told him.

"It can never be all right . . . never."

"Yes it can," she told him. "You're going to make it right. You're going to go home. And you're going to find your mother and write your history in peace, and I shall be beside you, and all will be well."

He kissed the soft cheek that lay against his own, leaning over him, comforting him. "If I do not survive this voyage, I want you to—"

"Don't even say it!" she whispered fiercely, her hand going to his mouth, her fingers covering his lips. "I won't hear it! You must survive it!" Her red-rimmed and tired eyes filled with tears. "You have to see your mother," she urged.

His eyes closed. "Yes . . ."

She held him as the sun climbed higher in the eastern sky, burning off the night fog and ushering in the new day. Her tears fell across his wet cheek, mixing with his own, the taste of salt on his lips as he slept.

Tim Ryan tapped on the door at eight o'clock sharp, waiting for them to respond, tapping again before he heard movement within. "It's best we're off soon, before all are up," he told Victoria when he stepped into the tiny room. He barely had room to reach down to help the duke to his feet. "You're sure you're up to this?" he asked, unsure now that he looked at the man in the morning light.

"When one has no choice, one is always sure," Edward said, a tired smile trying to reassure Victoria.

Victoria stared at the man who now lived in her heart. She felt the love of him welling up within her, spilling over everything else in her life. "There is no proof—the Queen could not stop you later if you wished to visit your lands—"

"She can," he told Victoria quietly. "She could and she most probably would. She is no fool. This wound tells a tale far different than the one we told her men last night. And the fact that she knows a manuscript did exist—I told her myself it did and that you and I were working on it—when one cannot be produced, more and more weight has to be given to what James says, desertion or no. There's no other way, dear heart."

Her heart leaped at his last words, at the look in his eyes. Tim looked from one to the other. "Is that it then?" he asked.

Edward still smiled at Victoria. "Are we to argue more?"

"How can I argue with such logic?" She smiled back, determined not to show how much she feared for him.

"Good. Shall we then?" He motioned to Tim and they started out and down a long dingy corridor toward a narrow stairwell that led out to the street.

Victoria Station bustled with crowds of people, all converging upon it from different directions and then diverging toward the huge iron monsters that spewed steam from their engines, their sounds loud and grating as they wheezed to a stop or began grinding out of the huge building. Lost in the crowds, Edward leaned on Victoria, Davy running ahead to open the carriage door for them. Victoria missed a step, seeing a group of soldiers standing near the head of the platform. "Steady on," Edward said into her ear, and she grasped his arm tighter, letting him lean more heavily as they walked past the small group.

The train compartment opened from the edge of the platform, Davy there to help him up and then to reach for Victoria. She looked around them at the fresh-looking plush seats, the wood paneling, as Edward sat down heavily upon the bench facing her. She sat down across from him, smiling. "This is not only cleaner than what we just came from, I swear it is bigger by half!"

He smiled. "Not quite by half perhaps."

Davy settled down next to the duke, Victoria staring at him. "Are you to come with us?"

"Yes, ma'am . . . until we meet the ship."

"Good," Edward told her. "Now you can sleep. I shall be in the best of hands."

Davy grinned, holding up a bag he had stowed before reaching for the duke and helping him up. "We've got provisions enough for an army too, thanks to Tim. He said as how you should build your strength."

The train groaned, metal clanging against metal, the sounds loud and foreign to Victoria's ears. She sat back on the bench opposite Edward and Davy, staring out at the crowded platforms they were leaving behind. Little by little the train was picking up speed, its grinding sounds falling into a steady cadence beneath their carriage as the wheels clacked over the narrow track, heading west.

Chapter 28

THEY REACHED THE IRISH Sea by Wednesday, Davy sleeping on the floor between the two long benches, his cloak wadded up for a pillow, his young limbs curling up, his big feet pressing against the door of the carriage.

Stiff and sore from so many hours of sitting, Victoria gladly stood up with Edward, pacing the short length of the carriage back and forth while Davy curled up on one of the benches and napped on, glad of the softer berth for an hour or so. They would move until they could not, sitting down together, waiting for the next stop when they could walk the platform and find the loo, splashing cold water on their faces and turning blindly back toward the train and their destination.

The smell of the sea came all at once to Victoria's nostrils, sharpening her sense of smell and turning her toward Edward. "Can you tell?"

He nodded, his hands holding hers, reaching to bring hers to his lips. "We've almost made it."

She leaned back, content to be beside him, watching the young Davy snoring softly on the bench across from them.

Mike Flaherty met the train, watching for them, seeing Davy waving out at him and jumping off before the train came to a full stop. Mike lumbered toward the boy, letting the boy lead him back to their compartment.

Edward smiled gratefully at Mike when the Irishman

climbed up to sit down across from them, Davy hanging in the doorway, watching the others disembarking.

"I've got some news," Mike began carefully.

Edward's good humor fled. "Tell me quickly."

"It seems all did not burn in the grate. James found others to listen in the morning, including Carrington, who would do almost anything to get into the Queen's good graces since she's so upset with him for helping Prince Bertie fool around so much in his company."

"Tell me the worst of it." Edward watched Michael.

"The worst is that she's ordered you to be held and brought back to London. Not arrested, mind you, exactly. But held. She wishes to talk to you."

Edward let out a long sigh, Davy whistling softly in the doorway. "Cor," Davy said, shaking his head. "I'd hate to have the likes of her mad at the likes of me!"

"There are soldiers at the docks. Watching."

"What do we do?" Victoria asked.

"If it's on you're going . . ." Mike stared at Edward.

"It's on I'm going." Edward spoke decisively. "But I think it may have to be alone."

"Don't be daft!" Mike told him.

"You are an accessory—as are you," he told Victoria, "if you are with me and I'm caught. It's safer for you to take her back—"

"I'm not going back!" Mike stared at Edward as if he were mad. "I've stayed on here because of you. And because your mother, God bless her, was gone. Now you tell me she's alive and you're to go and I'm to stay? Don't be daft!"

"Nor do I go back," Victoria told Edward, speaking quickly when she saw him about to protest. "If I wanted safety, I should never have come with you in the first place."

"It was different then—"

"It was no different to me."

Mike stood up. "You two can argue all the way to the docks. But I think we'd best be getting out of here before someone thinks to look at the trains."

Victoria stood up. "He's quite right," she told Edward, earning a quick look before he turned to let Mike help him out of the car.

"How is the leg?" Mike asked him.

"Better," Edward said.

"The same," Victoria said. "It is not healing."

Mike shook his head. "You're a fool to do this and I'm a fool to let you."

"As you say, but do it I shall," Edward told them all.

Davy helped Victoria down, walking behind Mike and Edward, looking all about as they moved toward a waiting carriage.

The narrow street bent down toward the sea, the harbor only blocks away. A low-lying mist blurred the outlines of the distant docks, of the ships that rode at anchor.

Victoria stared at the ships, the reality of their plight coming to her for the first time since their precipitous flight from Bereshaven House.

All in between had been a blur of movement. Of strange places covered over by the smells of poverty and fear, of swaying train carriages and tiny rest stations where all was foreign and cold, strangers huddling together and waiting in lines.

A feeling of unreality had surrounded her, the world she was seeing far different from any she had ever experienced. Now, looking at the might and size of the ships they rode toward, she thought of the size and power of the machine that had carried them here; the world was changing about her.

She reached across the seat for Edward's hand, her eyes on the scene outside, her heart skipping beats. This was all real and she was leaving the land of her birth, leaving in such a way she might never be able to return.

She felt the pressure of his grip, reassuring her. Her eyes found his, seeking out reflections of her own fears within the depths of his dark eyes. He saw surprise facing him, surprise and doubt and something more. "Are you quite sure?" he was asking her.

The smile she gave him was very small. "I am sure of nothing save that the world is nothing as I imagined . . . it is so . . . vast and anonymous . . . and we are so anonymous within it." She leaned toward him, seeing Mike and Davy avert their eyes. "I keep thinking of the 'surplus' people of Ireland that left on all those ships to America, crossing an ocean with no idea of what they would find on the other side. With nothing but their fare given to them by the government which wished them gone, with nothing in their pockets when they finally went ashore in that foreign land . . ." She shivered. "They must have been so brave."

"Or desperate," Edward said quietly.

The coach pulled up onto the dock, the sunlight coming out to warm them as they stepped down, Edward moving slowly but aiding himself. As Victoria stared upward a huge shadow fell across them, the shadows of the weather rigging falling across the dock and then pulling back a moment later, losing themselves onboard as the ship pitched, eddying with the waters beneath her bow.

Sailors were all around them, filling the docks, running up and down the masts and decks and sides of the ships that sat at anchor. Victoria took heart. "They'll never find us. There are so many ships."

"Aye, but only one on its way to Ireland," Mike told her, dashing her newfound optimism.

Edward put his arm around her waist, pointing off to one side where foreign-looking sailors were pulling up sheets, the sails billowing in the wind. "We could run off to Portugal and travel the Spanish main."

She felt the warmth of his embrace and leaned back against it, safe within his arms. "As long as you are there."

Mike was hurrying them forward, Davy hiking back along the dock to see what all he could see and hear. Suddenly he stopped walking. "Hark there!"

Edward looked toward the gangway. Victoria saw first the oily-looking swells that lapped up at the sides of the ship, the harbor water dark and dirty looking. Then she saw the uniforms at the bottom of the gangway. Soldiers' uniforms, not sailors'. A small group standing about, idly watching the sailors as they carried out their duties.

"Turn round . . ." Mike was urging them to the safety of the carriage, Edward's face closed and expressionless.

Once they were inside the carriage, Edward looked toward Mike. "I will need pen and paper."

"What?" Mike looked at Edward as if he'd lost his mind. "Here and now!"

"Here and now."

Davy ran up to the side of the coach, looking in before he rose to the driver's seat outside. "Word's out about a reward for spotting a runaway nobleman. Fifty guineas."

Edward whistled, grinning, startling the boy. "That's a lot to turn down," Edward told them. "You'd best think twice."

Mike shook his head, the boy staring first at the duke and then at Victoria. "Has he gone delirious, then?" Davy asked her.

"No," she reassured the boy, smiling at him until he climbed up onto the driver's seat.

Mike spoke up to Davy. "Take us around to the other dock."

The carriage started to move, the horse pulling slowly around, Mike leaning back in his seat, staring at the duke. "Paper it is."

Edward nodded. "I have to leave provisions for Sylvia and Judith. And James."

"James!" Mike said, his face grim. "I'd leave provisions for James if I could! Meanwhile, thanks to bloody James, we don't know if you'll be able to make this ship, or have to wait for the next."

"When is the next?" Victoria asked.

"Sometime next week," Mike told her.

Edward shook his head. "No. We *shall* make this ship. One way or another."

"Well, at the moment I don't see how," Mike told him plainly.

"First we find some writing supplies and some refreshment. And a change of clothes for me."

"Clothes?"

Edward grinned at Michael. "Clothes."

Victoria sat back beside Edward, her eyes closing as they rode toward their destination. Something had changed in Edward, something lighthearted and gay was coming out, through all the pain and all the travail. He was happy. Her eyes opened. He sounded as if he were truly happy for the first time in his life. She turned to look at him, seeing a newfound light in his eyes. And she smiled into it.

The carriage stopped as it neared the other dock, Mike getting out to sit up with Davy and direct him out of the waterfront maze toward the little rooming house Mike had found for himself the night before.

It sat back upon a dusty little lane well back from the docks, a tiny place to find, with no sign to tell of its existence. Victoria looked around herself as they went in, seeing shabby but clean furnishings, crisp white antimacassars across the backs of the worn overstuffed chairs that filled the little parlor they were shown into, the woman who left them there reminding Victoria of Matron. Compact and sturdy, with plain good features and no hint of ornament about her. Serviceable, Matron would have said and been pleased to be called it herself.

Victoria sank gratefully to one of the overstuffed chairs, seeing Edward sprawled out in another. "We can stay here a bit," Mike was saying. "While you find your writing materials and I scout out the harbor." His voice lowered. "If there were to be a fishing boat that was putting out to sea before the *Irish Star,* we might be able to catch her out of harbor. For a price."

Edward leaned forward. "Wait." He stood up, favoring his hurt leg, and walking slowly toward Mike. Victoria watched them walk out to the little hall, Edward speaking softly, Mike listening. And then Edward came back in by himself to look down at her.

"What is it?" she asked, sitting up straighter at his look.

He hesitated. "I have asked Michael to arrange rooms upstairs."

She nodded, coming slowly to her feet in front of him. "You should rest."

He watched her. "I do not wish to rest. Victoria, there is no way to tell what may befall me now."

"Don't." She took a step nearer, to gaze up into his dearly loved eyes. "It has to be all right," she told him as inwardly she prayed that it would be. That they would have the chance of building a life together. "It will be all right," she said then, reaching to touch his arm. As she felt the fabric of his coat sleeve she became hesitant, looking up into dark eyes that gazed down at her with an intensity that turned her heart over within her. "What is it?" she asked softly, lost in his eyes.

"I want you."

Her heart seemed to stop beating for an instant, fluttering within her rib cage. When he saw her expression, he reached for her, the palms of his hands clasping her arms.

"Dear heart—" He searched her eyes. "Have I offended you? I have shocked you to the core, I can see it. Forgive me, forgive the words." His grip slackened on her arms. "I have never had the gift of speech; I know what I feel but never how to say it." He searched for words.

"I"—she swallowed hard, her heart hammering at her daring,—"want—you." Her words ended in a little rush as she felt him react to her words. His grip tightened around her arms, his arms pulling her closer, his eyes staring down into hers. Her eyes closed, afraid to look at him. "I love you," she told him, the words bursting out unbidden, something within her breast soaring as she spoke, something else tightening, binding her chest as if to tear her in two with her fear of rejection.

She felt him drawing her close. Closer. His arms wrapping around her, enfolding her against his chest as his head dropped forward. He buried his face in her hair, his arms answer enough for this moment.

Mike came in to find them thus, standing in the center of the room, holding each other close. He coughed a little self-consciously, waiting for the duke to raise his head before he spoke. "The paper and pen. And ink." He held a writing box in his hands.

Edward looked at Mike over Victoria's head. "And the room? Rooms," he corrected himself.

Mike averted his eyes. "I'll show you the way" was all he said.

He led the way to a narrow stairwell and up a few steps to a sharp turn and up a few more to a narrow hall. A door stood open at the near end of the hall, another short flight of steps rounding upward to another tiny hall.

Mike stood aside, letting Edward lead the way into a small room that overlooked the narrow lane outside, a glimpse of the channel out past rooftops and chimneys. Victoria stood with her hand in Edward's, not meeting Mike's gaze, her eyes on the plain planks of the wood floor, her cheeks crimson.

"I shall call you when I've finished the letters," the duke told Michael.

Michael nodded. And still hesitated in the doorway. "I have asked about the clothing . . . should I come tell you when it comes?"

"Of course."

Mike nodded slowly, avoiding the girl, his eyes on the bed. He hastily looked up, seeing the duke gazing placidly back. "Should I show the—Miss—her room?"

Edward's hand closed around Victoria's. "You may use the other room. I'm sure Davy would enjoy a chance at a bed after what he's just been through."

Mike turned away, reaching to close the door, leaving them to themselves. Once outside in the tiny hall, he stared at the steps, feeling his own cheeks reddening as he went downstairs.

Inside the little room Edward drew Victoria to him, leaning a little on her as they stood there, his leg giving out after the climb. She could feel his weight change.

"Are you all right?" she asked, her breath soft against his ear as she spoke.

"I have never been more right in my life!" He leaned back, shifting his weight and bringing her with him as he fell toward the bed, laughing at her sudden movement as she thought he was falling.

She found herself beside him on the bed, staring into his laughing eyes, seeing them change color, seeing their color deepen as he lost the laughter and drew her closer, his mouth seeking out her lips.

The room fled from her vision. Danger, the future, all the consequences of what she was doing fled along with the room, nothing left but the touch of his flesh against hers. He pulled at her clothing, ripping at his own, nearly demented until he could touch her naked skin, until he sank down against her, drinking in her breast, drinking in the feel of her skin as he slid his hands down her back, cupping her buttocks and drawing her closer against him.

He sought her breast hungrily, her body responding to his hunger, reaching to pull him closer, seeking out the sensations that pulsed through her now, wanting him closer, closer yet, closer still, until his weight was upon her, the feeling of his body covering hers as right, as natural, as breathing. He moved a little, groaning with a pain that coursed through his leg, and she stiffened, reaching out to help him, murmuring her worries for his pain against his cheek, his ear, his nose.

He stopped her, lifting himself up on his elbows, his lower body pressing even harder against her own. His eyes sought hers. "It's all right," he told her, his voice husky.

"Your leg—" She said no more, his weight shifting, the hard shaft between his legs pressing against her belly, stopping all thought. Her bones were melting within her as she reached toward him, drawing him closer, hearing small sounds she realized came from her own mouth, dredged up from deep within, responding to the low moans he made when she moved beneath him.

He reached to touch her belly, her stomach fluttering beneath his touch, the feeling urging him on. His eyes found hers, watching her in the soft afternoon sunlight as he pressed the palm of his hand downward, her legs no longer rigid, his hand pressing between them, opening them wider.

She felt his fingers searching against her, the feeling heating her blood, making her writhe under his touch. When his fingers dipped within her, her back arched toward him unbidden, her body reacting to him, her mind detached and floating along with the sensations that rippled up her spine and down her legs, waiting.

More. She wanted more and she didn't know what to ask for; she wanted more and more and more and suddenly something large and hard touched the soft flesh he was opening between her legs, something pressed against her and joined her flesh.

Her eyes flew open, her hand reaching to claw at his back. He was inside her and she would burst. She felt the force of his body thrusts, felt the tightness of her own flesh, and knew he would rip her apart. Tears sprang to her eyes, pain ripping through her, and suddenly he thrust past the pain and waves of pleasure began to build one upon the next, carrying her with them, with him, as he thrust deeper inside her and pulled back away only to thrust deep again.

When he pulled away, she reached up to him, her back arching, her body determined to hold him within itself, to never let him go. His body melted into hers, his lips seeking out her lips, his tongue caressing her tongue, his arms surrounding her, his legs encompassing her, driving deeper and deeper within her until she felt explosions begin to burst through her veins, rippling on and on as his body began to shudder within and around her, pouring forth into the heart of her.

Peace descended, their bodies replete, their senses exhausted. His arms were a safe haven, her breast the only home he had ever known. Each moved closer to the other, side by side now on the narrow bed, the world well lost while they savored the feelings that none other could know.

His eyes were closed, his dark hair resting against her flesh, his face snuggled close between the twin mounds of her breast. Her arms encircled his neck, her one hand lost in his dark curls, the other sliding down his back, to press against his spine. Content.

This was love, she told herself, and she had found it. In all the world, with all the people in it, she had been the lucky one to have found this man. This moment in time. Her eyes closed with the thought, her drowsy limbs calling her down into the deep sleep of a contented child.

Chapter 29

W HEN SHE WOKE, SHE felt bereft of part of herself, opening her eyes to see him gone from her arms. She sat up quickly, the sun low in the afternoon sky, the room empty save for herself and her clothing, lovingly placed neatly across the one chair in the room.

Near the chair was a small table and upon it was an envelope. Victoria stared at the envelope, fear chilling her. It took her a moment before she reached for her chemise and slipped it over her head, rising from the narrow bed to gingerly take hold of the envelope.

When she turned back, the sight of the disheveled bed, the rumpled sheets and pillows, brought a lump to her throat. She swallowed hard against it, sitting down on the edge of the bed and staring at the white paper in her hand before reaching to slowly open it and read.

My darling, it began, Victoria's heart leaping at the words. She reread them: *My darling, Michael is waiting for you below. When you wake, I shall be gone, and I hope, if all goes well, I shall meet you aboard ship and tell you of all that is in my heart. If, my darling, I cannot meet you, Michael will see to your safe return and future. There is more I need to tell you, but I want to see your eyes when I do. Trust me and pray for us all.*

The note was unsigned. She reread it and reread it again before she laid it on the bed and stood up, dressing as quickly as she could.

Dressed, she reached for her small bag of medical supplies, thrust his note within, and opened the door to the narrow hall and tiny stairwell.

Mike jumped up from a chair in the parlor she and Edward had waited in earlier. He came forward, his face showing his concern. "He said to wait for you, but I was almost ready to come get you before it got dark. We must hurry."

"What is happening?"

"I'll tell you as we go. Come *along*." He was already moving toward the street door, holding it open for her, motioning her to the waiting carriage and slipping in beside her. Davy was atop, releasing the brake and taking the reins. "Who is with Edwa—with the duke?" she asked Michael, fear in her eyes. "Where is he?"

Mike sighed. "He is at the docks."

"As are the soldiers!"

"Aye. At dusk, when all hands come back from the pubs and prepare to weigh anchor, he'll be with them."

"With them!"

"Dressed as a sailor, going aboard with the rest of the crew."

"But they'll know he's not one of them!"

Mike shrugged. "They take on new hands here and there. And he's money to grease their palms and a tale to tell, which they may believe."

"Or may not." Mike did not refute her words. "And if they do not," she continued, "they may go directly to the soldiers and tell them!"

Mike remained silent, his eyes straining ahead toward the docks, which were just coming into view.

"What are we to do?" Victoria asked quietly, earning a quick and grateful look from Mike.

"Aye, and there's the right kind of girl! Keep your head and keep going forward, and all that can be done will be done. You have tickets, I have them for you. For him and for you. You shall go aboard and wait."

"And you?"

"I shall hang about until I see him on board. Then I shall join you." He patted his pocket. "I have my own ticket here, so I can come at the very last, if necessary."

"And if he does not make it?" She stared at Michael.

He avoided her eyes. "His instructions are I should go on with you, get you out of harm's way and bring you back when all is safe for you."

"I will not go if he does not."

Mike looked at her then. And grinned. "I'm glad to hear you say that, my girl, for I could never disobey him. And I could surely never go and leave him to these hellhounds that are after him."

"Good," Victoria said, but she did not return his smile, her worries too overpowering. "We are agreed."

The carriage was stopping, Mike standing down quickly and reaching back for her. "I put two trunks aboard in your name. They hold all I could pack for the trip and get here in time."

She nodded, stepping down onto the windswept dock and staring at the soldiers that loitered near the gangway. Sailors moved here and there, going about their work as the afternoon waned.

Victoria followed Mike forward, seeing the soldiers come to attention as she neared. One of the soldiers reached to unhitch a rope that barred access to the gangway. He bowed a little. "Miss," he said, smiling at her auburn good looks.

She nodded, forcing herself to smile back. "Thank you, Lieutenant," she said softly.

"Sergeant, miss." He grinned.

"Oh." She smiled again, passing by him. As Mike watched her the soldier reached to place the rope back across the gangway. "Have to see your papers, sir, if you're to go on board."

Mike stared at the soldier, his expression mildly quizzical. "Why?"

"The Queen's orders, sir." The young sergeant glanced back toward his men, who lounged nearby, the lady's back to them as she was handed aboard ship. The young sergeant leaned in toward the older man. "Looking for a nobleman, sir."

Mike grinned. "Sure'n do I look noble to you, my boy?"

The soldier grinned. "Well, there's an Irishman in the bargain and that you do be looking like."

"Aye, and that I am. But it's not on board ship I'm going just yet. It's to wet my whistle first . . . do you know of a good place before I join her ladyship aboard?"

The soldier pointed across the dock to where the waterfront street ended, its cobblestones circling in front of a half-timbered public house. "They seems to prefer that one, at least the boys who came off her seem to."

Mike grinned. "Maybe it's Gaelic they're speaking inside."

The soldier grinned. "I couldn't say, sir . . . but it's ale for sure they're talking."

Mike moved off, walking slowly, gazing idly around himself as if he had nothing but leisure on his mind. If any had been able to look close, they would have seen him scanning the faces of the sailors he passed, watching them each in turn more closely than they realized as they passed by the older man with his ambling gait.

The pub was called the Sailor's Grog and it was packed to the gunnels with sailors and tankards of ale. Mike pushed his way inside, looking all about without seeming to, taking in the faces of the men who crowded around the bar, pushing for one more before they had to leave.

Mike settled himself at the far end of the bar, calling for a pint and pushing his coins out toward the man behind the bar. Mike planted his foot on the brass rail that ran the length of the bar and took a long draft of the brew, the foam sticking to his upper lip.

When he wiped it away, he saw him. Staring at him from the other end of the bar, a sailor's suit and cap hardly disguising the dark, curly hair and darker eyes from any that knew him. Mike nodded slightly and then ignored the man at the opposite end of the bar, determined not to have the others notice their exchange. The sounds of hearty conversation filled the room, bits of it floating past Mike as he stood and drank by himself. "I've been there! I've been there meself!" an old sailor's voice piped up nearby. "I've sailed old John Chinamen's seas and I've heard tales of them as didn't live to tell about it themselves."

Other voices overcame the old sailor's. "He came in at

the hawse-hole, that one, and look at 'im now, in charge of bloody all, I tell you, and a fiend to work under . . ."

"No, that was coming 'round the *Lizard,* that was . . . it were twilight till it was nearly gone midnight and still we was becalmed."

Mike could feel the men stirring around him, the hour near to ending, feet shuffling, the last of their pints being lifted before they began to straggle out toward the dock in twos and threes.

Glancing over at the far end of the bar, Mike saw a bunch of sailors take off together, their voices rising in raucous good humor as they berated their fellows for tarrying. The doors closed, the end of the bar empty.

Mike hesitated, standing up with others who threw their coins toward the pot boy and the barman and started out toward the cobblestoned waterfront street.

Mike moved slowly, staying with them, moving a little ahead once they were outside. He could see the first group of sailors bunched up near the end of the dock, talking for a minute, reaching for something from the dark-haired newcomer.

With the others Mike walked past the first group, rounding toward the soldier who had kidded with him before, stopping and looking back at the sailors who now came slowly forward, down the dock toward the gangway where Mike and the sergeant stood. Mike handed over his papers to the sergeant, leaning in a little. "You say there's someone you're looking for . . . how much is it worth to catch him?"

The sergeant glanced at the papers, handing them back toward Mike, curious. He shrugged. "There's a man who's giving fifty guineas to get the bloke back to face Her Majesty's wrath, they say."

"Fifty guineas," Mike repeated. "That's a small fortune."

"Split between us who take him and him who points him out, of course," the soldier amended.

"Of course." Mike hesitated. "And he's only wanted for questioning, isn't that it? It's not like the Tower or some such?"

"Questioning it says on my orders, sir. Why are you asking, if I might, sir?"

Mike leaned even closer. "You see the tall sailor with the dark hair, coming along with the others."

The soldier glanced toward the group and then back at the man beside him. "Yes."

"There was talk in the pub about how none of 'em knew who he was . . . and I took a look at his hands. Lily white. Like an aristocrat, you might say. Not a workingman's hands. Not a sailor's hands at all."

The sailor pulled his orders out from his blouse, glancing at the description that was given and back up at the men who were coming forward.

Mike was halfway up the gangway, heading for where Victoria stood watching. The sailors started up past the soldiers, a few friendly words of derision exchanged, and then the sergeant stepped forward. "Excuse me there, you sir, I'd like a word with you."

The sailors turned toward their dark-haired companion, backing away from him as the soldier came forward. He looked up toward the ship, a few steps away, seeing Mike halfway up, seeing Victoria in that moment, standing at the railing, staring down at him, too far away to see the quick worry that was in her eyes when she saw the soldiers start toward him.

He made a dash for it, racing up the gangway, shoving the sailor in front of him out of the way. The man nearly went over the side, pushed out of the way again as the soldiers came after. He reached Mike's side, Mike turning to block his way. "Let me past!" he yelled, "Mike!"

"I'm sorry—" Mike was saying, the soldiers grabbing on to his borrowed sailor's clothes, pulling him back. Mike wouldn't meet his eyes, slipping an envelope into his pocket as they pulled him back and off.

"Let me go!" he shouted, his voice rising toward Victoria.

She stared in disbelief and started for the gangway, toward where they were pulling him off. Mike was in her way, forcing her back.

She clawed at him, hearing the sounds of struggle below, seeing nothing as Mike hoisted her up and shoved her back from the railing toward a passageway that led to the cabins. She struggled against him and fell back. Righting herself, she started toward him, ready to claw her way through him when an arm came around her, pulling her back.

"What, leaving me now, are you?" Edward's voice came from beside her ear, turning her around to stare at him, her eyes widening.

"Stay back, out of sight!" Mike hissed, turning to block the view from the dock with his broad shoulders.

"I tell you, you've got the wrong man! He's on board! He's on board, I tell you! *Let me go!*" James's voice carried back on the seawinds as the soldiers carried him off, wrestling with him to keep a grip on him until they had him tied, his words muffled now as they strode with him toward the end of the dock.

Victoria sank back against Edward, her heart in her mouth, her legs like jelly now that it was almost over. She stared at Mike, who turned toward them now, grinning. "Shame on you," he was saying, "to doubt the likes of me! Tsk, tsk . . ."

Sailors' voices rang out, the sails being made ready. They hauled aft the main sheet, the men singsonging *ho-ee-oh, ee-oh-ho-oh,* the weight of the sail becoming heavier at each pull.

The bo'sun called out to the shantyman, the men suddenly seeming to desert their work, stopping in midstride, holding the muslin and the lines but not hauling it up.

"What's wrong?" Victoria asked, frightened they would not leave port, that he would still be in danger. And as she spoke the shantyman began: "Kitty is me darlin'", the man sang out, "the capt'n is a growlin', the ship she is a rollin', haul the bowline—"

The crew chipped in, together singing out, "Haul the bowline, the bowline *Haul!*"

And as the word rang out all lay back together. In one smooth motion more than a foot had been gained, the sheet as taut as an iron bar.

The chanting began again, the shantyman leading the men and all leaning back together, raising the muslin higher and higher, more and more tightly hauled until they hove it in place, a young sailor scrambling up to ride lookout high in the main top-gallant masthead.

Edward pulled Victoria nearer, leaning his head against

hers. "I've seen the cabins and the only one that's fit for you is my own."

"I see," she replied, looking up to see Mike watching them. "Then you must bunk in mine, I suppose," she told him, earning a quick shout of laughter.

"Lord, what a trial you are going to be to live with," he told her.

She straightened a little. "Live with?" she asked, trying to see behind his smile.

"Aye. Live with," Edward replied. He looked over her head at Mike. "Did you see to the delivery of the letters?" he asked.

"James'll find it in his pocket once they settle him someplace. The others I've sent on to Sir Thomas, as you said to."

"What are you saying?" Victoria asked as they walked forward toward the cabins.

He did not answer until they were inside his cabin, safely away from all ears. Then Edward looked toward Mike, reaching out to clasp his hands. "You're positive Davy is all right?"

"Right and tight and on his way back to London," Mike reassured the duke. "And I'd best find where my own bunk is before you toss me out."

Victoria smiled. "You shall have mine." She saw the surprise in the two men's eyes. "Of course you shall. After what I was ready to accuse you of . . ."

"You shouldn't make such fun," Mike began.

"I'm quite serious," she told Mike, and then turned toward Edward. "I shan't be using it in any event."

"Victoria!" Edward stared at her, as shocked as Michael. He saw her looking back at him, an amused expression on her face. Slowly he found himself grinning. He turned toward Mike himself. "She's right, you know. You should have it."

"Your grace!" Mike stared from one to the other, sure they had both lost their senses. He saw Edward drawing Victoria close.

"And while you're about it," Edward continued, "you might make the acquaintance of the captain." He was ushering Mike toward the door. "Tell him as soon as we're out to sea I'd like to have a moment alone with him."

Mike watched the door close in his face. "You're flouting convention!" he called out to them. "People will talk. Even on ships at sea!"

Inside the large cabin Edward looked over toward the bed. And then back toward Victoria. "This will be the first really comfortable bed we've made love in."

She blushed. "We've not made love in it."

"Yet," he told her, watching her pink cheeks, her gray-green eyes as they came up to look into his, her love shining out at him. A cloud crossed her expression, quickly banished, but he could sense it. "What is it? Tell me . . . you must tell me everything that worries you from this moment on."

"It's nothing . . . I just thought of poor Sylvia."

Edward reached for her. "Have I told you that I love you?"

She leaned against him, drinking in the touch of him, the scent of him. "No . . . you haven't."

He buried his face in her hair. "I love you," he whispered into it, moving to bring her face close to his, to watch her eyes. "I have never loved before . . . ever . . . as I love you now." He brought her to the bed, sitting down beside her, keeping her hands in his. "I tell you this, for you must make a decision that will affect the rest of our lives."

She stared at him, worry surfacing again. "What are you saying?"

"Let me tell you what I have to and then you shall decide. Agreed?" He watched her uncertainty and smiled at it, touching her cheek. "I am not coming back to England." He saw her surprise and reached to touch her lips. "Listen, please. Whatever befalls me in Ireland, I will stay. It is where I belong, and that I know, from the bottom of my heart. Now. I have left provision for Judith and Sylvia and James to share equally in the revenues from the English property. For Judith to have the use of The Willows for as long as she wishes. For James to have the town house, since he has no interest in the land or the business, and Judith does. Sylvia has the right to live in whichever she chooses, as long as she chooses, or the other two forfeit what they have. And the one right that does not devolve to them is that of sale." He saw her clouded eyes clearing at the words. "Never fear. He cannot sell off the property for his gambling debts or whatever. He will have one third of the profits from the English holdings to do with as he pleases. I wrote him and he will find the note in his pocket and verification at my solicitors." Edward grinned. "After he has convinced them all he is not me." Edward's grin grew wider. "When Michael told me James had forgotten to have them mention in the official report that there were twin brothers, I realized we might have a chance."

"But how did you get him to wear those clothes?"

"Michael convinced him. I came on board in sailor's clothes and worked on the rigging while Michael found where James was staying." He saw the look in her eyes and shook his head. "Let me finish. If you must interrupt, Mike was told the London gentleman was here and realized who it must be. Now may I finish?" He smiled and reached to take both her hands in his. "Michael found James and told him he was shocked that I would run off on all of them, Mike included, for some girl—sorry, my girl, but he said worse than that."

"Which James, of course, believed."

"Of course."

"But—" Victoria began.

"But me no buts. Are you paying attention?"

"Yes," she told him.

"Good. Mike told him for the fifty guineas he would find out where and when I was moving—that I would be fool enough to trust Mike—"

"Which you were," she pointed out, smiling now herself.

"Shush. Where was I? Oh yes, I was going to come onboard in sailor's rig so he was to come on board too, confusing the men I'd paid to help me by pretending to be me and calling the soldiers to sort the mess out."

"But you didn't have anyone on board helping you."

"No. But he would have done and he has many times played the game of pretending to be me." Edward's smile left when he thought about the past. Victoria reached to kiss his cheek.

307

"They should have been able to tell the difference. Sylvia included."

"Yes, you seem to have no trouble doing it."

"Nor will your mother. You have been awfully generous, you know."

He thought about her words for a long moment, turning to look directly at her. "I haven't been. Not really. You see, I couldn't face my mother if I'd done badly by James . . . I couldn't stand to tell her the truth about him . . . and—and there's something else."

"Yes?"

"We'd have no chance of building a life together, a happy life at least, with another's misery wearing us down."

Victoria sat up straighter. "A life together?" She repeated his words slowly.

He sat up straighter too, watching her, his heart in his eyes. "Yes. What I mean is, if you like. That is—that is the decision you must make. If you wish to stay in Ireland with me. Or if you'd prefer to go back. I should see you were provided for, you know that. No matter what. You must not feel you have to stay."

"Yes," she told him. "I know that."

He watched her every movement as she looked down at her hands, which were folded in her lap. He looked down at them too. "I shall not go back. Possibly not ever."

Her eyes closed. "I think I shall like Ireland," she said softly.

He reached to turn her so that he could see into her eyes again. "Say that again."

"I want to be where you are," she told him, seeing his eyes glisten momentarily. He brushed at them, looking away, and she reached to turn his face back toward her own. "Wherever that is."

"In that case . . . I have something else to ask you."

"Yes?" She breathed the word. He reached for her, pulling her back with him onto the bed, smiling. "Yes!" she said again, laughing as he reached for her.

His lips reached to cover hers, his tongue touching her lips, gently opening them. A rapping at the cabin door brought them quickly to a sitting position, Victoria's hand going to her hair as Edward called out for them to enter.

Mike appeared in the doorway. "You said to ask the captain to stop in as soon as we were out of harbor." Mike stepped back, a large, portly man in a captain's uniform filling the doorway, coming just inside and doffing his hat when he saw Victoria.

"Oh, yes . . . good." Edward turned back to Victoria. "I almost forgot . . . will you marry me?"

She stared at him, a slow smile forming to meet his own, their happy laughter ringing out as the two men near the cabin door looked toward each other and then back at the couple who sat on the edge of the bed. Edward looked toward the captain. "I believe that means yes. How soon can you perform the ceremony?"

Mike spoke quickly. "But your mother—"

"Will no doubt want us to repeat the feat in front of God and God knows who all else . . . but I'm taking no chances. None." He reached for her, bringing her into his arms, reaching to kiss her as her arms went around his neck.

Mike coughed but they did not hear him. Their kiss became more impassioned, their bodies straining closer together, falling back against the pillows as the captain turned and stepped out into the passageway, reaching to close the door. He stared at Michael for a long moment.

"The sooner the better from the looks of it," he told Mike, walking away as Mike looked back at the closed cabin door and then up at the sunset colors of the sky above.

"Ah, well . . . Siobhan . . . and I can't protect him from everything, now can I?"

Whistling an Irish jig, Mike went in search of a spot of poteen from the Irish lads below decks.

Inside the darkening cabin Edward held Victoria in his arms. "You never did answer, you know."

"Answer what?" she asked him, snuggling close.

"You never answered whether you will. Whether you'll marry me." His eyes closed, content to lie beside her.

"I answered that the very first time you came to my room. At The Willows . . ."

"You did, did you?"

"Hmmm . . . you just didn't know it . . ."

When he leaned to kiss her, she was already unbuttoning his shirt.